THE CHANGING TIDES

THE CHANGING TIDES

Fall of the Imperium Trilogy
Book 2

Clifford B. Bowyer

HOLLISTON, MASSACHUSETTS

To my parents, Marilyn and Warren Bowyer: you have been my strongest supporters, my unfailing inspirers, and my biggest fans. I love you and truly appreciate all that you have done and sacrificed for me.

ACKNOWLEDGMENTS

Bringing the world of The Imperium Saga to life is a process that is fueled by moments of inspiration, research and development, and taking an idea and running with it. But not all ideas are necessarily good ones! Thus, it has always been vital to me to have an outlet where I can receive feedback and constructive criticism, whether I wish to hear it or not. I am fortunate to have such individuals in my life, and wish to acknowledge the efforts of the following people:

My mother and my father, who remain my biggest supporters and champions of my efforts. The pride that I see when I look into your eyes and that I hear in your voices, becomes an inspiration in itself.

My sister, Linda Karner, who has sacrificed many days to help with the more mundane aspects of supporting an author. Including a most vital service: access to my niece and nephew for their enthusiasm, excitement, and insight.

The rest of my family, including my sister, niece, nephews, uncle, and cousins, who exuberate such excitement and enthusiasm that I can hardly wait to get home and write.

David LaPointe, who has always been the first to read the raw manuscript and let me know exactly what he thought was good and bad.

Jayson Palmer, my Fantasy expert, who is available whenever I have a pressing concern or just need someone to listen as I talk about an idea.

Tom McWeeney and Jeromy Cox, my art team, who took a scene that expanded over one hundred pages of manuscript and managed to capture the spirit for the cover.

My editor, Kerrie McNay, for gently pointing the way, and even making me laugh and smile with some of her added commentary.

And finally, to all of my readers, with whom the fate of the Seven Kingdoms continues to hang in the balance.

Thank you, all.

CAST OF CHARACTERS

Solara	mystral female from Suspinti
Sora	mystral female from Suspinti
Tiot	timber wolf male from Dartie
Ferceng	troll male from Falestia
Thamar	dwarven male from Vorstad
Theiler	dwarven male from Vorstad
Baldock	dwarven male from Tregador
Arifos	elven male from Madrew
Ashwin	elven female from Xylona
Mylvannan	frost elven male from Akkammanavar
Heirn	elven male from Xylona
Vaz	white tiger male from Trespias
Vella	white tiger female from Trespias
Winton	human male from Danchul
Prime Minister Torscen	human male from Dartais
Rawthorne	human male from Falestia
Durgin	human male from Suspinti

Imperial Security and Investigation Authority:

Captain Adonis	adlesian male from Adlai
Cylnta	worral female from Mage's Council
Sergeant Darkler	human male from Tenalong
Dozzer	human male from Dartie
Nextra	human female from Dartais
Ortrill	human male from Trespias
Doctor Podeis	human male from Falestia
Commander Quince	human male from Danchul
Tink	human male from Suspinti

Tarleskazrin
Akkammanavar
MOURNING MOUNTAINS
Vohlmuth
FALESTIAN MOUNTAINS
Arenberg
RED MOUNTAINS
SENYA FALLS
KREBLA
Redland
LAKE SENYA
BLACKSTOCK MOUNTAINS
LAKE SUPRETTA
Turning Leaf
NORTHERN MOUNTAINS
Wildwood
ISLAND OF NO RETURN
Trespdor
Underwood
Korland
PIRROS RIVER
Shimendyn
LAKE OF TEARS
HORNED
BLOODY RIVER
FORBIDDEN PEAKS
TENALONG
Birshedine
DRYXAS RIVER
NEKROS LAKE
SUSPINTIAN FOREST
FORBIDDEN FOREST
Tenland
SUSPINTI
BLACK PEAKS
Border Town
DIN
TENALONG EVERGLADES
RIVER OF TEARS
Comonor
ARDAN RIVER
NORTH HORWOOD FOREST
Xylona
Purington
Larridge
LAKE CRESPEN
DANCHUL
SOUTH HORWOOD FOREST
DANCHUL RIVER
Vorstad
VENTELL MOUNTAINS
Estonis

N
FALESTIA
ORDELL MOUNTAINS
OLBRUS RAPIDS
ADLAI
Carnelian
HN MOUNTAINS
DARTIAN WOODS
Faylinn
DARTAIS
CUPTON RIDGE
BOLE RIVER
RIVER
LAKE CUPTON
LAKE PERCOTI
Bellmore
DARTIE
Water Haven
PERCOTI WOODS
Edgewood
MU FOREST
Trespas
Kramden
Arkham
Lowiskia
Aquatica
FROCOMON
GREEN MOUNTAINS
QUIRCH WOOD
Benny Bay
CARRION MOUNTAINS

THE CHANGING TIDES

PROLOGUE

Adonis was exasperated; this was the old woman's third recitation of her tale. The ebony-skinned warrior knew from years of investigations that eyewitnesses to a crime were very unreliable, and that a simple question was, more often than not, answered from a variety of perspectives. However, the more people he spoke to from the small Suspinti village of Korland, the more frustrated he grew.

Much of the story was the same: a beautiful woman with an almost siren-like voice had entered their village and somehow had mystified the men; she walked out one night and every male member of the village, regardless of age, was swept up in her wake and followed her into the Suspintian Forest. The men had been gone for days, and the women left behind were forced to fend for themselves.

To this point, almost every eyewitness agreed on the events. Of course, the descriptions of the siren varied, some even claiming that she was a hideous beast. Adonis figured that this was more emotion and the women's egos speaking, so he let the discrepancies in their observations slide.

It was at this point that the stories began to twist a bit. Nobody seemed to know or agree with what truly happened—or if they did, they refused to speak about it. He had heard dozens of variations so far, but as Captain of the Imperial Security and Investigation Authority, discerning the truth and finding justice was his job.

He had personally founded the organization with the intent of bringing prosperity and order to the land. Since then, his team has more often been referred to as ISIA, or simply the Authority, but their goals never changed. Their visit to Korland was not to hear about a se-

1

ductive vixen luring the men from the village, but to ascertain who had murdered her.

As he continued to listen to the old woman, he knew that every word from her mouth had to be carefully monitored; she, like many others, was hiding something. He listened as she spoke of a mystery woman who had come to save the day; as if this traveler was some kind of goddess or heroine, setting out to find the men and returning with them in short order. Of course, nobody could point out why a dead body was lying at the edge of the forest, why it had over one hundred stab wounds, or had any clue as to who did it.

Leaning forward, Adonis held up a finger to silence the woman. "Who was this mystery woman?"

"I don't know," the old woman answered after pausing to think for a moment.

"What did she look like?" he pressed on.

"She wore a cloak," she answered more quickly.

"A Mage's cloak?" Adonis tried to clarify.

"I'm not certain," the woman answered.

Adonis looked back and spotted one of his agents, Cylnta, a Paladin from the Mage's Council who had joined his cause. Though she now wore the standard Authority uniform—all red with two yellow stripes on the left side of the shirt and trailing down the pants' legs—she still wore her Mage's cloak draped over her shoulders. "Did it look like hers?"

"Oh no," the woman replied.

"So it was not a Mage's cloak then?" Adonis tried to clarify.

"No," the woman said. "No it wasn't."

"What color was it then?" Adonis continued.

"Captain, I am sorry, but it was dark," the elderly woman tried to explain.

"Too dark to see what she wore or who she was?" Adonis asked incredulously.

"I'm afraid so," the woman smiled warmly back at him.

"How about height?" he asked in mild frustration. "Was it too dark to see how tall she was?”

“I don’t know, maybe between five and six feet?” the woman guessed.

“Was it closer to five or six?” he asked.

“Perhaps in between,” she smiled again.

“Perhaps,” he repeated. “Was she human? Elven? What?”

“Again Captain, I’m afraid I cannot help you,” she said. “Would you like a drink?”

“No, I would not like a drink,” he declared sharply, emphasizing each word.

Next to him, a second agent leaned forward. “I would love a drink,” she said. “How generous of you to offer.”

“Well, I’ll get it right away,” the old woman smiled as she stood up and began to walk away.

“What did you do that for?” Adonis asked in awe.

The woman next to him smiled compassionately. She had long, wavy black hair, a very tanned complexion, and an angelic face that Adonis knew from personal experience had won the hearts of many men. He had first met Nextra several years before when she had seduced King Sarlec of Danchul and almost had become his second wife, though Adonis had put an end to that deception. Since then, he has come to rely upon her insight and ability to read the attitudes and desires of others.

“What?” he pushed on.

“You know she’s lying, I know she’s lying, and she knows she’s lying. Getting frustrated and hostile isn’t going to change that. She’s an old woman. There’s not much you can do that she’s particularly afraid of. That’s why she is the spokesman of this village.”

“When she comes back, you finish the interrogation then, I’m going to see what some of the others have found out,” Adonis instructed.

“Interview,” she corrected.

“What?” he asked as he was standing up.

“Interrogation has such a derogatory sound to it. I will continue the interview over a nice drink with her,” Nextra smiled.

"You do that," he said. As he turned to walk away, he saw the old woman walking back with a tray, three glasses and a pitcher of some dark-colored liquid. The smile on her face appeared sincere and pleasant. The same look that he had seen for the past few hours, and one he suspected hid a much darker ulterior motive.

Adonis straightened his long navy blue overcoat and then walked over to his first officer, Commander Quince. "Commander, tell me you've had better luck than we've had?"

At six-foot-two, Quince was stern and imposing, softened by his short blonde hair and light-blue eyes. His uniform was always in perfect condition, and the man unfailingly appeared commanding and in control. He had been recommended by General Kronos when the Imperial Guards were first being formed to protect the palace, and Adonis has never regretted the decision to take him on staff. Quince was a very successful and motivational leader, having earned the respect of his men both as an Imperial Guard, and now as part of ISIA.

"Nothing new to report, sir," he declared. "Ortrill and I are still getting the same story, but nothing to help with the victim."

Adonis glanced at Ortrill who was standing several feet behind Quince. The man defied all logic in Adonis's eyes. He was a practical joker who acted as if being serious would kill him. His hair changed color almost daily from one vibrant hue to another, this time dyed in a bright orange with spikes. Despite his oddities, the man had the ability to see a combat move once, and mimic it to absolute perfection. With the man's twin swords at his call, Adonis was quite willing to accept the eccentric jokester.

"Do we know anything more about the victim?" Quince asked.

"I was just about to go ask the good doctor," Adonis answered.

Adonis led Quince through the small village to the edge of the forest. As they passed Cylnta, he beckoned her to join them. The trio passed Dozzer, the former Lumnia champion from Dartie. He nodded to them as they exited the village and continued to maintain his watch in case anyone else tried to approach the remains of the victim.

Three other members of ISIA were near the body: Doctor Podeis was conducting his examination, Sergeant Darkler was observing, and

Tink, the boy-genius, was vomiting in a nearby bush.

"What news, Doctor?" Adonis asked.

Podeis—the man who had formerly been personally responsible for the health and well-being of Emperor Conrad and his family—turned around and looked up at Adonis. His grayish-white hair, receding as the years began to catch up to him, fell in short curls around his head. His greenish-blue eyes still showed a boyish charm, especially for a man that had seen as many tragedies as he had. Even when working on a cadaver, he was very pleasant, happy, and outgoing. As with all of the Authority agents, he wore the same red-and-yellow uniform with red boots and gloves, covered by a white lab coat.

"Captain, welcome, welcome," he greeted.

"Have you found anything?" Adonis asked.

"Based upon the depth and size of each wound, I would conclude that this was done by a small knife, possibly even a normal household utensil, such as a kitchen knife," he explained as he brushed his gloved fingers over the wounds to point them out.

As he spoke, Tink stepped back again to vomit into another bush.

"The kid can't handle it," Darkler remarked with a deep voice as he jabbed his thumb towards the seventeen-year-old inventor.

"I'm fine," Tink struggled to reply.

"Why don't you go get some fresh air," Adonis offered.

As Tink looked back up, one of the magnifying glasses that were attached to the headset he wore fell in front of his eyes, making the eviscerated corpse appear many times larger. Taking a deep breath, he turned and vomited again. After several deep breaths to steady himself, he smiled and agreed. "Perhaps Dozzer can use some help guarding the gate."

"I think he might indeed," Adonis agreed.

As Tink walked away, Doctor Podeis regarded the departing figure. "Poor lad—may he never grow accustomed to seeing such sights."

"Good thing Ortrill wasn't here," Quince commented. "Tink would never hear the end of this."

"Then let Ortrill remain in the dark," Adonis instructed them all. "What else have you got?"

Darkler stepped forward. "We have a name," he informed them. "This is Jayde, a lieutenant for the Hidden Empire."

Adonis did not doubt his sergeant's words. Darkler had grown up surviving the swamps of Tenalong, and had even scoffed at an offer from Lady Salaman to join the Hidden Empire. Though he was only five-foot-two, he was one of the toughest men Adonis had ever met—a fact that had been realized by the leader of that criminal organization.

"What would she be doing here?" Quince asked.

"Probably looking for some more slaves to put to work. Send Jayde out with her seductive mind-control and lure enough slaves to last the Hidden Empire for a few months," Darkler deduced.

"That tells us who she is, but not what happened," Adonis replied. "We certainly aren't going to figure it out using normal investigation techniques."

"These people have banded together with their story," Quince agreed.

"I'm sure we could break someone in time, but I just have this feeling that we are needed elsewhere," Adonis commented as he stroked his fingers through his goatee. At six-foot-four, Adonis was a very strong and physical presence. His well-groomed black hair, braided in cornrows, and ebony face—more often than not—intimidated the masses of the realm. Upon his face he wore shaded glasses that covered his blazing red eyes.

"Cylnta, are you ready?" he asked.

As a member of the Mage's Council, Cylnta had mystical abilities that she used to help Adonis in his investigations. The worral knew that Adonis preferred to discover the clues through a thorough investigation, but her abilities were invaluable to determine what had exactly happened.

If his dark complexion shocked those facing Adonis, many more hid from the worral. She was reptilian with a green-scaled body that blended with a variety of shades. Her eyes were yellow with black slits, like those of a snake, and they were always in motion, examining her surroundings, often looking in two directions at once. Of particular distinction with her was that in the dark, she could release a bioluminescent glow, a trait of her subterraneous-dwelling race.

The Paladin stepped forward and nodded. "I am prepared," she answered in a very clear and easy to understand dialect. Sergeant Darkler, who had lived for a time with the reptilian rasplers, was always amazed at how clearly Cylnta spoke.

Cylnta sat down and crossed her legs. Focusing both of her eyes on the body of Jayde, she slowly closed them and took several deep breaths to help herself focus and concentrate. A small light-blue mist appeared in front of her and began to swirl. A scene from history began to replay within, and the five Authority agents watched the events as they truly occurred.

They watched as a woman—who was indeed cloaked, thus shrouding her features—walk into the village with a bound Jayde behind her. The men of the village rushed past them, joyous to be reunited with their wives, mothers, and children. The cloaked woman handed the binding to the little old woman that Adonis and Nextra spoke with, and received a small pouch in return. She tossed it into the air a couple of times, as if weighing it, and then spun around and strode back into the Suspintian Forest.

The little old woman followed for a moment, with Jayde in tow. She then tied her to a tree, and walked away as a mob of women stood there, guarding the siren. Her absence was short lived—she returned with a cutting knife, and stabbed the Hidden Empire lieutenant in the stomach three times before standing back up and handing the knife to another woman, who bent down and likewise stabbed the screaming seductress.

The Authority agents watched the brutal stabbing again and again as every single woman of the village took her turn with the knife. Jayde was dead long before the final woman struck, but she shared the same grim satisfaction on her face as the old woman when she first attacked.

The last attacker stood up and handed the knife back to the old woman, who smiled in the same polite expression that Adonis had become familiar with, and then they untied Jayde and all walked back to the village, leaving the bloodied woman behind.

The light-blue image faded, and Cylnta opened her eyes.

"So, now we know," Doctor Podeis whistled. "Wow."

"What do we do? Arrest every woman in the village?" Darkler asked.

Adonis continued stroking his goatee, wondering exactly what they would do. How could they remove every woman from an entire village? Yet, they had all participated in the slaying of this woman. Even if she was evil and worked for the Hidden Empire, no one deserved such a fate.

"Captain!" Dozzer yelled from the edge of the village's wall. "We need you!"

Adonis turned and looked at the huge man who was waving towards him and jogged back towards the gate to Korland, Quince and Darkler by his side. "What is it Dozzer?"

"A rider sir, from Trespias," he informed as he pointed deeper into the village.

"Thank you," Adonis offered as he jogged towards Geist, the personal messenger for the Empress. Ortrill and Nextra were standing with him, and he could see the man battling fatigue. "Geist?"

"Adonis, at last I have found you," he wheezed. Geist was a short, thin man who had a gift of reaching his destinations quickly. To see him so winded, and his horse looking like it was pushed close to death, he knew that the messenger had vital news to report.

"Take a moment to collect yourself, my friend," Adonis offered. "You are here now, and clearly you have found me."

"Thank you, but time is of the essence," he struggled to state between breaths. "King Sarlec is dead."

"Sarlec?" Nextra asked, her voice reduced to a whisper. Though she had once been seducing him and trying to amass her own fortune, she obviously did have legitimate feelings for the man.

"What happened?" Adonis asked, putting a finger up to silence Nextra.

"Unknown—the Empress found him in his quarters," Geist relayed.

"Was it murder?" Adonis asked.

"Again, we are uncertain, though Centain feels confident that foul play was involved."

"I trust Centain's judgment," Adonis commented. "If he suspects foul play, I would bet that he is right."

"I concur," Quince chimed in—he too had known Centain, having served directly below the man before agreeing to join ISIA.

"Is there anything else you can tell us?" Adonis asked.

"There is much going on at the palace," Geist stated a little more clearly as he slowly regained his breath. "The unification talks are not going well: the royal families oppose them, and the Empress is struggling."

"Unification talks?" Adonis asked.

"Oh yes, you probably haven't heard," Geist said. "Warlord Braksis had received multiple reports of organized movements against the Seven Kingdoms. The Empress is trying to unite all of the creatures of the realm to oppose this threat."

"What organized movements?" Quince asked, seeking further clarification.

"The Dartian hunters, the fisherman of Arkham, orcs, hobgoblins, goblins, and even something known as a Shadow Mage," Geist replied.

Adonis glanced at Cylnta, who shrugged her shoulders. He knew that there were problems—when he was bringing Dozzer into ISIA, Braksis had only recently returned from quelling a revolt in Dartie—but an organized effort was something beyond what he was aware of.

"What does this have to do with Sarlec's death?" Adonis asked.

"King Sarlec is one of the Imperium's strongest supporters. Centain feels that his death is directly related to an attempt to weaken the Imperium."

"Very well," Adonis said. "I shall leave immediately."

"What do you want to do?" Quince asked. "We haven't yet finished up here."

"You remain here, finalize the details," Adonis instructed. "Make it look as formal as possible, and then just return to Trespias; we're not going to arrest every woman in this village."

"Very well," Quince answered.

"I need to return to Trespias as quickly as possible. Cylnta, Doctor Podeis, Sergeant Darkler, and I will leave immediately. The rest of the team will stay with you."

"Understood, sir."

"I will go with you as well," Geist offered.

"No," Adonis answered firmly. "You stay here with Quince. You need your rest and can return with them."

Geist glanced over at his mount and reluctantly agreed. Without rest, food, and water, his horse would perish during the two-week return trip to Trespias.

"Darkler, pack up our belongings and make sure that Doctor Podeis doesn't leave anything behind. We're leaving within the hour."

"Yes, sir," he bowed and then jogged back to the crime scene to collect the doctor.

"Cylnta, I'm going to need you to tax yourself a bit here," Adonis commented.

"What did you have in mind?" she asked.

"We need to get back to Trespias as soon as possible," he stated, allowing her to draw her own conclusions.

"I shall make some preparations," she replied. "I warn you, though—by the time we reach Trespias, I will be exhausted. It will take me some time to rest before I will be of any use to you again."

"I understand," he replied. "We need to shave time off of the return trip—two weeks is unacceptable."

"I will get us there sooner," she promised.

"I know you will," he answered confidently. As he watched his people going about their business, a dark red mist began steaming from his eyes, escaping above his glasses.

Thirty minutes later, with Cylnta sitting behind him on his horse, Doctor Podeis and Sergeant Darkler sitting on the wagon with a six-horse team ready to pull them, Adonis raised his hand and signaled them to leave. As soon as they were outside of the walls of Korland, Cylnta's eyes closed, and the horses leapt from the ground and began galloping through the air, storming forty feet above the landscape.

CHAPTER 1

"The Empress, she's gone!"

Winton lay where he fell, backhanded by the celestial bounty hunter. He could hear voices of confusion and chaos around him, but they seemed to be far away as he struggled with consciousness.

"Water! The Sovereign needs water!"

"Guards! Seal all of the exits!"

Get up. Winton slowly opened his eyes. The last words were too clear to him, not an echo from his consciousness. *This is the moment we have been waiting for. Working for. You will not miss it because of a slap to the face.*

He recognized the voice, though he could not understand where it was coming from. He knew that it was Zoldex, but it sounded as if his trusted advisor was speaking directly into his mind.

Get up! The shout came more forcefully.

Winton put an arm down and started to lift himself. Again, the world swirled around him and he felt as if he would lose consciousness, but he knew that he had to rise. The voice of Zoldex kept prompting him.

Good, good. Now, remember the deception. You must be convincing or all is lost.

Reaching up, he braced himself on the stone alter and used it to support him. As he looked out, his eyesight continued to blur slightly, but shapes and voices began to converge.

The door and part of the wall to the audience chamber had been demolished in an explosion. Winton saw several people trapped underneath in the rubble, including a few members of the royal families and ministry. Kings Lorrents of Falestia and Euristies of Frocomon were helping to dig them out.

Large vines trapped several of the Imperial Guards and appeared to be suffocating them. Several untangled guards and the burly King Palenial of Dartie were attempting to cut the vines and free the men.

The aquaticans were struggling with consciousness as much as Winton, though their blue skin was beginning to look brittle and crusty. The Sentinel continued to call out for water for Sovereign Arianna, a call that Arbuckle and Trivett, two of the gnomes from Underwood, answered. They both ran out of the chamber searching for water, leaving their third companion, Zeppenfeld, behind, studying the skin of the aquaticans and babbling on about how fascinating their condition was when they needed water.

Looking down, Winton saw the proud Captain of the Guards lying face down with a dagger jutted in his stomach. The final Imperial Guard in the room, along with the beautiful Queen Zerilla of Suspinti, rushed to his side and turned him over. Zerilla shouted out for a medic—the Captain was still alive.

The only other people still in the room that were relatively unharmed were Prime Minister Torscen, who was glancing around at the carnage with complete disdain; Queen Celenia of Dartie, lost as usual in her own grief-stricken turmoil; and Queen Dornela of Dartais, who was actually sitting on top of her husband, Rentios, preventing him from helping anyone else.

Stop wasting time! Do it now!

"Guard, is there any word on the Empress?" Winton spoke, his words more authoritative than he would have thought possible.

The man who was checking on Captain Centain glanced up at the young Danchul King. "We do not know anything, sir."

"What are you waiting for?" he screeched, gaining the attention of several others in the room.

"We are trying to save as many lives as possible," the guard reasoned.

"The life of the Empress, my beloved Karleena, is more important than that of a guard or a few troops. Assemble as many men as possible and try to find her!"

Arianna studied the man. Though she needed water badly in order to survive, the man's words struck her as wrong. In the past few weeks, she had come to know Karleena quite well, and not once did she mention Winton in terms of affection. Certainly not as a beloved. As she tried to speak, only undecipherable gasps came from her parched lips.

Her proud Sentinel misconstrued her intentions, thinking that she was calling for water. "The gnomes will be back soon my Sovereign."

"Soon, soon. Yes, very soon," Zeppenfeld agreed.

The guard glanced at Zerilla, who nodded and began applying pressure on Centain's wound. He then stood up and looked around. "Sir, from all indications, over a hundred Imperial Guards were killed today. We could not possibly put together a group large enough to pursue the abductor."

"You are an Imperial Guard!" he spat at the man. "Your priority, first and foremost, is to safeguard the Empress! Find her!"

Torscen took a step forward, regarding Winton curiously. He knew that if Karleena was gone, and Winton somehow claimed the Imperium as his own, that his own stature would be increased significantly. Smiling to himself, he knew where the vote of the ministers would lie.

"Perhaps the Guardsmen could assist," Zerilla offered as she continued applying pressure on Centain's wounds. "They could fortify the defenses and also conduct a search."

"Yes—have them conduct a search, but forget about defenses. I want every guard searching Trespias for the Empress," Winton instructed.

"I'll see to it, sir," the palace guard replied, and then headed out of the chamber.

Torscen walked up to Winton and looked the man in the eyes. He could read the son of his biggest adversary, King Sarlec, well. This whole scene was nothing more than a carefully laid-out façade. One he hoped to become involved in quickly before the newly crowned king faltered. "Might I suggest using the personal guards of the royal families to defend the palace?"

"Yes, that would be good," Winton agreed. "They could help the wounded as well."

"Most generous sir," Torscen said.

"Royal families, we need your personal soldiers and escorts to replenish the Imperial Guards. What do you have available?"

Zerilla looked up and shook her head. "I only came with a small escort. No more than four men and my elder son, Trong."

"That will not help," Winton concluded. "Anyone else?"

Glancing around, any member of the royal families that hesitated in their relief efforts to bother replying came back with a negative nod.

Euristies yelled out: "The unifications talks were peaceful. We had no need to bring our own private armies."

"There is one who might be able to help," Torscen chimed in.

"Speak, good Minister," Winton offered.

"King Garum arrived with a considerable contingent of his own men."

"Yes, Garum and his men would do nicely," Winton agreed. "Have him released and make sure he agrees to allow his men to serve the palace for the time being."

"I shall do so immediately," Torscen practically sang with joy as he made his way out of the room.

"How could you release Garum?" Zerilla yelled in protest. "He's a criminal, possibly the man responsible for the death of your father!"

"Not to mention this," Lorrents added, becoming interested in the conversation.

"His men are nothing more than thugs," Zerilla continued. "They are not loyal to the Imperium, only Lady Salaman and the Hidden Empire."

"Accusations," Winton waved away their concerns. "As the Prince of Danchul, I have known Garum for many years. He is misunderstood, that is all."

"What gives you the authority to make these decisions?" Dornela sneered, clearly searching to increase her own station in the hierarchy of the Imperium.

"My father was one of the strongest supporters of the Imperium. His efforts, along with Emperor Conrad and Admiral Morex's, helped to found the Imperium. That fact alone should be enough; but truth be told, my claim goes deeper."

"Then speak up boy, what is this alleged claim?" Dornela pressed.

"Karleena and I were to be wed," he announced matter-of-factly.

"Wed?" Zerilla asked, shocked by the revelation.

King Palenial stopped his rescue efforts and regarded the man who always seemed to exist in his overbearing father's shadow. The last he knew, Sarlec had been trying to arrange a union between Karleena and Winton, but the Empress displayed no real interest, and the boy himself seemed far too embarrassed to ever act upon such a discussion. Deep down, he doubted the sincerity of the new king's declaration.

"Yes, wed," Winton confirmed. "The decision was made and a date set. My father was most ecstatic about it, but he died before we made the formal announcement. Then, we did not feel it appropriate to declare our plans until after the unification talks had been conducted."

Every person in the room regarded the man for a moment. They each shared their own doubts. Winton and Karleena were complete opposites, but none of them could truly argue the words that he was saying. Without proof of deception, Winton would be the future Emperor, so until Karleena was found, they would allow him to play the role. After that, let the Empress dictate his fate.

Arianna struggled to speak once more; an accusation filled with rejection of primal fury toward the deceptive man was burning inside of her. She saw right through his lies and wished to speak out, but nothing more than a strained gurgle escaped her lips.

CHAPTER 2

"The Walls of Trespias, at last!" Thamar announced as the seven traveling companions reached the top of the hill and looked down at the capital of the Imperium. "It has been too long since I have set my gaze upon this place."

"I was not aware you had been here before," said Ashwin, the princess of Xylona.

"You were not yet born when last I was here," the red-bearded dwarf explained. "Help build those walls, I did!"

Ashwin did not doubt the words of her honorable companion, but was likewise confused. The Imperium was established long after the Race Wars, in a time when humans dominated the land, and more often than not, discriminated against the other races. If dwarves had assisted in designing and building the human capital, she suspected that it was not a widely known fact.

The young princess had only seen three and a half decades, and knew that the Imperium was founded fifteen years before her birth. Though young for her people, she had been adamant when speaking to her father about journeying to Trespias to represent the elves of Xylona. Her father, King Echalas, reluctantly agreed, but took several safeguards to insure her safety, including her traveling companions: Arifos, Mylvannan, and Heirn.

Arifos was a Madrew elf that had mystically appeared in Xylona during a raid by hobgoblins, one that overwhelmed the noble elves and almost saw the end of their home. The pink-skinned elf's materialization turned the tide. He saw the attacking hobgoblins and leapt into battle unquestioningly. His two enchanted lightweight scimitars, Phistala and Aurlestyl, were swift and brutal and he cut his way through the hobgoblin ranks. As they attempted to flee, he lowered his swords and dropped his foes with his bow—Unamalastra, the Impaler.

Though Xylona has always prided itself on having some of the greatest elven warriors of all time, they all had to bow to the abilities and might of their newfound ally. King Echalas immediately welcomed Arifos and offered him a new home with them amongst the trees. Arifos had his own quest, but he had agreed to stay with a desire to forge new alliances in an unknown land.

As his prowess with his blades and bow were displayed in each and every subsequent hobgoblin attack, he was awarded the highest prestige in all of Xylona: the gift of an honor blade. Though Arifos still preferred his own blades—which he had crafted himself—he acknowledged the honor of receiving the Xylona sword, keeping Skrenlar strapped to his back.

Mylvannan remained more of a mystery to her. He was like no elf she had ever seen before: His ivory skin was always chilling and cold; his snow-white hair was long and flowing; his eyes were quite striking—she had caught his ice blue gaze regarding her more than once. Known as a Frost elf, he hailed from Akkammanavar, a city deep in the icy peaks of the Mourning Mountains.

Ashwin knew that Mylvannan had the blood of a Xylona elf also flowing in his veins. Even still, his appearance, though striking, was far different than anything she had ever seen before. Even his wardrobe and weapons seemed out of place to her. He had a skin-tight—though extremely malleable—white and light-blue body suit that encased him from his neck down to his toes. Above that, he wore an ice-blue mithril breastplate, so finely designed that it would impress even the finest artisans. The same detail and design was put into his boots that rose to his calves. Over his shoulders he wore a long white cloak.

He also carried an honor blade with pride, given to him by his mother, Mywinn, before he left Akkammanavar to seek out Xylona. It was the sword known as Frostlartil, and in his hands, it has only grown in fame. He also had two serrated swords that he kept sheathed on his belt, as well as a pair of serrated daggers in his boots.

The final elf on this journey, Heirn, was also of royal blood. King Echalas originally wished to send Heirn to represent Xylona, but Ashwin argued that only the descendant of the King himself could properly speak for their people. Though this was agreed to, Heirn, her cousin, would still be the diplomatic representative to advise her on how Xylona should proceed with the unification.

Heirn had long blonde hair, and blue eyes that always remained stern and serious. He was garbed in a light green tunic and pants. He also had a light brown vest, with matching gloves, boots, and cloak. Beneath his vest he wore mail for protection. Like the other two elves, Heirn was also a wielder of an honor blade of Xylona, Martristlit, his principle weapon, though he also carried a longbow.

The young princess knew that these three renowned warriors were sent more for protection for her than to represent the interests of Xylona. They were as effective as an entire convoy of elves, one of the reasons she knew her father was willing to allow her to go in their care. As Ashwin traveled alongside of them, she vowed that one day she too would have the privilege of wielding an honor blade, and that she would be considered amongst the greatest warriors her city has ever known.

The three dwarves that accompanied them were no less famous throughout the land. The brothers of Vorstad, Thamar and Theiler, had almost three centuries worth of stories of their feats, including their efforts to forge an alliance between the dwarves and the elves of Xylona, a truce that has been mutually beneficial to both kingdoms over the centuries.

The third dwarf was a prince himself: Baldock of Tregador. He was the second son of King Kendall, and had answered Thamar's call for help when the orcs and hobgoblins continued to besiege Vorstad and Xylona. Though three inches shorter than Thamar, the black-bearded dwarf was much stockier and stronger.

He was fully armored in illistrium, the precious mineral that the Tregador dwarves had discovered deep in the depths of the Northern

Mountains and finely crafted into nearly unbreakable weapons and armor. Ashwin considered Baldock's wardrobe to be slightly excessive: beneath his armor, he wore a hauberk, chainmail pants, and a coif. The mail was enough to cover his entire body, from its hood to sleeves to leggings, but the dwarf placed still more illistrium protectors over him: he had a spangenhelm helmet, a breastplate with spiked shoulders, a fauld to protect his abdomen, gauntlets on his hands and extending up his arms, greaves that encased his knees down to his shins, and armored boots.

Strapped to his back was his famed battleaxe, Splitter. It was a weapon well-known amongst the dwarves of Tregador—the head of the axe always glistened when in its wielder's hand. The blade itself was engraved with the image of Feldrin, the dwarven God of Fury. Though he preferred his axe above all other weapons, he also had a short-sword fastened to his waist.

Hanging loosely over his shoulder by its guige was an immaculate shield. It was round with an orb embedded in the center of a six-pointed star made of illistrium. Surrounding that was another six-pointed star that stretched to the ends of the round shield. Upon these points were dwarven script that roughly translated to say, "*He who carries this shield carries a mystical void.*" The two stars rose from an orange field, outlined with intricately crafted silver designs resembling the head of an axe.

"Arifos, what do my eyes see?" Thamar asked pointing towards a shadowy-shape flying off in the twilight.

The pink-skinned elf followed the dwarf's finger and regarded the figure. "It is a flying stallion," he replied.

"Are ye daft, there ain't no such thing as a flyin' stallion!" Baldock interjected in a deep guttural voice.

Thamar turned and regarded the armored dwarf, one eyebrow raised higher than the other. When he had marched north to Tregador, he had seen several flying stallions soaring above the Suspintian Forest; he surmised that Baldock was only familiar with the creatures that threatened the mines of Tregador and considered everything else little more than a rumor or myth.

"Nevertheless, it *is* a flying stallion, black in color, with a celestial rider," Arifos concluded.

The three other elves regarded the fleeing figure and concurred with Arifos's observation.

"Did you say celestial?" Thamar asked in mild shock.

"Yes," Arifos answered.

"He appears to be carrying a sack," Mylvannan added.

"A sack that is moving," Heirn agreed.

Thamar stroked his red beard and then glanced back at his brother, who answered his concerns with a stern glance. "There has not been a celestial in these parts for over a thousand years," he said. "I do not think this bodes well in light of everything that has been happening of late."

"Bah! The celestal, celestlee, celiaste—whatever it bein'—probably is here fer the same reason we are," Baldock offered.

"Perhaps," Thamar answered quietly.

"Celestials are quite common where I am from," Arifos declared.

"I do not like what I be hearing," Thamar declared shaking his head. "Nor what I be thinking. Braksis's Empress is trying to unite the races against Zoldex, and you are telling me that something that no longer exists here, but is common in the land of Zoldex has just left the palace with a sack that clearly be having someone in it?"

Heirn mounted his horse and glanced one last time at the figure flying to the North. "The dwarf is right, we must hurry. There is no guarantee what we will come across, but we must go now."

The elves and dwarves mounted their horses and ponies and followed Heirn as he led the way towards the Walls of Trespias. They were still close to twenty minutes from their destination, and then an additional thirty before reaching the palace. As they rode on, they each clung to the hope that the unification did not collapse before they even arrived.

CHAPTER 3

Arbuckle and Trivett ran through the corridors of the palace. Around each bend, they found more signs of destruction and bodies of the fallen Imperial Guards. The emissary of Wei Lau had been swift and brutal, leaving none standing in his wake.

Arbuckle skidded to a halt, his eyes wide with awe as he looked down at one of the bodies: it was the corpse of a minister, and not one of the guards. Upon his tunic was a brooch, crafted with gold and several sparkling jewels within it. Reaching down, the gnome quickly unfastened the trinket and dropped it into one of his pockets.

"No time, no time!" Trivett chastised him, more for stopping than for stealing. "We must hurry!"

"I'm coming, I'm coming," he quickly retorted.

"You explored the palace—how do we find water?"

"The kitchen!" Arbuckle answered. "This way!"

Before Trivett fell in step behind his fellow gnome, he leaned down and picked up a small dagger that one of the Imperial Guards had dropped. He quickly tucked it in his pants along his back, feeling more confident that he now had some form of protection; though, looking around, he knew just how little the dagger would really serve him if they confronted the attacker.

The two continued down the hall and around several more corners. Arbuckle kept yelling "This way," and "Over here" as he ran. The two then stopped at a dead end.

Trivett held an angry scowl on his face. "You led us to a dead end!"

"I led us to a hidey-hole!" Arbuckle beamed.

"I thought I told you not to go looking for hidey-holes!" Trivett scolded.

"If you don't want to take it, we can try to find water elsewhere," Arbuckle offered as he feigned innocence.

"No time!" Trivett yelled. "Lead on."

Arbuckle reached out to a stone brick and pushed it with both of his hands. The stone started moving backwards, leaving a small gap just big enough for the small gnomes to crawl into. Once both were behind the wall, he replaced the brick and winked at Trivett.

"How did you find this?" Trivett asked.

"I could smell the food behind the wall and was hungry!" Arbuckle answered.

"Please tell me you didn't steal food?" Trivett pleaded.

"Only a little," Arbuckle reasoned. "They never knew a thing, though!"

"Oy!" was all Trivett could say in reply, slapping his forehead.

On hands and knees, Arbuckle led them through the narrow passage for several moments, then paused. "Time to go down," he said.

"Down?" Trivett asked.

"Down," Arbuckle affirmed. Turning around, he swung his feet ahead of him and allowed himself to drop down a small passage in the tunnel.

Trivett rushed to the edge and listened below for Arbuckle to hit the bottom. As he strained to see in the dark tunnel, Arbuckle stood up and flicked his nose. "What did you do that for?"

"I said we're going down, not falling!" Arbuckle snickered. "Come on."

Mumbling to himself, Trivett put his legs in front of him and hopped down as well. The lower level was only a small drop, and he shook his head wondering why he allowed Arbuckle to fool around so much sometimes.

"This way," Arbuckle said.

After climbing down, the tunnel was large enough to allow the two to walk. They headed straight down the tunnel and arrived at an open grate at the other end. Arbuckle held his finger up to his mouth to signal Trivett to be quiet.

"The palace chefs are still hard at work," he whispered.

"You mean they were oblivious to the attack?" Trivett asked incredulously.

"Looks that way," Arbuckle answered. "I don't think they would be too happy about us barging in this way."

"How did you get in last time?"

Arbuckle smiled deviously. "Wait for my signal!"

"How come I get the feeling I'm going to regret this?" Trivett moaned.

Arbuckle pushed the grate open slightly and crawled out of the tunnel. Moving along the wall, he reached behind his back and pulled out a small slingshot. He placed a small stone on it and pulled it back, launching the pebble into the next room where it clanked and clanged loudly on several pans.

One chef spun about. "Oh no, not again!" and ran into the other room. Three others soon joined him, determined to find whatever was causing the ruckus, all of them certain that it was an elusive rat.

Arbuckle smugly walked over to the grate and bowed with his hand stretched out for Trivett to enter the kitchen. "After you, sir," he said.

"You're enjoying this too much!"

The two quickly rushed over to the large keg that was marked "Water," and began filling a bucket for each of them. While they waited, Arbuckle strained to lean over and pick up an apple, biting into it and smiling at Trivett.

"Is there anything you won't steal?" Trivett asked.

"I won't steal the dagger you took," Arbuckle answered.

"How did you know?"

Arbuckle just nodded knowingly. "My bucket is full."

"Mine too," Trivett quickly answered. "How do we get past them?"

"Be ready to move quickly," Arbuckle explained.

"I really don't think I'm going to like this," Trivett said as he rubbed his free hand along his brow.

Arbuckle stepped as close to the entrance to the kitchen as he could to see the chefs. He then beckoned Trivett over and checked to make sure that they were both hidden beneath a cutting table. Satisfied that they were concealed, he took his slingshot out again and sent another pebble at the cauldron with the left over stew in it.

The noise was loud enough to get all four chefs running back in crying that the rats had made it into the kitchen. As they dashed in, the two gnomes crept around the corner and silently out the door at the end of the storage room.

Back in the audience chamber, Zeppenfeld glanced questioningly at the aquatican Sentinel, who merely shook his head, indicating that unless Arianna received help soon, the Sovereign would perish.

He turned to regard the door where his two colleagues had rushed out to find water and hoped that they would return soon. As he stared at the rubble by the doorway, Prime Minister Torscen returned, accompanied by the most unorthodox king that Zeppenfeld had ever seen. It was as if the man had no care in the world for his own personal appearance and hygiene, and the mere sight of him turned the gnome's stomach.

"Emperor Winton," Torscen spoke loudly for all to hear the title as he walked into the room. "I have returned with King Garum, as you requested."

King Lorrents stepped in front of the two and spoke challengingly. "He is *not* our Emperor." The imposing highlander glared at the Prime Minister, his piercing blue eyes blazing through strands of chestnut hair. He wore a navy formal jacket and a blue and green plaid kilt. His muscular arms were crossed at his chest. He was a very strong and respected king: a man who fought for Falestia for half a century, very straight forward and direct.

"Minor details," Torscen waved off the intimidating man's comment. "He was betrothed to the Empress and as such would have been Emperor."

"*Would have been*," Lorrents sneered as Torscen brushed past him.

"King Garum," Winton began, his words full of confidence and motivation. "Prime Minister Torscen has indicated that you have arrived here with a large contingent of your soldiers. Is this correct?"

"It is, my Emperor," Garum bowed, glancing back to catch Lorrents's scowl, one that was shared by many of the faces of the royal families.

"Would you be willing to loan those soldiers to the palace for the protection of all within?" Winton asked.

"I would, my Emperor," Garum replied.

"Excellent," Winton answered. "Summon your men at once. They will protect the palace while the remaining Imperial forces search for the Empress."

"As you wish, my Emperor," Garum bowed again before leaving to summon his troops.

King Palenial walked over and held Lorrents's arm so he would not lash out. "Patience, my friend—let them play their game."

"How can you say that? The worst elements of the Imperium are now spreading their tentacles directly into the palace!" Lorrents spat.

"Only until Karleena returns," Palenial promised. "We should focus our attention upon that."

"You are right," Lorrents agreed. "But if Garum tries to extend his ties into Falestia, he will find my people ready to oppose him."

"He will find an enemy in Dartie as well," Palenial agreed.

Arbuckle and Trivett rounded the corner and paused as they heard laughter. Arbuckle put his bucket of water down, leaned against the wall, and crept along it to peer around.

King Garum was talking to one of his men as they physically detained another against the wall.

"They want the doctor so he can save Centain," Garum laughed. "They will find his arrival to be too little, too late."

"Please, let me pass," the doctor pleaded.

"You are not meant to pass," Garum replied with a snicker. "You are also not meant to repeat a word of this." In a more menacing tone, to emphasize his point, he added, "Ever."

"Please," the doctor repeated. "The good Captain will die."

"That's the point," Garum laughed again. "He dared to imprison me, to defy not only the King of Tenalong, but an emissary of the Hidden Empire! To imprison me is to openly insult Lady Salaman herself! For that alone, your assistance *will* come too late."

"Do not hurt me—I have a wife and three children," the doctor begged.

"You've heard of Lady Salaman?" Garum commented, watching the doctor closely to make certain he recognized the name. "Good, then you know that you should fear her retribution for going against one of her agents."

"How much longer, boss?" the large man holding the doctor asked.

"I trust he'll be dead in a matter of moments. Hold him here until I return with the other men. Then you can let him go."

"Yes, boss," the thug responded.

"If you try to escape," Garum added, "Crusher here will show you why we call him that." With a laugh, the Tenalong king walked down the hall, away from the eavesdropping gnomes.

Arbuckle looked back at Trivett, a gleam of mischievousness in his eyes.

"Oh no, not that look again," Trivett moaned.

"We need to get the doctor free so he can help Centain," Arbuckle concluded. "Besides, we need to go down this hall to get the water back to the Sovereign."

"I was afraid you would say that," Trivett answered. "No hidey-holes around?"

"Now you want a hidey-hole?" Arbuckle bemused.

"Then let's get it over with," Trivett decided. "The Sovereign may not last much longer." Pulling his dagger out, he stood poised to rush towards the large minion.

Arbuckle placed another stone in his slingshot and leaned out, carefully aiming for the man's head. Releasing the sling, the stone struck Crusher in his left eye, causing the man to drop the doctor, cry out in pain, and slap his hand to his head.

"Now!" Arbuckle screamed.

The two ran around the corner. Arbuckle placed another stone in his slingshot and waited patiently for Crusher to expose himself again. Not seeing an easy shot at the man's head, he launched his next projectile into his groin.

Crusher bent over in pain, leaving his head open again, where a third stone just missed his right eye and hit him on the cheek.

"Why ya little rodents!" he screamed. "I'll kill ya both!"

Trivett rushed behind the man taking advantage of his impaired sight, and brought the dagger slashing at his hamstring, cutting deeply. Crusher fell to the ground, no longer able to walk.

The triumphant gnome looked down at the man and smiled. "I may not want to fight or break the rules, but I still know how to get you where it hurts!"

Arbuckle rushed towards his companion and the doctor, the two buckets of water in his hands. "Come—Centain and Arianna need us!"

The doctor looked timid and paused before falling in step behind them.

"What is it?" Trivett asked.

"If I defy the Hidden Empire, they may kill my family," he reasoned.

"Life is full of hard decisions," Arbuckle sneered. "Get over it."

"Arbuckle!" Trivett scolded. Turning to the old man, he continued, "You're a doctor, right?"

"Yes," the doctor agreed.

"Isn't it your credo to do everything you can to help a patient?"

The doctor grimaced and knew that the gnome was right. "Very well, lead on."

"About time," Arbuckle said. Before jogging off, he took a moment to kick Crusher in the arm, an action that caused the giant man to begin ranting and raving about how he would find them and kill them for this.

The three returned quickly to the audience chamber and rushed to their respective patients. Arbuckle and Trivett dropped next to Arianna with the two buckets, where the Sentinel began giving her water to drink and then wiping some along her body with a soaked cloth.

The doctor went to Centain and thanked Zerilla for helping to keep him alive for so long. He immediately opened his small bag and began working on the Captain's wounds.

Above them all, Winton stared sinisterly and promised himself that if Centain and Arianna lived, their saviors would die in their stead.

CHAPTER 4

As the traveling companions entered the gates of Trespias, with the exception of Thamar and Theiler, they all looked at the towering walls in awe. The two Vorstad dwarves merely smiled with pride at what Thamar kept reminding everyone was one of their greatest architectural achievements.

The guards atop the wall had watched them closely, but Thamar declared that they were friends of Lord Braksis and that they were there by request of Empress Karleena. After that introduction, the guards granted them entrance without delay.

They reached the groined vault that provided a crossroads to three different sections of the city. Thamar continued to march his pony forward towards the center of the city and the palace, but Arifos paused and looked at a path leading towards a mighty tower that stretched as high as the eye could see.

Mylvannan paused beside him and considered the tower. "What troubles you, my friend?"

"The Chosen One," Arifos whispered. "She's there."

Thamar turned and looked at the two. "What's the delay?"

"The Child of Prophecy is in that structure," Arifos declared.

"Then there is no safer place for her in all the realm," Thamar explained. "That is the Mage's Council, where all mystically-gifted individuals are trained from birth in their abilities. There is no better education in the whole land. Not to mention the thousands of Mages that will surround and protect her."

The pink-skinned elf kept his gaze on the Tower, torn between his duty to his people, and his oath to King Echalas to insure his daughter's safety. When last he had heard about the Chosen One, she was with Kai. If she were here now, something tragic must have happened, for Kai would never willingly leave the child's side.

"She is safe," Thamar repeated to emphasize his point. "Come, we must press on."

Arifos reluctantly turned away and brought his horse in line with Ashwin and Mylvannan. "I must return to this place and see that she is indeed safe."

"When this mission is complete, I will ride by your side," Ashwin promised.

"As will I," Mylvannan agreed.

Arifos did his best to hide his reaction, but he was truly touched by the friends he had made and this new life he led. It seemed to him as if the constant threat of battle, torture and death that plagued the first three hundred and twenty-nine years of his existence were little more than a nightmare. For the first time in his life, he felt awake and alive.

Though they were invited and welcome at the palace, all seven companions could feel the gaze of the people of Trespias following them, the scorn, fear, and hatred that were behind almost every face they passed. They were here to unite the races, but faced with the reactions of the people watching elves and dwarves moving freely in their city, the companions knew that they had a long road ahead of them.

"There," Thamar pointed to a large round building. "That is the entrance to the palace."

Stopping below the ascending stairs before the Chamber, the riders dismounted. Thamar glanced around and saw several children watching them. Reaching into a pouch fastened to his belt, he revealed a ruby that was the size of his thumb. "Take care of the animals and this is yours."

One of the children, wearing disheveled and dirty clothing, stepped forward regarding the ruby with awe.

"Another when we get the animals back," he promised.

"Sure thing, mister!" the boy beamed. He took the reins to

Thamar's pony and beckoned the others to come over, who each took one of the animals.

Thamar tossed the ruby to the boy and reached out and scuffed up his hair. "That's a good lad."

"Yer wastin' yer durned money!" Baldock growled.

"Better to pay the lads than to have to find new mounts for our return trip," Thamar replied in his normal gruff voice.

"Bah!" Baldock snorted. "Fear o' me Splitter should ha' been good enough!"

"If you are through, Master Dwarf, we should continue on," Heirn stated.

Baldock glanced up at the regal elf and huffed. "I'll be goin' when I be good an' ready to go!"

Behind him, the mute Theiler pushed the armored dwarf forward.

"What do ye think yer doin'?" he roared.

Glancing at the impatient scowls on his companions' faces, Baldock stepped forward. "Okay, okay, I be ready to go."

They ascended the stairs to the Chamber and glanced up at the statues that were constructed in honor of the founders and heroes of the Imperium. Men that had risked everything for what they believed in, and found their dreams come true.

As they reached the door to the Chamber, two individuals that were smeared with mud and wearing rags barred their way. Both men emitted a putrid stench, baring rotting teeth and rusted swords.

Thamar stepped ahead of the others and regarded the two. "We are the emissaries representing Xylona, Akkammanavar, the Madrew, Tregador, and Vorstad."

The two men looked at each other and then back at the dwarf. "Get out of here, little dwarf. The palace is off limits."

"My patience, too, has limits. We were invited and intend to answer that invitation," Thamar declared.

"The invitation has been cancelled," one of the men sneered.

"Be gone!" the other shouted.

"Ye dare to speak to the second son o' King Kendall in such a manner?" Baldock roared. "Ye will move or ye will be moved!"

Thamar turned and looked warningly at Baldock. Though Thamar was famed as one who leapt into combat and faced insurmountable odds, the black-bearded dwarf made him look like he was overly cautious.

Baldock did not notice the warning as the two men began laughing. He charged up the last few stairs, arms extended, and grabbed both men, continuing directly through the door, splintering it in the process. His scream did not stop from the moment he began his charge until after he stood alone in the Chamber and dropped the now unconscious guards. "Humph," he snorted. "Not be lettin' us pass, will ye?"

Thamar walked in shaking his head in disapproval. "We were invited!" he yelled.

"It doesn't matter," Heirn said as he viewed the fallen guards inside the Chamber. "Something is clearly amiss."

Arifos swiftly stepped in front of Ashwin, and with one fluid motion, reached behind his back and unsheathed his two scimitars. Stepping forward, he scanned the area for any signs of danger before looking back at the princess.

Mylvannan stood, with Frostlartil also drawn, next to Ashwin. With a nod to Arifos, he stepped into the room and approached the large plantlike mass that barred their path.

"What is it?" Heirn asked.

"A plant of some kind," Mylvannan answered. "There are guards trapped inside."

"Does it still live?" Heirn questioned.

Arifos slammed one sword into the ground and reached down to his leg where small throwing daggers encircled. Picking up one blade, he hurled it at one of the vines. As soon as the blade pierced it, the vine constricted further. "It lives."

"We must get past that to reach the bridge to the palace," Thamar advised.

"We could crawl around it," Ashwin offered looking at the sides where others had clearly passed the deadly plant.

"I'll check the path first," Arifos declared. Stepping forward, he moved swiftly to the side of the Chamber and entered the walkway that Ashwin had referenced. He paused and saw definite signs that others had passed this way. From the stench in the air, he concluded that it was companions of the two by the door.

He circled around the vines and found the opening on the other side clear.

"Who are you?" a voice demanded.

Arifos turned and saw another man similar to the ones out front. His appearance was slightly cleaner, but it had clearly been many weeks since he had seen a bath.

"I am Arifos," he replied.

"What are you doing here?"

"I am here to see the Empress," Arifos explained. "On a diplomatic mission."

"Then turn around," the man instructed. "This palace now belongs to us."

"And who are you to claim it?" Arifos asked.

"I'm the one telling you how it is," the man answered.

"Oh really?" Arifos smiled in anticipation. "Only one man?"

"Hey guys!" the man called out. Five more joined him, all as grungy as their companion. "How about six men, elf?"

"One, six—makes no difference to me," Arifos replied. "Let me see if I have this right: you wish to bar my path from seeing the Empress?"

"Absolutely," the man said.

"You wish to cause me harm?" Arifos asked.

"Only a few broken bones, nothing time won't heal."

"I see," Arifos answered. "Then I suggest you move aside now before you face something you cannot possibly handle."

The men started laughing at the elf, who merely crossed his arms across his chest, his index and middle fingers of each hand touching the opposite shoulder, and grinned at his opponents. Very few in the

Seven Kingdoms would recognize the Madrew insult he was giving them with his gesture.

"We'll wipe that smile off of your face!"

The first man lunged for Arifos with his fist. The Madrew elf dropped to his knees and brought his fists up, slamming the big man in the stomach three times before he even realized that the elf had moved.

Seeing their companion drop, the other five were quick to pull out their rusted weapons, which included a pair of swords, a mace, an axe, and a crossbow.

Arifos reached behind his back and unsheathed his two scimitars and crossed them in a fluid swipe across his chest, deflecting the first bolt. Stepping forward, he met the two swordsmen and parried both of their blows at the same time.

The two men continued their attack, but were enraged as the elf moved so quickly, both hands bringing his swords up to perfectly deflect each thrust regardless of how they struck.

"Out of the way!" the crossbow wielder called.

The two men moved aside, one swinging his sword high, the other low. Arifos saw the man in the middle squeezing the trigger and continued to grin at his opponents. He deflected both attacks and in a speed that defied their senses, dodged the bolt and brought both of his swords down, slicing both swordsmen.

The man with the crossbow quickly began reloading as his companion with the axe charged in. Arifos brought both blades up and caught the over-handed slash. He then allowed some slack in his arms and forced them back up, causing his opponent to raise the axe high over his head again. Arifos then brought his swords down and carved a cross along the man's throat.

The thug with the mace tried to charge in from the side, but Arifos leapt up onto the wall, took a step up and then kicked himself off at the man. With a leaping kick, his foot cracked into the man's jaw, breaking it, and sending him dropping to the floor.

Arifos landed on the ground with hardly a sound and sheathed both swords. The man with the crossbow was shaking as he tried to take aim at what he considered the now-defenseless elf.

"If you fire, you will die," Arifos promised.

The man looked visibly shaken, but did fire the bolt. Arifos raised his left hand and the bolt slowed down and halted directly before him. Twirling his finger in a circle, the bolt spun in the air until it faced the man with the crossbow.

"You're a Mage!" he cried out.

Closing his fist, the bolt resumed its flight as if it had never lost its velocity. It pierced the attacker in the chest and dropped him to the ground, staring in disbelief at the pink-skinned elf.

"Come on, elf! You could have left me some!" Thamar roared behind him.

Arifos turned to see his companions standing there and looking at the men he had just defeated. "I thought I told you to wait?"

"We thought you might have found some trouble," Thamar shrugged. Seeing the first man Arifos struck trying to stand up, the dwarf pounded him on the head with his fist and sent him back into unconsciousness. "Clearly we were mistaken."

"I thought the palace was supposed to be run by Imperial Guards? Some of the best and most dedicated warriors," Ashwin asked.

"It is," Thamar answered. "The guards were scattered dead in the other room. Many more trapped by that living salad, too."

"What happened?" Ashwin asked.

"There is no use in trying to speculate," Heirn cut off her remarks. "We must continue on."

Theiler bent down and regarded one of the men. Looking up at his brother, Thamar nodded his agreement. "Hidden Empire, they are."

CHAPTER 5

Hidden Empire, they are.

Centain felt trapped, useless, and vulnerable. Through his connection with the Harlocten plants, he could hear every word being spoken within the palace. He had overheard Garum threatening the doctor and the gnomes coming to his rescue. He had heard the mumblings of the royal families and their disbelief over Winton claiming the Imperium as his own.

Winton—that was the most frustrating development. He heard the young Danchul heir's claim that he was betrothed to Karleena, but knew that the man was being deceitful. He did not know to what gain, other than perhaps searching for power himself.

With his Harlocten plants, he heard everything that happened within the walls that he was sworn to protect. Even if Karleena had a relationship with Winton behind his back, he would have been aware of it through his precious plants. Since that was not so, he knew that his recovery was crucial, not only in helping the Empress, but the entire realm.

The dwarf's comment about the Hidden Empire was unsettling as well. He had always suspected Garum's ties to Lady Salaman, but to have her forces marching freely through his palace was unthinkable. Yet there was nothing that he could do to stop them.

He knew that the doctor was working on his injuries. He could no longer feel anything, nor could he even open his eyes. However, through the Harlocten plants, he heard the doctor and Queen Zerilla working frantically to save his life.

Crusher, who did this to you?

It was the damned gnomes!

They will suffer for this!

The doctor better not be working on the good Captain, not if he knows what is good for him.

Centain tried to speak, to warn the doctor, but he couldn't even emit a sound. The words were clear in his head, but he had no way of relaying them to the man risking his life and that of his family to save him.

I'm losing him!

Doctor, tell me what to do.

Apply pressure there. Damn, the blood just keeps coming. I fear that he has internal damage as well.

Hurry doctor!

Pausing to consider this, Centain wondered if he truly was that close to death. Was his life at an end? No matter how hard he wished to stop Lady Salaman, expose Winton, or rescue Karleena, would his life be lost before any of that could be accomplished?

Right around this corner.

Are you sure, Thamar?

Trust me! See, the audience chamber.

Guards, stop them!

What? We are invited guests!

Let them pass.

We bring news that may be of use to you.

What kind of news?

We have seen the destruction of the palace, the lives lost. Before arriving, we saw a celestial astride a winged steed flying north.

North you say? Impossible!

The conversation suddenly cut off. Centain wanted desperately to hear more, but the silence was deafening. What was happening? Why couldn't he hear anymore?

"What is that?"

Zerilla continued to apply pressure on the wounds but glanced up at the doctor. "What is what doctor?"

"There is some kind of vine wrapped around his neck and body," the doctor replied.

"Like the ones that are binding the men at the door?"

"Better not to take the chance," the doctor decided. Reaching into his bag, he pulled out a small scalpel and carefully began cutting the vines of the Harlocten plant from around Centain's body.

CHAPTER 6

Winton glared at the newcomers as they entered the audience chamber: two red-bearded dwarves, a heavily armored black-bearded dwarf, two elves with blonde hair, a pink-skinned elf, and an ivory-skinned elf. A most peculiar band.

Before they even spoke, a voice entered his thoughts. *Arifos. He must not be allowed to wander freely.* Winton turned to face the newcomers, more cautious with Zoldex's warning.

"Guards, stop them!" he called out.

Several of the men that Garum brought with him ran to heed the instructions of Winton. The companions tensed, reaching for their weapons.

Thamar stepped forward in protest. "What? We are invited guests!"

Queen Zerilla glanced up at the newcomers and was shocked to see a pink-skinned elf, just like Kai, the savior of her own home. "Let them pass!" she cried out.

"Zerilla, keep applying pressure," the doctor instructed.

"I am sorry, doctor," Zerilla responded. Looking up at Winton but keeping her hands firmly on Centain, she explained: "These travelers are allies to Suspinti. Not a threat."

"We bring news that may be of use to you," Heirn offered.

"What kind of news?" Lorrents asked, taking interest in the newcomers.

"We have seen the destruction of the palace, the lives lost," Heirn explained. "Before arriving, we saw a celestial riding astride a winged steed flying north."

All within the room fell to silence. The celestial that the elf was speaking of had to be the same one that abducted the Empress.

"North you say?" Winton asked doubtfully. "Impossible!"

"Do you doubt the words of the emissaries of Xylona and Vorstad?" Thamar growled challengingly.

"They are here to deceive us!" Winton continued. "To set us on a wild goose chase! We all know that Aezians are to the south!"

"He traveled north!" Thamar roared.

"He went south and back to Emperor Wei Lau!" Winton stubbornly replied.

Arianna could feel her strength returning. Her voice had likewise returned, though it was scratchy and little more than a whisper. The gnomes had done well to find water for her and her people, but most of them were still very weak.

She wanted desperately to confront Winton, for she feared that he was lying and could not be trusted. Seeing the dwarven and elven emissaries though, she felt a minor reprieve, for they were placing doubt upon the new ruler already. Doubt that would fester until hopefully the others could discern the deception on their own.

As she listened to the growing argument, she had little doubt that Karleena was indeed being brought north and not south. Though she had never met this red-bearded dwarf, she instinctively felt that he was an honorable individual and could be trusted.

Slowly, she stood up, to the protest of her Sentinel who wanted her to stay seated until her strength fully returned. Arianna refused. She was here to represent her people; and if the unification were to succeed, Karleena would have to be found quickly.

"Your Majesty, you do not have to listen to such clear distortions of the facts," Torscen offered.

Baldock charged past Thamar and Theiler, pushing them aside, and looked up at the Prime Minister. "A distortion, ye say? Yer talkin' to some o' the most noble individuals I ever had the privilege to be knowin'!"

"Is that supposed to impress me?" Torscen sneered. "Or frighten me?"

Thamar walked forward and clamped his hand on Baldock's shoulders. "There are no threats. I am a personal friend of Lord Braksis, and am here under invitation."

Lorrents took immediate interest in this. "Lord Braksis you say?"

"Yes," Thamar replied.

"He is my nephew. I would like to let him know of what has happened here this day. When was the last time you saw him?"

"I saw Braksis last at Xylona, where he and Solara both received medical attention," Thamar answered.

"Medical attention?" Zerilla jumped up in concern.

"My Queen, I need you to keep pressure on the wound!" the doctor scolded.

"I'm sorry doctor," Zerilla apologized as she sat down again, her thoughts no longer on the welfare of the Captain.

"They were attacked by hobgoblins, the same ones that have been assaulting Xylona for some months now in the name of Zoldex. They were rescued by Captain Travers and returned to Xylona for medical aid."

"Which we promptly gave them," Ashwin offered.

"What happened then?" Lorrents prompted.

"They continued north, towards the home of his father," Thamar declared.

"Lies," Lorrents spat. "His father is dead. Murdered by my own son."

"I know the tale of Rawthorne's treachery well," Thamar answered. "I was referring to the man Braksis now considers his father, Ferceng."

Lorrents seemed appeased and returned to his efforts to free the Imperial Guards trapped in the vines.

Winton watched the newcomers and knew that he had to eliminate them, somehow. He also saw Arianna struggling to stand up, and could see in her eyes that she wished to challenge him.

"Until we can determine exactly what has happened here today," Winton began, "I'm afraid that all non-humans will need to be incarcerated."

"Incarcerated?" Thamar bellowed. "My brother and I are sons of Vorstad! This is a prince of Tregador, and she is a princess of Xylona! You dare to demand our incarceration?"

"Until we figure this out," Winton calmly replied. "Yes."

Arifos unsheathed his two swords; Mylvannan and Heirn raised their honor blades; Baldock gripped Splitter in both hands; Theiler gently pounded his club in his open palm; and Thamar's fingers grew white as he tightened his grip around his hammer. Ashwin stepped forward and bid them to lower their weapons.

"We are invited guests and will not fight," she declared.

"What are ye sayin'?" Baldock demanded.

"We will show our intentions by acting peacefully," she adamantly replied. "Look around you, there has been enough fighting and destruction here already. We shall not add to it by fighting our allies."

Heirn lowered Martristlit and nodded his consent. "Peace begins here," he declared.

Thamar glanced at Theiler and then likewise lowered his hammer. "Braksis will vouch for us," he concluded.

Several guards, similar in garb and stench to the ones they fought outside, stepped up and claimed their weapons. Arifos, Mylvannan, and Baldock seemed neither convinced nor particularly pleased to turn over their weapons, but all ultimately relented.

A pair of guards approached Arianna who shot a warning look to her Sentinel.

The tall aquatican stepped forward and batted the men away. "No scoundrel shall lay a hand on the Sovereign!"

"Get them!" Garum ordered.

Several men pursued the aquaticans. The Sentinel remained behind, delaying the foes as two others—the only ones strong enough to move after the celestial's attack—grabbed Arianna and rushed towards an adjoining room.

The Sentinel picked up one of the Imperial Guards' fallen staffs and began twirling it above his head. As the first man came close to him, he brought the staff down and hit the man on the side of the shoulder, knocking him aside. He then brought the staff up and knocked a second man over.

Stepping backwards towards the room where the Sovereign was led, he moved slowly, stopping any who tried to get past him. Before he left the room, he nodded his appreciation and respect to the gnomes for helping him to save Arianna's life.

Meanwhile, the two aquatican guards that were with Arianna had reached a window. One picked up a chair from the room and continued to strike the pane of glass until it shattered. Looking down, he turned around. "It is a long drop, but it does lead to the sea."

Arianna stepped up to the window and looked down. She wondered if she would survive such a fall in her current condition.

Just then, her Sentinel backed into the room. "Sovereign, go!" He swung the staff and knocked another pursuer to the ground. Behind him, another door burst open and a dozen other men rushed in, separating him from Arianna and her aides.

"No!" Arianna screamed.

The closest aquatican to her pushed her out the window and she fell to the water below. Screaming in defiance, she spun around in the air, executing a perfect dive into the water.

After she pierced the water, she felt the pain of the impact from falling from such a height, and was rendered numb for several long minutes. As she continued to sink, she began to feel as if the sea itself were rejuvenating her.

Crashing into the open air, she looked up hoping to see her Sentinel and two remaining guards join her. Her wait was in vain. She continued to watch the window until the following morning, without even a glimpse of her noble Sentinel. As the hopelessness of the situation overcame her, she wept and prayed that, one day, their efforts of the past few months would ultimately be realized.

CHAPTER 7

He watched her in silence as she methodically went about preparing to leave. Though he had argued and continued to tell her that there was hope, that his efforts to protect Braksis had worked, he could clearly see the subtle changes in the woman.

When he had first met Solara, she had been playful, passionate, and someone he was very pleased to see his son with. Now, she was acting out her grief in a desperate desire to see Braksis avenged. Something he hoped was in vain, for he honestly believed that if his son were dead, he would know it.

"Please reconsider," Ferceng pleaded.

Solara stopped for a moment and regarded the troll. Her face was pained, as if another moment of sitting still would be the end of her. She could not stay, not while Braksis's attackers roamed free.

Turning away without a word, she fastened the clip that held her throwing knives around her leg. Standing up straight, she glanced at her armored form and her weapons. She picked up her two drantanas, lightweight mystral blades, and sheathed them in their scabbards crossed along her back.

"He is not dead, there is still hope," Ferceng tried to boost her spirits.

Picking up her final weapon, her elongated dragonrider sword, she inserted it in its sheath at her waist and turned to face Ferceng. "Alive or dead, my duty is clear."

"You are saying that in pain," Ferceng cautioned. "Do not rush headlong into oblivion because you are running from the truth!"

"I am not rushing, I am tracking," Solara reasoned. "And if I don't start soon, Tiot will not be able to pick up the scent."

"You may already be too late for the wolf to pick up their scent," Ferceng cautioned.

"I will track them myself then. Durgin will not be too hard to find. I should have killed him a decade ago when I had the chance. The other, I do not know him."

"What did he look like?" Ferceng asked, realizing that he had never even bothered to try and determine who had gone after his son.

Pausing for a moment, Solara recalled the image of the man as he had run past her. His look of satisfaction and pleasure aside, she recalled his physical description. "Long brown hair flowing freely down his back; a large and bushy brown mustache that trailed from his upper lip and down both sides of his mouth; approximately six and a half feet tall; muscles that nearly burst from his outfit."

"Rawthorne," Ferceng replied in a deep scowl.

"I have heard of him; he now has many injustices to atone for. My blades will find him, as they will Durgin," she vowed.

"Kill the attackers and then what?" the troll asked. "Then come back and pray you're not too late to find Braksis?"

"We searched for days; there is nothing more I can do here. Already, Durgin and Rawthorne may have escaped my pursuit. But I will find them, and I will show them that they will not live long with the glory of their kill."

"Do not lose yourself in your quest," Ferceng cautioned.

"I won't," Solara promised. "It is just something that I have to tend to."

With her comment, she whistled once and Tiot bounded to her side. With a slight nod to Ferceng, she turned and walked away from the place her friend had called home. She was confident that if Braksis truly did live, the Mage would find him easier than she would. She could only do what she did best, find Durgin and Rawthorne and make them pay.

As he watched her walk out, he lowered his eyes and sighed. "I fear you have already lost yourself, child."

Ferceng walked over to the boulder of ore he had selected to make Braksis's new sword with, and considered it for a moment. He had no doubt in his mind that he would finish the blade for his son, for he had no doubt that Braksis would return. As he stared at it, thoughts of other things he could do to help improve upon the design began flowing through his mind.

Closing his eyes, he knew that Solara's words—though hidden in revenge—were accurate. If Braksis were close enough to be found, they would have done so already. It was more likely that he was washed to sea, where anything could have happened. He prayed that his son was all right and would one day return.

"One day," he whispered. Standing back up, he walked over to the door and picked up Carnage, the battleaxe that Braksis had claimed after killing the tyrant Guldan. "First though, I will help you in another way."

With a quick look back inside, he stepped out of his cavern and mystically pushed the boulder doorway back in place with a gentle motion of his hand. He turned to watch as Solara rode off to the east with both horses and Tiot. He watched her until she was out of sight, then turned back and began walking southwest on a quest of his own.

CHAPTER 8

The first man that Solara was pursuing was oblivious to the danger he faced; though for a man who was once a ferocious and relentless Warlord, Durgin could not possibly be more frightened than he was if he knew who was coming for him. Perched beneath a tree along the edge of the Suspintian Forest, he slowly painted a small black skull onto his axe, a symbol of his first kill since returning to his old life.

As he continued painting, his hand shook and the image was so jagged and rough that one really had to strain to recognize it as a skull. Durgin did not care though, for in his eyes, the image was that of Lord Braksis, and the kill belonged to him.

Leaves rustled in the distance, and Durgin dropped his brush and the small tube of paint. He leaned against the tree holding his breath, looking into the woods, praying that nothing was there. If anyone did see him, they would see a once-strong man now pale white in fear.

Durgin listened for several minutes before daring to breathe regularly again. He placed the brush and vial of paint in a small pouch along his belt and grimaced at how far he had fallen.

He remembered clearly the days when he led his own band of marauders, how the villagers and townspeople fled before him, crying out in terror. His raids were swift and brutal. Even more, they were always profitable, regardless of whether it was by claiming jewels and riches, or by stealing the virginity of a farmer's daughter. He enjoyed and took just as much satisfaction in both acts.

That was before Braksis was sent by the Emperor to hunt him down and stop him. His forces were decimated, and though he had managed to strike a near-mortal blow to the young Warlord, it had been the greatest disgrace possible. He was brought down not by a knight or better fighter than him, but by a naked child.

The memory haunted him. Taunted him. Though he knew that the deathblow of Braksis was truly Rawthorne's, he took some satisfaction in knowing that one of his nemeses had been eliminated. Even so, he looked at his hand and watched as it trembled, unable to remain steady.

He had spent the better part of the past decade hiding in the swamps of Tenalong. He struggled to find what little sources of food he could to survive, too timid to seek out the Hidden Empire and join their ranks, a place he knew Rawthorne was now venturing towards.

Rawthorne—the name was like venom to him. The man was disrespectful, degrading, and even worse, right. Durgin shuddered at the thought, but he knew that where once he and Rawthorne may have been equals, he was now more a pitiful joke than a threat. Perhaps the former King of Falestia would have been right to end Durgin's life after they killed Braksis.

Perhaps, but as long as he lived, he prayed that he would never see Rawthorne again. Not unless it was as equals once more. The question was: how could he regain the mindset and presence of the man he once was?

A laugh broke his concentration. Like before, Durgin held his breath and tensed against the tree. As he listened, he heard children playing, and even music from a banjo. Gathering confidence, the former Warlord decided that it was time to take the first step to returning to his old life.

Standing up, he strapped his axe over his shoulder so as to appear less threatening, and then began walking towards the sounds of play. Concealed behind a tree, he saw three children running around with a fourth attempting to catch them. There was a wagon, a pony, two men, two women, and an older girl that looked no older than fourteen.

Durgin looked down at his shirt and saw the dried blood that had flowed from his nose when Braksis broke it. He wondered how they would react to him. Would it be in fear as before? In sympathy for his injury? Or would they merely laugh at him and turn him away?

Durgin stepped forward and walked towards the adults. One of the children, a small girl screamed when she saw him. The two men leapt into action and ran out, one holding a pitchfork, the other a hoe.

"Speak your business," one declared.

Durgin glanced back and forth, then down at his hand. The trembling seemed to have slowed down. Perhaps he could become the man he once was.

"Arlur, can't you see the man is hurt," one woman said.

"Stay back Quella, he may be dangerous," the man replied.

"Nonsense, if he was dangerous, he'd have that axe out already, wouldn't you?"

Durgin watched the exchange and began to relax. "I could use some bandages for my nose, a drink and food if you can spare it." As he said the words, they surprised him; he sounded so calm, but also innocent.

"How did that happen, mister?" the other man asked, still suspicious.

Durgin was not certain if these people were Suspintians or not, but if they were, most shared an incredible fear of the creatures within the forest. He decided to play on that fear. "My brother and I were journeying to Dartie—we planned on becoming hunters," he began. "A large white creature jumped out at us. It hit me in the nose, and I fear it rendered me unconscious. When I awoke, I was alone."

"Mama, was it a lupan?"

"Yes," Durgin answered the child's question. "It must have been a lupan."

"Where are you from, mister?" the man asked, still not satisfied.

"Fenland, capital of Tenalong," Durgin lied.

"Well, come on over here then and let me tend to your nose," Quella said.

"Thank you, m'am, I greatly appreciate this," he said.

As she led him over to the fire and sat him down, Durgin caught the eye of the teen-aged girl. He could see that she would be quite attractive when she grew up, if she grew up, he quickly corrected himself. A bit younger than he would have liked, but he was merely beginning, and why not start off with a sure thing?

As the images of what he was going to do to the girl swirled in his mind, he began smiling, feeling stronger than he had in many years.

CHAPTER 9

Winton sat in the throne room, marveling at his recent good fortune. He never imagined, that day that an old traveler had entered his life seeking asylum, that he would one day help the young prince to become an Emperor. The thought made him smile.

Someone knocked at the chamber door and Winton glanced over. "Enter," he ordered.

The Imperial Guard—one of the few that had survived—who had led the city's Guardsmen in their mission to try and find the Empress stepped inside and dropped to a knee.

"What news have you?" Winton asked, certain that the news—though very bad—would be delightful to his ears.

"The city's gates have been sealed—none may enter or leave," the guard explained. "We scoured the city, checking and rechecking every residence and building. There is no sign of the Empress."

"She is probably half-way to Aezia by now," Winton surmised.

"What are your orders, sir?" the guard asked.

"Assemble the royal families and ministers," Winton declared. "I wish to make a an announcement."

"As you wish," the guard replied. He stood up, bowed respectfully, and walked out of the room.

Winton watched the man leave and pondered his next move. According to Zoldex's instructions he still had much to do. The next few minutes were critical, though he would later have other matters that required his attention. But first, the royal families needed to leave the premises if his reign should continue.

Another knock on the door interrupted his thoughts. "Enter," he summoned with little enthusiasm.

Prime Minister Torscen and King Garum walked into the throne room. "You sent for us?" Torscen asked.

Winton regarded the two for a moment: of all the people he would address this day, these two were his greatest allies. "Yes, in a few moments I will be announcing a declaration of war."

"War, my Emperor?" Torscen asked.

"Yes, with the Aezians," Winton explained calmly. "To recover the Empress, of course."

"Of course," Torscen grinned cunningly.

"What of the threat to our own land?" Garum asked. "The reason we were brought here in the first place?"

"Ah yes," Winton said. "I do believe that the lesser races of our fine realm are being slaughtered, but a plot against the humans is pure folly, do you not agree?"

Torscen and Garum exchanged glances but said nothing.

"After all, you, King Garum indicated that there is no orc city with one hundred thousand orcs, am I correct?"

Garum watched the new Emperor carefully. He knew that the orc city was there, but was under instructions by Lady Salaman to never reveal its existence. He did not know whether the city belonged to her or not, but he knew better than to defy the leader of the Hidden Empire.

"You are correct," Garum answered.

"Excellent, then there really is no threat," Winton deduced. "Therefore, our efforts should be focused on recovering the Empress."

"I agree completely," Torscen said.

"I trust I can count upon support and loyalty from the both of you?" Winton asked.

"Of course," Torscen quickly answered.

Garum nodded, though he knew that if Lady Salaman desired him to work against Winton, he would do so without hesitation.

The door swung open and Palenial stormed in, the other royal families and ministers behind him. "What news have you heard?" he demanded.

"I fear that the bounty hunter has somehow managed to elude us. Karleena is most likely half-way to Aezia by now," Winton declared.

"A slight exaggeration," Euristies scoffed. "It would take three months just to sail there."

"Then perhaps we still have time to catch up to her," Winton was quick to reply. "Has Admiral Morex returned yet? We can have him begin pursuit."

"There has been no word from Morex, I am afraid," Torscen stated.

Winton tried to hide his amusement—Zoldex had assured him that Morex had already been dealt with. "A pity," Winton declared. "How about Lord Braksis? He would certainly know how to recover the Empress!"

"He too, I am afraid, has not returned," Torscen replied in a sorrowful voice. "I am afraid that *you* must make the decision on how to rescue your fiancé without them."

"Yes," Winton said as if in deep contemplation. "I see that the decision does fall on my shoulders." He gazed at every individual in the room, then set his eyes on King Garum. "We were brought here to defend against an orc army being bred in your kingdom, Garum, yet you claim that this is not true. Are you certain?"

"I am," Garum answered. "I sent my best scouts to find the orc city, and they returned without incident or cause for alarm."

"Very well," Winton answered. "Without substantial evidence to support the unification, I feel that our new priority is the safe return of the Empress. Send messengers immediately—recall all Imperial troops and request volunteers. If we must go to war with the Aezians, then so be it."

"Is this not a bit premature?" Lorrents asked. "Your actions today may leave us defenseless."

"I do not doubt that other races are being attacked. However, we have not concerned ourselves with the affairs of non-humans for centuries. We shall not do so now either."

"That is a pretty stubborn attitude," Zerilla added. "If not for an elf, Comonor may no longer stand!"

"Then let us all hope for a swift return of the Empress, and then she can resume the unification talks herself," Winton conceded.

"Should we not send emissaries first? Attempt to determine if Wei Lau truly has the Empress?" Lorrents suggested.

"And waste even more time?" Winton asked condescendingly. "You heard it yourself: the voyage to Aezia is three months. You would have messengers travel three months there, three months back, then have our armies take another three months before we can get to her? Surely such a course of action will see her dead!"

Palenial and Lorrents shared a look, and then both stepped back. The two had already decided amongst themselves that they would take steps within their own kingdoms to continue the Empress's mission, and if that meant that Dartie and Falestia were to stand alone against the rest of the Imperium, then so be it. For now, they would stop arguing and merely observe, seeking out allies in the other royal families.

Zerilla marched directly in front of Winton and spoke harshly, something none thought she ever could do. "What if the dwarves and elves are right, and you are too self-centered to even ponder their words? What if it is the bounty hunter himself that is deceiving us and the Empress has really been brought north instead of south?"

Winton found himself trapped in the scenario. He could not stubbornly ignore the information that he received, but Zoldex specifically instructed him to force the Imperium into war with the Aezians. "Very well," he said in defeat. "I shall summon the Mages that were appointed to assist the Empress. They shall go to Wei Lau and try to procure the release of the Empress."

"Thank you," Zerilla stated.

"But," Winton said, his hand held up to silence everyone in the room. "I want the military recalled, assembled here, and ready to go to sea. Once the Mages have the information for us, our enemies will learn what it means to attack the head of the Imperium."

"An excellent plan, my Emperor," Torscen chimed in.

Winton glanced for acceptance from the royal families, but found none. Zerilla was somewhat appeased by this compromise, but he could see that the rulers of the Seven Kingdoms did not support him. "You should all return to your kingdoms. Prepare your people for the upcoming war. Lead them and guide them, for they need you now."

Reluctantly, the royal families began to leave. Several paused to speak to each other, but Winton was glad to see them actually walking out and preparing to leave Trespias.

Torscen was the last to depart. As he closed the doors behind him, Winton could hear his parting words: "Very well done."

Not a moment after the door closed, a swirling blue image appeared next to him, revealing Zoldex as clearly as if he were in the room with him. "Was your deception successful?"

"Yes," Winton replied. "The royal families are all leaving Trespias and the Imperial forces are preparing for war."

"Excellent," Zoldex said. "You have done well."

Winton grimaced.

"What is it?" Zoldex demanded. "What do you hide?"

"The royal families are not convinced that Wei Lau is responsible," Winton explained. "They wanted emissaries to go first."

"How did you handle it?" Zoldex asked, showing no signs of anger.

"I said that the armies will still prepare for war, but that the Mages assigned to the Empress will go forth to Aezia."

Laughing sinisterly, Zoldex nodded his approval. "You did well. This will eliminate the Mages by sending them on a wild goose chase. By the time they return, it will already be too late."

"I will find the Empress's corryby as soon as we have concluded this conversation," Winton explained. "They will be sent from the Seven Kingdoms this very day."

"Yes," Zoldex said. "That will be acceptable. You must be cautious though."

"With the Mages?" Winton asked.

"With anyone that knows the truth of your deception," Zoldex answered. "Dispose of your father's body, make certain that Centain does not recover, and eliminate Sharnesta."

Winton considered this. He could easily burn his father's corpse. Dealing with Centain and Sharnesta would be trickier though: the Captain was under a constant watch by the doctor, and as for eliminating Sharnesta, how would he do it?

As if reading his thoughts, Zoldex answered him. "Sharnesta may need a long vacation; after all, it has been quite some time since she had been home."

"Yes," Winton agreed. "With the Empress gone, it is the perfect excuse to visit her family's ancestral home."

The image of Zoldex smiled and began laughing sinisterly once more. He had chosen wisely. The sniveling fool was a good puppet, and he was the puppet master.

CHAPTER 10

Deep in the dungeons of the palace, the visiting emissaries each dealt with their incarceration in different fashions. Ashwin kept turning her father's ring around her finger, and tried to remain calm while waiting for her fate to be determined.

Looking down at the ornamented black-gold band, she knew that her father had given it to her to help assure her safety. It was a ring of power named Imperius, the Ring of Imperviousness. She wondered, if her sentence was to be hanging or beheading, how exactly would the ring protect her?

Regardless of its mystical safeguards, she was glad that when her captors took her longbow and dagger, that they did not also remove her ring. For some reason, as long as she had the ring on her finger, she felt that her father was close by, and that they would manage to escape from such a sullen place.

She wondered if her father had been right: he had been opposed to her presence in the unification talks, but she had been adamant. Conceding, he had handed over the ring, as well as Arifos and Mylvannan—the two greatest warriors protecting Xylona from the hobgoblin attack—as protection. Now that they were all imprisoned, she could only hope that her foolish ideals would not be the downfall of them all—but especially of her father, without the services of the two famed elves.

She glanced over at them. They were so different from her: Arifos with his dark-pink skin and long, braided silver hair, light-blue strands scattered throughout; and Mylvannan, cold to the touch, with his ivory skin and snow-white hair. Considering her own pale complexion, she was amazed at how different the elves of the world could be.

Neither elf appeared distraught in any way. They stood together watching the guards in the hall. They did not speak, but she could see their eyes moving constantly, absorbing every detail of their surroundings.

Feeling chilled in the dank dungeon, Ashwin tightened her pine-green cloak around her. Her full-length lighter jade-green sleeveless dress and white laced-sandals provided very little protection when in such conditions. Beneath the cloak, she rubbed her bare arms repeatedly to try and ward away the goose bumps that were appearing all over her exposed skin.

Seeing her plight, Heirn walked over to his cousin and removed his own brown cloak, draping it over Ashwin for added protection.

"You will freeze," she observed.

"I am not as vulnerable to these conditions," Heirn replied. Without allowing another word of protest, he walked back to where he had originally been and continued to observe the gnomes, who were talking and giggling to themselves, hunched over and acting as if what they were doing was of vital importance.

The dwarves were dealing with the imprisonment in their own way. Thamar, one who typically tells tales and was very rarely quiet, sat in the middle of the large cell and stared at the doorway leading back up to the palace, as if expecting someone to come down and release him.

His brother Theiler acted as if he had not a care in the world. He was curled up along the wall, deep in his own slumber. His beard fluttered silently with each and every deep breath.

That fact was something that everyone in the room was wishing of the loud and boisterous Baldock. Though his weapons were removed, his armor remained. He paced the length of the dungeon, clanging with each step, and complaining loudly about the fact that they had surrendered. His tirade was relentless, and as the days went on, he still seemed full of energy and bluster.

The door that Thamar was patiently watching opened, and a

small, squirrelly man walked over with trays of food—if one could call it that—for the prisoners. It was the same man that delivered the food each time, and if the prisoners complained about what they were being fed, he snickered and spat in their meals.

Thamar jumped up quickly, showing no weariness in his legs. He rushed to the barred door and glared at the man. "I demand to see Warlord Braksis," he ordered.

Pausing in his rant, Baldock's brown eyes widened with a glimmer of hope. He regarded the squirrelly man and Thamar, with thoughts of vengeance dancing through his head for this injustice.

"Braksis no here," the man replied in short squeaks.

"Solara then," Thamar pressed.

"No here," he repeated.

Reaching his hand through the bars, the dwarven warrior grabbed the man by the collar and pulled him into the bars. "My patience is growing weary," he threatened. "I will see Lord Braksis, Solara, any member of the Imperial army, or even of the royal family."

"No here, no here," the man kept repeating.

The giant jailor, who stood at nearly seven feet, walked over, laughing in amusement. "Go ahead, kill him, dwarf; it just means you'll starve. This fool means nothing to me."

Setting his gaze on the jailor, Thamar could see that the man spoke the truth. He cared not for the servant, and by his own actions, the dwarf potentially was ruining any hope of being let go.

Releasing his grip, the server dropped to the ground and crawled away from the bars. The guard merely shook his head and laughed again.

"I want to speak to Lord Braksis," Thamar repeated. "I am a friend and ally of his."

"In here, little man, you are nothing but what I say you are," the jailor explained.

"I am Thamar, son of Thron, proud warrior of Vorstad and thrasher of mine enemies," the dwarf roared in defiance. "You will bring me an appropriate official to speak with or you will learn what it means to defy a true dwarven son!"

"Yeah!" Baldock roared as he charged the gate, bumping against it. "Ye be doin' what he be sayin' or ye be facin' our wrath!"

The jailor merely laughed in reply and took a step closer to the bars. "If someone were to come down right now, it is more likely that they would be authorizing me to torture and kill you than to release you."

Thamar held the man's gaze for a moment, and then stepped back. Returning to where he had been sitting since the start of his imprisonment, he sat down to wait some more. He was confident that they would soon be free, and he silently vowed that this man would be the first to feel his hammer.

Baldock spun around and eyed him incredulously. "Ye're just gonna be sittin' down again? Bah!" With a deep gurgle, he turned and spat at the jailor.

Wiping the spittle from his face, the guard rushed towards the bars in fury. The smile on the proud dwarf's face made him pause. Pivoting, he turned and walked over to a cabinet that held a variety of weapons. "Perhaps I'll begin torturing you without the instructions of the new Emperor."

"Stop yer jabberin' and bring it on!" Baldock encouraged him, hoping that the jailor would be foolish enough to open the cell.

The man paused for a moment, then pulled out a spear and walked back to the cell. "I would so very much enjoy that, don't tempt me."

"Yer moth'r was an orc!" Baldock tried to goad the man, but the jailor simply laughed again and walked away.

Seeing that he failed to convince the human to open the door, Baldock returned to his pacing and raving. With the exception of the three gnomes in the corner—who had all resumed their incessant chatter and gleeful squeals—the rest of the prisoners remained quiet and considered what options they possibly had left.

Ashwin began turning her father's ring again. She did not doubt that the giant jailor would take great pleasure in torturing them. She wondered, not for the first time, if the ring would help keep her from crying out.

CHAPTER 11

Studying the black splotch on the ground by the tree, Solara dabbed her fingers in it to see if it was still wet. The paint had already dried and crusted. Frowning, she looked at the scuffmarks along the ground and a deeper indentation left by a large figure.

"He was here, Tiot," she concluded. "Not too long ago."

The timber wolf watched her intently as if hanging on every word. He then turned and focused his gaze away in the direction they were heading and growled.

Stepping slowly and looking at the ground, Solara agreed. "Yes, he went that way."

Not wanting to lose the tracks, Solara returned to the two horses and took them by the reins. She originally was going to bring only her own horse, Myst, along with her, but decided that if she brought Braksis's horse as well, she could keep switching mounts and travel more quickly. Something she was grateful for, now that the tracks left by Durgin were discovered more frequently.

With horses in tow, Tiot led Solara to an opening where a wagon sat by the forest in a clearing. Solara felt tense, on edge, but saw no signs of danger from the timber wolf. Taking no chances, she tied the reins of the horses up on the branch of a nearby tree, and then removed her sword before approaching the wagon.

She pointed towards the forest, and Tiot, aware of the nonverbal command, began to circle around the wagon. He entered the Suspintian Forest and moved slowly to avoid making noise, keeping his gaze on the wagon at all times.

Solara reached the wagon and moved slowly around it, wondering if Durgin, or simply a wayward traveler would be surprised by her presence. Even as she thought this, she suspected what she would find, for barely a sound could be heard.

Stepping in front of the wagon, she lowered her sword and hung her head in sorrow. Her failure to kill Durgin those years before had ultimately led to the sadistic man's pleasure, and her growing remorse.

She saw two men, two women, and worst of all, four small children, all lying limply, blood and vicious wounds on their battered bodies. They truly had no chance against their adversary, and succumbed to his ruthlessness.

Solara had witnessed many hardships in her twenty-five years—most of which began the day Durgin had first entered her life—but never before had she thought she would feel so guilty, as if the massacre of a family with children had been her own fault.

Stepping out of the forest, the timber wolf walked over to her and glanced up, as if it could sense her very thoughts.

Solara bent down and rubbed Tiot behind the ears. "Don't worry, we'll get him," she promised.

Glancing up, she saw a clear morning sky. Not a bird in sight. Searching the ground around her, she also saw no signs of other predators. "No scavengers yet," she observed. "He was here recently."

Bending down, she gently rubbed a finger along one of the children's deep wounds and looked at the blood now soaking her fingers. "The blood is still wet," she said, privately damning herself for not arriving early enough to save this family. "He is close."

Tiot began sniffing the ground and went back into the forest, leaving Solara alone with the corpses and her thoughts. She promised herself that she would find Durgin and make him suffer. As dedicated to her mission as she was before this, she knew now that she had to find him even more quickly before he could inflict any further harm.

Stepping over to the remains of the fire, she lowered her hand and could feel the heat. It had only recently burned out. Perhaps she was only two hours behind her prey. She knew that she could reduce that gap quickly, especially with Tiot guiding her, but she had something that she needed to do first. Another delay that she hoped would not pain her further if she found more signs of Durgin's brutality.

Sheathing her sword, Solara walked over to the children first and gently carried their battered and broken bodies over to the wagon. Placing each of them inside, Solara could no longer fight the tears that overwhelmed her and began flowing freely from her eyes.

Moving the four adults a little more slowly, she managed to place all eight bodies inside the wagon. Stepping back, she watched them in silence for a moment, praying that whatever deity they revered would protect their eternal souls.

Finding two stones where the fire had died out, she struck them together to light some kindling that was piled for future use, undoubtedly gathered by the children, singing happily as they carried out their chore. She lit a torch and tossed it inside the wagon.

The fire took several moments to begin burning the wooden wagon, but it was soon engulfed in flames, along with the remains of the butchered family.

Turning away, Solara looked at her body, covered in blood, and picked up a dress she saw lying on the ground next to a broken crate. Using it as a towel, she wiped off as much as she could, though she knew she would not truly be clean until she found someplace to take a proper bath.

Pausing, she glanced at the bloodied dress. It was too large for the children, but far too small for either woman. Dropping it, she began searching for other signs. She found nine plates, nine glasses, and more clothes that would fit a young girl growing into womanhood.

Placing two fingers to her lips, she let out a long whistle, and Tiot soon trotted up to her side. Solara already had both horses ready to go. Glancing down at the wolf frantically, she spoke her fear. "He has a young girl with him. We must find them quickly."

Tiot responded by jogging off into the woods, with Solara leading the horses in pursuit. If Durgin had taken one of the girls, there was a good chance that she was still alive. Solara only hoped that she would find her in time.

CHAPTER 12

Standing before the double doors of the Empress's private chambers, Winton grinned with the thought that this, the most well-guarded room in the entire palace, would soon belong to him. Pushing the doors open wide, he strode in and scanned the splendor of the place. No other room in the palace was as luxurious, lush, or magnificent.

Stepping over to the large pool that served as Karleena's private bath, he stirred the water with his fingers. The warmth of the water surprised him, and he decided then that he would thoroughly enjoy bathing in this room from this day forward.

Glancing around the room, Winton wondered where the Empress would hide the corryby that allowed her to speak to the Mages. Without even having to search, he found it beside her bed on a table.

"This is too easy," he snickered as he approached the mystical communication device. Dropping onto the bed, he felt more comfortable than he had ever known, a remarkable feat considering that his entire life as the prince of Danchul was one that existed in a perpetual paradise.

With the corryby in his hands, he looked it over and wondered how exactly it was meant to work. He had never seen the Empress when she was communicating with the Mages, and without mystical abilities of his own, he was clueless.

He pushed at the small orb at every angle, shook it, and tossed it in the air. Nothing managed to make the mystical communicator work. In frustration, he called out. "Just show me the damned Mage!"

A gentle glow appeared within the orb, but nothing else happened. Winton studied it for a moment and decided that the device worked through verbal commands. Coughing for a moment to clear his throat, he steadily commanded the corryby, "Show me Mage Master Askari."

In response to his words, the corryby continued to glow, and small beams of blue light lanced up from the orb, ultimately swirling and forming the shape of the aquatican Mage. The image of Askari regarded Winton for a moment with a puzzled expression.

Winton had never seen the aquatican sibling of Arianna before. Like her, he had pale blue skin with pointed ears and commanding blue eyes. Unlike his sister though, he had long, flowing aqua-green hair, compared to her darker chestnut shade. The image of the man was striking, and even just in this mystical form, Winton could feel that Askari maintained a strong aura of leadership and respect.

"Forgive my silence, but I anticipated the call of the Empress," Askari apologized.

"I only wish that she were able to contact you herself," Winton mournfully began.

"The Empress is ill?" Askari asked.

"Far worse, I am afraid," Winton declared. "A bounty hunter sent by Emperor Wei Lau has kidnapped her from us."

The image of Askari pondered the words, but did not respond.

"Where are you now?" Winton asked.

As if sensing duplicity, Askari ignored the question and boldly asked: "Who are you?"

"I am Winton, son of Sarlec, and recently-crowned King of Danchul," he proclaimed.

"Recently-crowned King?" Askari repeated for clarification.

"I'm afraid my father, too, has recently been taken from us," he sighed mournfully. "Foul play is presumed."

The Mage continued to stare at Winton. "Why are you, then, the one to contact me?"

"The Empress and I are betrothed. Something my father had been encouraging for quite some time," Winton explained.

"From prince to Emperor," Askari mentioned in passing, allowing

Winton to come to his own conclusions about the Mage Master's reasoning.

"Where are you now?" Winton repeated.

"My apprentice Cicero and I are approaching the floating city of Estonis to meet with the avarians."

"I'm afraid that I will have to ask you to alter your mission," Winton said. "The recovery of the Empress is of utmost importance."

Askari maintained his stern gaze. If Winton's comments were received as welcome news, he did not display it, something that the new Emperor was mildly frustrated by.

"The Imperial forces are preparing for war. Before we do so, the royal families have decided to send you to Aezia first in hopes of diplomatically securing the release of the Empress."

"Though this is not part of our directive, I shall do so immediately without consulting the Mage's Council," Askari replied. "However, I would caution you on engaging in a second war."

"A second war?" Winton asked.

"Yes, for the Seven Kingdoms are surely at war right now. I have witnessed this on my own and have seen how quickly things are deteriorating. Do not withdraw Imperial forces until I have returned. If you do, the Seven Kingdoms will fall before the Empress sets foot back in her homeland."

"Then let us all hope that your mission will be a success, and that the Empress will be safely returned to us soon," Winton concluded.

Without another word, the image of Askari flickered out, and the corryby stopped glowing.

"What do you mean that you hope that the Empress will be safely returned?"

Winton spun around to see Sharnesta standing and looking accusingly at him. "Sharnesta!"

"Speak boy," she commanded. "What are you doing in Her Majesty's private chambers? Where is she?"

Standing up, Winton resumed his sorrowful expression. "You

have not heard then? I would have thought that you of all people would have known right away."

"Known what?" Sharnesta scowled, growing more frustrated and concerned.

"Sharnesta, I fear that something dreadful has happened," Winton said with a sniff. "The Empress has been kidnapped."

The handmaiden stumbled backwards for a moment before she regained her composure. Her hand shot up and clutched her chest. "Why have I not heard this?"

"I am at a loss," Winton said. "We have been trying to keep the news a secret, but it has swept around the palace quickly. Have you not questioned what was happening when the Empress had not returned these past few days?"

"The Empress usually provides me with her itinerary, yes," Sharnesta admitted. "However, with the unification talks, she has been under an incredible strain. I merely assumed that she was busy with her efforts."

"If only that were so," Winton replied.

Glaring at the young man, Sharnesta resumed her scowl. "What gives you the right to enter the Empress's private chambers? How did you get past the guards?"

Grinning evilly, Winton stepped closer to the woman that acted like a mother to the Empress. "I am allowed admittance because we were betrothed, of course."

"Rubbish," Sharnesta scoffed. "The Empress would never become intimate with you, no matter how much your father pushed for such a union."

"I am sorry to hear you say that," Winton declared. With a flick of his wrist, he rammed a small dagger into Sharnesta's stomach. His expression of joy danced as he saw her confusion and then the rationalization of what was happening to her.

Pulling the dagger out, Winton rammed it back in again and again, the entire time, smiling to Sharnesta and whispering to her that everything would be all right.

As life left the woman, Winton released his grip and she dropped to the ground. Blood seeped out from beneath her corpse onto the floor.

"Oh look at what you've done now," Winton whined. "You've made a mess on my new carpet."

Bending over, he wiped the blood from his dagger on Sharnesta's dress, and then sheathed it. Stepping back towards the door to leave the chambers, he heard a blood-curdling growl. As he turned, all he managed to see was a giant white paw slashing down at him.

CHAPTER 13

Though he remained in the middle of the floor, Thamar was becoming enraged. His patience had quickly come to an end and he demanded action. He knew from Braksis that the Imperium was honorable, yet their jailor was nothing more than a thug that probably worked for the Hidden Empire. He could not understand what was going on or why, but he was determined to find out and do something about it.

When Askari and Cicero had arrived at Xylona, missing Braksis by mere hours, they stressed the importance of the Empress's unification talks to help defeat the forces of evil that were becoming unified and plaguing the land. This summons was like a beaming light guiding the races into a bright and prosperous future, one that Thamar jumped at, one that had since crumbled around him in the dank dungeon.

Two of the gnomes were still chatting incessantly, whereas the third began walking around the back of the cell and gently knocking his knuckle along the wall. Determined to figure out what they were up to, Thamar stood up and walked over to the gnomes, almost bumping into the pacing Baldock.

The Tregador dwarf emitted a low growl of annoyance and continued his ranting as he paced the floor with a loud clanging from his armor.

"You be planning something?" Thamar asked when he reached the gnomes.

Trivett and Zeppenfeld looked up in an expression of pure innocence as if they had no idea what he could be referring to.

"Don't be playing games with me, gnomes," Thamar gruffly

barked. "Our time of sitting here and rotting is at an end. Can you get us out or not?"

Trivett glanced over at Zeppenfeld who was beaming and bobbing his head quickly. "As soon as I remember whether it was three ounces or four!" he joyfully explained.

"Three or four what?" Thamar asked.

"He blew up one of the palace's towers," Trivett explained.

"I be seeing that when first arriving," Thamar said as he stroked his beard. "You did that?"

"Yes!" Zeppenfeld jumped up and started to dance in place with his hands moving up and down quickly. "It was only two!"

The exclamation gained stares from everyone else in the cell, and Thamar considered them for a moment before returning his attention to the gnomes. "What's he doing?"

"Have to find a spot to blow up!" Trivett declared.

"Then we leave?" Thamar asked to confirm what he was hearing.

"Oh yes!" Trivett said. "Unless he blows us all up in the process."

"There are tunnels enough running through this place," Thamar replied, as if remembering a prior journey to Trespias.

"Arbuckle agrees," Trivett said. "He found many tunnels since we arrived here!"

"I'll spread the word," Thamar offered. Leaving the gnomes to the final preparations, he walked over to Theiler first and woke his brother up with a gentle nudge to the shoulder.

Theiler opened his eyes and looked as if he had been awake and alert for hours.

"We be leaving soon, be ready," he said, to which Theiler nodded that he would be prepared.

Glancing at Baldock, Thamar decided that the loud dwarf would be the last one he would tell. No use letting the jailor in on their plans when the Tregador dwarf begins laughing and boasting of it.

He walked over to Arifos and Mylvannan and whispered two quick words: "Be ready." Neither acted as if they heard him at all. Their gazes remained fixed on the jailor, but he knew the two battle hardened elves were more than ready to take action.

Kneeling down next to Ashwin, he considered the defeated look in her eyes. "What's wrong, child?"

She looked up at the dwarf that was so well-known to her people and almost broke down into tears, something most unbecoming of an elven princess. "I caused this, I was the one who demanded to go."

"Don't be foolish, girl; if anyone is being to blame, it would be me, for I was the one who said to lower our weapons," he explained. "Don't you be worrying, though—there will be story and song aplenty about our valiant escape from this infernal place."

"Our escape?" she whispered.

"Be ready—the gnomes are tinkering with a way to open a new door."

Heirn bent down next to Thamar. "I overheard," he said. "Not a moment too soon. I am almost tempted to taste the filth they call food."

Thamar raised his head and bellowed in a deep and boisterous laugh. "That was a good one, my friend!"

"What are you laughing at, *dwarf?*" the jailor asked, practically spitting the last word with contempt.

"I'm laughing at you," Thamar said. "What are you going to do about it?"

"Insolent dwarf!" the jailor roared as he began fumbling with the keys to open the cell door.

Baldock stopped his pacing and walked closer, his eyes gleaming with anticipation of the chance to strike a blow to their captor.

Thamar turned and looked at the gnomes. Arbuckle and Zeppenfeld were leaning next to the back wall and working on one of the large stones. They jumped up and ran back to where they had originally been sitting.

"Down!" Thamar roared. With the exception of Baldock, who had yet to be told, all of the prisoners dropped to the ground and covered their heads with their arms.

The Tregador dwarf glanced around in confusion. "What are ye all doin'?"

The explosion from behind him knocked him forward towards the bars. The entire cell became dense with smoke and flying debris. A scream of agony was heard on the other side of the bars, and coughing from all around them.

With the smoke and dust clearing, Thamar stood up and saw that two of the bars had been forced apart. The jailor was running for a weapon. Moving quickly, Thamar squeezed through the opening and charged the jailor.

"I promised you that you would feel my hammer!" he roared. "I have no hammer, so you'll have to feel the wrath of a Vorstad dwarf instead!"

The jailor spun around with his spear and shot it out at Thamar, who dodged quickly and barreled right into the taller mans legs, knocking him down. With the two on the ground, Thamar crawled up his body and brought both fists pounding down on his head.

The jailor squirmed below him and tried to shake the rampaging dwarf off, but Thamar's one hundred and seventy pound frame kept him pinned down on the ground. After a few moments and several more hits, the bloodied jailor stopped moving, and Thamar stood up triumphantly.

Jogging back to the cell door, he saw a greasy and dirt smeared Baldock stuck in the same opening he squeezed through, trying desperately to get through and attack the jailor on his own.

"Let me through, ye durned bars!" he roared in annoyance.

"He is dead," Thamar declared.

"Ye be stealin' all o' me fun!" Baldock cried.

"Fear not, noble dwarf," Arifos comforted as he helped pull Baldock back from the bars. "We will face many foes this day."

"Yes!" Baldock shouted in joy, his eyes aglow with the prospect.

Thamar crawled back through the bars and regarded the hole in the back wall. "Most impressive," he said. "Remind me to always have a gnome nearby whenever I am in a bind such as this!"

"I hear guards coming," Heirn explained. "Most likely to investigate the explosion. Let us be off."

"Let 'em come, I says! I'll be takin' 'em all on!" Baldock roared.

Theiler reached up and hit Baldock on the head, an action that got the Tregador dwarf to spin around and regard his companion. "Ye'll be explainin' yerself fer that!"

"My brother is mute and need not explain himself. His actions are clear, we must go," Thamar declared as he ran towards the opening.

"Yes, yes! Run, let's go!" Arbuckle offered as he waved people into the tunnel. "Into the hidey-hole!"

As the door slammed open and a handful of guards poured into the dungeon, they found only a dead jailor, a broken cell door, and a hole in the back of the cell mocking them—the prisoners had escaped.

CHAPTER 14

"This way!" Arbuckle cried out as he led the group down the dark tunnel. Like all gnomes, he had the ability to see well in the darkness and judge their surroundings with a clear precision, an ability that had allowed the gnomes to develop an extensive tunnel system and live underground in the community of Underwood.

The passage they followed was little more than a sewer. There was water flowing along the ground, though none of the escaped emissaries had any desire to see what condition the water was in. There were several side-tunnels that turned the entire system into a maze, but Arbuckle was confident that he was leading them in the right direction.

When they had first escaped, they could all hear pursuers coming after them. With the myriad of tunnels that could be taken though, they soon lost track of the guards and were assured by the heightened hearing of the elves that they had eluded their pursuers.

Arbuckle took a turn into a tunnel on the left-hand side and continued running down it. "To the left, the left!" he called out for others to follow. "This way, this way—quickly!"

Further down the passage, they could see light—a clear sign that they were moving in a better direction. Arbuckle skidded to a stop by a large opening where the water from the sewer flowed over a cliff and down into the ocean below.

Arifos, who was only a few steps behind the gnome glanced out and studied their surroundings. They were on the far side of the palace, furthest away from Trespias. The opening they had come to would allow them to either climb down to the rocky shoreline that formed the base of the island where the palace had been built, or up to try and make their way back into the palace itself.

"Down we go," Arbuckle announced when everyone had reached the ledge. After his recommendation, Trivett spun over the ledge and began climbing down the cliff face, Zeppenfeld inches behind him.

The Madrew elf continued to look up. "I am not going with you," he announced.

Arbuckle glanced at the elf, stunned. "Why not?"

"I will not leave my weapons behind," he vowed confidently.

"Nor will I," Mylvannan concurred.

"I would be likin' Splitter back!" Baldock agreed.

"You are fools," Heirn declared. "I have an honor blade of Xylona up there myself, but we are defenseless. We would be better-off returning to Xylona and selecting new weapons."

"They surely wouldn't be expecting us," Thamar offered. "Surprise would be on our side for a change."

"The dwarf is right. Besides, with the exception of my honor blade, my weapons were all hand-crafted," Arifos added. "I created them in a time when there was no hope in my homeland, and I desperately wished to change that. I could not repeat the process even if I were to try."

"I, too, have an honor blade of Xylona," Mylvannan commented. "It has been mystically enhanced by the Frost Queen of Akkammanavar. I will not leave it without at least trying to retrieve it. I will go with Arifos to recover the weapons."

"Then what are we all waiting for?" Thamar burst out. "We have a climb ahead of us!"

"I could show you some hidey-holes and help you find your weapons," Arbuckle offered.

"Arbuckle! What are you saying?" Trivett asked, pausing from his climb down. "We need to return to Underwood and let the gnomes and centaurs know what is happening here."

Arbuckle glanced back and forth, torn between his choices. He clearly wished to return to the palace and help his new comrades in their search for their weapons, but he also had a duty to his own people.

"Return to your home, noble gnome," Arifos answered for him.

"My weapons are calling to me already. I shall follow that like a beacon."

"Well, if you don't think you'll be needing me?" Arbuckle hesitated, clearly disappointed.

"Arbuckle!" Trivett screamed. "Come on!"

"I'm coming, I'm coming," he answered quickly. "Good luck, and may we all see each other again someday."

"Yes—there will be many tales to tell of this day," Thamar agreed. "We shall enjoy them before a raging fire, my friend."

"Princess, you shall go with the gnomes," Heirn instructed. "We shall meet up with you later."

Ashwin returned her cousin's gaze with contempt. "Do not try to protect me Heirn, I can fend for myself. I am coming."

"Your father would be most displeased if he knew that I allowed you to walk into danger!" Heirn cried in protest.

Thamar patted him on the back. "You didn't let her walk into danger, you let her climb in!" with a boisterous laugh, Thamar glanced up the face of the island mountain and then back at Baldock. "How is he supposed to make it?"

"I'll be makin' it, don't ye be worryin'!" Baldock promised.

Heirn stayed focused on Ashwin, who ignored his warnings and walked to the ledge. Arifos and Mylvannan had already begun ascending the cliff, and she quickly followed their progress, leaving the disapproving Heirn behind.

Thamar and Theiler began climbing after Ashwin, though their progress was noticeably slower as they climbed up. Baldock began after them; cussing and complaining the entire time he scaled the cliff face. Though he promised he would be fine, his declarations that this was no place for a dwarf soon filled the dawn air.

Heirn waited for the dwarves to show a definite sign of progress before following them. In his mind, all he could visualize was the armored Baldock dropping from the ledge and sending them both hurtling into the rocky shores below. Rubbing his temple with the thought, he stepped out and began climbing as well. He only hoped that they were making the right decision.

CHAPTER 15

The doors to the Empress's chambers burst open and a screaming Winton fell out. His right hand firmly grasping his face, blood seeping out between his fingers. "Help me!" he cried out in a mixture of fear and agony.

A white tiger leapt from the room and slammed into the Danchul heir, knocking him back into the wall with a violent impact. With a feral roar from his assailant, Winton cowered down to the floor fully expecting his life to be over.

"By the gods!" a man yelled from down the hall.

Winton heard the noise, but could not take his uninjured eye from the creature before him. It's emerald eyes bore into him with an unspoken promise that he was about to die.

Several guards charged the white tiger, only to have their path barred by a second as it jumped out and stood poised to attack in front of its companion. Emitting a roar of its own, the guards slowly began to creep backwards and away from the creature.

"Stop them, you fools! Save me!" Winton cried.

From around the other corner, more guards ran out, spears and halberds extended as they slowly approached the two creatures. The first white tiger inched closer to Winton, placing its face right in front of his.

Frightened beyond words, the bleeding man began to wet himself and tremble in terror. It then spun around and the two white tigers charged right through the line of guards, separating them with ease.

"Sir, are you all right?" one guard asked as he reached down to help Winton.

Winton continued shaking, unable to control himself. In that moment, he could still feel the warm breath of the white tiger; its claws slashing his face; the touch of its frame as it barreled him into the wall.

"Sir?" the man repeated.

"A doctor," Winton wheezed. "Get me a doctor!"

"Yes sir," the guard replied.

"And find those damned cats and kill them!" he roared in agony.

The man stood up and began barking commands. "Go find a doctor. You, stay here with the Emperor. The rest of you, come with me."

Still trembling, the blood seeping through his fingers, Winton passed out.

Vaz and Vella, the two white tigers that belonged to the Empress, knew that something was wrong and desperately wanted to find and help their master. They could sense that she was not there, and as they made every turn and saw Garum's thugs running rampant instead of the palace guards, they knew that enemies surrounded them.

In the Empress's chambers, they had been aware of Winton entering the room. Though they thought his presence odd, he had been an ally of the Empress, and also the son of one of her closest advisors, so they did not think anything of it. When they observed him murder Sharnesta though, the line had been crossed and Vaz leapt into action.

As they moved freely through the palace, both tigers could sense that there were still honorable individuals nearby, though certainly a minority compared to normal. Moving quickly, they began heading towards that group, hoping to unite with them against a common foe.

"There they are!"

Vaz turned around and looked at four men as they rushed towards the two. Each man held a spear in hopes of attacking the creatures from a distance. The white tiger sprinted towards them, leapt up against the wall and sprung over their spears, crashing head-first into two of the attackers.

The tiger had the throat of one man firmly clenched in its mouth, squeezing tightly as he convulsed below. The other had been rendered unconscious by the impact of the six-hundred-and-fifty-pound tiger.

As the others turned in confusion, Vella batted one aside with her front paw, and then leapt on top of the last man, pinning him down. With a slash of her claws, the man beneath her was dead, his throat torn out.

With several more of Garum's men running down at them, Vaz turned and roared a warning. The men did not pause, nor did the tigers as they both sprung into action, quickly eliminating their vast opponents.

As he regained consciousness, Winton almost passed out again immediately as he saw a needle above his eye and moving towards his face. "No!"

"Someone hold him down. I need him still," the doctor ordered. Two men dropped to Winton's side, one holding his body down and the other with his hands firmly on each side of his head. "Be still, sir."

Winton tried to comprehend what was happening, his thoughts lost in memories of the white tiger attacking him. As the needle entered his face, he cried out in agony, his wounds still fresh and painful.

"I must stitch these," the doctor tried to explain. "Stop struggling, I am almost through."

"The pain," he whined.

"Yes, I am sure the pain is exquisite. I will give you something for that when I am done with this."

Winton tried not to wince or cry out, but never before had he personally been hurt, and he did not like this feeling at all. He tried desperately to hold on to who he was: he was the son of Sarlec, prince of Danchul; in his home of Larcridge, he had been very popular and had very rarely been without many women nearby, all wishing that his gaze would turn their way.

His life had been pure bliss, as his muscled and tanned body pointed out. He had never had to work or fend for himself. Now, suddenly, all of that was taken from him. True enough, he had brought most of it about, but at this moment, he wondered who exactly he was.

His father was dead at his own hand, poisoned by a deadly toxin he had added to his father's wine, a man who he now realized had given him the perfect life that he was accustomed to, even if he had been unable to give himself freely to his son.

Now, his most prized attribute, his looks and ability to attract women, was now permanently etched from his being with one slash of a tiger's claw. How far he had fallen, and how much further he would fall, he did not know.

Lying there in pain and agony, he wondered whether his agreement with Zoldex was one that would sentence him to eternal damnation. If so, it was too late to turn back. Everything that he had worked for, until now, had come to pass. He was the Emperor, for all intents and purposes. He would not lose that because of his failing identity.

"That should do it," the doctor said as he carefully examined his work. "A nasty wound to be sure, but you will heal."

"Will I be scarred?" Winton asked, hoping desperately that the answer would be better than he anticipated.

"Those five claw marks will remain with you forever," the doctor answered calmly, "but your eye has been spared. You will be able to open it again in a week or so after I remove the bandages and stitches."

With a rising fury, Winton pushed the doctor aside and marched back into the Empress's chambers, slamming the doors behind him. He walked over to the bed and dropped down, looking at the corpse of Sharnesta beneath him.

Knowing that he would need to somehow eliminate her body, as well as that of his father, so that none could ever track the deaths back to him, he decided that he would have to get both bodies together and eliminate them at the same time.

Bending down, he picked up Sharnesta by the shoulders and began dragging her lifeless corpse. A trail of blood was left behind, but the palace was painted with blood after the recent deaths, and he hoped one more incident would go unnoticed. Once things settled down, he would commission decorators and servants to come in and return the palace to a more pristine look.

He backed through the doors, forcing them open as he went through. The hall was empty, with the doctor and two men already moving along their business. Winton was grateful that the man that had kidnapped the Empress had also eliminated almost the entire Imperial Guard, or else he would never be able to safely get away with what he was doing.

He could hear screams and roars in the distance, and knew that the Empress's pets were still alive and causing chaos throughout the palace. He only hoped that he could finish what he was doing and then find someplace safe so that the tigers could not come back and attack him again.

The quarters where he and his father had stayed were not too far from the Empress's, and he reached the doors without incident. Tearing through the barriers that the guards had erected, so that none could go in until after Adonis returned, Winton opened the doors and walked inside.

He dragged Sharnesta over to where his father lay and dropped her by his side: two confidants of Karleena, both silenced and unable to challenge his claim to the throne. Turning away, Winton called out to the air: "Zoldex, I need you!"

Without any delay, a pale blue translucent image appeared before Winton, regarding him as if Zoldex were in the room beside him. "What went wrong?" he asked, glaring at his scarred and bandaged face.

"The Empress's pets did not like me killing Sharnesta," Winton replied.

"Have you dealt with them?" the icy voice of Zoldex asked, a hint of more pain to come in his voice if the answer was no.

"They are being hunted down as we speak," Winton hastily answered.

"See to it that they are," Zoldex ordered. "Why have you called me?"

Winton walked back to the two corpses and pointed down. "I need the bodies removed before someone from ISIA arrives."

The image of Zoldex paused for a moment. "This ISIA could threaten your rule?"

"Royalty is not above the law in the Imperium," he answered sternly.

With a flick of his wrist, the two bodies began to glow and smolder from the inside out. Winton watched as they combusted and left nothing more than a scorched floor and ash.

"That eliminates the evidence," Zoldex said. "However, there is one more person you must deal with."

"Captain Centain," Winton whispered.

"That is correct," Zoldex agreed. "Will he die?"

"It is touch-and-go, but the doctors are working valiantly on him."

"See to it that they fail," Zoldex insisted.

"I will handle it personally," Winton promised, though he was uncertain how exactly he could manipulate the demise of a man that was regarded as a hero of Trespias.

Satisfied, the image of Zoldex flickered and vanished. As it did so, three words crept into Winton's head: "Don't fail me." The threat was apparent—failure was not an option.

CHAPTER 16

The progress of the elves and dwarves as they climbed the cliff-face of the island to the palace was a slow and stressful one. Arifos and Mylvannan led the group, moving the quickest, but they frequently had to pause and even climb back down to help one of the others.

Baldock had soon begun to lag behind, his barrage of complaints echoed through the chasm. The lack of climbing abilities of the Tregador dwarf bothered none as much as Heirn, who struggled to remain far enough behind Baldock, so that when he fell—and Heirn was confident that he would indeed fall—the surly dwarf did not bring him down with him.

Arifos was the first to reach the foundation of the palace. There was a small ledge that he could safely climb onto and stand upon with ease. He quickly scanned the smoother surface of the palace walls hoping that he could find some way to help his companions climb the rest of the way up. About twenty feet above them, he located a row of small windows. Turning to consider the others, he knew that few of them could make it up the smoother surface.

"I will go ahead and find a rope or something to help hoist you all up," Arifos suggested.

Mylvannan, pulling himself onto the ledge, walked over to the structure and rubbed his fingers along the smooth wall. "This is no worse than the icy peaks of my homeland. I shall join you."

"Very well," Arifos replied. Glancing at Ashwin as she, too, pulled herself up, he continued. "Remain here and help the others up to this point. We will be back shortly."

Ashwin did not appear pleased, but nodded without protest. Arifos and Mylvannan then slowly began their ascent.

Breathing heavily, Thamar reached Ashwin below the foundation of the palace. "What doesn't kill me makes me stronger," he wheezed.

Ashwin smiled at the unusual dwarf. "We're not up yet," she observed.

"I didn't say that this made me stronger yet," he retorted, garnering a giggle from the elf. "We're to be waiting here?"

"Yes," she agreed. "Arifos and Mylvannan feared that we would not all be able to make it up the smoother surface."

Thamar considered the two elves' progress. They were almost to the windows and moving far more quickly than anyone else had been. "For the best," he conceded. "Dwarves may be great fighters, builders, and miners, but climbers? No, I think not."

In unison, both leaned over and looked further down at Baldock. At that moment, his left arm kept reaching up trying to find the next cropping of the ledge, only to slip down. With a flood of vulgarities, he kept trying again and again.

"He'll be making it," Thamar surmised as his brother joined them on the ledge. "If my brother and I can make it, then Baldock can make it."

"You and your brother do not have the disadvantage of being so heavily armored," Ashwin surmised.

"That same armor that troubles him now will come in useful when facing our enemies," Thamar quickly reminded her. "Not that a true son of Vorstad ever needed that much armor to instill fear in the hearts of our enemies!"

The dwarves certainly were different, Ashwin pondered. She had been raised as an ally to the dwarves of Vorstad, and was used to their adventurous style, demeanor, and skills. Those from the Halls of Vorstad truly were great warriors, as well as architects of grand structures.

Seeing Baldock though—along with the four hundred dwarves he led to Xylona after Thamar requested assistance in the war against the orcs, goblins, and hobgoblins—she began to see how different they were. Not physically, of course, for a dwarf was a dwarf, but everything else was like night and day in her opinion.

The dwarves of Vorstad, as Thamar pointed out, did not wear armor. Some may have chainmail, but they preferred not to be weighed down by the armor, allowing them to be more mobile and flexible. The dwarves from Tregador had spent their lives mining the powerful metallic ore illistrium, and the warriors from their homeland were encased in it. Though slower than their Vorstad counterparts, she knew that the armored dwarves had a reputation of being some of the greatest warriors and blacksmiths in the realm, and seeing hardly any chinks in the armor, she understood that they would likely be able to defend and outlast many enemies as well.

The differences went deeper than that, though. In knowing Thamar, she had always thought that his thick and heavy accent was relatively strange compared to that of her elven kin. After meeting Baldock and his comrades, her opinion had changed remarkably. Now, Thamar and the dwarves of Vorstad were like great philosophers, with dialects so clear that it amazed her. Listening to Baldock, half the time she couldn't even understand what he was saying.

She wondered how different all of the races were based on their upbringing and habitat. Just looking at Arifos and Mylvannan, a Madrew elf and a Frost elf, she could see remarkable differences from herself. She wondered if she would ever meet other elves from around the realm. She had heard rumors, but never had been able to meet any personally.

The elves of Turning Leaf were the closest to Xylona, but she had heard many tales of their arrogance and sense of superiority to all other races. When Thamar searched for allies, he had stopped at Turning Leaf and was turned away: the affairs of others were of no interest to the elves. Considering how valuable the alliance with Vorstad has been, she could not even comprehend how her northern cousins could be so close-minded.

The Suspintian Forest was also the home of a second elven community in addition to Turning Leaf, Wild Wood. Though she had heard little of them, she wondered from what she had heard if these elves would be more like the dwarves of Tregador in her eyes. Allegedly, these elves were more tribal, living off of the land and behaving far more savage than any would ever expect from an elf. Hearing these rumors, she was curious if an elf of Wild Wood would regard her as an ally, or attack her on sight.

The only other elven city in the Seven Kingdoms was perhaps the most famous and respected: Faylinn, home of the Elandeeril, the maiden unicorn-riders. She recalled the stories of the elves that were divinely hidden and protected deep in the Dartian Woods. Only an honest, true, and noble soul could ever hope to find their grand city. Those that were not as honorable would find themselves overwhelmed by the Elandeeril, and never heard from again.

At the young age of thirty-five, she hoped that she would be presented with the opportunity to meet and experience all of these differences on her own. The unification talks she was sent here to partake in had been her first step to experience what the rest of the realm had to offer. Something she anxiously hoped would still be open to her.

"Durn!" Baldock screeched as his hand slipped from the ledge. "Stupid durned ledge. Let me up!"

Thamar and Theiler leaned over and both grabbed the armored dwarf by an arm and hoisted him onto the ledge. "Breathe easily, my friend; we have a minor respite before we must climb again."

"More climbin'?" he cried in protest. "This durned mountain will be the death o' me!"

"It's not a mountain," Heirn mildly reminded the dwarf as he climbed onto the ledge with a scowl. "It's an island."

"It's a blang durned mountain if I be sayin' it's a blang durned mountain!"

"Let us just say you are both right," Thamar smiled disarmingly. "It is an island mountain that the palace is planted upon."

Heirn glanced at the dwarf in frustration, but did not comment. Baldock was not as generous. "Blasted island mountain, eh? Well, this blang durned island mountain then will be the death o' me!" Pausing, he glared at Heirn. "Does that be meetin' yer satisfaction, elf?"

Ashwin smiled to herself, recalling once again how different they all were. Seeing them here on this ledge, she was certain that she would one day be able to meet the other elves. Perhaps they would be as different from her as Baldock and his kin were from the dwarves of Vorstad. Regardless, she was looking forward to discovering that.

CHAPTER 17

Arifos reached one of the windows and placed his palm flat against it. Using his inherent mystical abilities, he channeled energy through him and shattered the glass. Moving swiftly, he crawled inside and landed in a defensive crouch.

As he scanned the room, he saw several beds along the back wall, bureaus, closets, and the emerald colors of the Imperial Guards. Noting that nobody was around, he stood back up and reached his hand out to Mylvannan to help him enter the room.

Mylvannan crawled in and looked around himself. "This must be the quarters for the Imperial Guards."

"Yes," Arifos agreed. "With most of them dead, we probably do not have to worry too much about being discovered."

"Agreed," Mylvannan said. "I'm going to check to see if there are any weapons lying about. Why don't you see if you can find some rope to help the others up?"

Arifos nodded and darted towards the doorway on the far wall. Peering around, he saw that the hallway was clear and walked through. He moved swiftly, though not a sound could be heard from his elven footsteps.

At each door he came to, he paused to open it and peer inside. He found many more barracks for the guards, but no sign of people at all. He circled around and checked several passages to make certain that they were indeed alone, and was satisfied by his search.

Returning to several rooms, he began searching for anything that could be used to help the remaining dwarves and elves climb the twenty-foot wall. Room after room, he found nothing that could assist them.

Pausing to contemplate, he glanced up, his attention caught by the shimmering flowers that were attached to leaves and vines along the entire ceiling. He noted that the flowers continued to change colors as he walked past them. Each one that he stood near blended into a vibrant red.

Ignoring the alluring flowers, he regarded the underlying plant that appeared to have no end anywhere within the hallway or rooms, covering every inch of the ceiling. Reaching up, he tugged on one vine and could feel the strength within it. The flowers closest to him then changed from its reddish hue to a bright yellow.

Moving quickly again, Arifos began scanning the rooms for a small dagger. Finding one, he reached up and began sawing through the staunch vine. The process was not easy, but he did manage to cut through part of the plant and pull it down enough to hold onto it. The flowers in that area wilted and died before his eyes.

Placing one hand over the other, he began walking down the hallway pulling the vine that he severed free from the wall. He was amazed at how intricate this plant was as he managed to safely secure over fifty feet—more than enough for what he needed.

He coiled the vine until he had it all in a large bunch that he could easily carry. Satisfied with his work, Arifos headed back to the room where he had left Mylvannan.

After a few steps, a slamming door dropped him into a defensive posture. He strained to hear whatever was coming, and could discern the staggered breathing of someone who had been running. Dropping his vines, Arifos backed up against the wall and began walking cautiously towards the heavy breathing.

As he came to the next corner, he peered around and saw a man backing away from a door as if he were terrified by what was there. Curious, Arifos stepped into the corridor and towards the man. Though he had never seen him before, he could recognize the man's foul stench and wardrobe as one of the thugs that seemed to be controlling the castle.

He silently walked up right behind the man without alerting him at all. As he reached up to hit the man by the neck and knock him out, he paused and tapped him on the shoulder instead.

The man screamed and spun around. His face turned from horror to a look of confusion. "You're not a cat," he mumbled.

Arifos regarded him for a moment and considered the words. "Who are you?"

The man seemed to regain his composure with only an elf before him, a pink-skinned elf at that, and reached both arms out for Arifos's neck as if he were going to strangle him.

Arifos swiped his hand in the air and a wave of mystical energy knocked the man backwards and hurtled him through the door he had come from, splintering it. The Madrew elf quickly walked towards him to end this little conflict, unsatisfied with how it had turned out, but the man was glancing up and down the hallway, his terror apparent.

"What frightens you so?" Arifos asked, but the man was unable to answer, lost in his own private nightmare. Feeling pity, Arifos grimaced and then uttered the command: "Sleep." As he did so, the man yawned and fell into a deep slumber.

Stepping through the splintered doorway, Arifos glanced back and forth himself. He did not see anything out of sorts, but as he closed his eyes and concentrated, he could hear screams and roars in the distance. Something out of sorts was definitely happening at the palace.

He pivoted around and calmly walked back to the pile of vines. They would have to move swiftly, but whatever was wreaking so much havoc in the palace could be used to their advantage. He hoped that they could recover their weapons and be gone before anyone else even discovered them.

The two white tigers continued moving throughout the palace. They could not understand why the halls were filled with the appalling figures that they kept facing, nor did they know what happened. All that they knew was that these men felt wrong to them, as if they were dark and sinister—a real threat to the palace.

Every turn that they made seemed to bring them in direct confrontation with more of these horrid individuals. No matter how many they incapacitated or killed, dozens of others appeared ready to join in the hunt.

The two were tiring and desired a much-needed reprieve, one that never would be granted as long as they remained within the walls of the palace.

A net dropped on Vella, ensnaring her. Four men rushed forward, tumbling to the ground, spears pointed at the captured white tiger. Vaz, who had just finished facing a score of foes himself, darted around the corner and became enraged by the sight before him.

With a blood-curdling roar, he sprung straight at the men, who looked up in shock and fear, seemingly unprepared for the raging tiger. Vaz knocked two down with his first leap, both men immediately losing consciousness. With a swipe of his front claws, a third fell to the ground, clutching his stomach as he tried to keep his intestines from falling out.

The fourth saw the white tiger's ferocity and slowly began to back off. Another growl spun him around and he sprinted away as swiftly as he could. Vaz watched him flee and then lowered his head and grasped part of the net in his mouth. Pulling back, he managed to tear it, freeing Vella.

Vella sprung up and shook her head, grateful to be free. The two paused there for a moment, listening intently and trusting their senses. They had been trusting their instincts and moving towards the honorable individuals, but all that they encountered thus far was resistance. Deep down, they knew that their path was right, though neither animal truly understood how they were being called, and continued to look for the heroes they sought.

Arifos returned to find a frustrated Mylvannan. He had searched many rooms but only managed to locate a handful of daggers. Though they weren't much, it was better than being unarmed.

Uncoiling the vines that he had cut, Arifos tied one end to a support beam in the middle of the Imperial Guards' quarters, and then tossed the other end out the window. Ashwin and Heirn soon joined them, ascending the vine quickly. Thamar and Theiler took a little longer, but with the vine to support them they, too, managed to climb much more quickly than their prior progress.

Baldock remained the problem. He could not hold onto the vine, and no matter how many times he tried, he kept slipping back down to the ledge and launching into a tirade of complaints and insults.

Arifos returned down the vine to the surly dwarf and helped tie the vine around him. He then pushed from below as the remaining companions above continued to pull. Slowly, the armored dwarf was lifted into the barracks. As he was dragged through the window, all in the room collapsed, glad that they finally got the dwarf inside.

Dropping head first, Baldock was not pleased with how things turned out in the least. Sitting up, he began punching the floor where he fell with his armored gauntlets. "Dang blarned floor!" he roared. "Ye stupid blang durned floor!"

Thamar chuckled at the spectacle, but then stood up and examined the dagger that Mylvannan handed to him. "May all of our enemies this day be as easy to overcome as the floor was for Baldock."

Sitting in the windowsill, Arifos regarded the Tregador dwarf as he continued to spit insults and slam his fists down on the floor. Glancing at the others, he cautioned them all. "Something is happening: I came across a man that was terrified. I also heard screaming and roars."

"Roars, you say?" Thamar asked as he rubbed his beard in contemplation. A smile crept onto his face and glee in his eyes. "An unexpected ally we have this day! Come."

He moved out the door with Theiler in stride behind him. Arifos dropped from the window and joined them, as did Mylvannan.

Heirn reached forward and grabbed Ashwin by the arm. "They

are mad," he declared. "Stay close to me and don't take any chances."

Ashwin regarded her ring again for a moment and felt that whatever happened, she would not be harmed anyway, and that hopefully Heirn would not jeopardize his own safety for her. As he marched out after the others, she glanced down at Baldock who continued to pound relentlessly on the floor. "You can put that aggression elsewhere. We undoubtedly will be in battle soon."

The dwarf jolted to a halt and glanced up at the elf with anticipation. "May all that reside here learn what it means to be makin' an enemy o' Baldock o' Tregador! Second son o' King Kendall hisself!"

Pushing himself up, Baldock grabbed Ashwin by the hand and started running after their companions. "Come on, ye durned stupid elf! We be havin' battles to wage!"

Ashwin tried to hide her chuckle, but couldn't help herself. What an interesting band of adventurers she had been aligned with. She only hoped that they all managed to survive this encounter and continue to share many adventures together in the future.

CHAPTER 18

Mylvannan considered the pink-skinned elf for a moment. Since they began working their way through the palace, he had seemed so sure of himself as if he knew exactly where they were going—something that the Frost elf could not fathom.

Arifos neared a corner and held his hand up, halting the group. He peered around and saw three men running down the corridor, weapons drawn. Once they were out of sight, he lowered his hand and began following the men.

"Do you know where you are going?" Mylvannan asked.

"Yes," Arifos answered in a whisper. "Phistala and Aurlestyl call out to me."

Puzzled, the Frost elf paused to look intently at Arifos. "Your swords?"

"Yes," Arifos confirmed.

"They are sentient?"

"Not sentient in a way that they have personalities of their own, but they have been forged by my own hand and are imbued with mystical energies—energies that are as clear to me as if they were beacons of light shining in the dark."

Satisfied that Arifos did indeed know how to guide them, Mylvannan beckoned for him to continue leading the way. He hoped that they would reach their weapons soon. Though he was more than capable of using the dagger that he had found, he still preferred the serrated swords and daggers of the Frost elves, as well as his Xylona honor blade, Frostlartil.

As one, the two elves turned and looked back in awe at their companion, Baldock. Since entering the palace, Arifos had been directing them swiftly and silently, hoping to avoid any confrontations and using the guards' obvious distraction to their favor. The burly dwarf though sounded like an army marching, his armor clanging incessantly with each step.

Heirn saw the obvious displeasure on the faces of the two lead-elves, and turned to regard Baldock himself. His patience had been growing thin with the Tregador dwarf for quite some time, and thinking that this creature would somehow jeopardize their actions only enraged him more.

Baldock stopped and looked up at the scowling Heirn. "What be yer problem, elf?"

"You are too loud," Heirn scornfully pointed out. "Be silent or be silenced."

"Oh ho!" Baldock roared. "A challenge by the durned stupid elf!"

"Not a challenge," Heirn clarified. "A promise. With you being so loud, it's amazing that we have not had to fend off every single guard in this place."

"Bring 'em on!" Baldock smiled with glee, fire dancing in his eyes. "I'll barrel right through 'em! No more o' all o' this durned sneakin' around."

Ahead of them, Arifos held a hand up again to silence them. Baldock either did not see the signal or no longer cared to act stealthily, for he began laughing as if he were about to get his heart's desire.

A silent nod from Thamar sent Theiler into action. The mute dwarf pivoted and sprung onto Baldock quickly, his hands firmly clasped around the Tregador dwarf's throat.

His coif protected him from the attack, but his words still came out as a panted gurgle as he tried to summon the others to assist him. "Somethin' has possessed the silent one! Get 'im off! Get 'im off!"

Arifos could not believe their misfortune. He knew that they were close to their weapons, and this was the moment that the dwarf decided that he wished to abandon their stealthy advance through the palace—a moment when several fully-armed men had come around the corner, their curiosity peaked by the noise.

"How many?" Mylvannan whispered.

"At least fifteen," Arifos replied. "Fully-armed."

Mylvannan turned and raised his open hand and flashed his fingers three times to communicate to the others that there were fifteen. In response, Ashwin pulled out her dagger and took several deep breaths to calm herself. Heirn and Thamar were oblivious—both were consumed with the struggle between the increasingly loud Baldock and Theiler.

Ashwin stepped over and tried to pull Theiler away. The red-bearded dwarf's grip was like solid stone, immovable. "We have true foes," she said. "No use fighting amongst ourselves."

"Theiler," Thamar stated authoritatively. His brother immediately released his grip and backed away.

Baldock reached up and rubbed his neck. "Ye got fire in yer eyes, ye do! I like it!"

"Enemies approach," Ashwin cautioned.

"Bring 'em on!" Baldock repeated his prior challenge. "I'll take 'em all on! Show 'em what it means to be fightin' the defender o' the mine!"

Arifos, overhearing Baldock's continuing bluster, looked back with a grimace and raised his hand. As he did so, the dwarf floated off of the ground and hovered in the air.

"What trickery is this?" Baldock cried.

Concentrating, Arifos brought Baldock towards him floating through the air and flung him around the corner, increasing the dwarf's momentum as he went, directly towards the oncoming guards.

Baldock flew through the air screaming at first, but then when he saw the opponents he was barreling towards, began laughing maniacally. As he crashed headlong into them, he began swinging his arms quickly, punching anything that was close to him, his laughter growing even louder and more boisterous.

Mylvannan glanced at Arifos with a smirk on his face. "Very nice," he said.

"Why fight it?" Arifos asked with a grin of his own. "If the dwarf wants a fight so badly, let him fight."

Thamar and Theiler both charged around the corner and quickly entered the fray. They both held their daggers and began swiping at the hamstrings of the guards, dropping them quickly to the ground writhing in agony.

"We can't let Baldock have all of the fun!" Thamar roared as he jabbed his dagger into the stomach of another guard.

Theiler, quiet as always dropped to the ground, crawled through the legs of one man, leapt up behind him, and plunged his dagger into the man's back.

Heirn and Ashwin rounded the corner as well, though not as swift to join in on the fighting. They watched the progress for a moment and carefully selected their foes. Heirn moved in first, seeing a man struggling to stand up, using his sword for support. The Xylona elf swiped the dagger at his throat, forcing the man back to the ground as he clutched his neck, blood entering his lungs. Heirn scooped up the man's sword and entered the fray.

Mylvannan began to come around the corner to join his companions, but Arifos grabbed his wrist and held tight. "We should help."

"No, the tide has already changed in our favor," Arifos observed. "We should take advantage of not having the loud dwarf and recover our weapons. We will meet up with them then."

Reluctantly, Mylvannan nodded his assent and followed Arifos down an opposite corridor, taking one last moment to look back at his companions fighting valiantly. He hoped that they did not just make a grave error.

Baldock continued laughing as he pounded man after man. He paused and looked around, surrounded by battered and bloodied bodies. Smiling triumphantly, he searched for his next target. Another guard rounded the corner, and Baldock roared as he charged the man and slammed directly into him at the waist, forcing the air out of his lungs and causing his spear to fall.

Forcing him to the ground, the berserk dwarf raised his two hands and began pounding them down on the man's chest, continuing to hammer down at him. He could hear ribs cracking beneath his rampage, but did not cease until his foe had stopped moving and was dead.

Standing back up, he scanned the halls, looking for signs of another target. Seeing three more soldiers running towards them, he chortled and charged them as well. It had been quite some time since he had been truly able to cut loose, and he meant to savor every moment of it.

Thamar and Theiler's attacks were no less effective, though far less bloodthirsty. They moved in tandem, a pair of warriors who had obviously fought side by side in many a battle: they anticipated each other's actions, and when one left an opening, the other quickly filled it. Their opponents fell swiftly, and the number of adversaries dwindled before their combined might.

Heirn preferred a bit more finesse. He found another sword-fighter that was quite good with the blade: the two danced around in a waltz of death, neither giving into the other, both pressing on relentlessly. Lunges, thrusts, slashes—each move was properly countered, and the two found themselves at an improbable stalemate.

"You are good," Heirn complimented his foe.

The man, who had a scar below his right eye, did not acknowledge the compliment. He merely increased the ferocity of his attacks and continued to push Heirn back. In his mind, if he could get the elf with his back against the wall, this particular skirmish would be over, and he could boast the kill of yet another elf of Xylona.

Ashwin was entranced by the fight between her cousin and the warrior. She had never seen a sword fight last so long, and was amazed that one so skilled would be working alongside the other thugs that had fallen so quickly and easily. In her distraction, she suddenly caught a glimmer in her peripheral vision. Spinning quickly, she saw a man lunging towards her, his sword aiming straight for her head.

Not knowing what to do—being the least experienced of the companions—she faltered in fear. The man never reached her, though—a magnificent animal leapt out and caught the man's arm in its mouth and knocked him off of his target.

The beast was a large white tiger with black slashes. Ashwin was struck by the oddity of the sight. For a moment she had thought that her life was at an end, but then this beautiful creature came and saved her. She wondered whether the animal was a friend, or if it would turn on her as soon as it was done with her attacker.

The white tiger released the man's arm, and turned to face him. The man clutched his punctured and bleeding limb, trembling as he stared into the depths of the creature's shining emerald eyes.

With a roar from its majestic throat, the man began whimpering and scurried away. The white tiger monitored him as he fled, then turned and studied Ashwin for a moment. Seeing her there, the tiger knew that she had finally found the ones that they had been searching for.

Ashwin reached out, making gentle and soothing sounds as if she were talking to a baby, and rubbed the tiger on the head. She watched its eyes close, and knew that this animal was no threat, but a true ally.

Baldock walked back around the corner, splattered blood dripping from his armor, and a smile etched on his face. "Now that is what I be callin' a good fight!"

Thamar and Theiler paused in their dance of death, looking for an enemy of their own, only to find dead bodies all around them. Seeing Baldock glaring at something behind them, they turned and focused on the fight between Heirn and the final man left standing.

The two continued their duel, neither opening a hole in their defenses. Their attacks were in perfect sync, and it was obvious to all watching that the two fighters' skills were nearly identical.

Heirn did not wish to lose his focus on his foe, but he could see that his companions had survived the attack and that his foe was the last one standing. "It appears you are alone."

His opponent smiled briefly and spoke for the first time, "The way it should be," his voice scratchy and deep. Other than his scar, the man seemed quite out of place with the beaten thugs that surrounded them. He was clean-shaven, had his long auburn hair tied in a ponytail and he clearly had recently bathed. He wore a deep mahogany brigandine with a sea-blue shirt and earth-brown gloves. His pants, more of a saddle-brown, were tucked into black boots. Strapped around his waist was a black belt with a pair of jewel-hilted daggers.

The dwarves, Ashwin, and the white tiger circled around the fight. They could all see how good this man was, but felt confident that, with their own skills and abilities, he had no escape.

"Might as well give up," Thamar offered. "You won't be walking from here if you keep fighting."

The man forced his sword forward quickly and knocked Heirn off balance, sending him stumbling backwards. He then turned and regarded the dwarf. "Vorstad," he said. "By the color of the beard, you wouldn't be a son of Thron, would you?"

Thamar was clearly impressed. "You know of us?"

"I know," the man replied. Glancing around, he regarded the others. "A dwarf of Tregador, no doubt."

"If ye know that I be from Tregador, then know that ye are outmatched," Baldock replied.

"No doubt," the man mockingly replied. In his peripheral vision, he saw Heirn trying to stand back up. In one fluid motion like lightning, he slashed his sword down and stopped it directly at the elf's throat, gently nicking him. "You can stay where you are."

Resting his gaze on Ashwin, he smiled in a roguish manner. "A beautiful young princess you are, daughter of Echalas."

Ashwin stared hard at him, but her expression revealed that she was unnerved that the man had known who she was. She watched his gaze drop to her finger, and she instinctively balled her fist.

"My, my, if it isn't Imperius," he said. "I thought that all rings of power were accounted for. I will have to look into this further."

"Who says you will be left alive to look into anything further?" Thamar asked in a deadly stern tone. "Speak now, how is it that you know so much about us?"

"Let us just say that the allies of Xylona have interested me," the man replied. "I make it my personal duty to know all that I can about you."

"Yet you are here—clearly you are either misguided or an agent of evil. Which is it?" Thamar demanded.

"Who cares?" Baldock stammered. "Let's just take 'im!"

"Spoken like a true Tregador dwarf," the man replied. "Oh please, take me—*if you can.*" The final three words were spoken more deeply, as if a challenge.

"Who are you?" Ashwin asked.

"Since the lady asked so politely, allow me to introduce myself," removing his sword from Heirn's neck, the man bowed politely, though he never took his eyes from his foes. "I am Kabilian, assassin-extraordinaire."

"Kabilian?" Heirn asked. "I have heard the name." Focusing on the sword of the assassin, his eyes widened in horror. "That is an honor blade of Xylona!"

"So it is!" Kabilian joyously exclaimed. "Pandring by name. Its former owner I assure you did not wish to part with it, but such a finely crafted blade just begged me to take it."

"Why you..." Heirn yelled as he leapt towards the assassin. Kabilian stepped aside and with reflexes like lightning brought the sword down and sliced Heirn's arm, forcing him to drop his own blade.

"Temper, temper, good elf," Kabilian warned. "When we were merely fighting, it was magnificent. In anger though, your efforts are but a mockery of what you are."

"Enough of this," Thamar called out. "You clearly are a threat, and for that, you will face Thamar, warrior and thrasher of mine enemies!"

"Oh goodie," Kabilian retorted condescendingly. "Show me what you've got, dwarf."

Thamar did not have a chance to swing into action though, as Baldock stormed past him and tackled the assassin. His arms pumped quickly as he continued punching. Kabilian struggled to reach an amulet hanging on his chest, and with one last grin, ignoring the pain of the dwarf's assault, he clasped it and vanished from sight.

Baldock fell straight to the ground, and glanced around wondering what happened to the man. "No fair! He was mine!"

"There is more to that one than meets the eye," Thamar observed. "We would be wise to follow Arifos and Mylvannan's lead and find our own weapons."

"Agreed," Heirn said as he wrapped a torn cloth from one of the thugs' shirts around his slashed forearm.

Glancing down at the white tiger, Thamar smiled to Ashwin. "It seems you found the Empress's pride and joy."

"Excuse me?" Ashwin asked.

"The white tigers," Thamar clarified. "There should be another one around here somewhere."

Ashwin stroked the fine cat's head again and started scratching her behind the ear—a spot the tiger seemed particularly fond of.

Stroking his beard, Thamar quickly raised his finger with the memory of a story Braksis once told him. "Vaz and Vella if I remember it correctly—one male and one female."

Theiler nodded his head in agreement. He confirmed the names.

Ashwin continued stroking the white tiger's head. "You must be Vella then." The tiger growled in response and then darted down the hall that Arifos and Mylvannan had taken.

"Looks like we have our own tracker now," Thamar smiled appreciatively. "Let's get moving!" The companions, no longer concerned with stealth, ran after the white tiger and towards their friends.

CHAPTER 19

The two elves moved quietly through the corridors. Ahead of them, they could hear several screams and growls. Arifos raised his hand to slow down Mylvannan and they approached more cautiously.

Peering further down the hall at the sight before them, they saw a large white tiger advancing upon several more of the thugs. The men were backing away in terror of the approaching beast.

"We can use this to our advantage," Arifos declared. "Our weapons are down this hall, we are almost there; with this distraction, we can move freely."

"Agreed," Mylvannan said.

The two crept along the wall, carefully watching the battle before them. The white tiger lunged forward and shouldered one man aside, rendering him unconscious. A second man screamed and started to retreat, with the third falling as the tiger turned around and leapt onto his back.

"An efficient cat," Arifos commended the animal.

As they continued forward, Arifos stopped, his attention caught by a man standing in a doorway with a crossbow. He raised the weapon, aiming at the white tiger. With a slight tightening of his finger, a bolt soared out at the tiger.

Arifos lunged quickly himself and caught the bolt in mid-flight. Spinning back around, he sent the bolt back towards the shooter with even greater velocity using his mystical abilities to propel the bolt, piercing the man's chest.

Mylvannan stepped forward and smirked at Arifos. "Is this your idea of moving freely and not getting involved?"

"Perhaps I erred, but I could not allow the bolt to hit the cat," Arifos replied.

The white tiger turned and regarded the two for a moment. With a long spring, it launched directly between them and into the room where the man with the crossbow had been standing. As it landed, the two elves heard several more calls and cries, as the giant tiger attacked several other men.

"Do we continue on?" Mylvannan asked.

"No—those men could have gotten us while we were distracted. Let us help the tiger defeat them," Arifos decided.

"Very well," Mylvannan concurred. Picking up his dagger, he smiled at the prospect. Though he preferred fighting with his own weapons, it had been a long time since he fought anything or anyone at a disadvantage. He hated to be out of practice—something that he surmised was about to change.

The two elves entered the room and saw the white tiger standing atop of three men, pinning them down. Five others remained and were moving towards the tiger. Arifos and Mylvannan swung in quickly and stood before them, barring their path.

"You will not touch the cat," Arifos threatened.

The men did not heed the warning and came in, their weapons poised for the attack. The two elves separated, splitting their enemies. Three went after Arifos, the other two at Mylvannan.

Mylvannan jumped up and grasped onto the vines that covered the ceiling and flung himself out, feet first. He connected with one man, breaking his nose and toppling him to the ground. He then swiped with his dagger, slicing the second man across the chest.

Reaching down, Mylvannan chopped at the back of the first man's neck and rendered him unconscious. He then glared at the second man who was clutching his chest. Rather than fight, the man ran from the room.

Mylvannan considered the battle and realized that it was no true test. When he was younger, he learned his skill on the icy peaks of the Mourning Mountains. He fought against the sentient Frost giants, Ice trolls, quiltoth, and yinzella. The other creatures of the icy regions were no less dangerous, and he had bested cryobarrim, the deadly fargesbeck, and even a hydra. No, he thought, these humans were no challenge for a hunter of his abilities.

Arifos took a slightly different stance against his three foes: he opted for a defensive posture and waited for the men to come to him. The impatient thugs did not make him wait long, and rushed him one at a time. Arifos dodged sideways with the first thrust and brought his dagger down and dug it into the man's spine.

The second warrior paused, swinging his blade wildly. Arifos flipped his dagger around, caught it by the blade, and sent it hurtling at his second opponent. The man tried to parry the throw with his sword, but missed and dropped as the knife pierced his chest by his heart.

The third man was less cautious, thinking Arifos defenseless. The Madrew elf spun around his attacker, grabbed him by the head, and twisted with all of his might, snapping the man's neck. As he, too, dropped to the ground, Arifos glanced over to see that Mylvannan had likewise concluded his conflict and was waiting for him.

"Shall we find our weapons now?" Mylvannan asked.

Arifos glanced down and saw that the white tiger seemed at peace and no longer threatened; he had also defeated the three foes he had been perched upon. "Yes—the sooner we are out of this place, the better."

Mylvannan watched the pink-skinned elf walk back into the corridor and down the hall. Arifos remained a mystery to him. He definitely had his own ideals and values, and was an honorable soul, but Mylvannan felt that the Madrew elf was often too harsh and unforgiving to those that he fought against. He wondered what it was that made him the way he was.

CHAPTER 20

He paused at the doors leading to the infirmary and gently touched the bandages on his head. He had no desire to see the doctor again after being told that he would be scarred for life, but Zoldex had insisted. Pushing the double doors open, Winton entered the large medical room and scanned the area for his target.

In the middle of the room, he saw Centain lying on a table, unmoving. He stepped forward, but a young nurse barred his path.

"Do you need something for the pain, my lord?"

"Out of my way, woman," he screeched. "I wish news on the Captain!"

The doctor rushed over, hearing the harsh words from Winton, and hoped to come to the aid of his nurse. "Is there something I can do for you, sir?"

Winton brushed past him and walked over to the Captain. Studying the man with his one good eye, Winton could see that his breathing was irregular, and his wounds certainly looked fatal. "How is he?"

"Not well, I am afraid," the doctor confirmed.

Winton tried to hide his smile at that simple declaration. "What are his chances?"

The doctor lowered his head solemnly. "I fear that all I can do now is keep him comfortable. If we had some of the waters of Shimendyn, a healing potion, or even a Mage Healer, he would recover."

The thought of so many options that could save the Captain stung him. "Do we have these things?"

"Alas, we do not," the doctor frowned.

"Can we get them somehow?" Winton continued, trying to gauge

106

what efforts the doctor was taking.

"The Mages that were appointed to the Empress have not returned. Without them, we have no way of contacting the Mage's Council," the doctor explained. "It is truly tragic—they share the city with us and have the answer, but we cannot get to them and ask for their assistance."

"Yes," Winton uttered. "A tragedy."

"Unless we can get one of these mystical remedies, there is nothing more that can be done," the doctor concluded. "His injuries are just too extensive to heal with conventional medicine."

"I will do my best to procure one of these remedies," Winton stated. "Perhaps they could heal my own wounds?"

"Oh yes," the doctor said enthusiastically. "If we could get a Healer or a potion, there would be more than enough to help you both."

"I will have my best riders go out to try and get some for us then," Winton offered.

"That would be ideal, sir," the doctor said.

"Yes, please keep me appraised of the Captain's situation," Winton ordered.

"As you wish, sir," the doctor bowed.

Pivoting, Winton turned and walked out of the room. Centain was as good as dead already. If he did send out riders, he would do so only after the Captain was dead, merely to have the potion for himself. As for the honorable Captain, there was no use threatening his own position by trying to kill the man. All that he would accomplish was more witnesses that could incriminate him. Zoldex would just have to be satisfied that Centain would die soon enough on his own.

Satisfied that his new position as Emperor was secure, he headed towards the throne room, snickering. Sitting on the chair that had only been occupied by Karleena and her father Conrad before her, he knew that he had finally found his destiny: the Age of Winton had begun.

CHAPTER 21

"Right through there," Arifos pointed.

"Not a moment too soon," Mylvannan replied. "I can hear more guards coming this way."

Arifos paused for a moment and listened. There were more men on the way. "To hunt us or the cat though?"

The two glanced at the white tiger that they had fought alongside, and wondered why he was here and who he was. The tiger returned their gazes and then darted down the hall in the opposite direction.

"Why do you think he did that?" Mylvannan asked.

The tiger stopped at the end of the corridor and growled into the distance. He then turned and ran away. The two elves listened as the call rang out: "There it is—after it!" Both leaned flat against the wall and watched as another twelve men charged in pursuit of the white tiger.

"Never mind," Mylvannan said as he shook his head. "The cat's a smart one."

Arifos stepped forward and tried the knob to the door. "Locked," he stated. He moved his two arms over his head, circled them around and brought them both darting out towards the door, stopping inches from it. A shockwave of mystical energy launched from his fingers and hammered into the door, splintering it.

"That's a handy ability you have there," Mylvannan complimented.

"Most of my people have mystical energy flowing through them," Arifos explained. "Some more than others, but a trait we all share."

"In my homeland, only the Frost Queen and her Attendants are gifted mystically," Mylvannan replied. "A wondrous gift indeed."

The two walked into the room and were shocked to see their

weapons lying unattended upon a pair of tables. "How come I get the feeling that this is too easy?" Mylvannan asked. "Nothing in life is this easy."

Arifos studied the room before entering and nodded his agreement. "I neither see nor sense any kind of mystical traps, but caution is advised."

"Especially since you shattered the door," Mylvannan added with a chuckle.

"Agreed—other guards may come investigating," Arifos said as he took the first step into the room. He moved cautiously—though he did not sense any traps, he also did not wish to blindly walk into one.

He picked up his belt first and strapped it along his waist. Skrenlar, the honor blade of Xylona that he was presented with, was sheathed in its scabbard on his left side. He fastened another leather belt around his leg, small loops encircling it that held tiny throwing blades. He then picked up his quiver and slung it on his back.

As he picked up Unamalastra, he bowed his head, touching it to the tip of the weapon. Opening his eyes again, he pulled the bowstring back and nodded his approval. He then slung it alongside his quiver.

Mylvannan regarded him curiously. "What were you checking for?"

"Unamalastra is mystically enchanted," Arifos explained. "It will work for me alone."

"What do you mean?" Mylvannan asked as he sheathed his two serrated daggers in his boots.

"The draw weight of Unamalastra is so high that it is all but impossible for any but the strongest individuals to even pull back," he stated. "Yet I can wield it with ease and no strain."

"Is that why the hobgoblins who felt the Impaler's sting were launched into the air upon impact?"

"Yes," Arifos confirmed, thinking back to his encounters with the hobgoblins at Xylona.

"Again, your abilities are most impressive," Mylvannan commended.

Arifos reached down and picked up his two prized possessions—

his twin scimitars, Phistala and Aurlestyl. These were perhaps his greatest achievement. As he twirled the two blades, his mind drifted back to when he first crafted them.

In his homeland, his beloved city Lovilien, the vile Zoldex and his followers had established themselves as gods. Though the Madrew did not believe this, they had little they could do against the powerful magic users who seemed to live for an eternity. As gods do, they demanded satisfaction from the people by the surrendering of their flesh to the whims of their own designs. This desire was ultimately their undoing, their greatest failing, for when they mated with the Madrew, their magical abilities were passed along to their descendents; before long, most Madrew had the same mystical energy flowing in their bodies.

Arifos remembered his desire to fight against these false gods. He could see with his own mystical powers that their deities were no real gods, but men—but his people were too frightened to face Zoldex. The elders remembered the stories of those that had attempted to rebel and were slain brutally for their efforts. Though he did not wish to submit, Arifos kept his desire to strike back in check. Until, that is, the day that the false gods decided to make things more personal for him.

He had two younger sisters—beautiful, exotic, and so full of life. He can still remember their smiles and humor to this day, their innocence and purity. The worst part of the memory was the fact that they idolized their older brother, and where Arifos wished to fight back, they agreed as well, even if they did not truly grasp what that would mean.

Two eternals came to them one day and desired their submission of the flesh. Unlike so many before them, they refused, and told the false gods to be gone. The eternals did not appreciate the rebellious attitude and made a very public spectacle of the two young elves, slaying them in front of their entire community in order to deter further disobedience.

Arifos had not been there; if he had, he certainly would have been slain alongside his sisters in a moment of passion and anger—a death he would not regret if it meant his two beloved sisters were allowed to see even one more sunrise. Fate was not so kind. He had been away with a hunting party facing trolls that had wandered too closely to Lovilien.

Upon his return, he had found his people somber and quiet. Many had stared at him, but if he tried to speak to them, they turned their heads away in shame. He was confused and knew not what was wrong until he found his two sisters, still on display for all to see as an example of what happens to those that disobey their deities.

He remembered dropping to his knees, tormented, the image of his beloved sisters burned forever in his mind. He did not know how he had gained the strength to go on, nor did he even realize what he was doing, but he did rise that night, collected the brutalized bodies of his sisters, and left Lovilien with them for an old and distant ally.

He traveled by wagon for three months before reaching Krahiell, the home of the closest neighboring dwarves. He remained there for several years, fighting alongside the dwarves against Rock trolls, orcs, goblins, and zurkith. In payment, the famed blacksmiths taught him their craft. He mined their precious ore beside them, and soon crafted his two scimitars. Before he was done, he embedded the essence and purity of his sisters, and named them in their honor.

The weapons held more than just their essence. With every touch, he could feel them, and knew that they were with him. Against a foe of darkness, they would cut deep, mystically allowing his thrusts to overcome his foes' defenses. If facing a foe that is true of heart, the innocence of his sisters would shine through and the blades could not possibly bring harm or injure them.

He did not return to his people right away. He remained with the dwarves for a while, and when he reluctantly left, he traveled alone, fighting for what he believed in and facing the forces of evil at every turn. He found another elven civilization, Evanthia, and remained there for a while as well, amazed at how different his distant cousins were when not tainted by Zoldex and his fellow false gods. Seeing these elves, all reminding him of his sisters and what they could have been if born in a different homeland, he returned to his people and led a revolt against Zoldex.

Though the false gods were banished from the land, it brought little satisfaction to him: his sisters were dead, his people scarred for generations. Before he could even ponder this further, the demons and the hordes of darkness began to sweep the land, and again, Arifos found the only peace he could: his unrelenting slaughter of evil creatures.

He twirled the two swords and placed them into the scabbards along his back. He turned away from Mylvannan, hoping that the Frost elf would not see the single tear that trailed from his eye.

Mylvannan had caught the tear, but said nothing. He could see the torment in his companion and wondered if he would ever truly learn who Arifos was. He was the greatest warrior he had ever seen. Though he hated to admit it, the Madrew elf's abilities surpassed even his own. Yet when he attacked his foes, he did so with a ruthlessness and bloodlust that never seemed satiated. Yes, he thought, Arifos was indeed plagued by his past, and may the gods help any who fueled his fury.

Mylvannan placed the two serrated swords of his people into their scabbards fastened to his belt, and then lifted Frostlartil, his honor blade of Xylona, and reflected for a moment how his own enchanted weapon had been just as impressive as that which Arifos wielded. Before placing this in its holder along his back, he silently thanked the Frost Queen for her own mystical additions to such a fine weapon.

Hearing a low growl, the two quickly pulled their weapons and glanced up at the source. They saw a white tiger sitting on the top of a wardrobe studying them.

"Is it the same cat?" Mylvannan asked.

"Yes," Arifos replied.

"He must have dealt with his pursuers, then," the Frost elf speculated.

"So it would seem," Arifos returned.

"No!" a cry came from the hall. The two elves turned quickly, recognizing the voice of Ashwin, the elven princess both were sworn to protect.

CHAPTER 22

The two elves spun around to see Ashwin rushing towards them, a frantic expression on her face and her arm outstretched. "No, don't hurt the cat!"

Mylvannan smiled and stepped forward, his arms motioning downwards for her to remain calm. "Fear not Ashwin—we would never harm such a magnificent creature."

Visibly relieved, Ashwin sighed deeply. She glanced up at the tiger, which dropped from his perch and walked over to her, brushing affectionately against her leg.

"The cat likes you," Heirn said as he walked into the room, accompanied by Vella.

Ashwin smiled at the notion and bent over and grabbed both tigers by the neck, one in each arm and hugged them. Vaz leaned over and sent her toppling to the ground, exposing his belly for her to rub. With a giggle, she began to do so.

Arifos watched the exchange and then glanced at Heirn. "It would be best to recover your weapons, then we should be off."

"I agree," Heirn said as he tossed the sword he had been using aside.

"This is no place for pleasantries," Arifos commented more sternly, this time directed at Ashwin, who glanced up and grimaced at the remark.

Heirn walked over to the table where the weapons were scattered and slung his quiver and longbow over his shoulder. As he lifted Martristlit, his honor blade of Xylona, he took several swipes in the air and nodded in approval.

"It will be good to fight with such a well-crafted blade again," Heirn observed. As he ended his comment, his eyes lowered to the makeshift bandage on his arm where Kabilian had struck him. He vowed to himself that he would meet the so-called "assassin-extraordinaire" again, and then, with Martristlit in his hands, would prove exactly who is the better swordsman.

Heirn sheathed his sword and then leaned over and collected Ashwin's weapons as well. "Here, cousin," he said as he handed her her own longbow, quiver, and dagger.

"Thank you, Heirn," Ashwin said as she took each item and placed it in its proper place.

"Ah, noble elves—you have found our weapons I see," Thamar said as he walked into the room. "And Vaz, too, if my eyes are not deceiving me—for now that I see them together, I know for certain that the one who fought with us is the female."

By his side, Theiler nodded his agreement. The white tiger that had saved Ashwin was clearly not as large as the one that now lay before them. There was at least a hundred-and-fifty-pound difference between the two.

"Looks like they have a new mother," Thamar grinned at Ashwin as he pointed out how the tigers followed her every move.

"That would not be appropriate," Heirn commented.

"Why not?" Ashwin quickly asked.

"Look at them—sure, they can fight here by our sides, but how will we ever feed them once we are on the way back to Xylona?"

Thamar bellowed loudly. "Fear not, noble elf, for all cats are predatory creatures. I would bet that it is we that would be the ones needing to find food more so than them."

"Thamar is right," Ashwin chimed in. "They perhaps could even help us find food."

"Besides," Thamar was quick to add. "We couldn't leave them here surrounded by enemies!"

"Valid points," Heirn conceded.

Mylvannan and Arifos exchanged a glance. They had both seen

the white tiger fighting and knew that the two pets would be substantial allies—both in escaping from the palace and on their long journey home. If Heirn had protested too loudly, both would have stepped in and vouched for the beasts.

The familiar clanking of armor quickly sounded the coming of Baldock as he charged into the room, saw all of his allies, then lowered his arms to rest on his knees, bent over, struggling to maintain his breath.

"Never before have I seen a dwarf so winded," Thamar laughed. "They must make those of us from Vorstad of sterner stuff, I be thinking!"

"If ye be thinkin' that, then I would be more than happy to be provin' ye wrong!" Baldock wheezed.

Heirn glared at the armored dwarf and sneered. "Perhaps you would not be so winded if you were not garbed in so much armor."

Baldock stood up straight, his eyes opened wide in fury. "Listen here, elf—I be wearin' the armor o' the Centrinell fer o'er a century defendin' me own people. There be nothin' wrong with me armor!"

"You're too young to be winded so easily," Heirn added. "What explanation do you have then?"

Baldock scratched his black beard for a moment in contemplation. In complete stubbornness, he raised his chin and smiled. "It was the durned trip here."

"The trip here?" Heirn asked incredulously. "How did that wind you?"

"I be used to runnin' everywhere. When we came here, we be havin' mounts!"

Thamar started laughing and hit Baldock on the back with his open hand. "Then we will run all the way home my friend! Yes?"

Baldock's stern gaze dropped for a moment, a look like an animal trapped, then smiled triumphantly remembering his own argument. "Ye'll all be strugglin' to keep up with me!"

"That'll be the day," Heirn whispered as he shook his head disapprovingly.

"Come, collect your weapons so we can be off," Arifos prompted them.

Baldock's eyes opened wide again in anticipation. Nimbly, as if never winded, he moved quickly and picked up Splitter, sighing with relief, quickly replaced by joyous laughter as he rubbed his fingers over his famed illistrium battleaxe. "With Splitter in me hands, I be ready to take on all o' the foes in this here castle!"

Heirn was about to retort with a snide, "You would," but looking at the dwarf, now holding his axe, he seemed as if his fatigue were nothing more than an exaggerated act. As the axe head glistened, he wondered if the weapon somehow imbued strength into its wielder. After all, it was engraved with the mark of Feldrin, the dwarven God of Fury. Perhaps with that mark, in a dwarf's hand, the wielder would never be winded or allow his own fury to be satiated. This was something he would explore further after they were gone from this place.

After a moment of admiring the craftsmanship of his people, Baldock picked up his short-sword and placed it in its scabbard. He then lifted his round shield and turned to face his companions with that in one hand and his axe in the other. "I am ready," he announced triumphantly.

The two Vorstad dwarves glanced at each other and smirked. Thamar then nodded to Baldock. "Such spirit! I like it!"

Theiler walked over and quickly picked up his own sword and club, then returned to the door to glance out in case anyone was coming. Though his weapons neither glistened nor embodied mystical enchantment, he too was ready to face any enemies that may stand before him. He never needed more than his sword in any fight. Glancing down at the griffin claw fastened to his belt, he knew that this sword was better for him than a score of mystical weapons combined.

Thamar took the dagger that he had been using thus far and placed it in his belt. This soon was joined with his own dagger, as he slid it in next to his new one. Slowly, he reached out and lifted his large mallet. Dwarven writing was etched into the head of the hammer, marking it as a weapon forged for a noble and honorable house of

Vorstad. A studded strap wound around the top of the mallet, binding it to its handle.

He swiped his mighty mallet in the air several times and regarded his companions. "We should not dawdle, but leave this place immediately," he grimly advised. "I fear that it has been overrun by the very enemies that we sought an alliance against."

"I see no hobgoblins or orcs," Heirn commented.

"Yet I have learned that there is one man that is behind the hobgoblins and orcs that we *do* face. The same man coordinated the rebellions in the Imperium, the raids of the Suspintian Forest, and much more that I am unaware of, I am sure."

Any that looked at Arifos in that moment would have backed away in fear of the Madrew elf's fury. In a burst of primal rage, he uttered one word, a name, in such contempt that it left his companions speechless. "Zoldex."

CHAPTER 23

"We're almost there," Adonis tried to encourage Cylnta, a comment he had been making for several hours now. "We will see the Walls of Trespias soon."

The two flying teams continued to bob up and down as the exhausted Paladin strained to focus. The news of King Sarlec's death required their haste, but she had been struggling to keep their team flying towards their destination, with only minor periods of rest, for four days. She feared that she was beginning to lose the battle.

"There!" Adonis called out. "The Walls of Trespias!"

The call seemed to revitalize Cylnta who flickered her yellow slit eyes several times to focus on her task. The horse carrying her and Adonis rose slightly into the air and leveled out. Behind them, the wagon carrying Doctor Podeis and Sergeant Darkler did likewise.

"Curious," Adonis said to himself. The closer they got, he was struck by the oddity of the fact that the gate leading into Trespias was closed. In his thirty-six years, he had never once seen the entrance to the vast city blocked.

Glancing back at the fatigued Mage, he beckoned her to bring them to the ground and rest for a while. Cylnta gratefully eased the two teams down and then immediately closed her eyes, instantly falling asleep.

Adonis led the horse up to the gate and glanced to the Guardsman on the wall. "I am Adonis, Captain of the Imperial Security and Investigation Authority. Why is this path barred?"

A turquoise and gold garbed sentry peered down from atop the wall and studied the people at the gate. "ISIA you say? How do I know that you are no spy? Sent here to create further havoc? I saw you coming out of the sky! An *Adlesian* no less!" The last comment was spat at the ebony-skinned man, an insult to his homeland and heritage that Adonis had lived with his entire life.

"Looks like he doesn't know you, Captain," Darkler said. "Want me to scale the wall and teach him the error of his ways?"

"At ease, Sergeant," Adonis ordered. "We are all allies here." Looking up again, he called out to the guard. "I was summoned by Geist, personal messenger of the Empress herself. My mission is most urgent and delays are unacceptable."

Pausing for a moment, Adonis hardened his gaze and spoke more threateningly. "You are not causing me a further delay, are you?"

"The messenger of the Empress, you say?" the Guardsman asked.

"Yes, Geist by name," Adonis said, impatience creeping into his voice.

"There is no Empress, so be gone!"

Shocked by the statement, Adonis looked to Darkler, who was already springing into action. In a moment, he leapt and was climbing up the door, two daggers being used to hoist him up and help his assent.

The Guardsman became panic stricken and called out for reinforcements. He then pulled his own sword and lifted his shield to wait for the advancing foe.

Darkler leapt over the ledge and stood before the Guardsman. His glare was vicious enough to force the younger man to step back and cower, even though he was fully armed and his foe only carried a pair of knives. "No Empress?" he said through gritted teeth. "That's blasphemy!"

"Leave, or face the wrath of the Guardsmen!" the young soldier struggled to sound bold.

Darkler kept walking towards the man, but did not raise his weapons in any threatening way. The guard lunged forward, and Darkler dodged to the side, dropped his two daggers, and grabbed the Guardsman by the arm. With a flick of his wrist, he applied pressure and forced the man to drop his sword.

Smiling, Darkler raised his elbow and slammed the guard in the nose. He stumbled backwards, blood spurting from the wound.

A dozen other men rushed forward, all garbed as Guardsmen of Trespias. One man with a turquoise cape halted before Darkler and held his hand up for the others to likewise stop. He held the sergeant's gaze for a moment and then shook his head disapprovingly as he recognized the man before him.

Glancing over the wall, he saw an annoyed Adonis staring back up at him. "Idiot," he growled under his breath. Standing straight, he looked at Darkler and resheathed his sword. "My apologies, Sergeant Darkler, but this guard is young and foolish."

"No harm done," Darkler said.

The caped man glanced at his bleeding guard and realized that Darkler meant no harm to his own people. He knew the reputation of this man, and if the short brawler had to cut his way through the city to get to his destination, he would not have a care in the world.

"We are under a lot of pressure," the man said trying to rationalize the incident.

"Why?" Darkler asked. "Something more than a murderer?"

"A murderer?" the man asked, confused for a moment.

"King Sarlec," Darkler prompted.

"Oh, yes, most unfortunate," the guard nodded. "But no—the Empress has been abducted and the palace guards have been almost completely slain. The capital is in chaos. We were instructed not to allow anyone in or out."

Darkler was a man that knew the advantages of keeping a good poker face. He had grown up surviving in the swamps of Tenalong, and not getting into too much trouble with Lady Salaman of the Hidden Empire. He was normally unreadable, but the news he heard was most unsettling.

"Open the damned gates," he instructed. "Now!"

"Yes, of course," the caped man replied. "Anything for you and Captain Adonis."

Darkler quickly descended the stairs and stood by the gate waiting for the others. Adonis looked down at him and could see the turmoil on his face.

"What is it?" Adonis asked.

"It might just be the fall of the Imperium," Darkler speculated.

Adonis watched the man for a long moment, unable to speak. His father, Arkus, had been sworn to protect Emperor Conrad. That vow of allegiance and protection was passed on to him. Even when Conrad died, his oath was transferred to Karleena. Seeing the look on the sergeant's face, he suddenly wondered if his decision to create ISIA would come back to haunt him. If anything had happened to the Empress, he knew that he would be plagued forevermore; no matter how much good he did in the realm.

Bringing the heels of his feet down hard, he dug into his horse and began galloping swiftly towards the palace. He only hoped that things were not as bad as he feared.

CHAPTER 24

"Hey elf," Thamar whispered to Arifos, "the cats might be taking your job away."

Arifos glanced down at the red-bearded dwarf, not certain of what he was implying.

Seeing that Arifos was not grasping his meaning, Thamar shook his head incredulously. "Do I need to be spelling it out for you? The cats have taken the point. *They're* leading us now, not you!"

"As fer me," Baldock burst out, not bothering to whisper. "The elf should be leadin' us! We be trustin' a pair o' beasts to be gettin' us out o' here in one piece!"

"They know this palace and have enhanced senses," Ashwin explained in a whisper.

"Enhanced senses?" Baldock laughed. "I be seein' the pink one, he be havin' enhanced senses hisself!"

Heirn quickened his pace and placed a hand on the top of Baldock's armored head. "If you keep talking so loudly, we'll have every remaining guard in this place swarming down upon us."

"Bring 'em on!" Baldock roared. "If I told ye once, I told ye a hunnerd times—I prefer a good fight where I can be sinkin' me axe into someone's skull to all o' this durned sneakin' around!"

"It is curious, we have left dozens, maybe more lying unconscious or dead," Arifos stated. "How many more could they have left?"

"I be thinking of this myself," Thamar nodded his assent. "Our foes do seem to be endless. Let us hope that the cats get us out of here swiftly—for though I enjoy a fight as much as Baldock here, I feel that it is of utmost importance to relay what has happened here to Kings

Chaddrick and Echalas."

"Finally, a dwarf that I can agree with," Heirn said.

Theiler spun around and glared at the elf, his look threatening and warning at the same time.

"My brother does not like it when you be speaking poorly of us," Thamar explained. "We be allies, and looking for more, as was our mission. Fighting amongst ourselves would not solve anything."

"Forgive me, noble dwarf," Heirn said with sincere respect in his inflection. "I was merely attempting to point out that some dwarves, those from Vorstad, can think and see things rationally rather than blindly running into each foray."

"Regardless of your intent, keep your opinions and snide remarks to yourself. Even in apology, you now insult another of our band," Thamar cautioned him sternly.

Baldock glanced back and forth with an expression of bewilderment. "Who'd he be insultin'?"

"Enough of this," Arifos instructed. "We will have time for these petty arguments *after* we escape from this foul place."

"Agreed," Thamar said, his gaze still focused on Heirn. He squinted his eyes for a moment at the elf, then pivoted around and walked in front of Arifos and after the two white tigers. Theiler scurried to catch up, and then fell in step alongside his brother.

"What just happened?" Baldock asked, still confused. "Who'd the elf insult?"

Ashwin bent over and smiled at the armored dwarf. "He was insulting our enemies."

"Well, in that case, what's all o' this bickerin' about? Let's go find us some more guards and show 'em what we can be doin' now that we be havin' our weapons back!"

Ashwin stood up beaming and followed the surly dwarf as he eagerly charged after his dwarven companions, hoping to be in the lead if another threat tried to oppose them. With a wink at Heirn, she continued after them as well.

"Fools," Heirn whispered as he shook his head.

Arifos nodded to Mylvannan who continued on with Ashwin, leaving him behind with Heirn. "That was inappropriate," he cautioned.

"The dwarves are idiots. Baldock didn't even know we were talking about him," Heirn complained. "How King Echalas ever thinks that we will be able to fight alongside of each other is beyond me."

"You have been an ally of Vorstad for centuries, is that not true?" Arifos asked.

"Well, yes," Heirn conceded. "You can see the differences though between Thamar and his ilk and the dwarves of Tregador. Baldock may be good in a fight, but he's a brute that prefers to barrel his way through his enemies rather than display any finesse, style, or appreciation for combat."

"Do you think Thamar and Theiler are the same way?"

"I told you no," Heirn spat back defensively. "Even though they speak more eloquently and seem to have a better grasp of things, they still are more reckless than I would like."

"Oh really?" Arifos asked.

"Yes—deny that you have seen the fire in their eyes when battle is upon us, their cheers and songs as they leap into action. The dwarves cannot be controlled."

"The world is full of many creatures," Arifos stated. "I myself spent a good number of years amongst dwarves in my own homeland. Where you see recklessness and incompetence, I see pride, honor, and a belief that they could stand up to any foe—be it another dwarf, or even a giant or dragon."

"Like I said, foolish."

"Not so," Arifos quickly replied. "Though they have confidence to face these foes—and not even once does doubt or insecurity enter their minds—they are not naïve. They know that these creatures could overcome them and kill hundreds—perhaps even thousands—before they are brought down, but the dwarves would risk those hundreds and thousands without a solitary regret, for they would die fighting for their ideals and beliefs.

"Do not judge the dwarves too harshly, Heirn," Arifos continued.

"In my homeland, I've watched armies of dwarves fall before the evil horde that swept the land. With each dwarf that fell, those that remained grew even more determined to defeat their foe. Their abilities and efforts continued to double, and not even one of them complained or admitted defeat."

"They are all dead, I presume?" Heirn said, feeling that Arifos proved his point for him.

"Many, yes," Arifos conceded. "Yet the spirit and ideals of the dwarves lives on. I respect them."

"Some self-restraint would be good, is all," Heirn said. "If they knew that they would die facing their foe, would it not be better to have pulled back until a strategy could be formed to face the enemy?"

"Perhaps," Arifos solemnly replied. "My people fled—a mere fraction of the Madrew that once populated the land. Against the forces of darkness though, how far can you pull back? Sooner or later, you must make a stand, and fight for your beliefs. I fear that you will not find very many allies like the dwarves that are ready and willing to do this.

"Why are you here?" Arifos asked bluntly.

"I am representing Xylona in the unification talks," Heirn replied. "My King's wishes."

"Do you believe that Xylona will fall without allies?" Arifos continued to press on.

Heirn did not reply; he just closed his eyes for a moment and thought of his homeland. Though he did not like Baldock, he admitted that without the dwarves' aid, Xylona would have fallen long before to the constant barrage from the hobgoblins.

"I remember when I first arrived," Arifos reminded him. "Xylona was burning. The elves were falling back. The hobgoblins were winning."

"Yes, and you saved us," Heirn said in mild annoyance. "That is why you were awarded Skrenlar."

"What if it was not me though, but the dwarves of Tregador, or centaurs, or gnomes, or rasplers that came to your aid?"

The expression on Heirn's face darkened at the prospect.

"Do you hold these other races in contempt for not being born elves?" Arifos asked.

"Of course not," Heirn quickly retorted.

"Yet you do not like them, nor do you like having to rely upon them," Arifos observed. "Unless you change the way you view the world, unless all of the races change the way they view the world, the unification will fail, and the forces of Zoldex will sweep the land.

"All will die," Arifos somberly predicted. "I have seen it before, and hope that I will never see it again."

"I am here, aren't I?" Heirn asked.

"True, but you do not believe," Arifos said. "You see Baldock as an annoyance, and not as an ally or part of your salvation. We all will have roles to play in this upcoming war—and yes, it will be a war."

"This land has done nothing but fight war after war—some that last centuries. This will be no different."

"If that is the way you feel, then perhaps I am wasting my time trying to speak with you. I know Zoldex. I have looked into his eyes and have seen the blackness of his heart. I may not know exactly what he is planning here, but I assure you that it is well thought-out, well-schemed, intricate—and when his plans come to fruition, it will be devastating if we are not ready for it."

"I never thought you were so pessimistic, Arifos," Heirn said. "Somehow I expected you, above all others, to rise to the challenge."

"Do not misunderstand me—in this upcoming battle, I will be in the thick of it. I will see more than my share of enemies falling by my blades. But I will also see many of those I call allies and friends perish as well."

"You think that coming here, to meet with the humans, would have changed anything?" Heirn asked with a sneer.

"Did Captain Travers not come to Xylona and fight so valiantly with his men that he, too, was awarded an honor blade of Xylona?"

Heirn turned away in defeat. The human had fought well at Xylona.

"Humans, dwarves, and elves all fought side by side against the hobgoblins at Xylona," Arifos reminded him. "We fought well, yet still King Echalas feared that his city would fall without further allies. That is why we are here."

"Very well," Heirn admitted. "I see that we need the unification to be successful. What we've seen here though tells me that it will fail."

"Only this attempt at it," Arifos rebutted. "Zoldex has grabbed some power; he will extend his reach further. As he does so, more and more will be willing to talk and try to unite. We will be there to help guide them and merge all of our forces."

Taking a deep breath, Heirn nodded in agreement. "I shall apologize to the dwarf."

"Apologize not with words, but with actions," Arifos advised. "They will respect you more for fighting by their side than for claiming that you respect their alliance."

"As you wish," Heirn said, rubbing his arm where he had been injured. He thought to himself that he had already fought alongside the dwarves, and that his perception of them would not change because of one conversation. Realizing that, he wondered if he was indeed prejudiced against the other races, and knew that once they were out of here, he would ponder that more as well.

"Let us catch up," Arifos recommended. "We do not wish to fall too far behind the others."

As they began to follow the path of their companions, neither elf could possibly have realized that the others were all fighting desperately for their lives. That soon, events would unfold that would change all of their lives forever.

CHAPTER 25

The companions slowed down to a stop. Vaz had paused before entering a room, the hair along his back standing on end, indicating that he sensed danger.

The three dwarves and two elves stood behind the two white tigers and glanced around. This hallway only led to the room before them, the direction they had been led thus far. If there was danger waiting inside that room, they were not certain whether they should press on or double back and try to find another way out.

"I recognize this area," Mylvannan whispered. "We did come this way. The entrance to the palace is very close now."

Ashwin kept her gaze intent on the alert white tiger, still glaring at the door, a soft growl coming every few seconds as if their enemies were very near. "There is definitely something on the other side."

"Is it one or one hundred though?" Thamar asked. "We don't know what the cat be sensing."

"That is true," Mylvannan agreed.

"Who cares?" Baldock asked. "Let's just barrel down the durned door and pummel whoever be foolish enough to stand afore us!"

"He may be right," Mylvannan replied, a comment that received a stunned glance from both Ashwin and Thamar. "We have not yet come across any resistance that leads me to believe that we need to truly fear what is sent before us."

"You weren't there to fight Kabilian," Ashwin reminded him. "He fought as well as we did, even better perhaps."

"I do not want you to think I'm being reckless," Mylvannan explained. "We need to get out. We either can go ahead and face our foes, or turn back and continue searching for some other way off of this island. Ahead, we know there is a drawbridge. Any other ways, we'll probably have to do what the gnomes did and swim."

"I ain't swimmin'!" Baldock roared in protest. "With me armor, I'd be sinkin'!"

"Then ahead it is," Thamar agreed. "Do we wait for Arifos and Heirn?"

"That would be wise," Ashwin advised. "We should go in with full force."

"They may be a while," Mylvannan cautioned.

"What do you know?" Thamar demanded.

"Arifos merely wished to have a short conversation with Heirn," Mylvannan answered, not wanting to truly pursue this line of questioning.

"I want to be having a talk with him myself," Thamar agreed. "After we're out of here. The elf should have known better than to dally behind."

Ashwin listened to the conversation and then glanced back down the hall. She hoped that Heirn was all right. They were more than Xylona elves—they were also cousins, and she hoped that no harm came to him.

Without the opportunity to make the decision, the door before them opened and a man backed out of the room laughing. "I need to take a leak! I'll be back before the fighting starts."

As he turned around, he stopped short, a startled expression on his face. Directly in front of him was Vaz, with Baldock standing to his side, grinning fiendishly. As the man glanced around at the foes before him, he wet himself, cringing in fear.

Baldock reached out, grabbed him, and flung him through the door, splintering it as he did. "End o' the durned debate!" With those five words, he charged headlong into the room, his shield in front of him and Splitter raised, ready to swing. Vaz darted in behind him, followed by Vella.

Thamar and Theiler stood up and began to move after Baldock

through the door. As they went to enter, several arrows flew through and both dwarves skidded to a halt and backed away. "Figures the only one with the shield was the first one in!"

Glancing back at the two elves, Thamar slammed his hammer against the wall in frustration. "We need another door!"

Baldock rushed headlong into the room. His scream echoed through the chamber as he charged. Several arrows struck his shield and splintered along the illistrium. Reaching the first man he could, Baldock moved the shield to the right, momentarily opening himself up, and brought Splitter swiping at the same time, burying it deeply into his first target.

Without his shield to block his view, Baldock's eyes widened as he saw the room filled with archers and swordsman. "Where in Tanorus are ye all comin' from?" he asked as he yanked his axe back out of the fallen man. The only answer to his question was a stream of arrows launched directly towards him. He quickly brought his shield back up and crouched down, cringing as dozens of arrows struck his shield and splintered.

With the first volley ended, he jumped back up and rushed in at the next closest warrior. "Ye better not be scratchin' me shield!"

This thug was prepared, unlike the first, and parried Baldock's first thrust. The dwarf replied by punching out with his shield arm and clipping the man in the face. Blood began spurting from his nose as he fell to the ground.

No more arrows came towards him, and the surly dwarf thought that it could only be because he was so close to the swordsmen—they wouldn't want to kill their own, after all. With that in mind, he lowered his head and charged forward, knocking several over and getting deeper into the midst of his foes. Several strikes did hit him, but his armor was tough—almost as tough as the dwarf wearing it—and he continued swinging Splitter and his shield, ignoring any thrust that got through his defenses.

Passion burning in his eyes, Baldock was grateful to finally be able to cut loose and show his foes what it meant to enrage a dwarf of Tregador.

Vaz and Vella moved into the room swiftly and saw Baldock crouch down as a volley of arrows were launched his way. Realizing that this was a threat that needed to be dealt with first, the two white tigers charged the archers at the same time Baldock stood back up and charged the closest swordsman.

Vaz leapt high with Vella running in low. The archers raised their hands defensively as the two large tigers barreled into them, but their defenses were ineffective as claws and teeth began their devastating barrage.

Several archers ran away; a few more managed to elude the white tigers and find a different spot to try and stop the other companions from easily entering the room. The vast majority fell before the two white tigers—most rendered unconscious, but quite a few dead as well.

"You want another door, you've got one!" Mylvannan laughed. Raising Frostlartil over his head, the Frost elf called upon the mystical enchantment that the Frost Queen provided for him: "FRAAZAA!"

With the cry, a white mist began seeping from the blade as if the weapon itself had been frostbitten. With a downward swipe, Mylvannan slashed the wall before him, and a large portion of it turned instantly into a solid block of ice.

"Your door, noble dwarf!" he said as he reached forward and flicked the wall with his index finger and thumb. The ice structure before him crumbled and left a gaping opening for them to enter from.

Thamar's eyes widened in amazement, but only for a moment as he hoisted his mallet and charged through the new opening, his brother right beside him.

Mylvannan nodded to Ashwin and ran through the new doorway himself, Frostlartil still misting, ready to bring its chilling effect into the foray. Ashwin pulled an arrow from her quiver and leaned forward, sending one at a time at the remaining archers, hoping to eliminate her foes as quickly as possible.

She quickly assessed the situation in the room and saw that her companions had swiftly broken up their foes. The room was in total chaos—a definite advantage for the dwarves and elves.

With an arrow nocked, she leaned forward and sought out the archers. She could see the white tigers continuing their attack, and many archers scrambling to try and get away.

Several arrows launched towards her and she backed away through Mylvannan's door, using the wall as a barrier as the projectiles landed where she had been standing. Smiling, she leaned back out and instantly spotted the remaining archers as they were drawing their bows back again. With careful aim, she released her first arrow, watching as it soared and struck one archer between the brows.

Moving back to the safety of the wall again, Ashwin smiled to herself and drew another arrow. She waited, but no arrows fired back at her. Realizing that they were waiting for her to show herself again, Ashwin moved to the original doorway, bent around and launched an arrow, followed by two others in rapid succession. Each arrow hit its mark with deadly precision, dropping three more archers from the fight.

Two more left. Rather than returning to the other side—a move she knew would be predictable—Ashwin steadied herself and readied another arrow. Leaning forward, she giggled when she saw that her hunch proved correct, and she let it go, striking one man directly in his rib cage, below his left arm.

The second archer turned quickly to fire at her, but not as swiftly as Ashwin had pulled another arrow and sent it rushing towards him, a messenger of death. The arrow pierced his throat and in gasps for air, the archer dropped his bow and fell to the ground, clutching at his throat and writhing in agony.

Ashwin scanned the room for a moment and was satisfied that all of the archers were out of the battle. As she nocked another arrow, she walked into the room and began launching them with deadly efficiency at the swordsmen confronting her friends.

Baldock lost his shield in the midst of the close combat, but did not even pause to consider it. He just grabbed his axe with both hands and continued to swing it towards anyone that got close to him. A smile was etched on his face as the bodies began piling up near him. He knew that when he had killed everyone in the room, he would find his shield again. There was not a doubt in his mind of that fact.

Something behind him pushed against him and he spun quickly to see a dead body with an arrow jutting from it. For a moment, he thought that the archers had decided that it was worth killing their own allies to stop this devastating dwarf—a thought that boosted his already overcharged ego—but then he saw Ashwin as she continued to send arrows throughout the room.

Taking a moment, he glanced around, ignoring his own carnage, and saw his allies had all joined in on the fight. "Outnumbered?" he laughed. "Humph. Bring 'em on!"

With a blood-curdling roar, he leapt at the closest standing man and brought his axe down, embedding it in his chest. "Yes!" he roared. "Bring 'em all on!"

The two white tigers scanned the room and were satisfied to see that the archers had all been dealt with. They glanced at their dwarven ally—who had now been joined by the others—and knew that they did not require further assistance.

In the back of the room, Ashwin was alone, launching arrow after arrow. Vella left the bloody remains of the archers first and returned to the elf, Vaz quickly behind her. They realized that the young princess was the least defended and were determined to make sure that her volley of death did not cease. They would protect her and make certain of that.

The two red-bearded dwarves may have entered the room after Baldock, but if score had ever been kept, it would have been a close contest, as the brothers methodically moved through the swordsmen, leaving only bodies in their wake. This was a fighting style both had been accustomed to for almost three centuries, and their movements were swift and sure.

The sons of Thron did not hesitate at all as they faced insurmountable odds. To them, the more the merrier, for then they would have enticing tales to talk about in the years to come.

Thamar spotted Baldock's shield, which now was being wielded by one of the swordsmen as he tried to defend himself from Ashwin. "I'll be back," he said to Theiler as he walked towards the man, his mallet pounding anyone foolish enough to get in his way.

He stopped directly in front of the man and glared up at him. "That be belonging to a friend of mine."

The swordsman began laughing. "Then take it back, if you can!"

"I was hoping you'd say that!" Thamar beamed. He took two steps and jumped up, clutching his mallet in both hands. He brought it down in a thunderous blow than knocked the shield from the man's hand.

The man stepped backwards and raised his sword, ready to counterattack. With a lunge, he felt that he had the red-bearded dwarf with ease.

Thamar spun aside and dodged the attack. "I be swifter than I look," he smiled.

"We'll see about that!" the man confidently replied as he stepped towards Thamar, swinging his sword again.

"It will do you no good," Thamar boasted as he easily dodged the attack again.

"Would you stand still and fight?" the man cried out.

"If you want me to do so," Thamar said. He raised his mallet and swung with all of his might, shattering the man's right knee with the thrust. "I usually save a swing like that for giants, but you'll do."

The swordsman dropped to the ground, howling in agony. His hands clutched his leg, now bent at an awkward angle.

Thamar stepped forward and glared down at him. "I am Thamar, thrasher of mine enemies!" he roared as he brought the pommel of his mallet down and bonked the man on the head. As he watched the man lying unconscious on the ground, Thamar picked up Baldock's shield and hung it over his back by its guige. "You're alive—that's more that you deserve."

As he glanced around the room, he noticed fewer and fewer foes still standing before them. Nodding his head in approval, he had to admit that he and his companions were a very effective fighting team—a true force to be reckoned with. Stopping, he saw a man shackled in the back of the room—a man wearing the armor of an Imperial Guard. Raising his mallet, he walked towards the palace guard, daring anyone to get in his way.

The crackling noise as another swordsman was turned to ice made Mylvannan pause. This last one had not turned right away. He actually had bled a little. He glanced at Frostlartil and knew that the enchantment was wearing off. No matter, he thought, for the battle was nearly won.

He glanced back in his wake and saw dozens of frozen statues representing the foes he had fought. He was raised as a hunter and warrior of Akkammanavar, a deadly and dangerous terrain to be raised upon, but he thrived on the life. These swordsmen were nothing compared to the vicious quiltoth and yinzella he grew up fighting. The Frost elves had also feared the overpowering Frost giants, but he found himself wishing that he could face a foe that could really test him like one of those old enemies of his people. Even the Ice trolls—which were jokes in his opinion, though deadly when in vast numbers—would be more of a challenge than these mindless foes that seemed glad to charge so blindly to their deaths.

As another man rushed forward to stab at him, Mylvannan easily deflected the blow, twirled Frostlartil around, and brought it swiping down, slashing the man's chest. Yes, he thought, the incantation was wearing off. This man did not turn to ice. The wound he had been inflicted showed signs of freezing, but he did not freeze. No matter, he decided, this battle was as good as done.

Glancing around, he saw Theiler using his club like a bat, knocking his last opponent down. Baldock too was quickly running out of enemies. Behind him, Ashwin stood ready with her bow, but no further arrows were released. The white tigers by her side kneeled down and rested, confident that the battle was won. Only Thamar was still moving, using his dagger to unbind a green-garbed soldier.

The battle was indeed won, with no casualties or, by the looks of it, serious injuries.

CHAPTER 26

Thamar cut the bonds from the Imperial Guard and then helped him to stand up. "Perhaps you can be shedding some light on what is happening here?"

"Thank you," the guard replied appreciatively. "The Empress was kidnapped."

"Something a little more useful and up-to-date would be nice," Thamar said impatiently, his arms crossed at his chest. "We already be knowing about the Empress. We were arrested shortly after."

"My apologies," the man said. "Everything has happened so quickly."

"Then it should be a fairly quick tale," Thamar smiled. "But for that to be so, you have to start telling it."

"Give me back me shield," Baldock cried as he stormed up to Thamar.

Thamar pulled it from his shoulder and handed it to him. "A simple thank you would suffice."

"I saw ye hammer it!" Baldock yelled. "What did ye have to be doin' that fer?"

"You wanted it back, didn't you?" Thamar asked, unable to believe what he was hearing. "Besides, it's a shield. It will get dented from time to time."

Baldock examined his shield. "This is special to me," he said, breathing a deep sigh of relief when seeing that the orb was not damaged, and only a small dent was added to the top where Thamar hit it.

"That's why I tried so hard to get it back for you," Thamar replied.

Baldock grimaced and looked like he was almost going to say thank you or possibly even cry. Instead, he turned and walked away, checking the door to make sure there were no other threats.

Mylvannan and Ashwin stepped behind Thamar and watched Baldock leave. Theiler walked slowly towards Baldock, not wanting to let the surly dwarf know that he was following him, but also wanting to be nearby in case any other foes were to attack.

"That one has many levels to him," Ashwin said as she watched Baldock walk out of the room.

"He's a good one," Thamar said with a hint of finality. Looking back at the guard. "Tell us the story."

"King Winton of Danchul has taken control of the Imperium," the man said. "Unofficially thus far, but he is the one ruling. One of his first acts was to secure an agreement with King Garum of Tenalong, which is where all of these men came from."

"Are they evil?" Mylvannan asked.

Thamar stroked his long red beard for a moment. "I have heard that Garum is in league with the Hidden Empire. Could they be the ones trying to take over the Imperium?"

"That was what I feared as well," the guard nodded. "It ultimately was what got me tied up."

"Perhaps we should visit this Garum?" Mylvannan suggested.

"Or at least the Hidden Empire," Thamar agreed.

"That could be very dangerous," the guard advised.

Thamar let out a deep and loud laugh. "Look around you—my friends and I are more than ready to take on Lady Salaman and her ilk, especially if they fight like this!"

"These are low paid thugs," the guard replied. "Do not let yourselves become overconfident when dealing with the Hidden Empire."

"He is right," Mylvannan replied. "For every hundred minions, there is bound to be one skilled warrior—one like that Kabilian who you encountered previously."

"Yes," Ashwin agreed, remembering the uncomfortable encounter. "We will have to be cautious."

"Bah!" Thamar snorted. "We'll take them down if that is who is behind this, then we'll get the Empress back where she belongs. If Arifos and Heirn would hurry up, we can be on our way!"

The two elves approached the entrance to the chamber in silence. Neither had spoken a word since their discussion, both lost in their own thoughts. For Arifos, it was his determination to deal a devastating blow to Zoldex, and hopefully bring about the tyrant's downfall, avenging his allies lost along the way. Heirn was lost in his own internal debate, wondering whether his own beliefs were the kind that would hinder the alliances that they desperately needed. The more he pondered it, the more he was frightened that unification was nothing more than an idealistic fantasy.

Arifos held his hand up to stop Heirn as he saw the crumbled wall, arrows jutting out along the hall, and other signs of devastation. Reaching behind his back, he removed Unamalastra, and strung it quickly. With an arrow nocked, he slowly crept forward, listening for any signs of battle, hoping that his discussion with Heirn did not lead him to find his allies doomed—an event that would leave him gripping his own internal demons, facing despair once more. Guilt was a terrible foe that never seemed to be completely vanquished.

Heirn unsheathed Martristlit and followed Arifos towards the crumbled wall. The two cautiously swung in—Arifos high and Heirn low—and both sighed in relief when they saw their allies standing unharmed amongst piles of broken and battered bodies.

Arifos lowered his bow and walked toward his allies. As the two elves joined the others, he saw the Imperial Guard and nodded at the man, their eyes locking for a moment.

"Well, elf, it's about time you showed up," Thamar chuckled. "Nothing we couldn't be handling without you, of course."

"I see that," Arifos replied as he scanned the room full of bodies. "Where's Baldock and Theiler?"

"Scouting ahead," Thamar answered. "The two cats are with them."

"Good," Arifos nodded in approval. "We should be moving on. We're almost there."

The Imperial Guard began to tremble, his whole body shaking uncontrollably, and his face twisted, as if searing in agony.

Thamar reached out and grabbed the man by the shoulders. "Hold him down!" he yelled out.

Arifos stared, not taking his eyes from the man, watching as the guard began to scream while his flesh began to eat away, leaving a rotting corpse behind. "Everyone back!" he warned.

Thamar let the man go and stepped back, grabbing his mallet and holding it up defensively. "What magic is this?"

The decaying body stood up. Where once there had been an Imperial Guard, now there were the skeletal remains of a man wearing a dark green cloak. In its hand was a long scythe that it held with decaying fingers.

"What is this?" Thamar repeated. His momentary shock aside, the red-bearded dwarf swung out with his mallet, but never hit his mark as the creature raised a hand and Thamar found himself hurtling backwards uncontrollably through the air.

Arifos quickly pulled back Unamalastra and launched an arrow at the creature. Its body convulsed where it was hit, but it turned back quickly and emitted a death-defying hiss at the companions.

It raised its scythe high above its head and brought it swiping down at Ashwin, who remained frozen in place in shock.

"No!" Heirn screamed as he lunged in front of his cousin and felt the blade plunge deeply into his chest. He struggled to remain conscious, but lost all feeling in his body. His sword fell to the ground with a clang, and he winced several times, his head trembling as the creature pulled the scythe back out and allowed him to crumble to the ground.

Ashwin dropped to her knees and cradled Heirn as his mouth opened and closed, the last moments of his life quickly fleeing him. "Heirn," she cried, tears flowing freely from her eyes. "Why?"

Thamar rushed back in, his mallet in hand again. "A Shadow Mage!" he roared, remembering the tale that Braksis had told about his encounter with the creature. "Only mystical weapons can harm them!"

"This is a servant of Zoldex," Arifos agreed. "We must be cautious." Another arrow from the Impaler pierced the Shadow Mage, again having very little effect other than to slow the creature down for a moment. "Mylvannan, get the others out of here—I will hold this one off."

Mylvannan paused for a moment, wondering if his enchanted sword could help in the fight. If Thamar was right, he could be more valuable to the companions by remaining.

"Now!" Arifos roared as he launched another arrow into the Shadow Mage. The creature glared at him, an eerie red glow coming from its eye sockets. Another chilling hiss escaped its rotted lips.

Mylvannan sheathed Frostlartil and dropped to the ground, grabbing the weeping Ashwin by the shoulders. "Come, he is dead."

"No!" Ashwin cried in protest. "We can't leave him."

"We must!" Mylvannan continued to pull.

"No," Ashwin whispered to herself. "Why did he do it? Why?"

"He loved you," Mylvannan said as he continued to try and drag her away. "That is why."

"But I couldn't have been hurt as long as I wore the ring," she wheezed as she began trembling again.

"Thamar, I need help!" Mylvannan called out.

The dwarf rushed over and glanced at the Shadow Mage. This battle he knew he was outmatched, and if he remained to help Arifos, he would surely perish. Realizing this, he decided that perhaps it was time to find a mystical weapon of his own before they encountered another of these beasts.

With the two clutching her shoulder and arms, Ashwin had no choice but to be dragged away from her cousin, who now lay very still, the blood seeping from his wounded chest and from his mouth the only thing she could see. As she was dragged away, her hand brushed against Martristlit, Heirn's honor blade. She tightened her grip along the hilt and dragged it from the room with her.

"No," she said one last time, shaking her head as she stared at the body of Heirn.

"He's dead!" Mylvannan shouted again.

"As will we be if we don't hurry," Thamar added. "His death would be in vain if you were to perish anyway."

The dwarf's comment struck her hard, and she stopped fighting them, allowing the two to drag her from the room and after their other allies, leaving Arifos alone to face the Shadow Mage. She stared at the pink-skinned elf as she was dragged from the room and hoped that she would see him again.

Arifos launched one last arrow at the Shadow Mage and then placed his bow back in its holder on his back. He was uncertain why the bow, mystical in its making, was having no effect. He presumed that it was perhaps because while the bow itself was mystical, the arrows that were actually impacting his opponent were not. In one fluid motion, Phistala and Aurlestyl were in his hands, as if extensions of his arms. "If magical weapons are all that will kill you, then prepare to die."

The Shadow Mage paused for a moment and dropped the scythe. As the blade hit the ground, it vanished as if it had never even existed. The creature then raised its hands, and two swords mystically swirled into existence. It stepped forward and the two combatants slowly began circling, sensing out each other's abilities.

Arifos knew that this creature before him was a direct servant of Zoldex. Deep down, he felt that all of the years of persecution, of slavery and sacrifice, would all be erased by the death of this creature. With a smile on his face, he began attacking the Shadow Mage in earnest. "I'm going to enjoy this, demon!"

CHAPTER 27

Cylnta slowly opened her eyes, though they burned and told her that she had not slept nearly enough. Struggling to see around her, she saw Doctor Podeis glancing down compassionately at her. "Doctor?"

"I'm sorry to wake you, I know that you have already been through such an ordeal just getting us here this quickly, but the Captain needs you," Podeis said in his sympathetic, grandfatherly way.

Cylnta stretched her arms and neck, then stood up and jogged in place for a moment. "I'll be fine now—thank you for your concern, Doctor."

"Once this is done, I'm ordering you to bed," he smiled pleasantly.

Cylnta snickered. "That's one order I'll be happy to carry out."

"Come—they are inside the Chamber already," Podeis informed her.

The two walked up the stairwell, past the giant statues of the heroes of the Imperium. Cylnta glanced up at the image of Jeffa, a current-day member of the Council of Elders. He had a very interesting life as a Paladin—fighting wars, making friends, and becoming famous. She wondered if one day other Mages would see statues or any symbolism of what she had accomplished with her years in ISIA.

When they entered the circular building known as the Chamber, Cylnta paused as she saw the room in utter turmoil. A large plantlike structure was near the end, with limbs of Imperial Guards jutting out from the constricting vines. Adonis and Darkler were both kneeling next to it and speaking to each other.

"What's going on?" she asked the Doctor.

"Your guess is probably better than mine," Podeis replied. "Apparently the Empress has been kidnapped."

"Kidnapped?" Cylnta gasped with a startle.

"Yes," Podeis confirmed. "Come—Adonis wishes to use your mystical abilities to learn more."

The two walked into the Chamber and directly over to their colleagues. Adonis turned around and nodded to his Paladin associate. "It appears I cannot allow you to rest just yet. Your services are needed."

"I understand," Cylnta replied.

"I want to know exactly what happened here before we move on," he ordered.

"Very well," Cylnta agreed. She sat down and crossed her legs. She wiped both eyes a couple of times to remove any fatigue that remained, and then focused on the entire room and especially the plant structure before her. She took several deep breaths, and then a small light-blue mist appeared and began to swirl in front of her. The image began to clear, and they watched as events that had already occurred were replayed again.

A cloaked man walked into the Chamber and was confronted by one of the guards. He stretched his hands out and spoke to the newcomer. The man swiped his arms out to the side, removing his cloak and revealing a creature with stars that swirled through his body.

"What is it?" Darkler asked.

Cylnta stared at the image for a moment. "A celestial," she said.

"Continue," Adonis instructed her.

The light-blue image began swirling again. The guards quickly pulled their weapons and prepared for battle. A few began muttering something to themselves.

"Can you include sounds?" Adonis asked.

Cylnta breathed deeply. She could easily recreate a visual representation, but to have the actual conversations was very difficult for her. With her already weary state, she wasn't sure how long she could keep it up. "I'll try," she replied, very little confidence evident in her voice.

What do you think he is?

I don't know. I've never seen anything like it.

The first man stepped closer, his arm still held up in warning. *Okay buddy, back it up or we'll have to do this the hard way.*

The celestial did not move, but all of the ISIA agents could feel the tremors when his icy voice spoke. *I am Nitorum, let me pass or die.*

"Nitorum," Adonis repeated the name, committing it to memory.

I think you have it mistaken. There are fifteen of us in the Chamber alone, and over a hundred Imperial Guards in the palace. Now why don't you come with me and we'll make sure that nobody regrets what happens here today?

The celestial identified as Nitorum reached into a pouch on his belt and removed a small organism. He squeezed it gently and the guard closest to him began coughing and gagging as he struggled to remove his helmet. As it came off, the ISIA agents all shuddered as they saw the man's face decomposing in the image.

"Nice guy," Darkler uttered sarcastically.

Nitorum pulled out two knives that were curved like scimitars and began slicing his way through several more guards. The agents noted that the celestial was a very experienced fighter—in moments, he managed to find and slice into unprotected areas of the armor.

He then sheathed his two knives on his belt and removed another small organism. He tossed this one at the remaining guards, and when it hit, it began to grow rapidly into the large network of vines that now remained in the Chamber. It bound the remaining guards, and as they struggled, the vines appeared to constrict even more, crushing and strangling them alive.

The celestial nodded in satisfaction at his work, then walked calmly on towards the drawbridge. As he exited the room, the light-blue image vanished, and Cylnta slouched down a bit, even more tired than she was.

"Amazing," Darkler said. "I've seen my fair share of assassins and brutes, but that one is gifted. Its like his work is an art."

"An art of death," Podeis was quick to point out.

"How long ago was that?" Adonis asked.

"No way to know for sure," Cylnta replied.

Doctor Podeis walked over to one of the corpses. "I would estimate maybe a week, possibly a bit more."

"A week?" Darkler sneered. "And they left the bodies here to rot? Don't they have any respect any more?"

"Cylnta, can you get rid of this thing?" Adonis asked.

Cylnta stood up and almost fell over. Doctor Podeis was quick to catch her and help her back up.

"She's tired, Captain—you pushed her too hard just trying to get here," he said.

"If I knew that this was what happened, I would have pushed even harder," Adonis replied. "Could you remove this, please?"

Cylnta closed her eyes and focused. She tried to remember her training and performed a quick revitalization spell. She knew that the effects would not last. She had been using the spell practically since they first began their return to the palace. Each time, the effects and refreshing feeling wore off sooner and sooner.

"I am ready," she announced. She raised her hand and a small spark flashed from her fingers. They danced over to the plantlike structure, and it ignited into a raging inferno. Cylnta closed her eyes and concentrated—the strain was almost unbearable—but she controlled every flame, burning only the vines and leaving the bodies of the guards unsinged.

With another wave of her hand, the flames died out, leaving only a steaming ground where the vines had been, and the bodies of several of the palace guards.

"Thank you," Adonis stated as he walked through the steam and towards the drawbridge. As he reached it, he glanced around and saw some blood. "I need you to tell me what happened here as well."

Cylnta sat back down and focused on the blood. Once again, a light-blue mist began swirling, and the agents began to watch events as they unfurled. They watched an elf step out onto the very spot that they were, and have his way barred by a single man.

"Wait a minute," Adonis said. "That's not Nitorum."

"Looks like an elf," Darkler agreed. "And that looks like a hired-hand. Hidden Empire perhaps."

"I don't understand," Adonis replied. "Is the elf an ally of the celestial?"

"Perhaps," Darkler speculated. "But I wouldn't trust the guy he's talking to as far as I could throw him—and trust me, I can throw these guys pretty far!"

Adonis glanced at the short man and knew that he spoke the truth—He had first met Darkler in one of the most disreputable bars in all of Trespias, a place where the darker elements of the city gravitated. When he walked in there, these same ruffians were waiting on him hand and foot, cleaning the bar and making repairs. Darkler had single-handedly managed to turn the tavern around, though he must have injured quite a few in a brawl before the attitude adjustment.

"Can we get sound again?" Adonis asked. "Perhaps that would shed some light."

Cylnta concentrated. Her body began to tremble, but words did start to come out, though not as clear as before.

I am Arifos...I am here...Empress.

"Wait a minute, is he here to get the Empress, to help the Empress, what?" Adonis asked.

"I am sorry, my revitalization spell is already wearing off. I cannot get any better than that," Cylnta apologized.

"Very well, just show us the image then," Adonis conceded.

They watched as five more men, similarly garbed as the first joined the scene. They began to attack the elf, who sprung into action and quickly took out five of the men, and approached a sixth, who wielded a crossbow.

"This one is good too," Darkler nodded.

The man with the crossbow fired the bolt, but it halted in midair as the elf raised his left hand. It then rotated in midair, and launched back at the man who had fired it, plunging the bolt deep into his chest.

"He's a Mage," Darkler concluded.

"Do you know him?" Adonis asked.

Cylnta shook her head. "No, I have never seen him before, but there are many Mages that I have never met."

"Something to look into further," Adonis decided. "Continue."

A dwarf entered the image, his mallet raised and ready for battle. Another pair of dwarves and three more elves soon joined him. The seven of them then walked over the drawbridge and to the palace.

As the image dissipated, Cylnta looked up at Adonis. "That's it."

"I didn't see the celestial," Adonis pondered. "Are these elves and dwarves allies of his, or of ours?"

"They were fighting men that looked no better than Hidden Empire lackeys," Darkler pointed out.

"Yes, but those men seemed to be guarding the entrance to the palace," Adonis replied. "Come—too many questions and not enough answers. We will learn more inside."

CHAPTER 28

Swiping his axe, Baldock continued to hammer at the carpet along the ground. It was highly fashionable and quite beautiful, though that fact was lost on the surly dwarf. He had been striking it for almost ten minutes. Theiler and the two white tigers were watching and looking at him oddly.

"Ah ha!" he shouted with glee as he dropped his axe and ripped a large fragment of the carpet loose. "Got it!"

Theiler continued to watch the Tregador dwarf with mild interest and a bit of confusion. He had seen Baldock moving around and bringing his axe down to create a rectangular pattern, but with the carpet torn and free, he wasn't certain what his companion had in mind.

Baldock glanced over at Theiler and winked. He then started to rub the carpet along his armor trying to clean as much of the blood from it as he could. "Those durned thugs bled so much on me I might wind up rustin'!"

If Theiler could still laugh, his eruption would be loud and boisterous; instead, a large grin creased his face and he nodded approvingly.

Vella looked back down the hall, crouching down, her ears flattening and every muscle on edge. Theiler noticed the change in the white tiger's behavior and studied the way they had come. He could not see anything, but did not doubt the instincts of this predatory creature.

The male, Vaz circled around and began moving swiftly along the wall. Theiler raised his club, leaving his sword in its sheath.

"What?" the oblivious Baldock asked.

Theiler pointed down at Vella, which did nothing to communicate his thoughts to Baldock.

"What?" he repeated. "Ye want to eat the cat?" he asked as he saw Theiler's club gripped in his hand.

Theiler shot Baldock an incredulous look and almost hit the armored dwarf over the head with his club instead.

"What in the hordes of Tanorus are you doing? We need help!" a familiar cry came from down the hall.

Theiler recognized his brother's voice and darted down the corridor to help Thamar. Baldock just shrugged and continued wiping blood off of his armor.

When Theiler reached his brother, he was shocked by what he saw: both Thamar and Mylvannan were clutching one of Ashwin's arms and practically dragging her along with them. He found this curious, for though Thamar was small, he knew his brother had more than enough strength to carry the elven princess on his own.

"A Shadow Mage," Thamar relayed with dread. "It took the life of Heirn."

Theiler winced at the announcement and could see why Ashwin was so shaken. As a dwarf, if anything happened to Thamar, his first reaction would be outrage and an overwhelming desire for vengeance; but after that, he knew that his world would truly be shaken to its core. He could sympathize with the young princess.

"Where's Baldock?" Mylvannan asked.

Theiler jabbed his thumb back down the corridor to where he had left the Tregador dwarf and Vella behind, almost sticking Vaz in the eye; the stealthy tiger had come out of the shadows and silently moved up behind him, surprising the dwarf.

"We need to hurry and leave this place," Mylvannan indicated.

Theiler sent a curious glance at Thamar.

"Arifos is holding the creature off while we escape," he mournfully declared.

Theiler looked like he wanted to rush back and help their Madrew ally, a passion and fire in his eyes that Thamar likewise shared. Mylvannan saw the danger of this and let go of Ashwin's arm.

"You two take the princess. I'll join Baldock and find the exit."

He kept his gaze on Thamar expectantly for a moment, and when he saw the red-bearded dwarf nod his assent, he turned and jogged down the corridor.

Theiler kept his gaze on his brother, hardly believing that they were leaving Arifos behind.

"The elf is tough," he sighed. "If any of us could survive that battle, it is he."

The two dwarves each held on to Ashwin, helped her stand up, then began walking after Mylvannan. Vaz remained behind them for a moment as if he, too, was drawn back to the battle between Arifos and the Shadow Mage, but then turned and joined the others.

Arifos quickly learned that he had underestimated his opponent. He saw the decaying figure before him and had assumed that his own swiftness and skill would easily allow him to strike out at this creature. He had also thought that this creature was more likely to focus on magic as it had done with Thamar. He quickly found both assumptions to be very misleading, and almost life threatening.

A downward thrust by the creature's two swords was easily blocked, but the strength behind them forced Arifos to his knees. He could hardly believe that something that appeared to be closer to a skeleton than a man could be so strong.

As a Madrew elf, he was far stronger than the elves he had encountered in this realm. Not only because of his mystical abilities, but also because of the blood of the eternals that plagued all Madrew by flowing through their veins. In this encounter though, he realized that those despised self-declared gods that had left them with longer life spans, increased strength, vitality, and mystical abilities, might have helped save his life.

Building up the mystical force in his arms, he channeled his energy through the swords and sent the Shadow Mage stumbling back a moment, giving him an opportunity to stand and prepare himself again. The Mage did not give him much time—though it had backed off, it merely spun into another dance of death, twirling the blades with such precision that Arifos needed to recall his training to save him again.

The more he fought this creature of darkness, the more he realized that he had become cocky with his easy victories over the hobgoblins, and even the humans he faced here in the palace. Neither were a challenge to him, nor did they even offer him a contest worthy of a warrior. Here though, he faced what he knew was a true warrior of Zoldex, a creature from his own homeland.

With Zoldex's name saturating his thoughts, he pressed the attack again himself, swiping his swords high, then quickly bringing them down to the sides and low, slashing up in an attempt to gut the creature. Each move was perfectly defended, and with an ease that defied reason.

Accepting the fact that this fight may cost him his life, a sense of calm flowed over the pink-skinned elf. All of the injustices that his people had been through suddenly seeped into his swords, and he was a vessel of retribution: as long as he lived, no creature of Zoldex would be safe.

Increasing his cuts and thrusts, Arifos feinted to the right, then stabbed quickly with the sword in his left hand. For the first time since the encounter began, one of their swords struck its mark. The Shadow Mage hissed, its eyes glowing as they bore down at him.

Arifos did not care though; he had learned what he wished. Where he struck, thick red ooze began slowly flowing as if coming from the bones of the creature itself. Arifos smiled again, his confidence returning tenfold. "If you can bleed, you can die."

Mylvannan pulled at the door in mild frustration; it did not budge. "It must be bolted from the other side."

Baldock glanced at the Frost elf and grinned. "I wouldn't be worryin' too much about that then."

"This is the way out," Mylvannan reminded the dwarf. "Would you rather turn around again?"

"Nope," Baldock smiled knowingly. He stepped back a few paces, then turned and ran as quickly as he could towards the door. With each step he built up momentum.

Mylvannan's eyes widened as he saw the dwarf barreling directly towards him. He leapt to the side just as Baldock stormed past and crashed through the door, splintering it before him. In one attempt, the armored dwarven battering ram removed the final obstacle barring their freedom. Almost.

"I don't like this, Captain," Darkler shook his head. "Those men we passed at the gate are definitely not the kind of guards I think we want defending the palace."

Adonis took a deep breath in frustration. He failed to understand a lot that was transpiring, but he did not like what he was seeing. Not at all. The palace had been under siege, the Empress apparently kidnapped, and then criminals somehow wrested control of the place. This was not a good day by Adonis's estimation.

As he reached out to open the door, he was about to realize that the day was worse than he thought. He could hear clinking and clanging of armor, sounding like an entire battalion charging headlong into battle. Reaching down, he pulled his sword, Crimbaya, from its sheath.

"Prepare yourselves," he instructed too late, the door before him splintering to pieces as a dwarf plowed through and struck him directly in the chest. As Adonis fell, Crimbaya spun away to the far corner of the hall. He was sprawled on his back, clutching his chest and struggling to get air back in his lungs.

The dwarf lying atop of him looked down with a puzzled expression. "Who are ye?"

Adonis did not reply, but he recognized this dwarf from Cylnta's images. He was one of the dwarves that had been with the elf that attacked the guards on the drawbridge.

Darkler lunged out and tackled the dwarf, sending him sprawling away from the Captain. With the armored warrior no longer on his chest, Adonis could breathe again. As he stood up, he saw an ivory-skinned elf with snow-white hair and ice-blue eyes moving directly towards him.

Darkler paused after he tackled the dwarf. He saw a sword lying by a slain Imperial Guard and tossed it to Adonis, knowing that his Captain was defenseless. The act cost him as the dwarf shook his head several times as if clearing his vision, and then returned the favor by plowing directly into Darkler headfirst.

Mylvannan stepped through the door and quickly scanned the hall to see four enemies: a dark-skinned man, a short man who seemed more than willing to exchange blows with Baldock, an elderly man, and some kind of reptilian creature. All four were similarly garbed in red uniforms with a pair of yellow stripes along their shirts and down the sides of their pants. The dark-skinned man caught a sword and stepped towards him.

"FRAAZAA!" Mylvannan cried out, activating the mystical enchantment on his sword for the second time that day. He swung his misting blade at the ebony-skinned warrior's sword, and upon impact, the sword turned to solid ice and shattered.

The man dropped the blade and countered with a punch, hammering Mylvannan in the jaw. The Frost elf fell backwards, crashing into the wall and slumping down to the ground. The blow had been incredibly strong and would make one of the dreaded quiltoth proud, he thought.

Thamar and Theiler jumped through the door, leaving Ashwin behind with the white tigers and stepping between Mylvannan and his foe. Their weapons were drawn and the two Vorstad warriors were ready for action, a part of them still wishing to make amends for leaving Arifos behind.

As Mylvannan struggled to stand up, he saw that the elderly gentleman had tossed the ebony-skinned warrior another sword. "No," he called out forcefully. "Get the princess out of here: this fight is mine."

Thamar bit his lower lip, hating the idea of leaving any fight behind. Reluctant, he nodded to his brother and both returned to the doorway and helped Ashwin back through as Baldock and Mylvannan fought. The two white tigers remained close to the elf, but did not act as if threatened at all.

The reptilian woman stepped before the dwarves and held her hand up. "I will not allow you to pass."

Thamar smiled and emitted a low growl. "Lady, that is the best news I have heard all day."

The two combatants proved to be fairly equal in skill as the battle continued. Four blades moving so swiftly that any onlooker would think that they were mere mists. Sparks emitted with each contact of the swords.

The Shadow Mage had not opened another spot that Arifos could take advantage of after the initial wound. In addition, it seemed to ignore the wound as if it had never been harmed, even though thick globs of its blood now marked its steps along the ground.

Arifos lunged with his right arm while parrying with his left, his two swords perfectly matching every move and countering against his foe. As the battle continued on, he began to wonder if the Shadow Mage would ever tire. Though he was physically fit, he questioned how long he could keep this pace up against a creature that seemed immune to its own injuries.

The creature brought its two swords straight in, and Arifos parried them both out, leaving both bodies momentarily exposed. Taking the initiative, he jumped forward and kicked the creature in the chin.

As he landed on the ground, crouching down, he pulled his swords in and dug both into the Shadow Mage's waist, thinking that he had finally gained a decisive victory. The creature did not even flinch.

Rolling backwards, Arifos stood back up and glared at his opponent. The jaw he had kicked had broken free and was hanging from the Shadow Mage's face. Both slashes also had been deep and more of its blood oozed from it. Other than that, the creature did not even appear inhibited as it stepped after him, both swords twirling, ready to press the attack again.

Taking a deep breath, he muttered, "At least I won't hear any more of your hissing."

In the distance, Arifos could hear the echo of Mylvannan's enchantment. As he began deflecting the Shadow Mage's attacks once more, he found himself torn between where he was and where he should be. His companions were just and true—as good of friends and allies as any could ever ask for. If they were in trouble, he wished that he could be fighting by their side. As he deflected another thrust, he returned his focus on the Shadow Mage. This was an agent of Zoldex, an ancient enemy of the Madrew. He was where he belonged.

Cylnta stood with her hand outstretched, mystically barring the way of the dwarves. Every fiber of her being was straining to merely maintain consciousness, but the battle they found themselves in had a reviving impact, providing her with an adrenaline rush. She only hoped that it would last long enough to defeat her foes.

"I am Thamar, son of Thron, warrior and thrasher of mine enemies!" the dwarf cried as he leapt through the air, his mallet held over his head. He brought the hammer down with all of his might, sending ripples and cracks along the protective bubble she had erected around herself.

Thamar stopped and looked for a moment in confusion as he

stood inches from Cylnta and had not touched her. Raising his mallet, fire in his eyes, he began hammering away at the protective barrier with thrusts so powerful that the Paladin wondered how long her defenses really would hold up.

A ferocious roar came from behind her and Cylnta turned just in time to see a large white tiger barrel into her. The Paladin dropped to the ground, her spell broken, and consciousness fleeting.

Thamar glanced furiously at Vaz. "Damned cat! Don't you know that a warrior needs to get into a fight?"

Seeing that Vaz was not paying attention, he spun and glared down at the elderly man in the back corner. The man raised both arms in a passive manner. "I'm no fighter, you have nothing to fear from me. I surrender."

Thamar nodded. "I accept your surrender. You have the word of a true son of Vorstad that you shall not be harmed."

Glancing back at Theiler, he beckoned him on. "Get the princess out of here. Take the *cats* with you," sneering, for the memory of a dwarf was long indeed, and he would remember that Vaz had ended his battle for him.

Theiler nodded and picked up Ashwin, who was still in a state of shock. Though her eyes were open and her hand still clutched desperately onto Heirn's honor blade, Martristlit, she stared blankly at whatever happened to be before her. Her thoughts were trapped back with her cousin, and she was oblivious to the current skirmish.

Thamar considered the rest of the room. Baldock was fighting with the shorter man, and Mylvannan was engaged in swordplay with the dark-skinned warrior. Trying to decide whom he would help the most, he heard the tiger's growl and saw several of the thugs charging towards Theiler and his group. In an instant, his decision was made.

When he heard the roar of the white tiger, Arifos knew that he could no longer afford to delay. His companions and friends were perhaps fighting for their very lives. He had to find a way to defeat this creature, and quickly.

The Shadow Mage did not leave any other openings though. He did not know what else he could do to injure the thing, for he had already struck several mortal blows, and the creature merely shrugged them off.

"I do not have time for you any longer, demon!" he shouted.

The Shadow Mage did not respond, its jaw merely hanging slack.

Seeing one chance, Arifos back-flipped away, being grazed along the back with a sword as he spun. He flipped several times so that he was far enough away from the creature, though it was quickly pursuing him.

He then stopped, slammed one sword into the ground, and thrust his balled fist up towards the ceiling. In that instant, he sent a cascade of mystical power launching from his fist and towards the vine covered ceiling. His first attempt had no effect. Repeating his actions again and again, he wondered if he would be in time, as the Shadow Mage continually closed in on him.

Then he heard a crack. With another thrust towards the ceiling, the entire structure above the Shadow Mage collapsed in vines, rock, and debris. Arifos covered his eyes, shielding himself from the dust and debris that filled the room.

As the dust settled, he picked his second sword up again and walked over to the collapsed ceiling. What he saw troubled him immensely: the bloody and battered body, not of the Shadow Mage, but of the Imperial Guard that they had been speaking to prior to the transformation.

Arifos glared at the dead man for a long moment, and silently vowed that he would face the Shadow Mage again. That the next time, he would not be so cocky and reckless, and that then he would show the creature why he was the greatest Madrew warrior that ever lived.

As he heard another growl, he left his thoughts behind him and sprinted down the hall towards his friends.

Baldock laughed as the small man he fought sent a fist towards him and he lowered his head so that all that he hit was his illistrium spangenhelm. The man pulled his hand back and shook it several times, wincing in pain.

"Ye'll learn better than to be doin' that, I reckon!" Baldock continued to laugh.

The man rushed back at Baldock in almost dwarven fashion, as if a berserker rage had overcome him. Though they were foes, Baldock continued to laugh. He liked this little man; he liked him a lot.

The man pulled two daggers and started to strike and jab, though he found no openings in the dwarf's armor.

Baldock held his axe and shield wide allowing the man to see how hopeless his attack was, still laughing as the thrusts continued. Then the man tackled him again and sent them both sprawling into the wall.

"Good!" Baldock cheered. "I gave ye an openin' and ye took it!"

"Time to go!" Thamar called out.

Baldock glanced over at the red-bearded dwarf, an expression of sorrow on his face. Looking back at the man struggling with him, he sighed. "This has been fun, we must do it again sometime!"

As he finished his statement, he rammed his shield into the man's face. He then lowered his shoulder and hit the man with his spiked shoulder pads, and then finally lifted him and slammed him into the wall, leaving the dazed Authority agent behind.

Theiler slowed down as he saw the onrushing guards. He gently put Ashwin down and pulled his club out. He need not have bothered though—the two white tigers bolted ahead and began viciously attacking the men.

Their initial lunge alone knocked three men over, rendering them unconscious. A few swipes, bites, and pressure from their massive forms soon had the rest of the guards out of the way.

Theiler shook his head and bent down to pick Ashwin up again. The tigers may be taking some of the fun away from them, but he had to admit, they were swift and effective. He liked these cats, a lot.

Adonis knew that he was outnumbered. He had seen both Cylnta and now Darkler fall before their foes. The elf facing him was also extremely gifted with a sword and deflected each of his attacks. He had hoped to defeat the elf quickly and assist his troops, but all hope of that was lost now.

"I do not understand," he growled. "You appear to be someone that is worthy of battle. I see that my allies are unconscious and not dead. Why then did you kidnap the Empress?"

"I sense that you are noble and are not like the others that we have fought—I take no satisfaction in this fight," Mylvannan replied. "However, you are disillusioned."

"Disillusioned?" Adonis asked as he thrust Crimbaya at the Frost elf. "Did you not attack the palace?"

"You err. We, all of us, were invited guests of the Empress."

"Yet you attacked the guards when you arrived," Adonis accused.

"We attacked, yes. But those were not the guards of this palace. You will see that much is transpiring here. Things are not as they appear."

Adonis had a feeling that the elf was not trying his hardest in this fight. Deep down, he knew that to be true. He wondered if what he had said was factual: were these elves and dwarves invited guests? Was this some kind of misunderstanding? He hated not having all of the facts. That was something he intended to change very shortly. Right after he finished this fight.

Another elf leapt through the door, a pink-skinned one. He swiped an open palm and Adonis felt himself hurtling through the air. Right before he hit the wall and fell into unconsciousness, he knew that he had just met a Mage.

"My apologies for the interruption my friend, but we must be off before more agents of Zoldex reveal themselves," Arifos called out.

Mylvannan nodded his agreement and looked down at the ebony-skinned man he had fought. He hoped that he was right about this man and that he was not evil. If not, leaving him alive would be a mistake. However, he trusted his instincts, instincts that were honed on the icy peaks of the Mourning Mountains. They would meet again one day, and when they did, he hoped it would be as allies.

Arifos led the way down the corridor and after Theiler, Ashwin, and the white tigers; Mylvannan, Thamar, and Baldock moved swiftly behind them. They crossed the drawbridge, went straight through the Chamber, and then lost themselves in the winding back-streets of Trespias.

CHAPTER 29

He stood there watching them leave. The assassin known as Kabilian regarded the companions with mild amusement and newfound interest. After all, he was more than an assassin: he was a collector of rare valuables, especially mystical objects.

Reaching up, he placed his palms on his helmet and slowly lifted it from his head, returning Kabilian to the normal spectrum, and making him perfectly visible to all who would look at him. His helmet of invisibility was a valued item to him. He knew of only three that existed in the entire realm; he was proud to know that he owned two of them.

He lowered the helmet and dropped it into an unusually small satchel attached to his belt. This he had acquired long ago from the first Mages he had ever met. The Mages had the intriguing ability to design fascinating things. Very practical as well. As the helmet went in, it faded and vanished instantly. Kabilian knew that the satchel also held a variety of other items that he had accumulated: the hair of a lupan, a claw of a koxlen, and the tooth of a dragon. These three items could actually summon each of the great beasts to come to his side and defend him if need be.

The satchel also held a pair of scepters, a few rings and other assorted jewelry with enchanted abilities, and a variety of potions. All of these items and more were stuffed inside the satchel, but it looked no larger than a pocket as it hung from his belt. The satchel contained a nearly infinite void that would allow him to place as much as he wanted within it, and with little more than a thought, he could pull out the item he desired.

Reaching down and concentrating, he pulled out a small vial filled with a glowing cerulean liquid. Taking a deep breath, he could still feel the throbbing from the cracked ribs he had received after being attacked by the Tregador dwarf. Flicking the cork off with his thumb, Kabilian drank the contents of the vial in one swig, instantly feeling a burning sensation sweep throughout his body.

He flexed his fingers a couple of times until the pain started to wan. He took another deep breath, relieved that the healing potion had worked again. Though his ribs were certainly not completely healed, they would not pain him as much as they had been.

Reaching back into his satchel again, Kabilian removed a small red ruby. It was round in shape and was about the size of his thumb. He held it up to his eye and glanced at the fleeing companions, the world around him turning a deep wine red, including most of his quarry.

Arifos did not appear as the others, though. Rather than a dark red, he actually burned in a bright and shining crimson through the ruby, as did both of his swords, his bow, the sword of Mylvannan, and the ring of Ashwin.

The ruby had the distinct ability to perceive mystical auras and bring them forth to the viewer. Kabilian always found it comforting to know that he could tell exactly what was mystical and what was not before attempting to acquire an item from someone. Though he definitely made exceptions—such as Pandring, the honor blade—but more often than not, he focused on enchanted weapons.

The armored dwarf that had attacked him caught his interest. He sensed that the axe and shield were somehow mystical, but the dwarf did not appear through the ruby at all. It was as if a shadow existed where the dwarf stood. Kabilian moved the ruby away from his eye and looked at the dwarf freely. *Most curious,* he thought.

As they fled towards the back-streets of Trespias, Kabilian knew that he would have to learn more about the dwarf from Tregador. In his line of work, information was everything. Without it, he would fall victim as easily as he had to the armored dwarf. If not for his amulet and its ability to transport him away, he would surely have died under the dwarf's ferocity.

That would not be the case in their next encounter.

"Hey, there they go. Why didn't you stop them?"

Kabilian did not even stop watching the companions as they fled. He knew that the speaker was one of Garum's people. Though they were theoretically allies in this venture, he reported directly to Lady Salaman and considered the mindless minions of Garum to be beneath him.

"Come on, let's get them!"

Kabilian sighed. He knew that these fools would have no chance against the foes they were so intent to track down and confront again, but he had no desire to do so himself until he had visited Tregador personally and learned as much as he could.

Without saying a word or looking, he raised his right hand and flicked his wrist, activating a mystical bracer that he wore, launching a small drug-tipped dart at the lackey. He did not need to turn to know that it hit him in the throat and his life would be over before he even hit the ground.

"What did he do to Groano?"

"Get him!"

Kabilian lowered the ruby and returned it to his satchel. He turned and faced this petty annoyance and saw three more men. *Hardly worth the effort,* he thought. Reaching down, he pulled his two jewel-hilted daggers. As the men rushed towards him, he whispered an incantation and both daggers extended in length to full-length swords.

With a smile on his face as he saw the men pause with confusion, Kabilian slashed both jewel-hilted weapons at the first man, creating a cross along his throat. He then spun to the left and ran the next man through, piercing the man's heart.

Glaring at the third man, he twirled both weapons and smiled. That smile, he had been told, was terrifying—those that saw it quickly realized that they were about to die. This man was no different. He lunged forward at Kabilian, who dodged to the side and tripped the man. As he fell on his chest, Kabilian spun his two weapons around and dug them deeply into the man's back.

His two swords then shrank back down to their original size. He used the shirt of one of the dead men to wipe the blood off, and placed them back on his belt. He hated wasting his time on such imbeciles.

Before he left, he studied the streets of Trespias once more but saw that the companions were lost in the winding back-roads. He knew that he would see them again. When that happened, he would be prepared for the Tregador dwarf, learn the secret of how he appeared as nothing more than a shadow to the ruby, and then acquire all of their mystical weapons as his own.

Smiling at the thought, he pivoted and walked back into the Chamber. First, he had business to attend to for Lady Salaman. It would be unwise to keep her waiting because of his interests. He knew he would meet the elves and dwarves again soon enough.

CHAPTER 30

Winton paced the throne room impatiently. He had been waiting for news that the two white tigers had been dispensed of after their brutal attack. He raised his hand and gently rubbed the bandages along the right side of his face. With his newfound injuries, he wondered if his handsome features would ever be able to attract a woman again. He remembered how many girls had fawned all over him for much of his young life. Now, all they would see is a scarred freak.

The rationalization did not sit well with him. Though he was now Emperor, he had never truly aspired for such a position. Rather, he merely wanted to receive his father's love and attention. How could that ever happen now that he had poisoned him?

Standing alone in the throne room, Winton began to wonder, not for the first time, if the decisions he had made of late were wise. Had he done things that would haunt him for the rest of his days? Sighing, he knew that they would. Even with that insight, he still did not really feel remorse towards the murder of his father. That thought shocked him. Could it be, was he so conceited that his only regret was the fact that he was scarred and disfigured in the process?

The doors to the room swung open and two men stepped inside.

"Do you not know how to knock?" Winton scolded them. "I am the Emperor now, and deserve some respect."

"My apologies, sir," the man bowed, mockingly.

"What news have you?" Winton asked as he waved away their sarcasm.

"Most of the men are dead," the man replied.

"Dead?" Winton repeated in shock. "Tell me that they at least succeeded in killing the Empress's pets."

"No sir," the man gulped.

Winton rushed to him and slapped him across the face. "No?" he screeched. "All I wanted was the two pets to be slain and you return to tell me that my men instead lay dead?"

The man looked up, anger apparent on his face. He had no respect for the self-proclaimed Emperor who stood before him, but knew that Garum wanted Winton to be obeyed—at least for now. "There was a prison escape, as well."

Winton's left eye widened in shock. "What happened? Why was I not informed?"

"I do not know," the man responded as he glanced back at his companion. "The elves, dwarves, and gnomes escaped though, and soon were joined by the white tigers. Together, they laid havoc to the palace."

"This is unacceptable," Winton roared. "Find them, kill them all!"

"I already told you, most of the men died trying to stop them already."

"I do not care for your pathetic excuses. Prepare whatever men are left. You will hunt them down and give them exactly what they deserve."

"As you wish," the man sneered in reply. With another exaggerated bow, he turned and led his companion out of the room.

As Winton watched them leave, he noticed Adonis standing in the doorway. "Adonis, what are you doing here?" Winton spun, walked over to the throne, and then sat down. He silently scolded himself, knowing that his voice trembled as he saw the renowned Authority agent.

Adonis walked in and was soon followed by three more members of ISIA. "You of all people should know why I am here," he said, his piercing gaze never leaving Winton.

As he watched the ebony-skinned man, Winton felt as if Adonis was looking straight into his soul. He did not enjoy the scrutiny and wished that the man would leave. This would be his first true test though, his first real adversary that could unhinge him and tear down all that he had accomplished. Adonis was far more dangerous than Sharnesta ever could have been to him.

"You have heard of the Empress, then?" Winton asked, trying to sound more confident.

"Yes, I have," Adonis replied. "Though that is not why I am here."

"What then?" Winton asked, momentarily confused.

"Your father," Adonis answered calmly. "Have you so soon forgotten about the murder of your own father?"

"My father?" Winton repeated in a near whisper. "Forgive me, Captain—these past weeks have been traumatic indeed. My father's murder, the Empress's kidnapping by the Aezians, and now those suspected as accomplices I have been informed have escaped."

Winton held Adonis's gaze and wondered why he said nothing. He glanced behind Adonis for a moment and recognized the worral, a Mage that was loyal to the Authority. He knew that she would uncover any deception he wove. All of his words had to closely resemble facts if he had any hope to leave this encounter without being discovered.

"Yes," Adonis finally answered. "I am sure that you are under a great amount of strain."

"I'm glad you understand," Winton said in relief.

"There are some things I do not understand," Adonis replied. "Perhaps you can enlighten me?"

Winton winced, and knew that he did not want the Captain to remain here before him for long, but also realized that he had little choice. With a wave of his hand, he beckoned the Captain to continue.

"Why is the palace overrun by hired mercenaries?" Adonis asked.

"Most of the palace guards were slain when the Empress was kidnapped," Winton explained. "King Garum had fortunately come to Trespias with many men and kindly offered them to the palace for its defense until the Imperial Guard could be rebuilt once more."

"I see," Adonis replied. "It was fortune shining down on the palace, then."

Not knowing how to respond, Winton merely shrugged.

"What happened to your face?" Adonis quickly changed the subject.

"My face?" Winton asked as he reached up and touched the bandages again. "It was the assassin that just escaped."

"Oh really?" Adonis said with an unreadable expression. "I must have misunderstood then, for when I first arrived here, you were chastising those two men for not being informed that the prisoners had escaped."

"My apologies, Captain," Winton offered as a bead of sweat began to trickle down from his forehead. "The white tigers somehow were joined with the escaping creatures. It was one of them that attacked me."

"The white tigers you say?" Adonis nodded as if he understood. "The personal pets of the Empress?"

Winton did not say a word, for he did not like where the possible insinuations were headed, regardless of how true the revelations could be.

Adonis changed the subject again. "So, you are the Emperor now?"

"Yes," Winton answered, "though it is not completely official. Prime Minister Torscen is making preparations."

"How did this come about?" Adonis asked.

"The royal families agreed before leaving," Winton replied.

"Why would they agree to this? What makes you any more suited to rule the Imperium than, say, King Lorrents or Euristies?"

Winton swallowed, then breathed for a moment. His next words were clearly lies, and he was afraid that the Paladin would reveal that. He could see no other way out though. "My father had been pushing for a union between Karleena and I for years," he said, hoping that the reply would allow Adonis to leap to the conclusion that the two were betrothed without him having to actually say it.

"I see," Adonis replied in his typical unreadable manner. "So you are the logical choice because of some connection between you and

Karleena then?"

Winton just nodded, not wishing to say another word.

"What about the escaped prisoners?" Adonis asked, changing the topic again.

"We suspect they are spies," Winton answered, "or at least in league with the Aezians."

"What makes you think that?" Adonis questioned.

"When they arrived, they tried to throw us off track, and claimed that the Empress was not being brought where we believed," Winton replied.

"How do you know they were lying?"

"They left dead bodies in their wake, Captain—how can you question their sincerity?"

"I myself fought them," Adonis replied. "Still, our investigation will explore all avenues." Tightening his eyes slightly, he added, "All avenues."

"I would expect nothing less from you, Captain," Winton replied, trying to act unaffected by the man's words.

"What of Centain?" Adonis asked.

Winton winced again; he had hoped that the meeting was over. "He was severely wounded in the battle with the kidnapper. We fear that he will not survive."

"I understand," Adonis said. "When the investigation is complete, I will temporarily resume my post as the Captain of the Imperial Guards and rebuild the palace's security network."

"I appreciate the generous offer Captain, but I hardly think that will be necessary," Winton shrugged. "Our first and foremost priority is in finding my beloved Karleena."

Adonis watched him for a moment, then nodded, turned, and walked out. His three companions followed without ever saying a word.

Winton watched them leave and, when the doors were closed, began trembling. Quite shaken, he felt that things were quickly unraveling around him. He needed Zoldex.

Jumping up, he walked to the doors and swung them open. He then marched down the corridor straight towards the Empress's private chambers and entered. He paused as he saw the blood stains both of where Sharnesta had fallen and where his own blood splattered the ground from the white tigers' attack.

Raising his nose in disgust, he walked over to the bed and collapsed upon it. Turning over, he stared at the ceiling and was a little surprised to see the plants along the ceiling change colors to a deep black. He knew that the flowers altered their appearance based on the moods of those around them. He wondered if the same color had shown in the throne room and if Adonis noticed.

"Zoldex!" he cried out. "Zoldex I need you!"

The familiar swirling mist appeared and revealed the form of Zoldex. "Do not shout, you fool—there are others who will overhear you."

Confused, Winton began to look around. Who was there? Then he stopped and glanced over at the door that Sharnesta had entered from—he had forgotten about the handmaidens.

"What do you want?" Zoldex asked impatiently. "I am quite busy at the moment."

"Busy?" Winton asked. "Things are falling apart all around me and you are busy?"

"You do wish for your reign to be a long and fruitful one, do you not?"

"Well, yes," Winton agreed.

"Then accept that I am busy fulfilling that destiny," Zoldex replied. "So make whatever you have to say quick."

"Adonis is back and I think he suspects me," Winton blurted out.

"It is of no consequence," Zoldex brushed the fear aside. "Soon, you will be too powerful for Adonis to even be able to think of touching you."

"How can you say that?" Winton asked.

"Your forces are already on the march," Zoldex grinned deviously. "All of the Imperium will soon tremble before you."

Not really satisfied or assured, Winton balled his hands into a fist and punched the mattress he was resting upon.

"What else troubles you?" Zoldex asked.

"Everything!" Winton screamed.

"You must remain calm. All will unfold as it was meant to," Zoldex explained.

"Is that why the elves, dwarves, and gnomes escaped? Is that why the white tigers have turned me into a freak?" he roared, his words rising in volume and intensity.

"The prisoners have escaped?" Zoldex returned, his own voice appearing to grow in anger. "How could you let this happen?"

"So even the mighty Zoldex is fallible," Winton replied, not at all comforted. "Do not worry, I have already ordered all remaining soldiers to pursue them."

"No," Zoldex immediately said. "Let them leave. They will meet their end soon enough when they reach their destination."

"Are you certain?" Winton asked.

"I have decided," Zoldex firmly replied.

"Very well," Winton responded, feeling defeated. When first he had met Zoldex, the man seemed more like a father than Sarlec ever had; now he was growing harsh and wrathful. He wondered again if all of this was perhaps a mistake.

"If that is all, I must resume my other preparations," Zoldex harshly explained.

"That is all," Winton whispered.

"Do not worry—I shall be with you soon." With those parting words, the image of Zoldex vanished.

Winton continued staring at the ceiling for a long moment. He was beginning to hate everything that was happening. He wished that he had some form of an escape, or at least a distraction. Slowly, a smile crept over his lips. He leaned up and glanced at the door to the handmaidens' chambers and realized that he had the best distraction possible.

Standing up, he began walking towards the door, his elation growing with every step.

CHAPTER 31

Adonis glared out the window of King Sarlec's quarters. His rage growing, a trail of red mist smoked from his eyes. He turned around and looked at his companions.

"What's on your mind?" Doctor Podeis asked.

"Sarlec's body is gone, the Empress was kidnapped, Centain is apparently close to death, and my every instinct is screaming that our new Emperor is behind it all somehow."

Darkler was kneeling along the ground and touching some scorch marks. "Well sir, it looks like two bodies were here, and both burned."

"So a Mage must be behind this, not Winton," Podeis surmised.

"Not necessarily," Adonis replied. "Winton is definitely on edge. He was trembling and sweating throughout our meeting. He is definitely hiding things. Cylnta, what could you perceive?"

"Unfortunately, nothing. There is some kind of barrier blocking my senses since we entered the palace."

"Could it be the pink-skinned elf? He was a Mage," Adonis reasoned.

"I don't think so," Podeis replied. "We shouldn't eliminate them completely, but the dwarf spared my life when I surrendered, and I believe that particular group is honorable."

"The elf I was fighting did seem to be holding back," Adonis agreed.

Darkler rubbed his chin where the dwarf had slammed him with the shield. "If that's holding back, I'd like to see them cut loose."

"I think you did," Podeis replied with a snicker. "Look at all of the bodies of Garum's men lying around."

"They were technically employed by the Imperium," Adonis replied.

"We all know that Garum is little more than a puppet for Lady Salaman," Darkler sneered. "These men are probably all her criminal operatives. No loss to the Imperium."

"Agreed," Adonis said. "We will have to explore all of these options. Eliminate suspects one at a time. First though, I want to check on Centain."

"Would you like us to continue examining the room?" Darkler asked.

"Yes, see if you can come up with anything here. Also, try to figure out whom the second scorch mark belongs to: if there was another murder, I want that investigated as well. Podeis and I will check on the Captain."

All four ISIA agents nodded and began carrying out their orders. With the barrier blocking Cylnta, this would be a real test of their abilities to discover the clues and bring the culprit to justice.

CHAPTER 32

"We are fortunate," Thamar explained. "There is no moon this night."

"We should still move quickly," Arifos responded. The two glanced over to Mylvannan who was gently caressing Ashwin's forehead. "How is she?"

Ashwin solemnly gazed at Arifos. All of the innocence and joy that he had seen in her eyes when they first set out for Trespias was gone. "You need not worry about me, I will be fine."

"Do not hide your feelings," Thamar responded. "The death of your cousin has hit you hard."

"Indeed it has," Ashwin replied as she tightened her grip on the sword Heirn once wielded. "I will see his death avenged, and live up to the expectations of a wielder of an honor blade."

All of the companions knew that her words seemed bold, but the elven princess was truly breaking inside. It would take a long time for these wounds to heal, but even still, she would never reclaim the innocence she once had. The way of the road had a tendency to do that to you.

"So, what is the plan?" Baldock asked.

"We leave the city, tonight," Thamar explained.

"Do we get our animals back?" Baldock wanted to know.

"The gates are sealed," Arifos explained. Shortly after they had escaped, he scouted the city and found the gates shut. They would not be leaving that way. "We must go over the wall and travel by foot."

"I told you that payin' those durned kids would be a waste," Baldock grinned.

"I stand corrected," Thamar relented.

"Will Vaz and Vella be able to make it over?" Ashwin asked.

The group turned to regard the white tigers, both of whom seemed to be following their every word. Without prompting, Vaz stood up, walked over to a nearby building, jumped up in one leap to a balcony on the second floor, and then used that to spring to the top of the city's wall. From there, he jumped over to the other side.

"It looks like we need not worry about the cats," Thamar replied with a laugh.

"Are we returning to Xylona now? To tell my father about Heirn and everything else?" Ashwin asked.

"No," Thamar shook his head. "We will stop at Vorstad on the way and report what is happening to the dwarves first, then move on to Xylona."

"Agreed," Arifos said, as he glanced back one last time at the Mage's Council and hoped that the Chosen One truly was safe being left behind in a city he now knew Zoldex had an influence in. As he turned away, he knew that he would return to Trespias. The future of the world may depend upon it.

"I watched the blasted cat go up, but how do we get over?" Baldock asked.

"We climb," Thamar responded as he pointed to Theiler holding a rope.

"More climbin'?" Baldock snorted. "Bah!"

The companions scaled the wall in the darkness of night. Vella joined Vaz on the other side first, and soon they were all reunited outside of the Walls of Trespias. Without another word, or even supplies for the road, the companions jogged off southward towards Vorstad.

CHAPTER 33

Shiel sat down and gently rubbed her forehead. She shared the same concern that many of the handmaidens had been asking her: Sharnesta had been gone for too long. Even the chefs that usually bring them their meals had stopped coming. She had taken two of the girls and went to the kitchens, but was shocked to find men of ill repute permeating the halls. Something had happened.

The cooks were happy to provide them with food, and also slipped Shiel the news that the Empress had been kidnapped. The servants of the palace were all discussing it. She even heard that Winton, the newly appointed King of Danchul, was poised to take control of the Imperium in Karleena's absence. Allegedly, the two were betrothed, though Shiel had never heard or seen any signs of that before.

The disappearance of Sharnesta was quite disturbing as well. She always kept the handmaidens focused and in control. She oversaw everything and made certain that neither the girls, nor the Empress, were ever left wanting. She was also Shiel's mother.

This last fact was why the other fourteen girls were looking at her for support and direction. There were fifteen of them in all, including her. Only five provided care for the Empress at a time, but with the extra women, they would always have handmaidens ready for whatever Karleena's needs may be, regardless of the time or duration.

At the age of twenty-five, Shiel was one of the older handmaidens that cared for the Empress. She had been trained practically since birth to follow in her mother's footsteps and lead the handmaidens: a role she feared she now needed to accept with her mother's disappearance.

Shiel stood at five-foot-seven, with long wavy auburn hair and tawny eyes. Though a servant to the Empress, she had lived a life of luxury herself, and was the envy of almost all of the other girls that she worked with. She heard many whispers when the girls thought that she wasn't listening, about how beautiful she was, or how perfect her body was. Though she would never feel that way about herself, she did have to admit that many of their comments were accurate.

Like her mother before her, she lived a very isolated life, and had personally never even left the palace. Other girls had traveled with Karleena in the past, but Shiel had always remained behind with Sharnesta to take advantage of those times to learn more about what it meant to be in service to the Empress.

She often wondered who her father was, as Sharnesta never spoke of him; add in the fact that she never left the palace herself, Shiel expected that her father was nothing more than some passionate affair with one of the Imperial Guards or Ministers. She had fantasies that he would be more than that, a forbidden love between her mother and one of the nobles or members of the royal families, but she could never really visualize her mother doing that.

"What are we going to do?"

Shiel glanced at the speaker and smiled pleasantly. "We will do what we always do. We will continue living as always and wait for the Empress to be returned to us. When she is, undoubtedly, she will need our tender care."

"What if she never returns?"

"The Empress will be back," Shiel said confidently. "I have no doubt about that."

"What about Sharnesta?"

Shiel lowered her eyes. This was one question she could not answer. She truly had no idea where her mother was. "I wish I had more answers," she sighed.

"You're not worried though?"

"No," Shiel said. "It is our job to tend to the Empress. As I said, we will be prepared for her return."

"What about those men that are around the palace?"

"Try to avoid them," Shiel recommended. "And never leave here without at least one other person with you. There is more safety in numbers."

"You're afraid they'll try something?"

"I do not like the appearance of them, no," Shiel agreed.

"Should we try to leave the palace?"

"And go where? This is our home," Shiel said.

"For you perhaps, I still have parents I could go to."

"If you wish to leave, you certainly may do so," Shiel answered. "We are not slaves here. We receive more compensation than we would ever dream of anywhere else in the Imperium. We also are clothed, fed, and have a roof over our heads. Our only real job is to tend to the Empress."

"Perhaps you are right."

Shiel stood up and walked over to the blonde-haired girl that was thinking of leaving. She sat down and gently caressed her leg. "Don't worry, if we think things are getting worse, we'll consider leaving. All of us."

"I'm afraid I won't be able to allow that."

Shiel spun around to see Winton standing in the doorway that led to the Empress's private chambers. "This section of the palace is private and does not allow admittance to any man."

"I am not a mere man, but the Emperor," Winton replied. "You were in service to the Empress, now you are in service to me."

Shiel stood up and walked over to stand directly before him. She struggled not to wince at his bandaged face. "We are in service to the Empress only."

"I have decided that you, all of you, will serve me," Winton grinned fiendishly.

"No," Shiel replied calmly.

"Oh yes, you will," he said as he removed a dagger from his belt. "All of you are now part of the Emperor's harem."

"A harem?" Shiel laughed at the absurdity of it all. "Surely you jest."

"You are free to leave if you do not wish to pleasure me," Winton offered. "I'm sure the afterlife will be glad to see you."

"What are you saying?" Shiel demanded.

"Those that will not willingly be part of my harem will die," Winton threatened.

"No," the blonde-haired girl began to sob.

"Let's see," Winton beamed with anticipation. "Which of you will I taste first?"

Shiel, horrified, glanced at the girls. She did not want any of them to submit to this, but how could she stop it?

"Her," Winton smiled as he pointed to the crying girl. "She'll do."

"No!" the girl cried. "I won't! I want to go home to my parents."

"Then they will see you when they join you in Tanorus," Winton sneered as he raised his dagger.

"I will go," Shiel called out. "Take me."

Winton stopped and looked her over, glancing up and down. Shiel felt very exposed. She was wearing only a one-piece red-laced chemise, her normal attire when she was preparing for bed.

"Yes," he said as he began licking his lips. "You will do quite nicely." He placed his dagger back in his belt and grabbed her by the arm, dragging her away.

Shiel glanced back at the others. "Do not worry about me." She could see in their expressions that words alone would not calm the girls down this night.

Winton dragged her into the Empress's room and over to the bed. With his left hand, he reached up and grabbed the back of her chemise, and with a violent pull, he ripped it from her body, tearing it along the seams. He then pushed her onto the bed and stared at her.

Shiel lay there, horrified by the man before her and what he was about to do. She had never before left the palace, and had never felt the tender caress of a man. Both things stood out in her mind as regrets this moment as her innocence and virginity was about to be ruthlessly stolen from her.

Thinking of the others, she knew that most of the girls were also virgins, and that it was far better for her to suffer this injustice than them. She only hoped that she could satisfy him enough so that he would not seek out the other girls for this mockery of affection.

With the girls on her mind, she sat back up and smiled seductively at Winton. Reaching her hands out, she helped him with his pants and prayed that this would be quick. She knew that after this moment, she would never feel clean again.

Winton's pants dropped to his ankles and he jumped on top of her, knocking her back to the bed. His hands reached out and he began fondling her breasts. His mouth was lapping at her throat.

Shiel closed her eyes and tried to bear it, knowing that this sacrifice was protecting the other girls, at least for this night. As he entered her, she let out a little cry, for he was not gentle or caring, as she had always envisioned. He was rough and brutal, acting as if he needed to prove himself in some way.

Shiel did not move, but merely allowed him to satisfy himself as she stared blankly at the ceiling and lost herself in thoughts of the other handmaidens she was protecting. If she had known that she too was a child of Sarlec though, her reactions would have been very different.

Kabilian stood by the bed, cloaked by his invisibility helmet, and watched as Winton continued to thrust himself at the handmaiden. He watched her eyes and saw that she was completely oblivious to what was happening. As if she was in a completely different world, unaware of the man and his brutal violation of her.

He may be an assassin, but certain lines should never be crossed. Taking advantage of a woman was one of them. Reaching down, he grabbed Winton by the shoulders and pulled him off of the woman and easily tossed him to the floor and away from the bed.

"What? Who dares?" Winton screamed as he scanned the room, seeing only the handmaiden he was bedding.

Kabilian pulled his helmet off and revealed himself to Winton.

His glare of pure contempt was enough to make Winton shuffle backwards for a moment.

"Who are you?"

"Who I am is unimportant," Kabilian answered, his voice deep and threatening. "Lady Salaman sends her greetings."

"Lady Salaman?" Winton gasped, his one good eye widening at the name.

"She is pleased that the arms of the Hidden Empire have extended so far," Kabilian explained.

"She's pleased?" Winton repeated softly.

"Yes," Kabilian answered. "And she expects to be well-rewarded for her support of your rise to power."

"Rewarded?" Winton said as he stood back up. "What did she do for me? Her people failed to even kill Braksis like I hired her to do! I have done this on my own!"

"She will be most displeased if I have to tell her that," Kabilian shook his head disapprovingly.

"I am the Emperor," Winton roared. "I don't give a damn what would please or displease her!"

Kabilian grinned at Winton—a look he could see sent shivers through the man. With a flick of his wrist, a small dart launched from his mystical bracers and impacted Winton in the chest. "Be grateful that this one is only drugged and not poisoned," Kabilian replied. "We will be in touch again, and next time, you better be more receptive to providing Lady Salaman what she wants."

Winton dropped to the ground, his body paralyzed, his voice unable to make a sound no matter how hard he tried.

"You will awaken in time," Kabilian said as he turned to walk away. As he glanced at the woman again, who was still staring at the ceiling as if catatonic, he turned back to Winton. "And if I find out you have been taking advantage of women again, I will be back for you. You will not find a second encounter so pleasant."

He walked out of the room and replaced the helmet on his head. As he turned invisible, he decided that with his mission complete, he would venture to Tregador to learn as much as he could about a particular dwarf. Smiling at the thought, he reached down to grasp his amulet, and transported away from the palace, as if he had never been there.

Shiel continued to watch the ceiling. She was terrified that either the man that attacked Winton or Winton himself would harm her for overhearing their discussion. She hoped that they would think that she was in a catatonic state.

As the man left, she knew that she was alone with Winton. She could hear his gurgling as he struggled to stay conscious, but then that too ceased. Sitting up, she glanced over and was satisfied that the brute was asleep.

She replayed the conversation in her mind over and over. Winton had apparently been involved with the Hidden Empire in an attempt to murder Warlord Braksis. An attempt that failed. He then boasted that he had done this on his own. She wondered if that meant that he was behind the abduction of Karleena.

That and more, she surmised. This man was far more dangerous than she ever expected. She only hoped that the words of his attacker would remain in his ears, and that he would no longer desire to hurt any of the girls.

Shiel stood up and walked over to the Empress's bath. She stepped in and began vigorously cleaning herself. She wished to get every scent, every touch of the vile man off of her. It was something she knew she would never be able to accomplish—for though she could clean her body, her mind would be scarred for life.

She stayed in the bath for over an hour, incessantly scrubbing her body. Then she remembered her original thought, and was afraid that Winton might kill her for overhearing the discussion. Afraid of that, she dried herself off and returned to Winton's side. Glancing down, she was glad to see that he was still unconscious.

Stepping back, she kicked him in his genitals. The intruder could have done it; she rationalized as she struck the man. She saw his face wince, but he did not move or stir other than that.

Thinking that this would be a long night, Shiel got back into bed and positioned herself exactly as she had been when the intruder pulled Winton off of her. She stared at the ceiling and resumed her attempted act of catatonia.

She did not know how long she lay there staring at the ceiling, but eventually, Winton did stir. He began groaning and moaning and walked over to her. Shiel maintained her focus and did not move her eyes from a single spot.

Winton waved a hand in front of her eyes and then shrugged. He reached over and tried shaking her by the shoulders. "Snap out of it," he slurred, still slightly drugged.

Shiel blinked several times as if coming out of a spell and looked at the man. He glared at her for a moment as if thinking, then turned and walked away. "Get dressed and get out of here."

Shiel reached for her chemise and wrapped the remains of it around her. She then ran from the room and to the safety of her friends and colleagues. Her ruse had worked, so far. She allowed herself to hope again that the words of the intruder would indeed sink in, and Winton would no longer desire the girls' presence in his bed.

CHAPTER 34

On the same night that Shiel allowed herself to be violated to protect the other handmaidens, a young fourteen-year-old girl desperately wished that her torment would stop. She could remember the happy times—before the vile Durgin entered her life.

She had been traveling with her family through the northern Suspintian Forest, as they planned to move north to Lake Supretta of Falestia. Months before, they had met a man who was looking for farmers and settlers to migrate there and begin a new community. He made the new settlement sound like a glorious haven where their family could prosper and thrive.

As residents of Korland, a Suspintian town that always lived in fear of the creatures of the forest, the move had been a sign from the gods for a better future: a new home where the children, and their children after them, could grow up without fear and make a decent living for themselves.

It was a dream-come-true. Even the road was full of exciting adventures, smiles, and a wave of optimism that none of them had ever truly felt before. Then a stranger walked into their camp.

She remembered as her father and uncle had run to challenge the larger man. He had been armed, but did not appear threatening at the time. It was as if he was disoriented and in need of assistance himself. He had told a story of how he and his brother had come from Fenland to become hunters, only to fall prey to a lupan, the cause of his apparent state and injuries.

Her mother had pitied the man and invited him in to dine with them. She had even taken an extra effort to make a better meal that evening for their guest. He had sat there the entire time telling stories of how the lupan had attacked him, and how his brother had met his untimely demise. The story was tragic and sorrowful, and the man had seemed on the verge of tears.

After dinner, the women had worked on his outfit, cleaning the bloodstains as much as they could while he talked more with the men. She remembered how he had seemed to become one of them that night.

That had just been an act though. She remembered awakening in the middle of the night to a scream. Her younger brother had awakened with a nightmare and wound up walking into a real one: their guest had just butchered the adults in their sleep, and turned his gaze on the children.

He came in quickly, as if the children would somehow offer more resistance than their parents, and slaughtered them all—all that is, except for her. With the blood of her family dripping from his axe, and splatters of it on his body, he had walked forward, licking his lips as if she were a meal to be devoured.

She had thought that she too was about to join her family, but instead of Durgin swinging his axe, he lashed out with his fist, rendering her unconscious. Since then, she had lost all track of time. All she knew was the ranting and raving of this mad man, with occasional outbursts when he would beat or violate her.

Though she knew she was still alive, that fact hardly registered. She felt dead inside, her spirit and individuality shattered forever. Even her name, Leora, seemed to be a distant echo or cruel memory. Now, she answered to the name, "Girl."

Once-upon-a-time, she had raven-black hair with sparkling blue eyes. Now, her face itself was black and blue, a reminder of Durgin's brutality. Her dress was disheveled and torn; bloodstains were caked between her legs where he ruthlessly stole her innocence from her. Her arms and legs were also cut and bruised from his harsh treatment.

"You listening, girl?"

Leora turned to face him, though she had to struggle to see him.

One eye was so badly swollen that she could not open it. The other she had to struggle to see through. She already knew what he was saying; he repeated the same rant over and over. However, if he suspected that she wasn't paying attention, he lashed out quickly. His temper, she learned, was like a volcano waiting to erupt.

"That's better," he snickered. "Wouldn't want you to miss any of this."

She struggled to peer at him and watched as he continued to paint skulls onto his axe. He had told her hours before—or was it days—that he would design one for every member of her family. He also took great pleasure in pointing out where her skull would be drawn.

"I was great once, great," he continued to say, "a Warlord that made any who saw me tremble in fear." He paused and glanced over at her. "You are trembling. Perhaps I am returning to the man I once was.

"Yes, I will be great once again," he vowed. "It began with the death of Braksis, and then continued with your family, and now you. What next though?"

He snapped his fingers and jumped up. Leora winced and tried to move further into the tree she was tied to, but could not get any further away from the man.

"It was a mystral bitch that caused me to fall from my greatness," he recalled. "It seems only fitting then that I kill some mystral now, to announce to the world that I am back.

"Yes, that is what I will do. I will find me some mystral." Laughing sinisterly, he looked up at the night sky, as if challenging the world. "Perhaps I'll even begin scalping them and adorning myself with my kills!"

Once, Leora knew she would have shuddered at the thought of this man scalping women and wearing their hair upon his body. Now, she was numb to the world. This man may torment her, beat her, violate her, but he could no longer hurt her any more than he already had. She was broken. If he killed her, then he would merely be setting her free.

"I'll be a Warlord again," Durgin smiled. "A great Warlord." Glancing over at the girl, he began walking slowly towards her, a wicked grin etched upon his face. "I'll show you what it used to mean to be a true Warlord."

As the morning sun pierced the horizon, Solara remained behind a hill, her knuckles turning white as she clutched the hilt of her sword. She had still managed to follow the trail of Durgin, but it was becoming increasingly difficult—some blood here, tattered clothing there, and signs of campsites—but these tracks were mixed with those of hobgoblins, creatures she now found herself trying to elude.

She listened to their guttural grunts and growled conversations as they passed near her. The patrols were increasing in frequency and she wondered how she could continue to avoid them while traveling with two horses and a wolf. Fortune had been shining on her, so far.

The hobgoblins passed by and she released the hilt of her sword, flexing her fingers to get the blood flowing again. She wondered how futile her mission was. Too much time had passed already since she had found the wagon. Surely, she would find the child dead—another failing upon her part.

With that thought in her mind, she almost wanted to pursue the hunting party of hobgoblins and slay them all for continually delaying her mission. That would be foolish though: she may have the element of surprise, but she had counted groups that ranged from five to fifty, and certainly could not encounter the upper numbers alone.

"Tiot?" she asked hoping that the wolf could still track the child by her scent. Solara reached into a satchel strapped to Blaze and pulled out one of the child's dresses that she had taken from the camp. She hoped that with frequent reminders, the timber wolf could find the girl.

Tiot darted off through the woods and Solara quickly began following him, glad to see that it was not in the same direction as the hobgoblins. She held the reins of the two horses, for this deep in the forest, she could no longer ride them freely, and had opted to walk and not burden them with her added weight.

She made it about thirty paces before she started feeling nauseous and ill. She could not understand why she had been feeling poorly of late, though she certainly had been neglecting her own health while pursuing Durgin.

Stopping suddenly, she bent over and began vomiting. She remained bent for a moment, her hands firmly on her knees. Taking several deep breaths, she stood up straight and wiped her mouth. She glanced at the two horses and shook her head.

"Whatever this virus is, it won't stop me from finding Durgin—no matter how sick and fatigued it may make me," she vowed. Hearing the confidence in her voice, she had to admit to herself that she did feel slightly better now. Whatever this was, she only hoped that she could complete her mission before her symptoms got worse.

A howl in the distance caught her attention—Tiot had found something. She grabbed the reins again and began running towards the timber wolf. She had not heard Tiot howl like that in some time, and felt that time was somehow short.

She found a small clearing and came to a stop. Tiot stood by a tree near the end of the camp. She saw the remains of a fire and the clear boot-tracks of a large man. As she stepped over to the fire, she grinned to feel heat still emanating from it. "Soon, you bastard—I'm catching up to you."

Tiot barked and she turned to regard the wolf. He stepped aside and revealed a broken and battered body tied to the tree. Solara's heart broke again as she saw the sight. Tears flowed uncontrollably from her eyes as she ran over—the realization that she was too late and had failed again would haunt her thoughts.

The child must have been no older than fourteen. Her entire body was badly battered, bloody, and brutalized. The remains of her dress were frayed and in tatters. Solara closed her eyes and chastised herself for being delayed by the hobgoblins.

"I'm sorry, I'm so sorry," she kept repeating.

Tiot walked up and started to lick the child's face. Solara was outraged at first, but then paused and leaned closer. She could hear the child breathing. Very faint, but the girl still lived.

She jumped up and ran to the horses, grabbing medical supplies and water. Her emotions were in a whirl, she was still horrified by what Durgin had done, but she clung to the hope that she could save this child, that if she could manage to save just this child, it would somehow make up for all of her shortcomings of late.

She dropped down on the ground next to the child again. Pulling out a small vial, she poured the contents into the mouth of the girl. It wasn't much, but it held some of the waters of Shimendyn from when she and Braksis had been there, what seemed like a lifetime ago.

The effect was hardly noticeable, and none of the bruises began to fade, but Solara was relieved to hear the child breathing a bit easier. Smiling at Tiot, she reached over and hugged the timber wolf. "You did it, boy," she said.

Looking back, her face turned to a scowl as she considered the rope binding the girl to the tree. She removed her dagger and cut the rope, allowing the girl's arms to fall to her side.

Solara then took the drinking water and dumped some on a small cloth. She used that to gently dab at the blood and injuries, hoping to clean some of them off. As she continued, she saw the girl struggle to open her eyes, though only one was able to do so.

"You are safe now," Solara promised compassionately. "I will not let anything else hurt you."

The girl winced from the pain as she tried to move.

"Rest now," Solara said.

"Who?" the girl asked in a nearly indecipherable whisper—the only word she seemed to be able to utter.

"I am Solara," she replied. "I will protect you."

The girl reached a hand up and tried to touch Solara's head. "Mystral?"

"Yes, I am a mystral," Solara replied.

The girl began coughing and gagging for a moment, but then struggled to tell what she knew, though it came out fragmented and with long pauses. "He... is... hunting... mystral."

Solara watched the child intently. She admired the strength of the girl for struggling to tell her. "You rest now," she said. "I promise you, he will not harm another as long as I live."

The girl leaned back and fell asleep. Solara took a deep breath and stood up. If Durgin was going to hunt down her people, she knew that he would find that they were not as easy a prey as a fourteen-year-old girl. He would soon come to that realization himself.

Watching the girl sleep, she thanked whatever gods might be watching her for allowing her to arrive in time to save her. She now had two goals: she would see both Durgin and Rawthorne dead, and she would also make certain that this child survived her ordeal and would one day thrive again.

CHAPTER 35

Winton sat on the throne in complete solitude. Everything he knew, or thought he knew, was nothing more than a memory. He knew that his life was at a crossroads, but could not clearly see what paths were open to him. He was King of Danchul, and very soon would be crowned the Emperor of the Imperium. This should be a lifetime achievement and moment of triumph, but thoughts of Zoldex pulling him from one side and Lady Salaman from the other made him feel trapped.

Was he truly to become Emperor, or only be a figurehead for one of those two? He did not know the answer. He only knew that events were hurtling past him with little time for thought and reflection. It was during those few times that he could pause to think, that he began to feel foolish and harbored many regrets.

A knock at the door startled him. Winton blinked several times to ward away the thoughts he was plagued with, and admitted the visitor. "Come."

Prime Minister Torscen glided into the room, his movement swift, and the smile on his face full of pride and satisfaction. "I have news, my liege," he said.

"What is it?" Winton asked, though he truly did not care about what Torscen had to say.

"Support for your ascension is in, sir—you are to be the official Emperor of the realm," he announced. "We shall arrange a formal ceremony for your coronation."

"That will not be necessary," Winton shrugged. "As long as I am accepted, that is all that matters."

"Sir, image is very important. The sight of a strong Emperor taking command is vital."

"Do I look strong?" Winton growled, ripping his bandages from his face, revealing his scars and disfigured appearance. "Do I?"

Torscen winced momentarily, but stepped forward again. "You may be scarred physically, but you are still a symbol of strength—the son of Sarlec and mate of Karleena, daughter of Conrad. You must see how important your appearance is to the realm? You are connected to the greatest men of this generation!"

"I do not wish to be seen," Winton sighed and turned away.

"Perhaps," Torscen whispered. "But perhaps you should see before you can be seen."

"What are you babbling about?" Winton asked. "I have no time for guessing games."

"If you would join me for a moment," Torscen stated.

"Where do you wish to take me?" Winton demanded.

"You will see," Torscen smiled.

Before he even realized what was happening, Torscen reached out, held his hand, and guided him from the throne. He led him out of the room and down the hall to an open window. From there, he waved his arm to show what was outside. "Behold."

Winton glanced out the window and was speechless.

"Magnificent, isn't it?" Torscen asked.

The streets leading to the Chamber were packed with tens of thousands of men, all staring at the palace. There were so many that the ground itself could not be spotted for as far as the eye could see.

"What is this?" Winton asked, his voice shaky.

"These are the people of the Imperium that have answered your call," Torscen answered.

"There are not this many soldiers in the Imperial Army," Winton observed.

"That is true," Torscen agreed. "What is even more true is the fact that the army has yet to return from their posts. What you see before you are volunteers."

"Volunteers?"

"Yes, the proud men of the Imperium who will gladly sacrifice their own lives to follow your leadership and help to recover the Empress," Torscen explained.

Winton shrugged and walked away from the window. "The Aezians would slaughter them."

"Why do you feel that way?"

"These are not soldiers: they are farmers and fishermen, fathers and husbands. What do they know of fighting a war?"

"There are soldiers in there as well—soldiers from each individual Kingdom's militaries—hunters too. Many of these people have a deep heritage of fighting wars. Would you ask them to do any less when the Imperium itself is challenged by a foreign power?"

"What about armor and weapons?" Winton asked.

"Many have their own. Those that do not will have them crafted for them. The blacksmiths have been working day and night since the Empress was abducted."

"Do we have enough ships to send them to Aezia?" Winton asked.

"More ships are arriving as we speak," Torscen grinned. "We will be ready for your order."

"When will the generals return?"

"Soon, I would guess. The messengers were dispatched immediately, but the Imperial army was spread throughout the realm. It will take time," pausing, Torscen led Winton back to the window. "Time for even more volunteers to hear the news and come to our aid as well."

"Yes," Winton agreed.

"Do you still wish to remain in the shadows?" Torscen asked. "Your subjects are waiting for you."

Winton took a deep breath and scanned the crowd once more. "Very well, I shall speak to them. First though, I wish to wear the armor of Conrad. I will address them in that."

"An excellent choice, my liege," Torscen nearly purred in satisfaction.

"Oh yes, and when the generals arrive, have them report directly to me."

"As you wish it, so it shall be," Torscen bowed.

<h1 style="text-align:center">CHAPTER 36</h1>

Adonis paused as he heard the crowd beginning to cheer. He stepped to a window and looked out to see a man garbed in golden armor and an emerald cape. The famed blade of Conrad, Ochroid, was being held high on display for those gathered around.

Shaking his head, he turned away in disgust.

"What is it?" Podeis asked.

"A fool trying to live in another man's shoes," Adonis replied.

Podeis stepped forward and looked out the window himself. He grimaced as he recognized the sword and armor of Emperor Conrad. "Those do not belong to him."

"Neither does the Imperium, but it doesn't seem to phase him," Adonis replied.

"He has the support of the ministers," Darkler pointed out.

"That makes me even more nervous," Adonis growled.

"Shouldn't we be joining the army there?" Darkler asked. "After all, we are soldiers of the Imperium."

"No," Adonis quickly retorted. "Things are getting out of control. We have no part in this war. Instead, we need to do what we do best: finding out what really happened, before the warmongers make things even worse."

"You don't think Wei Lau has the Empress?" Podeis asked as he stepped away from the window.

"I think there is more going on than anyone wants us to know about," Adonis answered. "We will figure it out though."

"Very well—what's next?" Podeis asked.

"Tell me what we have so far," Adonis instructed.

195

"I have run some tests on the wine that was in King Sarlec's room. I did detect a very potent poison," Podeis said.

"So it was definitely murder," Adonis deduced.

"Yes," Podeis agreed. "The culprit can eliminate the body, but undoubtedly, evidence is left behind."

"What else?"

"I made a thorough check of the bodies lying throughout the palace. Many of these guys I recognize from Tenalong," Darkler commented.

"Part of Garum's army?" Adonis tried to clarify.

"If they were, let's just say that they wouldn't necessarily take all of their orders from their King," Darkler replied.

"Hidden Empire?"

"Hidden Empire," Darkler confirmed.

"Have you checked on Cylnta recently?" Adonis asked.

"No," Podeis shook his head. "She just needs her sleep. She will be fine in another day or so—we really pushed her to her limits."

"I think that its time to pay Lady Salaman a visit," Adonis decided. Reaching into his belt, he removed a corryby that Cylnta had modified for each member of ISIA so that they could communicate with each other. "Quince."

He waited several moments after stating the name. Since they were not Mages, Cylnta had made it so that simply speaking the name of the individual you wanted would send your message to their corryby. Unlike the normal Mage communication device though, they were unable to create a visual image of the speaker without using mystical abilities.

"This is Quince," came a voice through the small orb.

"How are things in Korland?" Adonis asked.

"We said that we were going to arrest everyone, and then the old woman confessed and took all the blame herself," Quince replied.

"So you are just about wrapped up there?" Adonis asked.

"Close enough—what's wrong Captain?"

"We arrived to a little more than the death of King Sarlec. The

Empress was kidnapped, the Imperial Guard decimated, Centain is close to death, the Imperium is preparing for war, and Winton seems to be commanding it all."

"That's quite a circus," Quince said. "Do you need us in Trespias?"

"No, the clues are leading us to the Hidden Empire," Adonis indicated. "I want you and your unit to meet me at Border Town in Tenalong. We'll fill you in with more once we arrive."

"Yes sir," Quince replied.

"And Quince," Adonis quickly added. "Keep your ears open. I want to know what the rumors are throughout the Imperium. From here, it looks like every man in the entire realm is preparing to go to war and help rescue the Empress. That includes everyone in ISIA other than us. I would like to know what is really happening outside of Trespias."

"Understood, Quince out."

Adonis placed the corryby back in its pouch. He glanced up at Podeis and Darkler. "Get some rest. Cylnta needs another day or so—we'll give it to her. We'll leave here at dawn in two days. Keep your ears open until then, but don't let anyone know where we're going, or when we're leaving."

Both men nodded their agreement and walked out of the room. Adonis returned to the window and watched Winton as he addressed the people filling the street. Undoubtedly providing them with a motivating speech on how they would quickly win the upcoming war. Shaking his head in disbelief, he turned and walked away, wishing that the armor of Conrad were being worn by practically anyone but Winton.

CHAPTER 37

Walking back to Blaze, Solara stopped to check on the young girl and saw that she was still sleeping. She had been through so much; Solara only hoped that the rest would do her well, though she knew that the injuries the child suffered would take years to overcome. She was not much older when Durgin had first entered her life. He had killed her mother with no thought or remorse. That memory still haunted her, as she was sure this experience would do to the child.

She reached out and gently caressed the girl's head, looking at her battered face. The external injuries would fade soon enough, but Solara knew that the child would probably still feel them long after they were gone. Turning away, she balled her hands into fists, wanting to punch something—preferably Durgin.

Blaze's ears pricked-up and Solara reached for her elongated mystral sword. She knew that horses had exceptional instincts, and would not doubt that now—especially with both Durgin and the hobgoblins so close.

Tiot emerged from the dense foliage, and stopped beside her, turning back and growling.

"What is it boy?"

As if in answer to her question, the timber wolf headed back and led her through several trees. Solara bent over and stayed low as she followed. In an opening, they saw dozens of hobgoblins passing by. Their patrols were increasing. It was as if an entire army of hobgoblins were scattered throughout the forest.

Not only were they increasing in size and frequency, but with the child's safety to consider, they were becoming far harder to evade.

Each group she had seen was dressed differently as well: some wore armor or chainmail, others animal skins, some very little clothing at all. Each member of the group was similarly garbed, but very different from the overall masses of hobgoblins spotted.

This group was garbed in blood-red shirts and pants with chainmail draped over their chests. Their shoulder pads were iron, crafted into skulls with spikes protruding. Their knees were likewise covered with skulls and spikes. Some wore skullcaps, a few had cloaks or capes, but all were dressed similarly.

Solara watched them pass, her body tense, but ready to attack if she were to be discovered. As the last hobgoblin wandered from sight, she breathed a little easier and stroked Tiot behind the ear.

"Try to pick up Durgin's trail again—we'll be along shortly," she instructed.

Tiot darted into the clearing where the hobgoblins had been marching and straight across. Solara watched for a moment and then turned to lead the horses after the wolf. She sheathed her sword and walked back to where she had left the horses, and dropped instinctively as she heard the grunts and growls of the hobgoblins.

She tried to concentrate on what they were saying. Though she had never learned the hobgoblin tongue, a natural ability that all mystral possess is that of picking up languages quickly. The ability was more predominantly used when they protected the entire realm and needed to communicate with all of the races, but she knew that, given time, she would be able to decipher the language.

She inched forward quietly, trying to not make any noise. She did manage to understand a few words they said, but very little. At that moment, she wished that she had taken the time to study different languages. In hindsight, it would have been quite handy.

She clearly understood two words, "eat" and "kill." The rest of the dialect was too garbled for her to understand. Peering through a bush, she saw only five hobgoblins and breathed a sigh of relief. At least it wasn't as large a force as she had just observed, though she noted that these were wearing the same outfits as the ones she was watching. This was probably a hunting or scouting party.

As one reached for the child, Solara sprung into action. She removed one of her throwing knives and leapt through the bush in front of them, the blade hurled as she flew through the air. The hobgoblin reaching for the child pulled his arm back, screaming with the knife sticking right out of his palm.

Solara did not pause, pulling another throwing knife and hurtling it at the same hobgoblin, this one embedding in its throat—one part of his upper body that was not covered by armor or chainmail. The creature fell to the ground, gurgling as it began to drown in its own blood.

The other four hobgoblins were standing and staring at their fallen ally, as if their minds could not register what happened so quickly. Solara was not about to give them a chance to regain their composure. She reached behind her back and drew her drantanas, bringing them up in front of her with two quick twirls each. She then crouched down and lunged forward at the closest adversary.

The hobgoblin turned and looked at her coming. It growled and raised a mace, but his defense was uneven and he was unprepared for her skill. Solara easily evaded the mace and dug both of the blades into the creature's stomach. The chainmail protected him somewhat, but her ferocity and pent up anger forced the blades deep, dropping the hobgoblin back.

Solara pulled her two swords out of the dead hobgoblin and looked at the other three. Things were going well thus far.

"A mystral?" one of them said in the common tongue.

"Like the one we killed!" another replied.

"Like we kill this one!" the third roared as it charged her with a sword.

"Be careful," the first one commented again. "She might be a Mage like the other one!"

Solara wondered what they were talking about. These hobgoblins had apparently killed a mystral Mage. If that were so, she would not underestimate them. She waited for the first hobgoblin's attack, thankful that he charged alone. She parried his blow and sent her foot up into his jaw. She heard the crack and knew that she had broken it. He fell backwards with the blow and landed a few feet from her. She went in for the kill, but the other two were on her then.

One held a small single-bladed axe, the other a sword. They both ran towards her, and if she weren't fighting for her life and that of the child, she would have laughed hysterically as they bumped into each other and stumbled apart. As they glanced at each other in shock, Solara swiped her blades at the two creatures, striking each and drawing blood.

"Come now, boys—the fight is with me, not each other," she taunted them.

The hobgoblin with the axe was the first to retaliate, swiping his axe and striking a tree as Solara dodged out of the way. He began pulling, but the blade was deep and he could not get it free.

"Too bad," Solara said in mock sympathy as she thrust one blade into him all the way to her hilt. The hobgoblin squealed in agony, and then dropped to the ground when she pulled her sword out. Turning to the other one, she smiled. "I have all of this anger that has been building inside of me. It was so nice of you to give me a release."

The hobgoblin kept looking back and forth at its dead companions and looked like it was waging an internal debate over whether to try and continue attacking this lone mystral, or whether it would be better served fleeing.

Solara could see the indecision, narrowed her eyes into slits and glared at him. Raising her bloodied blades, she yelled out, "Boo!"

The hobgoblin screamed, turned, and ran away. Solara watched him running and then decided that she couldn't let any of them get away. If even one lived, they could warn all of the others about the mystral and child in the woods, and then she would have no hope of evading them.

Sheathing one of her swords, she unfastened another throwing knife and hurled it in the air with deadly accuracy. It dug into the creatures back and he dropped to the ground. Satisfied with the kill, she turned to find the hobgoblin whose jaw she had broken. Her worst nightmare was realized as she saw the creature holding the child, a rusted and jagged knife to her neck.

Solara paused, realizing that any quick movements on her part would certainly spell doom for the child. The hobgoblin was glaring straight at her, its mouth dropped open with a stream of blood flowing from its nose.

Even more troubling than the hobgoblin threatening the girl, was the child's reaction. She was awake, for her one good eye was open and looking at Solara. But it was not filled with fear, or hope that she would be rescued. Instead, all that Solara could see was a desperate anticipation of the knife slitting her throat and ending her torment. The sight broke her heart.

Solara heard a growl and then the knife dropped from the girl's throat. Solara dropped her other sword and lunged forward, catching the child as she fell. "I have you!"

Tiot had returned and had his jaws digging into the hobgoblins hamstring. Solara covered the child's eyes as the timber wolf continued his assault on their attacker.

She started to rock the young girl back and forth and tried to comfort her. Only then did the girl begin to cry. Solara wondered whether it was tears for what she had just experienced, or because she was forced to endure another day. It was a frightening thought, and she prayed that she was wrong.

Durgin continued through the woods, the vision of hundreds of mystral lying dead at his feet pervading his thoughts. All he knew was where he had first met the one that had hurt him; had defeated him. He hoped that others would be near there.

Without the girl to slow him down, he moved much quicker. Determined to find his quarry and take even greater pleasure with their deaths. He paused for a moment and recalled the silver-haired girl that had hurt him. He was not yet ready to face all of his demons. He would need to work his way up to her. Her entire race dying by his hands would be good practice before challenging her again.

He heard an almost roaring thunder in the distance. A smile creased his lips as he realized what it was. With eager anticipation, he began running forward, oblivious to the many branches that kept slashing at his face and body as he ran through them. He reached an opening and dropped to his knees laughing. He had found it. The waterfall where the two mystral he had met had been.

Glaring across the open water, he recalled the day a decade ago: it would have been his greatest triumph. He had fought Braksis, and though his men were lost, his tormentor fell by his hand. Then, the oddest thing happened—a naked child defeated him. Not a knight, nor a warrior, but a naked child.

Swearing at himself for falling before the silver-haired mystral, he vowed that her hair would be wound into his own. He would wear her hair as a symbol of his strength and determination. He would destroy the mystral and then his own demon. Then, and only then would he reclaim his true mantle of Warlord.

Wondering where exactly the mystral were, Durgin decided that he would remain hidden until he saw one, and then he would strike. Before he ended her misery, he would make sure she told him where the others were. Yes, he grinned, he would find them all and make them pay for what was done to him.

The hobgoblin walked through the forest, annoyed that he was sent back to find the missing unit. The others were eating right now. Several xiats were found grazing and they managed to capture a few of them. He wouldn't know how they tasted though, because he was stuck looking for the five missing scouts.

Without watching where he was going, the young hobgoblin tripped and landed face first on the ground. Growling in anger, he glanced back to see a body lying face down with a knife protruding from its back.

The hobgoblin crawled over and turned the body, dropping it back quickly when he saw small insects already crawling through its hairy reddish-orange hide. Pulling out his mace, he glanced around for an enemy, but could only see the other four slain scouts.

He checked each quickly and grew angry by the sight. They were all killed, and not even a single drop of blood from an enemy could be found. He pulled a knife from the hand of one of the hobgoblins and considered it for a moment. He was unfamiliar with the design, but was impressed by how well it was crafted. A very sturdy blade that was smooth and finely crafted of silver, but also incredibly light in weight. The hilt appeared to look like the scales of some kind of reptile, the detail of which was even more exquisitely crafted.

Tossing the knife at a tree, he watched it hurtle cleanly through the air and embed itself to the hilt. Smiling joyously, he pulled the other knife from the hobgoblin's throat and placed it in his belt. He danced over to the tree but was unable to pull the knife back out. Frustrated, he returned to the first scout he had discovered and pulled the knife from his back as well.

Two of these knives were better than none. He examined the bodies for anything else of value. He took one sword and a horned helm, dropping his own skullcap on the ground. Let the others eat a xiat, he thought—he had found something much better.

After checking every belt and pocket for any gold or valuables, the young hobgoblin decided that he had gathered enough information to report back to his chieftain. He did not know what killed these five, but decided that it must have been a band of warriors, a group that had surrounded them and killed them all. Whoever they were, they had finely designed weapons. Patting the throwing knives on his belt, he smiled and hoped that he could soon add more of these well-crafted weapons to his collection.

CHAPTER 38

"I'm thirsty."

Solara stopped and stepped back to look at the young girl. Other than when they first met and she had mentioned that Durgin was going after mystral, this was the first time she had spoken. "Good morning," Solara smiled. "Did you sleep well?"

"I'm thirsty," she repeated again.

Solara handed her a canteen full of water. "Drink as much as you want. There is a clear water lake ahead. We can refill our water then."

The girl winced as she tried to smile, but accepted the canteen and took several large sips.

"I'm Solara," Solara said in introduction. She had told the girl several times during the past couple of days, but this was the most alert the child seemed, and she hoped that she would finally learn her name.

"Thank you, Solara," she replied.

"What's your name?"

The child lowered her head as if searching for her name. In a near whisper, she said, "Leora."

"That is a beautiful name, Leora," Solara said. "I like it."

Leora looked up, a tear was streaming from her eye. "I almost forgot it. He only called me 'Girl.'"

"That's over now, Leora," Solara said, making sure she used the name to reassure her. "He can no longer hurt you."

"I can't escape him," Leora cried. "Whenever I close my eyes, I see him. When I open them, he's there too."

Solara stood up and walked over to the child. She sat down and embraced her. "We'll face this demon together. You and I."

"How can you know what I'm dealing with?" Leora shouted.

"The same man murdered both my mother and my mate. I will not lie and say that I know how you feel—he hurt you in ways that are unthinkable—but we do share the same demon."

Neither spoke after that. The two sat there, holding and comforting each other. It would be a long time before either recovered from the scars that Durgin gave them; but perhaps, together, they would find a way to survive and move on.

Durgin rolled over and opened his eyes. It was morning. Stretching, he felt tightness in his neck. He had not slept well. As he started to rub it, he stopped, afraid that even the slightest movement might reveal his presence.

Across the lake, he counted a dozen women; just like the two he had found that day long ago. He studied them for a moment and grinned as he recognized the mark of the mystral upon their brows.

Watching them in the water, bathing and giggling happily, oblivious to his presence, he felt aroused and excited. He wanted that feeling to last, and not lose it too quickly. He moved slowly back into the forest so he had some cover from the mystral women, and then began licking his lips as his eyes remained on the objects of his desire.

He stayed there for several minutes, building his desire until he was ready to burst. When he couldn't take it any longer, he started making his way through the trees and closer to the girls. Before this day was done, he would have at least a dozen more skulls to stencil onto his axe. Laughing to himself, he decided that perhaps he wouldn't kill them all—at least not right a way. A Warlord did need to taste the pleasures of his spoils after all.

The young hobgoblin ran through the woods with twenty others along with him. His chief had not been happy with the news. He saw the throwing knives and indicated that they were mystral weapons. Mystral!

Now, they were sent out to find the ambushers and kill them all. Retribution for the five lives stolen before their time. As he followed the others, he decided that he would stay behind them. He'd allow the older hobgoblins to fight and die at the mystral's hands, and then he would plunder the bodies again, hopefully adding to his collection of finely crafted weapons.

Smiling to himself, he began to think of how he could even begin to tell tales of his feats in battle. This mission would be his claim to fame. Even if he let others earn that fame for him, he was an opportunist and would grasp the chance; the mystral didn't have a chance.

CHAPTER 39

Solara paused to listen as she heard the roaring waterfalls of her home. Dragon's Myst was not far, and soon they would reach a clearing and be at the Lake of Tears. She thought the name ironic. It had been named that after the dragons left the mystral to fend for themselves and fled north to Darnak. The "tears" were those of the mystral left behind. She thought of the lake with different, more personal meaning now: tears for the death of her mother.

As she walked through the clearing, she glanced back to Leora and smiled. "This is where I grew up."

Leora absorbed the scenery before her. The waterfall, the lake, the flowers, and the trees, "It's beautiful," she said. "So peaceful."

Solara glanced back across and could see some mystral in the water. They had not noticed her yet. It was not that long ago when that had been her and her mother. At the same time, it was a lifetime ago.

She found it ironic that Durgin had led her back here, to the spot where their lives had both changed forevermore. She had gone from an innocent and idealistic child to a warrior and protector. He went from a tyrant and Warlord to a cowering whelp, scared of his own shadow.

"What are you looking for?" Leora asked.

Solara smiled. The child was quite intuitive. "I am looking to put an end to our mutual demon."

Leora leaned back in the saddle on Blaze, almost as if she were trying to back away and flee.

"Do not worry—I will not let him harm you again," Solara said. "I will see to that personally."

"I do not wish for you to die," Leora whispered.

"I will not," Solara promised her. "He has too much to answer for, to atone for."

As she was speaking to Leora, she saw the child pale and begin to tremble, her uninjured eye staring in fear, seeing something that terrified her. Solara turned and scanned the water where Leora was looking. Movement closer to the trees on the opposite side of the bank grabbed her attention. Her eyes widened as she clearly spotted Durgin. She drew her drantanas and began to step forward, into the lake itself.

"Remain here," she called back to Leora, almost as an afterthought.

At her feet, Tiot began to stiffen. Solara paused and looked down, not wanting to delay her pursuit of Durgin. How many of these defenseless mystral could he slaughter before she got to them.

"What is it Tiot?"

The timber wolf turned and looked into the forest. Solara glanced backwards as a bola soared out and hit her in the head. She plummeted into the water with a loud splash—the hobgoblins had caught up to her!

Durgin paused as he caught a reflection of light in his peripheral vision. He glanced across the lake and saw a silver-haired woman falling into the water and hobgoblins swarming out at her. He froze in terror, realizing that his nightmare was about to be relived in the same spot; but then he breathed more easily—the hobgoblins would eliminate her.

No, he thought—she would only die at his hands. The hobgoblins would perish. If she were powerful enough to stop him as a child, no band of hobgoblins would be able to defeat her. But their delay would give him enough time to build his own confidence and kill some mystral himself.

Before he turned away, he saw the child he thought he had left for dead. His hands turned cold at the sight. Could the silver-haired witch actually return his victims from the dead? If so, no matter how many he killed, she could send legions after him. He also spotted the timber wolf and felt certain that it was the pet of Braksis. Trembling, he hoped that Braksis would not be revived and unleashed upon him.

Pushing those thoughts aside, he returned his focus on the bathing mystral. Their attention was now on the hobgoblins and the silver-haired witch. Smiling in satisfaction again, he stepped forward, his axe in his hand. He saw a young girl; no older than the silver-haired one had been when she attacked him. He would not make the same mistake he did a decade ago. The child would be the first to die.

CHAPTER 40

Solara lifted herself from the water. Her head was ringing with pain from the bola. She was having trouble concentrating, her vision blurred—she saw three hands as she tried to focus on one.

Looking around, she kept blinking to regain her focus as she searched for her dropped swords. Hearing Leora cry out, she realized that she no longer had the luxury of time. She stood up and drew her elongated mystral sword, her only remaining weapon other than her throwing knives and dagger.

Tiot was already attacking one hobgoblin; his jaws firmly entrenched in the creature's neck. A pair of others was standing around trying to bat the wolf off of their comrade with maces and clubs. Another hobgoblin was grabbing Leora and pulling her from the saddle.

Solara stepped forward and almost fell over. She needed to focus—the child depended on her. Barely able to stand, she forced herself forward in a defensive posture towards the hobgoblins.

As several of the burly humanoids charged into the water at Solara, she watched as their blurred images started to fall backwards. Straining to see, she saw arrows piercing the hobgoblins. Only a few at first, but soon the hobgoblins had dozens of arrows jutting from their bodies, as if they were giant pincushions.

Solara shook her head, still trying to regain her focus, and turned to look behind her. Three fully armored mystral warriors stood on the top of a hill and were launching arrows down at the hobgoblins. She glanced back and saw the few survivors of the volley turning and fleeing back into the forest.

Stumbling over to Leora, she saw that the child was unharmed and breathed a sigh of relief. Leora seemed focused on something else though. Still struggling to concentrate, Solara turned to follow the child's gaze. Leora then raised her trembling hand and pointed.

Solara squinted to try and see, but knew what had to have captivated Leora's attention: it had to be Durgin. Solara shook her head again, blinked several times, and started back for the water.

One of the mystral reached out and held her. "Rest easy, Sister Solara, for you are back at Dragon's Myst now."

"No," Solara pushed her aside as her vision cleared just enough to see a dark figure closing in on the mystral in the water. "No!" she screamed in warning, but it was too late.

Durgin rushed into the water and brought his axe down, splitting the head of the youngest mystral as easily as he would split a melon. Pulling his weapon free, he moved to the next closest woman as she cried out, the last thing she ever would do.

The other mystral were now alerted and saw Durgin, a maniacal glare in his eyes as he pulled his axe from the chest of his latest victim and moved towards them. "Two," he called out. "Many more to come!"

The mystral began running and swimming away, fleeing as quickly as they could. Some rushed towards the shore where their clothing and weapons lay; others headed deeper into the lake; a few walked through the water, which was quite shallow, towards the waterfall.

Durgin watched them all go and tried to pick which group he would follow first. As he watched the girls that were heading deeper into the lake, he saw the silver-haired witch coming towards him, waist deep in water and still moving.

He could not believe his eyes. He had seen the hobgoblins swarming down on her, yet they were gone and she was still advancing. How could he ever hope to overcome that?

An unbridled terror began flowing through him. The thrill of the hunt was over. Every instinct was telling him to flee. He was not yet ready to face the silver-haired one. He still needed time to regain his strength and confidence.

Glancing at the fleeing mystral, he shook his head in regret and bit his lip. *There will be another time*, he thought, trying to rationalize his decision. Letting them live now would only enhance the pleasure, allowing them the opportunity to wonder when he would be back for them. With one final look at his nemesis, he rushed from the water and fled into the forest.

Solara reached the spot where Durgin had been. Several mystral were there now, fully armored and ready to face their attacker. Adrenaline and vengeance were the only things keeping her on her feet. When Durgin vanished from sight, Solara could not fight her own injuries any longer. She fell over and into the water.

Another mystral lifted her up and pulled her over to the shore.

"He must not escape," Solara whispered, teetering on unconsciousness.

"Do not worry, we will find that one again."

"He must pay," Solara protested even weaker than before.

"After we tend to your own injuries and bring home the dead."

Solara was no longer in any position to argue as she lost consciousness.

The young hobgoblin stayed hidden and watched the battle as it unfolded. He was impressed by these mystral. Three alone managed to turn the tide and stop the entire unit he was traveling with. He wondered if they were really powerful, or whether his own people were weaker than they thought they were. Either way, he found himself drawn to the mystral, and held little desire to return to his own kin.

He watched as several of the dragon-marked women led the two horses, a small child, and a wolf to the other side of the lake. All of them then headed towards the waterfall and vanished behind its crashing waters. The hobgoblin watched it all and waited for a long time after they left to make sure that none would return.

When he was certain that he was alone, he snuck out of his hiding place and began to search the bodies of his fallen tribe. As before, he found many pouches of gold and small jewels; no weapons that drew his attention though. With that thought, he turned and glanced at the lake. The mystral they attacked had two swords that she dropped!

He ran to the water and started searching for the lost weapons. He was glad that it was still daylight, for if it was night, he probably would have no chance of finding the blades. He saw something glistening under the water and he reached down. It was a sword—lightweight, like the two throwing knives, and just as finely crafted.

He continued walking along the water searching until he found the second one. Twirling both, he was quite pleased with his newfound weapons. As he started to walk back to the shore, he paused and regarded the body of one of the fallen hobgoblins. There were close to fifteen arrows sticking in him.

The hobgoblin pulled at one until he could get it out. The tip was crafted to look like the head of a dragon. Unlike the arrows his people used, these were entirely made of metal. He pulled all of the bodies from the lake and began cutting the arrows free from them. It was a slow and tedious process, but when he was done, he managed to fill two quivers with the silver dragon-tipped arrows.

The only bow he had was a hobgoblin bow he had found on one of his slain kin, but it would do for now. Strapping the two quivers to his back, he placed his bow over his shoulder, and both swords in scabbards he stole from a couple more hobgoblins. The scabbards were a bit large, but until he found something better, they too would suffice.

He glanced at his own sword and mace and tossed them aside with disgust. He had better weapons now.

"A creature after my own heart."

The hobgoblin spun around, pulling his two new swords and preparing himself for whatever faced him. It was a man that was better dressed than any he had ever seen before. Though he had a scar below his right eye, the hobgoblin knew that the man before him held a far better station in life than the villagers and farmers his people had been raiding thus far.

"Who are you?" he asked in the common tongue.

"I am Kabilian," the man said in a scratchy and deep voice. "I, too, am a collector. We share that passion." As he said it, he lowered his hands to reveal his jewel-hilted daggers.

"You cannot have my weapons!"

"Nor am I looking for them," Kabilian replied. "No need to get upset—you like mystral weapons; I tend to search for mystical items. There is no conflict of interest here, my newfound friend."

"You're an enemy," the young hobgoblin spat out. "Humans are enemies of hobgoblins!"

"That may be so, but when the hobgoblins fled, you stayed behind. You, my friend, are different. You are not a mindless minion. You are unique."

"Unique?"

"Yes, unique," Kabilian smiled disarmingly. "Tell me friend, what is your name?"

"My name?" the hobgoblin repeated, pausing—he had never been asked by anyone for it before, not even the chieftain asked his name when he had returned and reported the deaths of the scouting party.

"You must have one," Kabilian teased.

"Yes, a name," the hobgoblin said. "I am Cricktellik."

"Cricktellik, eh?" Kabilian scratched his chin as he pondered the name. "That won't do at all."

"That is my name!" the hobgoblin shouted.

"Oh, I know it is," Kabilian said. "A good name, too—but if you are going to travel with me, you need something shorter, something with more menace to it, something that just rolls off the tongue. Cricktellik is just too long, too confusing. You want something that will strike dread in your opponents' hearts!"

"Travel with you?" the hobgoblin asked in confusion.

"You certainly don't want to go back to your own kind, do you?" Kabilian asked.

"No," Cricktellik agreed. "I want more. I want better than what my tribe has."

"I thought you did," Kabilian beamed. "How about Crick?"

"Crick?"

"Yes, we'll just shorten your name," Kabilian nodded in approval. "Crick it is. I like it."

"Crick," the hobgoblin repeated.

"Out with the old, in with the new," Kabilian replied. "Now, shall we find you something a little better to wear as well?"

"Something to wear?" he said as he scanned the ground. "I can't fit into mystral armor."

"Indeed you can't, but I bet you the dwarves of Tregador could make you an illistrium suit of armor to die for!"

"Dwarves?" Crick asked skeptically.

"My next stop," Kabilian explained. "I was on my way there when you caught my attention. Care to join me?"

Crick glanced at the dead hobgoblins and nodded. "To Tregador, my new friend."

"Perfect," Kabilian slapped him on the back. "With my reputation, training, and generous nature, you'll be quite formidable and a good companion in no time at all!"

Crick watched him as they started to walk away. He did not understand this human, but he would study him. He had a confidence about him, a certainty unlike anything the young hobgoblin had ever seen before. If he were willing to take him as a traveling companion, and to teach him, he would learn whatever he could.

"Crick, my newfound friend, I believe this is the beginning of a wonderful partnership."

CHAPTER 41

His travels had turned from days into weeks with little to show for them. Ferceng stopped every traveler, worker, and individual he passed, asking for any information they may have on the Murky Death Clan, but nothing substantial was ever reported. It was as if the Tenalong orc city was mythological rather than real.

He considered several times the possibility that rumors of the vast orc city were spread to incite fear, and possibly leave this area of Tenalong open from outsiders. It would be a sound strategic move. After all, why actually grow an army larger than any orc clan ever had, if the paranoia of such an army was enough to keep strangers at bay?

The feasibility of an orcish army so large often caused him to pause and contemplate: orcs had horrid societal values, often breaking into factions, with rivalries amongst their own kind ensuing. They also despised staying in the same place too long, and often looked to expand their own territory, attacking villages, smaller towns, and even other races like the dwarves.

Orcs were also not known to be skilled in the arts of agriculture or other skills necessary to help a community survive. As such, they sent large hunting parties out to find food—whether it was through hunting or theft did not matter to them.

All of this and more he learned in the Academy when he was studying to be a Mage. Though he knew that there were always elements of a race that did not follow the ideals of their own kind—like the disciples of Krung, who were granted land by Braksis's father to cultivate, forming a prosperous and peaceful settlement that thrived to this day—Ferceng found it hard to believe that an entire community of orcs—one hundred thousand orcs—would be that different from most of their other relatives.

The numbers alone were mind-boggling. If a fifteen-thousand-orc mining colony had waged war with the dwarven city of Carnelian—a city twice their size—then why would an orc clan that clearly outnumbered anything around them refrain from trying to expand? Even more troubling, how could it be possible that nobody had ever come across this vast city?

He was determined to solve this mystery—not only for his son, but also for the sake of the entire realm. These orcs were not typical of a normal clan. If they were real—and he sincerely hoped that they were not—then the only possible answer to all of his questions was that they were building an army that would conquer the realm. That rationalization was most troubling of all.

That had been the fear of Braksis—if there really were one hundred thousand orcs ready to march on the realm, the humans would fall quickly. The Imperium's forces were a mere fraction of that right now. Each Kingdom also had its own army and defenders, but they too would be easily overcome. This conclusion was what led Braksis to so passionately convince the Imperium to try and put the differences of the races behind them and forge an alliance with the other civilizations of the realm. A noble goal, but one Ferceng knew would be far harder to accomplish than it was to conceive; unless, of course, the races had actual proof that the orcs were building an army. Proof he was determined to provide.

The last person he had seen had heard rumors that the Murky Death Clan could be found at the base of the Forbidden Peaks, where the Bloody River and Forbidden Forest meet. He had to admit, with names like that, the rumor certainly seemed plausible. He only hoped that they would pan out.

That report was given to him almost a week ago now. Since then, not a single soul had been seen. That wasn't completely unheard of in Tenalong—very few that were not born here ever wished to come to this Kingdom. However, he was no longer in the swamps; his trail led him west, beyond the swamps and on dry land again. Still, not a single home, traveler, or any sign of civilization.

Ferceng was not that old. He had not even reached his seventieth birthday, but he had seen and experienced a lot. Deep down, his instincts were telling him that he was close.

He had reached the Forbidden Forest three days ago and was now walking along the outskirts of them to find the Bloody River. Though he could use his mystical abilities to move more swiftly and cover more ground, Ferceng felt that it had been too long since he had been on a quest, and he did not wish to miss any details: the indentation of a footprint, a broken twig, or any other sign that something had gone the same way he was going. Thus far, he had not discovered anything.

In the distance, he could see the river. He would be there soon. He squinted as he tried to concentrate. There were people at the river's edge, fishing. Ferceng smiled to see other forms of life. None were orcs, but hopefully they could point him in the right direction.

Ferceng increased his pace and walked over to the riverbank with his hands stretched outward to show that he was not a threat. Many would see a troll and fear for the worst, so he hoped this group would be willing to speak to him.

There were two centaurs by a wagon, four gnomes, an elf, and three humans. Ferceng thought that it was odd to see this grouping together; centaurs particularly hated humans. Perhaps the unification would work after all.

"Good day," Ferceng called out pleasantly. He waited, but none of them even raised their heads to look at him. It was as if they were oblivious to what was happening around them.

He waited for a moment, and then grew concerned. He saw a small wooden bridge built further up the river and began walking towards it, the entire time he kept looking back at the fisherman, disturbed by the fact that not even one of them turned to watch him leave.

After crossing the bridge, he returned to the workers and walked right up to one of them. "Good day," he said again. As before, the elf just walked to the wagon and placed a small bucket of fish in it.

Ferceng leaned over and looked at one of the gnomes that were still sitting by the bank holding a fishing rod. It was as if the gnome was shining in the sunlight. He walked around and examined all of them briefly, and saw that all had the same substance on them. It was hardly noticeable, almost clear, but definitely something that made their skin glisten.

Taking a deep breath, he knew that what he was about to do would be frowned upon by his old instructors at the Mage's Council, but he did not have the time to properly study this minor intrigue. He reached out and touched one of the humans with the tip of his finger. The human did not react, only continued to return from the wagon, pick up his rod and begin fishing again.

Ferceng glanced down at his finger and saw that the tip was also glistening slightly. Raising it to his nose, he smelled it—there was no odor. He rubbed it between his index finger and thumb, and felt it squishing. When he looked at his hand again, it was on both fingers now. He wiped both fingers off on his pants, and when he looked again, was glad to see that the substance was gone. Whatever it was, he was certain he didn't want it to encompass him like it was doing to the others.

Deciding that these workers were under somebody's control, he decided to wait and let them lead him there, hopefully to the orcs that he was searching for. Walking over to a tree, he leaned down and rested while watching the fisherman fill the wagon with small buckets full of fish.

If this was for the Murky Death Clan, Ferceng concluded that at least one of his mysteries had been solved. The reason the orcs were not seen marauding nearby towns, villages, and kingdoms for food was because they somehow had created unthinking slaves to do the work for them.

The workers seemed to never tire. They were almost robotic in their movements, but they were efficient with their task. The wagon filled up and the centaurs began pulling it towards the base of the For-bidden Peaks. Ferceng stood up and began to follow them.

He saw the dug up ground where the wagon had traveled. The grass was mostly gone and dirt-ruts formed a path there now. He figured that he could have followed this route earlier, but he wanted to make certain that he found his destination, and these workers were his best lead.

They followed the path around the base of the mountains and continued on. Along the route, Ferceng saw large fields of farmland: rows upon rows of corn, grains, and even cotton; orchards ripe with fruit; and small kitchen gardens full of herbs and vegetables. As Ferceng continued on, he also found livestock being tended to. All of the people working this land—a myriad of races—had the same shiny exterior that the fishermen did.

Ferceng continued on and paused as the workers approached and entered a large gate that would rival the size and magnificence of the one built in Trespias. The base of the stone wall had wooden pikes built into them so that anyone attempting to invade would find scaling the wall a life-threatening endeavor. A deep ravine was also dug around the base of the wall. Ferceng glanced over and saw the bottom was filled with a bubbling liquid. He also spotted portions of several skeletons, the bones mostly dissolved from the liquid, and the remains decomposing.

A bridge led to the gate, which was now open. Several orcs were standing along the wall and peering down at him. Watch towers filled with orcs armed with bows were also scattered every fifteen to twenty feet. As he glanced around at the defenses, he took a deep breath to calm himself. He wanted to find the Murky Death Clan, and apparently he just had.

He walked through the gate following the workers, unchallenged by any of the sentries. As the fishermen continued on, Ferceng paused where he was and looked around. Not only were the walls of this city impressive, but also the structures inside were overwhelming: so unlike the orcs he had studied so long ago!

There were large structures built directly into the base of the mountains. They had five levels each and, he assumed, extended deep within the base of the Forbidden Peaks. How many orcs could be living in those buildings? He counted twenty structures just within eyesight, each one with close to fifty small openings on each level.

Not wanting to draw attention to himself, he resumed walking around. The area surrounded by the wall also held large structures. He approached one, a wooden building ornamented with skulls. He peered through a window and saw dwarves working away with their hammers, forging finely crafted weapons and armor—hundreds of which adorned the walls and were displayed on small wooden stands, waiting for someone to claim them.

Wishing to see what else was around, Ferceng approached the next building. Much larger than the last, this one was round with several long rectangular structures stemming off from it. Feeling daring, Ferceng stepped inside this building and walked around. Gnomes, dwarves, and humans were working in this building. He saw large weapons being crafted: catapults, ballistae, and battering rams.

He walked past the workers—who, like the ones he had seen before, did not even pause to look at him—entered one of the adjoining buildings, and saw that it was a warehouse. This particular one held hundreds of catapults. For the sake of thoroughness, he entered the other two warehouses and confirmed the scope of these massive weapons.

He exited the building and approached the next one. This structure was made out of a hard alloy—not as sturdy as illistrium, but very durable. Several smoke stacks protruded from the roof and dark clouds were emitting from it. Stepping inside, he found dozens of gnomes working together on potions and mixtures.

Like all Mages, Ferceng had taken a variety of courses in Alchemy and Potions. He looked over the shoulder of one gnome and watched him work, absorbing the details of all of the base elements and compounds being used. This group was designing a variety of things here, but most noticeable was an explosive compound that Ferceng surmised would be quite devastating.

As he exited the building, he heard shouting and cheers. Curious about what was going on, Ferceng made his way deeper into the compound, passing dozens of similar buildings as those he had already explored. He found orcs, thousands of them, all young, standing around a pit and cheering.

Ferceng stepped closer and tried to look over. The ground moved up into an elevation and then arched downward again so that wherever you stood you could see what was happening. As he peered down, he saw a dwarf and two rasplers fighting each other. Another dwarf lay dead in the arena.

He knew of gladiatorial combats, something that was quite popular during the Dark Ages, but he had never actually witnessed one firsthand. The dwarf was wielding an axe and charged one of the rasplers. With a swipe, the raspler was on the ground, clutching what remained of its newly severed limb, as its companion jumped on the dwarf's back and dug two claws into his shoulder.

The orcs present cheered as the dwarf maimed the raspler, and even louder when the dwarf fell himself. Ferceng did not pull his eyes away. Not because he was interested or drawn into the fight, but because the fighters below did not have the clear shiny membrane that the workers had—they were fighting with their own abilities and instincts!

Walking back down the hill and away from the pit, he saw a large wooden fence with guard towers along the outside. He did not wish to get too close to that area—there were many orcish guards patrolling there. He presumed that beyond the fence was where they kept their slaves and prisoners.

A large opening in the mountain caught his attention. Directly above it was a carved symbol of what looked like a giant bug with a long neck, rounded head, two pincers, six legs, and a round tail. Ferceng wondered what the symbol represented, as he had never seen any kind of creature like that before.

"Something I can help you with?"

Ferceng spun around and saw an older orc female standing before him. He was glad that he learned the orc tongue in his Mage's Council days. "I was curious about the opening," he said, curious that she asked if she could help him and not demanding to know who he was and why he was there.

"That is the entrance to the lair of the Binders," the orc replied.

"Binders?" Ferceng asked.

"Yes, the creatures that provide us with our slaves," she explained.

"Oh yes," Ferceng said as if he just remembered what she was talking about. "Perhaps you could answer a few more questions for me," he continued.

"We are both allies of Zoldex—whatever you wish to know, I would be glad to answer."

Zoldex, he thought. So Braksis had been right—the ancient rival of Pierce had returned. The Council of Elders would need to be warned, and soon. "That is true," Ferceng said to continue the deception. "I am surprised—I would have thought that I would see more warriors around?"

"We have begun our glorious purge of the south in the name of Zoldex. The damnable elves, dwarves, and humans will fall before our might as Zoldex has foreseen."

"Magnificent," Ferceng offered, playing his part to perfection.

"That is enough, I will see to our guest now."

"Oh, yes Father—as it should be," the orc bowed and walked away.

Ferceng regarded the newcomer. She had called him "Father," but he was certainly no orc. Though he wore a helmet, he could see lime-green eyebrows and lashes with blood red eyes studying him. This man was an eternal.

He wore mostly armor, with an orange bodysuit leaving only his arms bare. Over this he had a black breastplate with a skull hand-crafted into the middle. His legs had black slashes with jagged spikes sticking from the end, as did his boots and gauntlets. His helmet was also spiked down the middle with two larger horns jutting from the sides. Strapped to his belt was a sword with a hilt that matched the horns of his helmet.

"I have never seen you before, troll," he stated, stern and judgmental. "Who are you? What are you doing here?"

Ferceng thought for a moment. He had known that he was taking a monumental risk by even daring to enter this city, but things had been so easy for him up to this point. That ease led him to a story that he hoped would be believable.

"I am Ferceng, leader of the troll armies being sent north to create a presence for Zoldex in Falestia," Ferceng boldly declared, hoping that his outright lie would not be too unreasonable. He was making quite a few assumptions based on what he had already heard and knew.

"Can you prove what you say?" the eternal asked, daring Ferceng to offer some form of validity to his identity.

Ferceng reached behind his back and pulled Carnage over his shoulder. Though the axe had been the weapon of Guldan of Frocomon, Zoldex had enchanted it, a fact that hopefully would appease this eternal. "I show you Carnage, a weapon my ancestors claimed in battle with the dwarves of Vorstad. A weapon enchanted by Zoldex to lead my armies into battle."

"Enchanted how?" the eternal asked.

"This axe is unbreakable," Ferceng boasted. "What's more, it can slice through any substance known."

The eternal looked bored with the description and was not amused by the deception.

Ferceng stepped over to a large boulder on the ground. "Allow me to demonstrate the fury of Zoldex in a troll's hand!" He then raised Carnage high overhead and brought it down, splitting the boulder in two.

The eternal nodded in approval. "Impressive," he said. "I have seen other weapons similarly enchanted by Zoldex. You must be a troll of extraordinary talents and potential for Zoldex to have bestowed such a gift upon you."

"I do not like to boast," Ferceng replied in a challenging tone.

"I am sure," the eternal laughed. "I was unaware that the trolls were marching north."

"Does anyone truly know everything that Zoldex is planning?" Ferceng was quick to reply.

The eternal laughed boisterously. "Your words ring true," the eternal said. "I only hope that Zoldex is not spreading his forces too thin."

"Why do you fear that?"

"The orcs are laying siege to the south, the hobgoblins to Suspinti, and now I hear that the trolls will move into Falestia. Until our reinforcements arrive, we should focus on one area at a time. Conquer gradually."

"Yes," Ferceng agreed, though he truly wished to learn more about the reinforcements. A question he would not dare to ask this eternal, a man that was clearly much more intelligent and cunning than the orc he was previously speaking with. "By the way, forgive my ignorance, but I was never told that an eternal led the Murky Death Clan."

"Very few even know of the existence of Grool—my involvement is even more masked than that. Allow me to introduce myself—I am Benatar."

Ferceng noted both names—Benatar, the leader, and Father of the Murky Death Clan as the female orc had called him; and the city, Grool. "My gratitude," Ferceng replied.

"So what brings you to Grool?" Benatar asked.

"Many of my trolls had heard the stories of the one hundred thousand orcs of the Murky Death Clan. When we were informed of our advance to the north, many hoped that I could learn the secrets and expand upon our own numbers. My troops are weary of facing superior numbers."

"A valid concern, one reason why the trolls, and many other races, have been unable to persevere in the past," Benatar replied.

"We see eye to eye, then," Ferceng nodded. "I wish my own armies had as many as yours. How did you acquire so many orcs?"

"You can thank Zoldex for that," Benatar snickered. "He and I were old childhood friends. When he was banished from this land, he contacted me and told me to prepare for his eventual return. Though his message was short, images of grand armies and how to build them were burned into my brain. All I needed was to find the right location and group to begin expanding upon this goal.

"That led me to Grool. The Murky Death Clan numbered no more than ten thousand orcs. They had retreated beyond the swamps after being decimated by the combined forces of Xylona and Vorstad. They were a people defeated and without purpose. They were dying.

"When I arrived here, I could see the potential, and knew that I had found the foundation I needed. With nothing more than Grimifate, my sword," he said, patting the hilt of his blade, "I declared that I was the new leader of the orcs, and that any who dared to challenge that rule would fall victim before me."

"Did any challenge you?" Ferceng asked.

"Of course," Benatar laughed at the memory. "No orc would willingly sacrifice their own stature in society. Here, the strong survive, and the strongest rule. That was what they were trained and what they knew. I had to alter that fundamental philosophy."

Ferceng listened, thinking that many of his own doubts about the existence of this place were now being answered. The orcs that lived here during the Age of the Mage were like any other. Somehow though, this eternal changed all that. He had altered their entire society, beliefs, and culture. This was not a man to be taken lightly.

"The Chieftain of course was the last one to face me. He sent his best warriors first. I killed them all. The Chieftain was the last to fall. After that, the survivors named me their new Chieftain, a position I said was no more. Never again would there be an orc Chieftain of the Murky Death Clan."

"Orcs without a Chieftain?" Ferceng asked with a skeptical look. "Did that last?"

"For many centuries," Benatar confirmed. "After the orcs adjusted to their new philosophy of living, I named an orc as Chieftain, though even he bows to me, as I do to Zoldex."

"We all must have order and a hierarchy," Ferceng nodded his approval. "What else did you do to change the orc's behavior?"

"I told them that from this day forward, they were secluded, and could never be revealed to the rest of the world. That they were being bred for a greater purpose—namely to serve Zoldex."

"You must have been discovered, though," Ferceng said. "Look at all of the other races around this city."

"Yes, others have wandered near here over the years. We could not allow ourselves to be exposed, though. We killed many, captured the rest. No survivors would ever be allowed to leave this place."

"You are fortunate to have the Binders," Ferceng said, though he was truly fishing for information.

"Yes, the Binders have made things much easier. Any creature brought before them loses all will and independence. They are mindless slaves, doing anything that is asked of them."

"Anything?" Ferceng pressed.

"I could ask one to kill his own parent or sibling, and he would do so without a second thought," Benatar smiled proudly.

"I still do not understand how you could have so many orcs. That is what my trolls wish to know."

"Along with Zoldex's message, I learned that by adding the blood of an eternal into the provisions of the orcs would have unimaginable side effects. Though I provided only small doses, the orcs grew taller, stronger, and lived longer. Somehow, by mixing my own blood with their food and water, they absorbed the properties of an eternal.

"Fewer and fewer orcs died, rapidly increasing the numbers of the legions being formed. The population increased so much so that I could no longer provide enough blood to satiate the orcs, who were growing quite dependent upon it by then. So I took a raiding party back to the land of the eternals and kidnapped dozens of my kin. To this day, they remain imprisoned here, their blood being drained to feed the entire Murky Death Clan."

Ferceng listened intently, but his stomach was turning at the thought. It was similar to how the Mages propagate their own kind. He remembered the story of how Hergzenbarung, a Council of Elders member, had become a Mage. A Paladin had stumbled across a pair of lupans, who killed and ate him. Their offspring had somehow emerged with the mystical abilities of a Mage, and was brought to the Tower to be raised as one of their own, though many Gatherers died to claim him. The blood of the eternals must have had a similar effect upon the orcs.

"A near-eternal life," Ferceng nodded his approval. "That would be one way to increase my troll armies!"

"Do not get your hopes up," Benatar cautioned. "The process takes many generations, and the same could not be done for your armies in time to assist with the upcoming war. Perhaps when it is over you and your kind could also begin feasting on the blood of the eternals."

"A most appealing prospect," Ferceng agreed. "I feel that I have learned what I can. Enough to offer some hope to my own armies that, one day, we will number as many as the one hundred thousand orcs!"

Benatar laughed at the comment.

"What humors you?" Ferceng asked.

"Your estimates are very old," Benatar explained. "The orcs of the Murky Death Clan increase by almost twenty thousand a year, and every year more and more are born. We have well over three hundred thousand right now, half of which are marching to conquer the south."

Ferceng could not catch his breath—the numbers were staggering, far worse than even his darkest fears. "Most impressive," he said to keep the charade alive. "Good fortune with your conquest, then."

"And to you," Benatar replied. "May the trolls of Tenalong slaughter the unsuspecting fools of Falestia."

"It will be glorious," Ferceng nodded. "For Zoldex!"

"For Zoldex!" Benatar cheered in response. "We shall meet again, Ferceng—in Trespias, when we are triumphant."

"Yes," Ferceng agreed. "Until then." As he walked away from the eternal, he headed straight for the gate of the city. He did not wish to arouse any suspicion. The individuals bonded in slavery would have to remain that way for another day. For now, the civilizations that were still free needed him more. He hoped that he would be in time to warn them, for alone, none of them could withstand the force bearing down on them.

CHAPTER 42

"Are you certain?"

"I verified the orcs' march myself, my lord."

King Echalas clasped both hands and lowered his head so that his chin rested on them. The news was dire indeed. Ilias, swiftest of all elves had just reported that the orcs of the Murky Death Clan were on the move, straight towards them. To make the situation even worse, apparently there were far more orcs than they had anticipated.

At four hundred and ninety years old, Echalas had lived the dreams of his people, and saw them thrive. Xylona's history and heritage were deeply embedded in the tales of the warriors of their treetop city, the proud few who defended their home against all adversaries and earned the right to wield an honor blade.

To Xylona, no threat could possibly tear apart the home that they had made. All opponents quickly learned this time after time. Times were changing though: the forces of evil were allying themselves with Zoldex, and their assaults thus far had been relentless. In the past month alone, he recalled at least a dozen times the hobgoblins had almost breached their defenses. The war was not going well.

The people still believed, though. No matter how hard the war became, or how close they came to defeat, the elves of Xylona felt that they could, and would, overcome any threat. Echalas was not so certain.

They were fortunate to ally themselves with the dwarves of Vorstad—now with Tregador as well. Armies of the small humanoids were scattered below the city, defending it valiantly for their elven allies. Humans too had come to fight in the name of Xylona, though they were

230

recently summoned back to their own capital—a fact he pondered whether it was coincidence, or a sign that Zoldex's reach extended all the way to the throne of Trespias.

This last possibility was even more frightening than the orc army bearing down on them this day. He had spent many years fighting for Xylona, and then leading it. It had only been in the past century that he had found the time to begin a family of his own. He was fortunate to find Arleyn, his beautiful and, above all, understanding wife. He was even more fortunate the day his only child, Ashwin, was born.

Ashwin, though, was in Trespias. If the Imperium had been compromised, her safety was in doubt—a thought that would shake the foundations of the strongest father.

"How would you like to proceed, my lord?" Ilias asked when King Echalas did not respond.

Echalas closed his eyes for a moment, trying to push aside the fears and worries for his daughter. It was far better to focus on events that could be controlled, and that was how to handle the oncoming tide of evil.

He opened his eyes and walked over to a balcony that overlooked the North Horwood Forest. The morning was so peaceful, not a cloud was in the sky, a gentle breeze brushing the leaves of the trees. Below him, he saw several elves and dwarves laughing and joking. How could such tranquility be threatened so much?

The king turned back and beckoned his two visitors, Ilias and Jellanos, to join him. They could see that his contemplation was over. The elf that stood there then was the king that had led their people for three centuries, but served Xylona for his entire life. His long blonde hair did not flow as freely as it did in his younger days; his indigo eyes showed a deep compassion and love, but also a commanding logic that could not be denied. His shirt and pants were a myriad of green shades, creating a blend that could almost hide him in any forest region. His knee high boots were as white as the clouds, as was his cape that he had clasped around his neck. The clasp, handcrafted by his wife, was an intricate golden rose.

"When will the orcs arrive?" Echalas asked.

"Based on their speed when last I saw them, they could be here as early as the first light tomorrow; if they camp for the night, we would have even more time," Ilias reported.

"That does not give us much time," Jellanos stated. "I shall prepare for any injured we may have."

"No," Echalas ordered. "That will not be necessary."

"Surely you do not think we will fall?" Jellanos asked in shock.

"Not a single elf will fall before these orcs," Echalas sternly replied.

Jellanos and Ilias exchanged a glance. "My lord, the numbers against us are far too high. Odds are, this is one battle we may not win. To think that none will die, with all due respect, is a bit naïve."

"No offense taken, noble Jellanos," Echalas said as he took a deep breath. "None will need your services tomorrow, for none will remain to face the oncoming army."

"We're leaving Xylona?" Ilias stammered.

"It is not a decision I make lightly. I have spent my entire life preserving the values and fighting for Xylona. To abandon it is unthinkable. However, I see little choice: either we remain and fight for our home and perish, or we leave, live to fight another day, and allow our culture to grow elsewhere. I prefer the latter option."

"Yes, my lord," Jellanos nodded. "A wise decision."

"I will need to speak with Detroz, but begin preparations for our evacuation," Echalas ordered.

"I will go for him now," Ilias said.

As he left the balcony, Echalas turned and grabbed Jellanos's arm before he could leave. "I need to speak freely, old friend."

Jellanos nodded and stepped back onto the balcony. The doctor was one hundred and two years older than Echalas; he had been a mere pupil present when the current king was born, helping his predecessor with the delivery. There had never been many secrets between the two. "You're worried about Ashwin," he said, needing not ask the question, for the turmoil over his daughter was evident.

"I thought I was doing the right thing by sending her away. I thought I was protecting her from the constant attacks we have been undergoing of late. Now I fear she may have marched straight into the den of the enemy."

"Even if she has, she is well protected," Jellanos reminded him. "Three honor-blade-wielders are with her, four if you count the fact that Thamar was offered one and he turned it down."

"Is it enough though?" Echalas asked.

"I have never seen better fighters than Arifos and Mylvannan," Jellanos commented with conviction. "I have seen both of them turn the tide in many battles. Your nephew, Heirn, is also well trained and an accomplished warrior. He knows his responsibility and takes very few risks in life. If there is danger, he would steer Ashwin away from it."

"The dwarves might not be so willing to abandon glory," Echalas somberly added.

"I know not of Baldock, though he did appear a little wild to me. Thamar though has fought alongside us for a long time now. He may crave a good fight, but he always makes sure that his mission is completed. I would not worry."

"She does have my ring, too," Echalas said, trying to be more optimistic.

"That she does," Jellanos smiled. "See, nothing to worry about."

"What if they return here and find the city overrun?"

"You're thinking that Arifos would allow them to walk headlong into an enemy encampment?" Jellanos laughed. "I think not. He never walks blindly, even into an environment he thinks is friendly. I think he has seen far more violence and suffering than both of us combined. They will not be taken unawares."

"I thank you, old friend," Echalas smiled as he patted Jellanos on the shoulder. "I cannot speak these concerns to any other, and when I talk to Arleyn later, I must sound confident, or else she will see right through me."

Jellanos snickered. "She will see right through you anyway."

"You are probably right," Echalas had to agree. His wife always seemed to have the uncanny ability of seeing through his words and understanding the true meaning of his thoughts. Her gift was both a blessing and a nuisance at times.

"Ah look, the dwarf has arrived," Jellanos pointed inside the room. "I shall begin preparations for the evacuation."

"Have everyone ready to leave by nightfall. If the orcs can be here as early as daybreak, I do not wish to have a single soul left for them to attack."

"Yes, my lord," Jellanos offered a slight bow and walked out of the room.

Echalas stepped back inside the room and nodded at the dwarf. Detroz was an imposing individual. He was almost as tall as most elves, standing at four feet and eight inches. His wardrobe was almost entirely black: his shirt, pants, boots, and gloves. Upon his chest he wore chainmail, with a dagger and sword sheathed along his black belt. Even his horned helmet atop his brow was mostly black. The only thing the dwarf wore that had a slightly different tinge was his cloak, which was a dark, charcoal gray.

Though he wore dark colors, the wardrobe was not nearly as dark as the dwarf himself: his deep brown eyes always appeared challenging and imposing. It was as if everyone Detroz looked at was an enemy he was just waiting to tear into. His features were stone-hard and just as stern. This dwarf was unmovable and unshakeable. Echalas doubted that Detroz would even blink at the news that the Murky Death Clan was bearing down on them.

"Welcome Detroz," Echalas offered pleasantly.

"An honor," he replied in his normal deep and booming voice as he bowed, though never taking his eyes from the elf.

"I have heard that others call you the Destroyer of Orcs," Echalas said. "That title may soon be tested once more."

Detroz said nothing, but merely watched Echalas as he began pacing.

"I have received a report that the Murky Death Clan is on the march. They are heading this way."

"How many?" Detroz asked without hesitation.

"It sounds like they have even more than the hundred thousand that we were warned of."

"When?" he continued to question, his voice still full of confidence and showing no signs of trepidation at all.

"As early as first light," Echalas answered.

"You can count on the dwarves of Vorstad and Tregador," Detroz declared. "We will be ready."

"That may not be necessary," Echalas said, though he was inspired by the confidence of the dwarf. "We are leaving Xylona. Tonight."

"Are you pulling back to Vorstad?" Detroz asked.

"No, if we went to Vorstad, we would be trapped between the Murky Death Clan and the Severed Head Clan. It would be a glorious finale to both of our kingdoms, but would serve no purpose in the war against Zoldex. We will be traveling north to Turning Leaf, and trying to convince our northern cousins that it is imperative that we unite. We would be honored if you would travel with us."

Echalas watched the dwarf for a moment, but could not read him at all. His expression had not changed since he walked into the room. As he stood there, he thought of how his last statement could seem to be a violation of their treaty. The dwarves had assisted Xylona for months now, leaving their own home under siege. When the scales turned against them, the elves fled, leaving the dwarves to fend for themselves.

"I will send my fastest messengers to King Chaddrick so that Vorstad, too, has time to evacuate," Echalas offered.

"No," Detroz boldly said. "I shall lead the dwarves here back to Vorstad and see what my king's wishes are. If we are to fight or flee, we shall do as he decrees."

"Then I wish you a swift and safe journey," Echalas said. "I hope that one day soon we will fight alongside each other once more."

"Until that day," Detroz bowed, again not taking his eyes from King Echalas, and then turned and walked out.

Echalas watched the gray-bearded dwarf leave, and wondered for a brief moment if they could have defended Xylona as long as they had allies like Detroz fighting alongside of them. The risk was too great, but he truly hoped that he would have the opportunity to one day repay the dwarves of Vorstad for all that they had done and sacrificed for him.

As Detroz stepped outside onto the walkway, Grosskurth waited there to greet him. The light-brown-bearded dwarf wore off-white pants and a shirt, with a light tan cloak, boots, and belt. He had two darker leather straps across his chest, each fastening a scimitar to his back. He did not dress, nor did he fight like most dwarves. As Detroz regarded him for a moment, he thought that Grosskurth didn't act like most dwarves either.

"You already know?"

"That orcs are marching this way?" Grosskurth asked with a wry grin.

Detroz was not surprised. Grosskurth was a master tracker and scout, his abilities resembling the skills of a ranger more than that of a dwarven fighter. He could read signs that no other dwarves could, and never had steered them wrong in the past. If orcs were coming, he undoubtedly would have known about it first. "Did you go scouting?"

"Not necessary," Grosskurth laughed.

"Then how?" Detroz demanded.

"I followed you and listened to your conversation," Grosskurth admitted.

"That seems a bit beneath you," Detroz shook his head.

"I knew something was happening. After you were summoned, I overheard a few elves talking about leaving Xylona. I wished to know why. Purely coincidental that I overheard you two speaking. Right place, right time."

"I'm sure," Detroz said. "Is everyone down below?"

"Everyone but Graf," Grosskurth smiled.

For the first time, Detroz's expression changed. "Don't tell me he and some elves are going at it again?"

"I think you should see for yourself," Grosskurth snickered.

"I think that will turn my stomach," Detroz shook his head, regaining his composure.

"Perhaps," Grosskurth cryptically said. "This way."

He led them over several walkways and down a level to a round structure encasing one of the trees. As they stepped up to the door, Grosskurth turned back and smiled. "You may be disappointed."

"I'll risk it," Detroz said as he pushed Grosskurth aside and walked into the room without knocking to announce his presence. As he did, he stopped short, not certain he could believe his eyes: Graf was sitting on a large pillow, wearing white silken elven robes, talking to at least a dozen elven children.

"Then I jumped onto the back of the Rock troll and grabbed it by the neck like this," as he said it, he arched his arm and acted like he was strangling something.

"Ahem," Grosskurth called from the doorway.

Graf paused and looked up, glancing back between Detroz and Grosskurth. "Looks like I have some more tales to live children—that's all for today."

"Oh," the kids began moaning.

"Now, now, if we can, I'll finish up later," the black-bearded dwarf said as he shooed them away.

"Good bye, Uncle Graf," one of the smaller girls said, something quickly repeated by all of the children. One paused to give him a hug before she ran out the door with the others. Graf's lip seemed to quiver as he appeared overwhelmed by the sentiment.

"Uncle Graf?" Detroz asked.

"Not often I see you shocked," Grosskurth snickered. "I warned you."

"You're not going to tell the others, right?" Graf asked, a concerned look on his face.

"Tell them what?" Detroz asked. "What did we just come in on?"

"This is my family," Graf smiled proudly.

"You're the father of those children?" Detroz yelled in shock. "I know you talk about elven women having a thing for you, but I thought it was always just a joke."

"It's not like that," Graf said as he stood up. "About seventy years ago I saved an elf that was being attacked. I carried him all the way home. He wanted to thank me, though I said it wasn't necessary. They built me this little home for whenever I was in Xylona. My home away from home. His children liked my stories. Soon, others began coming to listen."

"Uncle Graf?" Detroz repeated.

"Filancen's children started it, and the others just picked it up," Graf smiled innocently. "Who was I to disillusion them?"

"Which ones were Filancen's children?" Detroz asked.

"None of them," Graf laughed. "They are older now, though they still visit me frequently. It's the younger ones that like the stories the most."

"You probably give them nightmares," Grosskurth laughed.

"I only tell stories with happy endings," Graf shook his head. Glancing back at Detroz, he studied his long-time companion. "You won't tell anyone, right?"

"Why is it such a secret?" Detroz asked.

"Image," Graf replied with a snort.

"Image?" Detroz asked.

"What I do here is for me," he said. "It's not very dwarf-like, but I'm happy. To tell you the truth, these kids often bring tears to my eyes. An odd feeling for an old battle-hardened dwarf like me."

"A dirty old dwarf," Detroz pointed out.

"Only with other dwarves," Graf replied. "I don't want the others to know. This is for me alone."

"Does Thamar know?"

"No," Graf snorted. "How did you even find me?"

"That would be me," Grosskurth smiled.

"Should have figured—you see everything that happens," Graf

snickered. "So what will it be? Is my secret safe?"

"Your secret is safe," Detroz said. "Though I must tell you, the attitude you have with the others is often ridiculed. You'd be better to stop trying to live up to this image you claim to be trying to preserve."

"If I didn't tell those stories of elven women and me, the others would begin to wonder where I disappear to and eventually find out. Filancen's two eldest daughters understood that. They even walked out with me one day, one in each arm and put on an act for Thamar and Theiler."

Grosskurth laughed boisterously. "I bet their expressions were priceless."

"They were!" Graf joined into the laughter.

"Enough of this," Detroz said to calm them down. "We have preparations to make."

"Preparations?" Graf asked. "Yes, what brought you here? What's going on?"

"The Murky Death Clan is on the march. We will not be here when they arrive," Detroz summed up his conversation with Echalas. "We must be prepared to march to Vorstad by nightfall."

"We will be," Graf nodded enthusiastically. He grabbed his single-bladed battleaxe from a mantle on the wall and started to walk towards the door.

"Ahem," Grosskurth said again.

"What?" Graf asked.

"If you want to keep the deception up, don't you think your armor would be better than an elven robe?"

Graf looked down and actually blushed. "Good point." He ran back in and grabbed his outfit. "I'll be right with you two."

Detroz and Grosskurth walked out to give him some privacy. As they stood in the trees, Detroz glanced down at the dwarves scattered along the ground, warriors from both Vorstad and Tregador. Soon, he thought, soon they would have the glory of slaughtering orcs once more.

CHAPTER 43

As her eyes started to flutter, Solara jerked herself awake and scanned her surroundings. She was no longer in the water, but she felt like she was someplace safe. As she looked around, a small grin crept onto her face: she was home.

She slowly got out of bed and walked over to an indentation in the wall. She glanced down and saw a stuffed dragon that had been given to her when she was a child. She recalled vividly that she had never been able to go to sleep without it. Seeing it perched there, she realized that since Durgin entered her life, she had never given her childhood a second thought. His actions had a way of forcing one to grow and mature.

Thinking of Durgin, she searched for her weapons and armor, but found none. All she had on was a loose-fitting laced green nightshirt, and the only other article of clothing she could find was a robe. Frowning at her options, she put the robe on and walked towards the sliding curtains that represented doors in Dragon's Myst.

Before she reached the doorway, a bout of nausea hit her, and she bent down gripping her stomach, breathing heavily. She couldn't understand what was wrong with her, or why her illness was persisting.

The curtains moved aside and a young woman with blonde hair that extended to her neckline, sparkling azure eyes, and a scowl upon her face walked in. Solara noted that she shared the same green dragon emblem upon her brow. As the woman studied her with a disapproving glance, she put her hands on her waist. "What are you doing out of bed?"

"You've changed, Sora," Solara said. "All grown up."

"No thanks to you," Sora quickly retorted.

"There were circumstances," Solara justified.

"There always are," she harshly added as she took Solara by the arm and led her back to the bed. "You look sick."

"Gee, thanks. Nice to see you too, sister-dear."

"I'm serious," Sora replied. "The hobgoblin's attack must have injured you worse than we thought."

"It's not the hobgoblin attack," Solara responded. "My head is still ringing and I'm a bit dizzy, but I'll recover."

"What is it then?"

"I don't know, some kind of illness, I haven't been able to kick it for a few weeks now."

Sora regarded her for a moment, compassion in her eyes, then she stood up and her features quickly returned to the state of anger she had administered when she first walked in.

"It is good to see you," Solara said, trying to calm her younger sister down.

"If it's so good to see me, why haven't you come before?" Sora screamed at her.

Solara breathed deeply to steady herself. She would rather face the hobgoblin hunting party alone than having to try and explain herself to her baby sister. "We are mystral. I followed the old code of our people."

"Old," Sora sternly repeated. "If you haven't noticed, the new code is pretty much staying in seclusion and not letting the world remember that we even exist."

"He risked his life to save mother and me," Solara said back, her tone increasing to match Sora's.

"Good job—mother is dead and you vanished without a trace," Sora scoffed.

"When I was able to, I returned and explained what happened."

"Sure, then you ran right off again because your knight needed you," Sora shook her head. "What about me?"

"What about you?" Solara repeated. "I'm just grateful that you were ill that morning. If you weren't stuck in bed yourself, you would have been with us. How would you have liked that? You would be dead, Sora!"

"Then I'd be dead. Instead, I had to grow up on my own. I was only seven at the time!"

"You look good to me," Solara commented as she studied her sister more closely. Sora's hair was in disarray, frizzled and frayed, but it looked good on her. She had on an outfit very similar to the one that Solara normally wore, only that she had thick, padded red gloves that extended to her elbows.

Sora glared at her sister without saying a word. Her contempt was obvious.

Solara rubbed her head and then returned Sora's stare. "I'm sorry," she said sincerely. "I did not wish to hurt you."

"You think being sorry will change anything?"

"I'm hoping that it's a start," Solara said. "We had a great relationship when we were younger. I want to reclaim that."

Sora emitted a boisterous laugh. "When I was younger, I practically worshipped you!"

"I never asked for worship," Solara whispered.

"Yeah, well I learned soon enough that it was misplaced."

"Sora, I regret leaving you behind. I regret you having to grow up on your own. I regret that that bastard came into our lives. But I do not regret the decision I made. I made it with the honor and ideals of our people, and I stand by it."

"I regret that bastard coming into our lives too," Sora agreed. "May Braksis rot in Tanorus for all eternity."

"Braksis?" Solara asked. She jumped up out of bed and stepped closer to Sora. "May Braksis *rot?*"

"Wrong bastard?" Sora asked innocently.

"Wrong bastard. I was talking about Durgin."

"Oh, sure you were," Sora said. "Of course. When you say bastard, I just thought of the one that took you away from me."

"He was a great man," Solara said while trying to repress a tear.

"Was?" Sora repeated. "Past tense?"

"Yes," Solara slumped back down on the bed. "I watched him die."

A small grin escaped Sora's lip, but she quickly sat down to comfort her sister. "What happened?"

"The same man that killed our mother, along with Braksis's cousin attacked him when he was alone and defenseless. I tried desperately to get to him in time, but I was delayed by goblins. When I finally reached him, I watched as he plummeted to his death."

Sora sat there, a myriad of reactions forming in her mind. She was resentful of the man that had taken her sister from her, but she just watched as Solara, her big sister, turned into a weeping baby at the thought of losing him. Seeing this, she could only feel compassion and sympathy for Solara.

The two embraced for several minutes, neither speaking again as Solara continued to cry. Then she backed away and tried to regain her composure. "I don't know what's come over me," she said with a sigh. "I usually don't break down like that. Instead, I try to focus my emotions and let them drive me."

"Drive you for what?"

"To find and kill Durgin and Rawthorne," Solara clutched her fist and boldly declared. "Where is my armor and weapons? As long as Durgin still breathes, I cannot rest."

"Hold on a minute," Sora cautioned. "You're in no condition to go after Durgin now, but you will be shortly."

"What do you mean?"

"The High Dragoness wishes to see you," Sora informed her. "She said that it was imperative. After that, several other members of the Sisterhood are already preparing to go after Durgin for what he has done. He will not escape."

Solara closed her eyes for a moment. "Zanafaly wants to see me?"

"Yes, she was adamant about it."

"Do you know why?" Solara asked.

"We'll find out when we get there."

Solara grimaced, wishing to resume pursuing Durgin now. "Where is the girl I was with, the timber wolf, and horses?"

"They are safe," Sora answered. "You'll see them again after you visit the High Dragoness."

"Very well, let's get this over with then," Solara said impatiently. She did not know how long she was unconscious for, nor did she know which way Durgin was going. Whatever the High Dragoness wanted, she hoped that it would not take long; the longer she waited, the colder Durgin's trail grew. That man would not escape her.

Sora led the way outside, and Solara had to pause as she looked at the caverns that were the home of the mystral—very little had changed since she was here last. The tunnels behind the waterfall were deep, and the mystral had created a network of homes, shops, and other facilities. Along the walls were crafted images of dragons, their heads pointed up and flames leaping from their mouths, illuminating Dragon's Myst.

The two sisters walked deeper into the caverns, descending to a lower depth. Solara spotted a woman that looked familiar. As she regarded her, the woman stopped and walked over.

"Sister Solara, it is good to see you up and about again," she said.

Solara regarded her for a moment. She had long flowing raven hair, the mark of the black dragon upon her brow, and eyes the color of the purest silver. She wore black dragon-scaled armor with knee-high boots, and a glove encasing her entire right arm, and another on only her left hand. She had two drantanas fastened to her belt, with a bow and quiver upon her back.

"I'm sorry, I know you were the one that helped me by the lake, but do I know you?" Solara asked, searching her memory.

"Don't tell me you forgot all about your old friend Atindra?" the raven-haired mystral asked with mock disappointment.

"Atindra?" Solara laughed. "By the dragons, you look great!"

Sora glanced back and forth. "What? So she lost some weight, what's the big deal?"

Solara glanced at her sister, horrified.

"Do not get upset with her old friend—I did indeed lose weight."

Solara looked back and tried to visualize her childhood friend in the woman she saw standing before her now. Atindra was muscular, and there was absolutely no sign that this was the portly child she once knew. "You do look great."

"Thank you," Atindra smiled. "I feel great."

"Are you the one helping me to go after Durgin?" Solara asked.

Atindra glanced over at Sora, then back to Solara. "I am preparing a hunting party to go after him now," she said.

"Excellent," Solara replied. "I look forward to us traveling together again. It will be like old times."

Atindra and Sora exchanged a glance again, and then she bowed to Solara. "We will speak again after you see the High Dragoness."

"You can count on it," Solara agreed.

Sora grabbed her hand and started to drag her away. "Come on, we need to go."

"I see you still haven't learned patience," Solara observed as she shook her head.

The two resumed their descent down the tunnel. They came to a long spiraling stairwell, and journeyed deep into the depths of Dragon's Myst. Once they reached the bottom, the dragon flames were no longer illuminating their path. Instead, a light-blue mist swirled around them, bright enough for them to see.

As Sora led Solara on, the elder sister regarded their surroundings. She had never been down here before, nor had she ever met Zanafaly, though she had heard many stories—none of which did justice to the craftsmanship and beauty of their surroundings. The blue mist was intoxicating, bringing forth a sense of elation, joy, and anticipation for where they were going. The walls of the circular cavern they entered were intricately crafted to appear like glistening dragon scales. Solara was quite impressed.

"We're almost there," Sora said.

She led them out of the tunnel and into a large opening. As Solara scanned the surroundings, she felt that this cavern was at least as large as the one that housed Vorstad. The illuminating mists were all around them, encompassing everything. Three mystral stepped forward, each wearing a long white ceremonial robe. Their shoulders were covered with golden dragon-scale shoulder pads. Upon their heads were finely-crafted helmets forged in the image of a dragon. Along their backs were folded golden wings of dragons. They also had strands of golden lace swirling up their arms and legs.

"Sister Solara, welcome," one of them greeted pleasantly. "The High Dragoness will be most pleased to see you."

Solara studied the room more thoroughly. She saw hundreds of the Dragonesses scattered around small bubbling pools in the ground. Some of the pools had mystral garbed similar to what she now wore, though in different colors. Tensing, she realized what must have been going on. The High Dragoness wished to see her because it was her time to become impregnated by the Essence of the Dragon.

"Thank you for bringing her, Sister Sora," one of the Dragonesses said.

"You're welcome," Sora replied as she glanced at her sister, seeing a betrayed look on her face.

"You may go now."

"Very well," Sora replied with a short bow as she backed away and left Solara alone with the three Dragonesses.

"This way," one Dragoness said as she led Solara deeper into the room. Taking a deep breath, Solara followed, hoping that she could find some way to talk her way out of this one.

CHAPTER 44

His lungs feeling like they were going to burst, Durgin kept forcing himself to take another step, and then another. Every few feet he glanced back, certain that the silver-haired witch would be there, laughing at him, taunting him. He had stopped to rest several times, and each time, he was awakened with the feeling that she was above him, laughing at him, and telling him that he was nothing, a pathetic excuse for a man.

Pausing by a tree, he breathed deeply several times and studied the forest behind him. Could he have lost her? Was he finally safe? A slight breeze flowed towards him; the leaves and grasses started blowing. Durgin's eyes widened, convinced that the witch was coming, and this was a sign.

Turning, he began to run again, knowing that soon he would reach the small town of Bimbadine. He hoped that there he could find some way to hide or escape from the silver-haired witch. He had plundered this town before; perhaps they would still fear him. Fear him enough to give him a horse to escape with. Yes, he decided. He would get a horse in Bimbadine and be gone before the witch could track him further.

Glancing back again, he continued running headlong into a tree. As he fell back, he hit the ground solidly, and lay there unconscious longer than he would have liked.

As he tried to stand up, he felt a lump by his left ear where he had hit a tree root. It sent excruciating pain pulsating through his neck and shoulder when he touched it. The pain was so bad he almost passed out again. The thought that the mystral were almost certainly upon him though kept him alert.

Studying his surroundings, he saw a trail of smoke off in the distance. Picking up his axe, he ran towards the dark smoke streaking into the sky. This time, he was much more cautious to make sure he did not run into anything again.

The smoke was coming from a small farmhouse. Durgin did not see anyone outside, but could hear singing and music within. He glanced around several times to make sure that nobody else was watching him, and then ran to the front door. As he got there, he kicked the wooden door in, and stepped inside with his axe firmly held in both hands.

The music came to a sudden halt, and Durgin studied the people inside. It was a large family, ten in all. It appeared to be a father and mother, three sons and five daughters. Durgin did not say anything, he only growled as he looked at the family, his axe ready.

The father stepped forward. "Now see here, you can't just go barging into people's houses like this!"

Durgin lunged forward, swinging his axe and plunging it deeply into the father's chest. He held him there for a moment as his eyes gleamed watching the pain of the man's last moments of life. When he was finally dead, he pulled his axe out, allowing the man to fall to the ground, blood beginning to seep around him.

Durgin smiled and scanned the room again. Some of the women were screaming. The three other sons were grabbing what they called weapons. One had a sword, but the other two only had a kitchen knife and the wooden leg of a chair. Durgin emitted another feral growl and charged into the room.

The young man with the sword tried to engage him first, but Durgin sidestepped him and watched the man trip over his father's body. Durgin then swung around and punched the son with the kitchen knife in the face. As he stammered back, Durgin swung his axe and severed his head.

More screaming ensued, and the young man with the chair leg charged, crying that he would pay for what he did. Durgin just waited for him, not even moving. As the wooden leg swung towards him, Durgin reached up and grabbed the smaller man's arm, halting his attack in mid-swing. He squeezed his arm so hard that the man cried out and dropped his weapon. Durgin then twisted his arm, and severed it with his axe.

As he fell back screaming, the brother with the sword charged in again. Durgin parried several strikes from the sword, and then batted it away. With both hands holding the axe high, he brought it slicing down as if the man's head were a melon.

With a maniacal glare, he glanced back at the only remaining man, the one with the severed arm. He hurtled his axe through the air, embedding it into the man's chest. "His crying was getting to me," Durgin snickered.

The six women continued to cry and scream, but none of them stepped towards Durgin to confront him, even though he was now unarmed without his axe.

"Quiet!" he screamed at them, his eyes looking as if he was lost in his own insanity. "I said quiet!" he roared again.

The mother gathered her daughters around, trying to shield their eyes and comfort them. She did not know what this villain intended, but after seeing what he had done, she certainly did not want to inspire his wrath to come down on them for being too noisy.

"That's better," Durgin said as he grinned sinisterly. Walking quickly, he searched the small farmhouse and found some rope. He then tied up each of the women so that they were unable to escape.

Satisfied with his work, he walked over and pulled his axe from his final victim, and then walked to the windows, searching the forest thoroughly for any signs of the silver-haired witch. Seeing that she was not there, a sense of relief overcame him. He managed to devastate another family, and his demon did not return. Perhaps she was not tracking him anymore after all?

He enjoyed that sentiment. Even if she were after him, he was growing stronger with each and every kill. Looking at the women tied up, he wondered whether he should just take a horse and flee, or whether he should perform the task of a true Warlord and enjoy the spoils of his victory.

The decision was quickly made. He needed to regain his confidence. He would flee later. Now, he had to perform his duties. Studying the six tied-up women, he saw one that looked very similar to the witch that was tracking him. Smiling, he decided that she was the perfect choice. She may not be the mystral, but she was close enough.

Reaching down, he untied her wrists and smiled. "You're first."

CHAPTER 45

Solara was led deeper into the large cavern where another small tunnel was located. The three Dragonesses led her in, and Solara stopped at the end as she saw a throne shaped like a dragon with its wings spread. High Dragoness Zanafaly stood in front of it and smiled at her. Along her sides were half a dozen other Dragonesses.

Zanafaly was similarly garbed as the other Dragonesses, but she had a long flowing dragon scale cape that dragged behind her. "Welcome, Sister Solara," she said.

"An honor, High Dragoness," Solara said as she dropped to one knee and bowed.

"It is good that you have returned to us," Zanafaly commented as she sat down on the throne.

"May I ask what is so urgent?" Solara asked as she glanced up at the one mystral that held more power and influence than even the queen.

"Well, I see that your time with the humans has deteriorated your mystral sense of decorum," Zanafaly frowned. "As you wish, though. You return to us without the one you were sworn to protect?"

"I have," Solara commented. "I fear that Warlord Braksis has perished."

"You were unable to prevent it?"

"I was," Solara confirmed.

"Very well, then your sworn duty has hereby been fulfilled. It is good that you have returned."

"I'm sorry, High Dragoness, but I have only returned because my quest has led me here," Solara started to explain.

"Fate has led you home," Zanafaly smiled.

"No, a murderous tyrant has led me here. He is one of the two responsible for murdering Braksis, and he also wishes to kill as many mystral as possible."

"I see," Zanafaly stated as if she was merely humoring Solara.

"I cannot possibly return until I have my revenge. These men will die at my hands."

"I am most disturbed by the anger and hatred that is deep within you, child," Zanafaly said as she stood up. "You must learn to release this and return to the Sisterhood where you belong."

"I will return when my quest is complete, not before," Solara challengingly replied.

"I'm afraid that I cannot permit that," Zanafaly calmly responded. "You are already beyond your twentieth year. It is long past time for you to perform the ritual of the Essence of the Dragon."

"No," Solara sternly objected.

Zanafaly studied her for a moment. "Arise," she said.

Solara stood back up and looked directly at the elder mystral.

Zanafaly reached out her hand and touched Solara's stomach. Her eyes widened in terror and she backed away hissing at Solara. "You have been soiled!"

Solara looked at her in shock. She could not understand how the High Dragoness could have possibly known about that one time that she and Braksis were together, especially by a mere touch alone.

"You have violated the laws of the mystral. You have allowed yourself to be soiled by a man," Zanafaly declared, her voice rising. The other Dragonesses in the room all looked horrified.

"I can explain," Solara pleaded.

"There is no explanation," Zanafaly said, regaining her composure. "Sister Solara, daughter of Selina, you have violated the ancient codes of the mystral. Our heritage and codes are sacred to us, and you have willingly defied them. Even your tone and demeanor with me has been confrontational. As such, I see no alternative other than to banish you from Dragon's Myst forevermore."

"Banish?" Solara gasped. She may not be ready to return now, but the thought of never being welcome home again was staggering.

"From this day forward, you will no longer be considered a mystral. You are dead to us." Raising her two arms, she beckoned the other Dragonesses in the room, who walked over and grabbed Solara by both arms and dragged her away.

Solara watched the High Dragoness as she was dragged out, the pure disappointment evident on her face. All she wanted to know, though, was how could Zanafaly know about her and Braksis?

CHAPTER 46

Standing with her back to the wall, Shiel waited as several guards walked by. Things were becoming much more dangerous and risky around the palace. If Winton knew that she was out, she thought that he would definitely lash out at her. An experience she hoped she never had to go through again.

When the guards passed, she turned into the medical facilities and saw the doctor leaning over Centain. She glanced around to make sure that they were alone and then walked all the way in. "How is he doctor?"

The doctor looked up. "Shiel? What brings you here?"

Shiel looked away, not wanting to face the doctor. She found a chair and sat down, avoiding his questioning glare.

"What is it?"

"I'm sorry, doctor," she said. "Is it possible that you could provide me with some bandages and medicine for the handmaidens?"

"Of course," the doctor said. "Is everyone all right?"

Shiel bit her lower lip, and then looked up at the man. "I'm afraid not," she said.

"Tell me, what's wrong?"

"It's our new Emperor," she said. "He seems to think that the Empress's handmaidens are now his own private harem to do with as he wishes."

"That's horrible!" the doctor said, aghast.

"Do you have anything?" she asked again.

The doctor smiled. "I may have exactly what you are looking for."

He stood up and walked over to a cabinet. Reaching in, he pulled out a small bottle. "Here you go."

"What's this?"

"Put two drops in his drink and he'll be sound asleep within five minutes."

Shiel giggled at the thought. "A sleeping potion?"

"Yes," the doctor smiled back. "Hopefully he'll be willing to have a drink first."

"I'll get him to drink," Shiel grinned cunningly. "Will you get in trouble for this?"

The doctor shook his head. "I'm already in trouble—ever since the attack on the palace, my life has been threatened many times. I get the distinct impression that people want this poor man dead."

Shiel stood up and looked down at the Captain of the Guards. "Will he live?"

"Doubtful," the doctor said. "There is nothing more I can do for him. I just wish that the people threatening me would realize that."

"There has to be something that can be done," Shiel said.

"I'm just trying to keep him alive. Maybe a healing potion or Mage Healer will show up and assist me."

"If I could help you, I would," Shiel said.

"No, don't worry, you have enough on your own mind," he said. "It's a shame we couldn't somehow smuggle you out of the palace."

Shiel's eyes widened. "Smuggle us out? Where would we go?"

"Well, I know you're not soldiers, but I have heard that Captain Angel is taking on recruits for a light-foot military unit—Warlord Braksis's suggestion before he left."

Shiel considered this for a moment. "Is the Captain in Trespias?"

"All military units were recalled by Winton. I would certainly presume so," the doctor surmised.

"Thank you, doctor," Shiel said. "You have not only helped us, but you may have provided us with options."

"Don't get caught," he said, his voice now serious. "Things are not the way they were when the Empress was here."

"Of that I am well aware," Shiel agreed. "Thank you again."

As she prepared to leave, she took one last look at Centain and wished that she could somehow help him. Perhaps, she thought, if they did escape, she could find a healing potion and somehow manage to get it back for the Captain. As she walked out, she smiled at the thought: that was exactly what she would try to do!

CHAPTER 47

Sora turned and was stunned to see Solara being escorted by two Dragonesses. Jogging over, she looked at the trio. "What's going on?"

"This one has been banished from Dragon's Myst. She is no longer a mystral. You are now a single child, Sister Sora."

Sora glanced up at Solara who had an unreadable expression on her face. "What happened?"

"She was deemed a heretic," the Dragoness declared loudly for any around to hear.

"Can I at least get my armor and weapons back?" Solara asked.

"You are no longer mystral, and will not be adorned with any of our things," the Dragoness declared.

"What about Leora, Tiot, and my horses?"

"Those outsiders will be returned."

"I should hope so," Solara commented, an underlying threat evident in her remark.

"Silence tramp!" one Dragoness scolded as she backhanded Solara across the mouth. "We will hear no more of your insolence."

Sora watched as the three walked away. Her mouth was open, confusion on her face. A hand was placed on her shoulder. She spun around and saw Atindra looking down at her.

"What does this mean?"

"This means that Solara is no longer considered a mystral. If you see her, you treat her as an enemy."

Sora pulled her shoulder away. "She's my sister."

Atindra nodded. "That she was; but in the eyes of the mystral, she is no longer."

"I won't accept that," Sora sneered. "If she's no longer a mystral, then I'm no longer a mystral."

"Consider what you are saying," Atindra cautioned. "There is no coming back if you follow this path."

"I wouldn't want to come back," Sora angrily snapped. She then ran back to her home. Once she stepped inside, she pulled out several satchels and began filling them with her personal belongings. Pausing, she walked into Solara's room and grabbed the stuffed dragon; smiling, she thought that her big sister might actually get a kick out of it.

With her bags packed, she went to a locked cabinet and opened it up. Inside were her two glaives, her prized possessions. The three razor sharp blades on each glaive were shaped like the wings of a dragon. She fastened them on her belt, and then withdrew her two drantanas and slid them into their scabbards over her back. The last weapon she took was her dagger, which she sheathed in her boot.

Glancing outside briefly to make certain that nobody saw, she walked back in and took Solara's armor and boots out as well. She knew that when a mystral was banished that they were not allowed to have any representations of their people, but she wasn't about to let her sister go after her mother's killer without being prepared. The elongated mystral sword, a dagger, and a few throwing knives were also there, all of which she placed in the last satchel. Knotting the straps and slinging the satchels over her shoulders, she walked out of her home, never to look back.

The Dragonesses led Solara beyond the waterfall and stood her in the open. She could see the horses, Tiot, and Leora. Tiot was tense and began growling at the Dragonesses. Solara shook her head no and raised her hand, beckoning him to calm down.

One of the Dragonesses then pulled out a small dagger and cut her clothes from her. "These are the ritual garments of those that receive the honor of being touched by the Essence of the Dragon. You do not deserve to leave with even so much."

Leora watched as the clothing was cut from Solara and cried out.

Solara knew that the poor child had been through so much, and there was no way she could know what was happening. Pausing to think, Solara herself couldn't quite understand exactly what was happening.

The other Dragoness threw some filthy clothes at her. "These rags were taken from the slain hobgoblins. Even they are too good for the likes of you."

"You are most generous," Solara sarcastically replied with a polite smile.

The Dragoness backhanded her again. "I have wasted all the time I will on scum like you." She spat on Solara and returned to the waterfall.

Solara reached down and began putting on the tattered hobgoblin garments. The mystral warrior that was standing with Leora, Tiot, and the horses walked past her without even a glance.

As soon as she, too, was gone, Leora ran over and hugged her. "Are you ok? I was so frightened!"

"I'm fine now," Solara said. "We will be better when we are away from here."

"Not dressed like that, you won't," Sora said as she stepped out from behind the waterfall. "Do you have room for one more in your party?"

"Sora, what are you doing? You could get in trouble just for talking to me."

"I guess I'm in real trouble then," she said with a grin as she reached into her satchel and pulled out Solara's armor. "Here."

Solara stood there for a moment regarding her sister. "You're sure about this?"

"You're not leaving me behind again," she said. "Where you go, I go."

Solara smiled, and then picked up her armor and wardrobe from Sora. "Thank you," she said.

"Anytime," Sora responded. "What are sisters for?"

Another figure stepped out from behind the waterfall. It was Atindra. "I see that there is no talking you out of this?"

"Nope," Sora stubbornly grinned.

"I figured as much," Atindra nodded. "I will make this quick. My group is going after Durgin at first light tomorrow. That gives you about a five-hour head start. If he is dead before we find him, I will not weep."

Solara nodded to her childhood friend. "Thank you, old friend."

"I haven't done anything to thank me for... yet," she grinned.

"Yet?" Solara asked.

"Well, if memory serves, you had two drantanas that you lost in the lake?"

"Yes," Solara slowly replied.

"Then two more are yours," she said as she tossed two sheathed drantanas to Solara. She also pulled a bow and three quivers full of arrows and handed them to Sora. "I know that neither of you are big on archery, but this could come in handy."

"Thank you again," Solara said. "I don't know what to say."

"Say nothing," Atindra replied. She pulled out one more box. "Here are enough throwing knives to last you a while."

Solara nodded her approval and gratitude.

Stepping over to Leora, Atindra smiled. "I know you are young, Little One, but I have this for you too." She handed a dagger to the child, which looked like a small sword in her hands. "It was mine when I was your age. We share the same shade of hair, so now we shall share the same weapon."

Leora glanced up at the smiling mystral and nodded her thanks as she took the dagger.

"That is all I can do for you," Atindra said as she turned and looked at Solara.

"You have done too much already," Solara returned.

"You know that with banishment, I am breaking the code by talking to you?"

"Yes," Solara admitted.

"Good, then remember that for when we meet again. A code means nothing to me when it concerns a good friend."

Solara and Atindra embraced, and then the raven-haired mystral returned to Dragon's Myst. Solara quickly finished dressing and arming herself, and then looked at Sora and Leora. "Let's go finish this."

CHAPTER 48

Solara followed Tiot, but did not really need to. The trail that Durgin left behind was obvious. It was as if the Warlord wished for them to know where he had gone. As she followed the path, she had a distinct feeling that he was heading towards the human town of Bimbadine, and once there, he could be preparing an ambush for them.

The morning sun was upon them, and Solara could make out a small farmhouse in the distance. She paused and glanced down at Tiot, who was tensing and ready to spring into action. The path they were following led directly to the house.

"What is it?" Sora asked. "Why did we stop?"

Solara turned and looked at her sister. "I think he is in that farmhouse. I want you and Tiot to stay here and make sure nothing happens to Leora."

"But—"

"No buts," Solara adamantly replied. "Protect Leora."

Sora glared angrily at her older sister, but refrained from saying anything else. Solara pat Tiot on the head and slowly made her way towards the farmhouse. She circled behind and hoped to be able to look inside and try to find out where Durgin was, if he really was still here.

She dropped low and began crawling along the ground, her eyes moving constantly to take in the details of her surroundings. She did not want to miss anything. Things seemed quiet though, at least in the yard. As she neared the building, she heard sniffles and whimpers, like people were trying to fight the urge to cry.

Crawling to the back wall, she paused, and then turned around so her back was against the building. Slowly, she rose up towards a window, hoping to peer inside and see if she could determine what was going on. As she glanced in, there was nobody there, and nothing out of place.

Closing her eyes to listen and concentrate, she heard a female voice, barely audible, whimpering, "Please don't," over and over. There were definitely people there, and Durgin was amongst them. She was certain. She just wasn't sure exactly where, and she didn't want to do anything foolish or impulsive and risk the Warlord taking any more lives.

As Solara began moving around the farmhouse to look into another window, she stopped short, hearing a knock on the door. She froze, waiting to see what happened. A loud bang came from inside, and then the front door opened. Solara could hear some speaking, and then heard the distinctive laugh of her sister.

Solara ran towards the front door and watched as Sora ran away, and a hunched over Durgin limped after her. She didn't want to let her sister face him alone, but she figured that Sora was faster, and hopefully could evade him until she made sure everyone inside was all right.

"Please don't," the silver-haired daughter begged. "Please don't."

"Shut up!" Durgin said as he grabbed her chin with his left hand to hold her steady. "You can't move. This must be perfect." With his right hand, he dabbed his brush in the ink and brought it up to her forehead, continuing to paint a dragon upon her brow.

The young woman was tied down to the bed. Each limb firmly restrained by rope to each of the four bedposts. She had thought that she was going to be violated by the giant, sweating man the night before, but he had been ranting and raving that he needed to prepare her, that he needed to conquer the silver-haired witch, and then he began painting upon her brow. She wasn't sure what he intended, but she was terrified.

"I said, stop moving," he screamed, tightening his grip on her chin.

A knock on the front door made him tense up. He released her and turned to look at the closed door to the bedroom. He started breathing more heavily through his nose, clearly annoyed by the disruption. Glancing back at the girl, he studied his work and frowned. "I'm not ready yet."

There was another knock, and this time Durgin leapt up, infuriated. He walked to the bedroom door and kicked it open, creating a loud bang as it swung and hit the wall. "How dare somebody interrupt me?"

As he walked towards the front door, he paused and glared at the other women tied up. "Not a peep out of you, or you're all dead," he threatened, smiling sinisterly, then turned away and opened the door.

Outside, he saw a short, blonde-haired mystral smiling at him. The sight of a mystral calmed him only slightly—this was not the silver-haired witch, but one of the creatures he had sworn to kill. "You picked the wrong house," he growled.

"I'm sure," Sora said as she spun and kicked him in the groin. As he fell backwards, both hands on his genitals as he cried out in pain, Sora began laughing and ran away.

"I'll kill you for that!" he roared with a pained squeak in his voice. He slowly started pursuing her at a hobbled limp, determined to make the mystral suffer for attacking him.

Sora paused at the threat, placed her thumbs in her ears, stuck her tongue out at him, and waggled her fingers. She waited until he was almost upon her, and then turned and ran further away, stopping to taunt him again when she was at a safe distance.

"I'll strangle the life out of you, bitch!"

Solara stepped inside the farmhouse, not certain whether she was grateful that Sora had disobeyed her and had made this easier, or whether she would kill her herself for putting her life in jeopardy. Once she saw the walls and floor covered with blood, she lost all thought of anger towards Sora, and knew that Durgin would not be walking away from her this day. One way or the other, this would end today.

As she scanned the room, she saw five women tied up and crying, with the remains of four men scattered around. She paused in shock when she saw Durgin's axe leaning against a cabinet. The fool had been so furious at Sora that he ran after her without any weapons.

Removing her dagger, she kneeled down next to the first woman and began to cut her bonds. "There is nothing to fear now," she tried to sound reassuring. "He is gone. I will protect you."

She cut the bonds of the five women, and saw that they were all still traumatized. Even when freed, only the elder woman moved, and that was to an adjoining bedroom to check on another daughter. With a terrified cry, she yelled out, "Tabata?"

Solara followed the weeping mother in and paused as she considered what she saw. The girl could be no older that seventeen and had silvery hair, similar to hers. She was tied naked to the bed, her legs forced apart by the binds. Upon her brow was a half-painted image of a dragon.

The mother stood in the doorway, stunned by what she saw. "Tabata?"

"Mother," the girl called back with a panicked sob.

Rushing past the mother, Solara cut the girl free. "Did he hurt you?"

"No," the girl said in a whimper. "I think he would have, but he was trying to finish what he was painting before he injured me at all."

Solara brushed her hand through her hair and revealed her dragon emblem. "He was drawing this."

The mother glanced at her, seeming to finally regain her composure now that her daughter was cut free. "What is going on?"

"That man killed my mother and mate. I had once hurt him, but did not kill him. I think in some sick sadistic way, he is trying to turn his victims into me since he cannot strike me down himself."

"Will you kill him?" Tabata asked, her eyes stern.

Solara nodded. "I shall."

"Then the world will be a better place," she answered. "Shouldn't you be going now? Make him suffer."

Solara did not need to speak again. She placed a hand on the girl's shoulder for a moment, and then turned and walked out. Durgin had a lot to answer for. He would be forced to atone for all of that this day.

"You're going to die, bitch!" Durgin roared. "Slowly. Like all of your stinking kind." He did not know why she had suddenly knocked on his door and attacked him, but all he wanted to do was strangle the life out of her. She was young, and in the back of his mind he considered her dangerous, but right now, he couldn't care less.

Bending down, he picked up a rock the size of his fist and hurtled it towards the mystral. She dodged easily, and then laughed again.

"If this is a throwing contest, you're going to lose." She then crossed both of her arms, and with a short leap, snapped both arms out and released two glaives spinning towards Durgin.

"No," Durgin cried as he dropped down, using his arms to try and protect his face. One of the glaives barely grazed his leg, but the other struck with much more accurate force, severing his lower right arm.

Screaming in pain, Durgin clutched his severed limb. The pain was excruciating. He almost passed out, but refused to allow another mystral child to stop him. Wincing, he struggled to see her again and watched as she caught both weapons, laughing at him, mockingly.

Durgin jumped forward and charged at her. Sora was unprepared, thinking that he was too hurt to continue. He rammed into her and knocked her down on her back. Straddling her, he took his one good hand, grabbed her hair, and began slamming her head into the ground. The only sound coming from his lips was a steady growl.

Sora cried with each blow, feeling as if her head was splitting open.

She tried to hit him with the two glaives in her hands, but her limbs felt weak, and she could hardly move. With another shove down, the world turned black, and she lost consciousness.

"Durgin!"

Durgin froze, too afraid to move. The voice was the same as that from his nightmares of the silver-haired witch. Slowly, he released his grip on Sora, and watched as her head slowly fell into the pool of their combined blood. Turning, he saw Solara, standing several feet away from him holding a sword and ready for him.

"Get away from her," she threatened.

Durgin's entire body trembled. He was not ready for this yet. How could he face the witch, especially now that he had lost a limb? He was too weak.

"I said, get away from her."

Durgin stirred, but as he stood up, he pulled one of Sora's drantanas from its scabbard. He kept his back to Solara for a moment as he breathed steadily to calm himself. Knowing that he could not postpone this fight, this final challenge to regain his former glory, he turned, snarling at the witch.

Solara held her elongated mystral sword and stood ready. She saw Durgin as he was attacking Sora, and only hoped that she was all right. If someone else important to her perished by the hands of this madman, she was not certain that she could handle it. As it was, she knew that this battle had to end quickly so she could get to Sora and try to save her.

She stared into his eyes and watched as he charged towards her, a drantana swinging at her head. Solara easily parried the blow and held Durgin's gaze. The man was feral, as if his humanity was lost. Each breath was an animalistic snarl. His attacks were little better, just swinging at her, hoping to knock her back with brute-strength alone.

Solara kept moving swiftly, making sure she was well-braced for his attacks. He was relentless, and though she easily blocked his advances, she was unable to counterattack at all. He kept coming and coming.

His bloodied stump shot out and hit her in the head. She backed away quickly, wiping blood from her eyes, but was shocked to see that he had dropped his sword and was screaming, clutching his arm again. It was as if he had forgotten that he had lost it.

Pausing for another moment, he bent down to pick up his sword and started running towards her. Solara pulled a throwing knife and hurled it with accuracy towards his left hamstring. The blade sunk deeply, but Durgin kept charging her. She removed several more knives in quick succession, sending them towards the rampaging warlord. Each one pierced his legs, but he ignored the pain and slammed into her.

As Solara dropped, she removed her dagger and rammed it up into the man's stomach. Durgin did not scream. He acted as if he was not even hurt. He just continued breathing heavily, a glare of pure hatred washed over his face. Not wanting to suffer the same fate as Sora, Solara turned the dagger in her hand and started pushing down with all of her might.

Durgin did not scream: he just stopped with a look of agony and shock. Using the delay, Solara pushed the two-hundred-and-fifty-nine-pound Warlord off of her. Jumping up, she smiled to see that the dagger hit its mark, jutting from his pelvis. "That was for Leora," she said.

Durgin pulled the dagger and winced. Slowly trying to stand up, Solara took another throwing knife and flung it straight at his severed arm. The blade dug into his bloody stump and Durgin dropped back again, tears flowing from his eyes.

"That was for my mother," Solara sneered.

Raising his head to look at her, Solara kicked him and sent it slamming back down to the ground. "That was for Sora." Pausing, she turned and started to walk away. She could hear Durgin struggling to get up behind her. She listened carefully for his movements. As she heard the drantana being dragged up off of the ground, she spun around, pulled her own two swords, and dug them into his chest. "That was for Braksis."

She held his gaze as the sword dropped from his hand. Confusion crept over his face as he kept blinking, his mouth moving open and closed slowly. Removing her two swords, she watched him crumple to the ground.

Solara jumped on top of him and sat there, staring into his eyes until she was certain that he was dead. "And that was for me," she whispered, not feeling any of the relief or satisfaction she had hoped to have.

Standing up, she ran over to Sora and bent down. She was still breathing, so at least she wasn't dead. Gently picking her up, she carried her back to the farmhouse, hoping that there might be some bandages or medicine available for her. Durgin was dead. Now it was time for the living to go on living.

CHAPTER 49

Atindra led fifteen mystral warriors, known as the Guardians, all fully armored and equipped with mystral weaponry. They arrived at the small farmhouse and Atindra ordered the others to fan out, using intricate hand signals designed by the mystral to communicate.

She silently walked over to the barn and saw the two horses that Solara had used in the stables. Things appeared calm, very calm. Deciding to take a risk, she walked up to the front door and knocked.

A silver-haired woman answered the door with paint upon her brow resembling a dragon. "May I help you?"

Atindra looked confused for a moment until she saw Solara inside. "I am here to see Solara."

The girl glanced inside, and Solara nodded her approval. She then stepped away from the door and allowed Atindra to walk inside.

Atindra glanced around and took in the surroundings. Solara was on the floor with several other women scrubbing at blood. "What happened?"

"Durgin," Solara answered with a single word.

"Has he been taken care of?"

"Yes," Solara answered. "Finally."

"That is a relief," Atindra replied. "What of Sora and your other traveling companions?"

"Sora was injured, but she will recover. Tiot and Leora were not involved."

"I see," Atindra said. "If Sora is hurt, she can return with us. I guarantee her care."

"No," Solara said after a brief pause. "She will stay with me as she wishes."

"You lead a dangerous life. You see that she was hurt right away," Atindra reminded her.

"She will not be in harm's way for long," Solara confidently replied.

"What makes you say this?"

"I am going to travel to Comonor. The Queen there owes me a small debt. I will seek information on the whereabouts of Rawthorne, and then leave Sora and Leora there in her care until I return."

"She will not be happy by that decision," Atindra pointed out.

"She is hurt now, and needs time to recover. Zerilla will be able to give her that time."

Atindra smiled and nodded. "Very well—then I wish you a safe journey, and may Rawthorne also be found and killed quickly."

Solara stood up and embraced her childhood friend. "Thank you, old friend."

"I must be off," Atindra answered. "If Durgin is truly dead, then we must be back to Dragon's Myst. No telling when more of the filthy hobgoblins will decide to show themselves."

"May the dragons look at you with fortune in your struggles," Solara answered. Both women smiled, and then Atindra turned and walked out. Solara watched her go and thought about everything that had happened since Braksis had died. Soon she would find Rawthorne, and then life could finally return to normal. At least as normal as it could be without the man she loved.

CHAPTER 50

Though Kabilian had never been to Tregador before, he was quite impressed by what he had seen already. They reached the base of the Northern Mountains where Tregador was located, only to see that they needed to follow a steep trail. Not wanting to use magic this close to the dwarves, Kabilian led Crick up the mountain on foot.

The trail was very smooth and had roped railings along each side of the path. The mountain on the other side of the railings was much higher than the passage where they walked, clearly showing the hard work and time the dwarves spent cutting the rock down to provide easy access to their city. The trail was also wide enough for at least three decent-sized wagons to be driven side by side to the dwarven city for trade.

In fact, as they ascended, several wagons were leaving Tregador and passed them. They had both centaurs and gnomes in the group, all of which eyed the two companions suspiciously. Several centaurs appeared ready to attack Kabilian and Crick on sight, but Kabilian bent over, bowed, and very pleasantly greeted them. The others in the caravan suggested they forget about them and keep moving.

Kabilian turned and watched them leave, waving at them. He knew that they were from Underwood. It was the only community that had both centaurs and gnomes working together—a very prosperous relationship between the two races. He had heard that Underwood was an open trade community to all races, with the minor exception of humans, whom the centaurs despised.

He was curious though—the wagons were filled with armor, lances, and other glistening weapons of extremely proficient craftsmanship.

He wondered if this armament was in direct correlation to what was happening in Trespias, or whether it was because of Crick's fellow hobgoblins and their increased presence in the Suspintian Forest.

As the group vanished from sight behind a bend in the trail, Kabilian turned and continued on the path. Behind him, Crick slowly followed, though he seemed highly timid and uncomfortable about what they were doing. Pausing, Kabilian glanced back at Crick. "There is nothing to fear."

"Easy for you to say—dwarves dislike humans, and will not trust you, but they will listen. I'm a hobgoblin—I'll be killed on sight!"

Kabilian laughed and then removed his left glove, which he tucked into his belt. Reaching into his satchel, he removed a silver ring with a red rose glistening on the top. Holding it up and smiling, he then held it in his bare palm and reassuringly patted Crick on the back. "There is nothing to fear, our salvation is in the palm of my hand."

Crick watched him suspiciously, not understanding how jewelry could somehow be their salvation. If this day resulted in a fight, he felt much more confident with his mystral swords, throwing knives, and arrows.

As they continued, Kabilian saw their destination and smiled with respect for the Tregador dwarves. Unlike most of the dwarves he knew—the warriors of Vorstad, and the miners of Carnelian—these dwarves actually appeared to live on the mountain, and not in it.

The trail led to a large city that could be seen on a flattened expanse of the mountain. Stone buildings towered into the sky with bridges and walkways connecting them. A large wall encased Tregador, with wooden gates as large as the mountain path. As he studied the city, Kabilian felt that the dwarves must have taken every stone they chiseled to make the trail and used it to form a glorious city to live in.

Beside the gate was a long curved horn. Kabilian looked around to see if there were any guards, and was shocked to find none by the doors or on the walls to the city. Bending over, he blew into the horn and heard a long and deep note come from the instrument. He held the note for several seconds, then stood and watched the gate.

"What now?" Crick asked.

"Now we wait," Kabilian shrugged.

Moments later, a bearded face opened a small peephole in the door and looked at them. "What do ye be wantin'?"

Kabilian smiled pleasantly and looked at the dwarf, though he could only see his eyes, nose, and some of his gray beard. He reached up and brushed his ear for a moment, touching several hoop earrings that he wore. Then, in perfect dwarven inflection, he responded. "We are travelers seeking to deliver information and also request a trade."

"Ye be a human and travel with a durned hobgoblin? Be gone, before I be sendin' the Centrinell to be gettin' ye!"

Crick looked back and forth, completely oblivious, for he could not comprehend the dwarven tongue at all, and did not know what his companion and the dwarf were saying.

"Appearances can be deceiving," Kabilian said. "Human and hobgoblin we may be, but evil we are not."

In response, the dwarf slammed the peephole.

Crick looked at Kabilian who only shrugged. "What did he say?"

"He said that they were going to have to properly prepare for guests as honorable as us," Kabilian smiled.

Crick turned his head sideways and gave his human companion a befuddled glare. Kabilian then bent over and blew into the horn a second time. He watched the door, but the peephole did not open again. Instead, he heard a gruff voice from behind him.

"That will be enough o' the blowin'!"

Kabilian turned around to see half a dozen dwarves, all similarly garbed as Baldock in extensive illistrium armored coverings, standing with weapons drawn. He pondered where they had come from. Clearly there was a secret passage or tunnel that allowed them to sneak up behind the visitors, but he had seen no signs of such when they came up the path. "Ah, noble dwarves—so nice of you to send an escort."

"We're not bein' no durned escort, unless ye be wantin' an escort to an early grave." The speaker stood in front of the others, his long, blonde beard and mustache, both reaching his waist. A coif covered his hair, but Kabilian assumed that it flowed almost as long underneath his armor. His gaze was piercing and unrelenting. This dwarf had been hardened by a life of violence and mistrust, and he certainly wasn't going to easily back down to a pair of travelers he considered enemies. He held a finely crafted mace in his hands, and had several small axes fastened to a belt encircling his waist. Kabilian assumed that they must have been throwing axes.

"An early grave?" Kabilian chuckled. "You amuse me dwarf. I assure you, though—we are not here for foul play."

"I'll be the judge o' why ye are here," the blonde-bearded dwarf answered. "And no matter how much o' the dwarven tongue ye be knowin', it won't be savin' ye."

Kabilian grinned in reply, "I did not mean to insult you."

A brown-bearded dwarf standing next to the blonde-haired one stepped forward, his warhammer firmly clutched in both hands. "Let's just be killin' them already, and be done with it. Ye know we can never be trustin' the stinkin' humans and hobgoblins!"

Kabilian reached over and sniffed himself by his armpit. "I will have you know, I take great pride in my personal welfare. However, if I require a bath, I could always return later today."

"Ye be havin' a quick tongue on ye," the brown-haired one said. "Perhaps I'll be cuttin' it out o' yer mouth!"

The blonde-haired dwarf held his arm out to stop his companion. "Who are ye and why are ye here?"

Kabilian bowed respectfully before answering. "I am Kabilian, an adventurer who fancies rare collectibles. My companion is Crick, a rare find himself. His tribe was slaughtered when he was nothing more than an infant, and oddly enough, he was spared when a mystral warrior found him and decided to teach him a more honorable code than that of his people."

To prove his point, Kabilian stepped aside and pointed towards the weapons that Crick was carrying. "These were gifts from his adopted mother before he left Dragon's Myst."

"Bah, this be rubbish!" the brown-bearded dwarf snorted.

"Me brother is right, yer story is farfetched. More likely that ye killed a mystral and stole her weapons."

Kabilian shook his head. "I wish there was something I could do or say to convince you. I assure you, I am not trying to deceive you."

"Ye expect us to be believin' this?" the brown-bearded dwarf snorted again. "Just look at his clothes! He be wearin' tribal colors o' a maraudin' hobgoblin band!"

"Alas, the mystral did not have any clothes that could fit a hobgoblin, so they were forced to garb him in the colors of other hobgoblins that they had slain. The outfit, though, is an insult to the noble Crick. He is most uncomfortable in these garments, and wishes to have something more similar to the mystral he knows and loves. A tribute if you will."

Kabilian glanced around, still seeing skepticism and doubt on the faces of the dwarves. He wasn't going to be able to convince them without help. He opened his hand and slid the ring onto his finger. "It was fortunate that I was passing by. I was on my way here from Trespias with a message from Baldock, and the mystral asked me to show Crick the way to Tregador, the home of the most famous blacksmiths in the entire realm!"

"Ye say ye be knowin' Baldock?" the blonde-bearded dwarf asked.

"Quite well," Kabilian answered. "We met in Trespias where he was representing the dwarves in the unification talks. As an adventurer, I of course was there to see if I could help out with the ever increasing hostilities in the realm. We spent many nights drinking and telling tales. A good friend, Baldock is."

"Don't ye be believin' him!" the brown-bearded dwarf screamed. "Lies on top o' lies, I tell ye!"

Kabilian glanced at the dwarf in awe. His ring typically impacted anyone within a ten-foot radius to him. The dwarf was well within its power, but did not seem phased. "Baldock told me that if ever I came this way, I would always be welcome in his home."

"Bah!" the dwarf snorted again. "Let's just be killin' him."

"Hold yer hammer," the blonde-haired dwarf said. Facing Kabilian, he lowered his mace. "Me apologies fer me brother. He is a suspicious one he is. Any friend o' Baldock's is a friend o' mine."

"I am glad to hear it," Kabilian smiled.

"Me name is Feldrin—I be commandin' the Centrinell until Baldock returns."

Kabilian looked at the dwarf curiously. "Feldrin?" he repeated. "You are the dwarven God of Fury?"

Feldrin laughed for several moments. "Me father be likin' the name. I be full o' fury though, don't ye doubt."

"Then an appropriate name it is," Kabilian said. Trying to probe for more information, he questioned Feldrin further. "Baldock did not mention the Centrinell."

"We be the protectors o' the tunnels," Feldrin explained. "Baldock be our general."

"Impressive," Kabilian said. "Curious that he did not mention it. Of course, he boasted about Rock trolls one night; perhaps I should have looked beyond his words."

"Many Rock trolls fell to our blades," Feldrin grinned triumphantly. "King Kendall hisself will be wantin' news o' his son."

"Ye can't be bringin' 'em in to see the King without proof o' their claim! What if they be assassins sent here to be killin' Kendall?" the brown-bearded dwarf protested.

"Assassins, Veldin? Bah!" Feldrin retorted. "I be tellin' ye, a friend o' Baldock is a friend o' mine."

"Will ye at least disarm 'em?"

Feldrin put his arms around his brother's shoulder. "No need to be insultin' 'em so. We'll be with 'em every step o' the way. I trust that if there is any foul play, suspicious Veldin will split their heads like melons before their plans can be revealed."

All of the dwarves with the exception of Veldin began laughing boisterously. Veldin continued to glare at the two visitors, watching them suspiciously, though he did seem somewhat satisfied by the fact that he could kill them if they tried anything.

Feldrin knocked on the gate and the doors slowly opened. Kabilian removed his ring and replaced it into his satchel while the dwarves were not watching. He then placed his glove back on his hand. As the dwarf led them into Tregador, Kabilian paused to see four ponies on each side of the doors pulling open the mighty barriers. Several dwarves stood on each side as well.

Feldrin nodded, and with the exception of Veldin, the other Centrinell members wandered off into the streets of Tregador. Glancing around, Kabilian was even more impressed now that he was inside the walls of the city: the streets were laid out in cobblestone; the buildings were impressive with chiseled dwarven markings indicating what each one was. They passed dozens of dwarves working at smithies, foundries, and other assorted manufacturers, all molding the illistrium that they mined.

He saw hundreds of dwarves hard at work, but also small taverns with laughter and dwarven hymns heard from within. Sitting on the stairway to one of the buildings, about twenty or so children were sitting, mesmerized by the stories of a gray-bearded dwarf who looked as if he had already seen five centuries in his lifetime.

A small group of eight dwarves caught his attention. He watched as they rolled four empty wagons onto a wooden platform. With one dwarf on each side, they began pulling at a rope and the platform descended.

"Where does that lead?" Kabilian asked.

Feldrin glanced over and laughed. "The mines are deep below us. Illistrium is found deep within the depths o' the Northern Mountains. The deeper ye go, the purer the elements. The lifts will be bringin' minin' parties into different sections o' the mines. We ha' hunnerds o' 'em throughout Tregador, includin' deeper shafts once ye descend into the mines themselves."

"Impressive," Kabilian answered.

"Right through here," Feldrin said, shoving two large wooden doors with both hands, revealing several steps leading to the pillared building. Inside, hundreds of dwarves were feasting at tables that stretched the length of the entire hall. Their conversations were loud, as if each dwarf was trying to shout over those speaking next to him. At the end of the hall was a smaller table that was slightly elevated and faced the entire dining room.

Feldrin led Kabilian and Crick into the hall and down the middle aisle directly towards the head table. Kabilian noted that as they walked through, the dwarves slowly quieted down as they each noticed the newcomers, all of their eyes boring into the two companions.

The head table had three chairs elevated higher than those to their sides. The dwarf in the center was clearly King Kendall, for he wore highly ornamented illistrium armor, with a golden crown atop his brow and a long crimson cape along his back. His long russet hair and beard were braided with golden laces woven through them. As Kabilian looked up at him, he could see that Kendall was the type of dwarf that commanded attention and respect. He assumed that very few that came before the dwarven king would ever leave feeling that they somehow managed to cheat the man.

To his left was a female dwarf who appeared almost elven by her dress. She wore a forest green sheath gown accented with a gauzy red and yellow-gold scarf around her waist, the long gold edges of which cascaded down the front; a matching shawl was draped around her bare shoulders. She was wearing a golden tiara, much smaller than her husband's crown, with her whitish-gray hair trailing loosely down her back.

On the King's right was a younger dwarf that resembled the Queen. They shared the same look and posture, though his beard closely resembled his father's. He was much thinner than the other dwarves around him, and as Kabilian regarded him, he thought that this was a dwarf that would never survive a physical confrontation. He was not even wearing armor like most of the other male dwarves. Instead, he wore a brown loose-fitting short-sleeve shirt tucked into blue pants. His boots matched the shade of his shirt, and extended to his calves.

Feldrin and Veldin both dropped to one knee and bowed before Kendall. Kabilian beckoned Crick to do the same, and they kneeled down slightly behind their two dwarven guides.

Without standing up, Feldrin, with his head still bowed, announced the guests. "Me King, I present Kabilian, an adventurer; and Crick, the adopted son o' a mystral warrior—friends o' yer son Baldock."

A few dwarves gave deep bellowing laughs at the introduction. Kabilian raised his head and glanced around. Some still stared at them with suspicion and awe. As he looked up at Kendall though, he saw a wide smile on the King's face.

"Friends o' Baldock, ye be sayin'?" Kendall asked. "Stand up, stand up. Welcome to Tregador!"

"Thank you, King Kendall," Kabilian replied, still speaking in the dwarven tongue. By his side, Crick continued to scan the faces of the dwarves that were all glaring back at him.

"So, did ye be meetin' me son in Xylona?" Kendall asked.

"Actually, Trespias," Kabilian answered. He watched the king who seemed to grow concerned by the news. His son appeared mildly annoyed, and the Queen was outright angry. The scowl on her face and venom in her eyes was very easy to read.

"Trespias?" Kendall repeated. "But I sent him with Thamar to be helpin' Vorstad and Xylona! What is he doin' in Trespias?"

"Actually, Thamar is with him in Trespias. As is Theiler."

"Why?" Kendall demanded.

"We were invited to Trespias to partake in the unification talks," Kabilian began, making certain to reference himself as part of the group.

"I've heard o' this," Kendall said as he slammed his fist on the table, the giant turkey leg he was eating rising off of his plate and falling to the ground. "Those durned Mages came tryin' to convince me to be sendin' me dwarves to Trespias. They be sayin' that the realm be in danger. I be tellin' 'em that the only help I be givin' is the four-hunnerd-strong I had me son lead to Xylona and Vorstad! I be tellin' 'em that they would not be gettin' any more help from Tregador than that! And ye be tellin' me that these durned Mages then went to find me son and be fillin' his head with ideas that go against what I already be decidin'?"

"I do not know what to say," Kabilian frowned. "Your son was at Trespias, as were representatives from Vorstad, Xylona, Underwood, and Aquatica."

"Bah!" Kendall roared.

"This be what happens when ye let that wretch ye call a son do things on his own," the Queen coldly chastised him. "Tyndall here would never ha' disobeyed yer wishes."

Tyndall raised his hand to brush off the comment, as if he agreed but did not wish to take the time to actually speak.

Kendall turned and glared at his wife. "Me son be the strongest and best warrior in Tregador. I would be thinkin' o' none better to ha' fightin' in our name!"

"Tyndall is yer first born son, and the true heir to the throne! That other son o' yers is too durned reckless fer his own good"

"Tyndall is not a blasted fighter!" Kendall roared. "No offense boy, but yer brother is the warrior. Ye are the thinker. Ye will rule with facts, figures, and ideas. That be fine fer the future o' Tregador. Fer now though, if Tregador must fight, Baldock must fight!"

"Kendall, ye are bein' unreasonable," the Queen screeched. "Ye should ha' drowned Baldock when he was born."

"Ye've gone too far, Vinielle! Not another word o' Baldock. If he went to Trespias, then he must ha' had a good reason to go!"

Kabilian smiled—clearly, the Queen disliked Baldock—and where the King originally was upset that Baldock went to Trespias without consulting him, now he was defending him from his wife. He could definitely find out the information he needed from this trio.

Allowing the two to continue their argument for a few more minutes while observing, Kabilian decided that he would try to change the topic. A daring move when facing the royal leaders of the dwarves, but if Kendall became too enraged, who knows how long before they would be able to discuss other things he hoped to achieve. "If I may interrupt, Your Highness?"

Kendall turned his gaze from Vinielle and looked down at Kabilian. His face was slightly red, as his temper was flaring. "What?" he screamed.

"I do not wish to interrupt, but Baldock told me the finest craftsmanship in all the realm was that of Tregador. He said that I should definitely stop here, let you know that he was all right and that he would report back to you as soon as he could, but to also request a suit of armor."

"Armor?" Kendall asked.

"Yes," Kabilian answered. "My companion may have the orange hide and fur of a hobgoblin, but inside, he is as noble and just as any mystral. To wear the garb of his wretched race is an insult to him. He hopes to acquire a finely-crafted suit of illistrium with dragon markings to remind him of his true home and upbringing." As Kabilian finished, he removed a large ruby that was bigger than his hand from his satchel. "The mystral provided me with this for payment of the armor."

Kendall began laughing boisterously. "The money o' a companion o' me boy is no good here. Ye will get the finest craftsmanship in the realm as promised, and all fer the low, low price o' ye joinin' me fer dinner!" Looking around, he beckoned one of the servers. "Another leg fer me, and two plates fer me guests!"

As the place settings were being prepared, Kabilian leaned over and asked Feldrin about the Queen. "Why does the Queen dislike Baldock so much?"

"Baldock be not a child o' the Queen," Feldrin explained in a whisper. "King Kendall be havin' a habit o' strayin' from the nest, if ye be gettin' me meanin'. Baldock be the child he had with one o' the servant girls."

"I understand now," Kabilian said. "So she tries to push Tyndall to the front while putting Baldock down?"

"It be more than that," Feldrin sternly replied. "She often be the one sendin' him on missions that would place his life in severe jeopardy." Snickering for a moment, Feldrin nodded conspiratorially. "Baldock has the last laugh though! Bring on Rock trolls, orcs, hobgoblins... er, no offense to ye, Crick—and Baldock will find a way to triumph!"

Veldin kept pacing behind his brother, never taking his eyes off of Kabilian, and muttering the same thing over and over: "Ye shouldn't be speakin' so much."

Kabilian took in every detail: every word being spoken, every action, and every relationship between the dwarves here. He knew that he was gaining information, and information is power in the right hands. Smiling to himself, he knew that when next he confronted Baldock, he would be very powerful indeed.

CHAPTER 51

Transmuted into a giant hawk, Ferceng perched on the roof of one of the buildings of Xylona. He had hoped to arrive at the elven city in time to warn them of the advancing orcs, but was shocked to find the city already overrun by hobgoblins. The burly humanoids were celebrating their victory over the elves by drinking their spirits and pillaging the city.

His heart broke as he watched the creatures cheering and roaring in triumph. Though he had been secluded for many years, he still loved the realm, and to see the forces of evil advancing and conquering the land like a plague, he could only weep.

Deciding that there was nothing that he could do for Xylona, Ferceng hoped that he could at least reach Vorstad in time and warn them of the invasion coming their way.

Stretching his wings, he tightened his grasp on Carnage with his talons and took to the air. As he flew away, he glanced back and wondered whether the Seven Kingdoms could truly withstand the forces aligned against them. He sincerely hoped so, but every piece of the puzzle he uncovered led him to think that the realm would fall, and the forces of Zoldex would usher in a new era under the domination of an evil tyrant.

CHAPTER 52

Shiel walked into the throne room and looked up at Winton, who was looking her over as if he wanted to devour her right then and there. "You wished to see me, my lord?"

"Ah yes," Winton smiled. "Today will be a glorious day. The generals have returned to Trespias and I will be issuing the orders to have them send forces to rescue the Empress."

Shiel watched him closely. The return of Karleena was more than she could hope for. If the Empress were back, then Winton would no longer be allowed to use the handmaidens as a harem. Hopefully, once she found out what he was doing, Karleena would banish Winton from the palace forevermore.

"You must be overjoyed with the prospect of her return," Shiel replied without showing any sign of her own desires.

"I am overjoyed," Winton smiled. "So overjoyed, that I will need your services."

"My services?" Shiel asked, taken aback that a man that was supposedly committed to the Empress, and was taking steps to see her rescued, was now looking to also continue to betray her behind her back. Not for the first time, Shiel wondered if this was all some elaborate deception. She was certain that if Karleena was truly betrothed to Winton, she would have known. If he was lying about that, could he be lying about her rescue as well?

Winton began licking his lips. "Perhaps a little preview of tonight's entertainment?"

"What do you wish of me, my lord?" Shiel asked, trying to mask her disgust.

"Come here," Winton instructed with his hand raised out.

Shiel slowly walked over, grimacing at the mere thought of this man touching her again. As she reached his side, she breathed a sigh of relief to hear a knock at the door.

"What is it?" Winton screamed out in anger.

The door opened and Prime Minister Torscen stepped in. "Emperor, the generals have arrived, as you have requested."

"Yes," Winton smiled. "Excellent." As he stood up, he grabbed Shiel by the waist and pulled her towards him. He then began kissing her and fondling her breasts. As he pulled away, he whispered into her ear: "Be ready for me in my bed chambers. I will be in shortly."

"As my lord wishes," Shiel replied. She watched him walk out of the room in disgust. Tonight would have to be the time. She must prepare the other girls. Determined with her idea of how to escape the clutches of Winton, she hurried from the throne room to return to the other handmaidens.

The three generals—Hinbar, Lowred, and Sevlow—all stood with their hands behind their backs, waiting for their instructions. They had received a summons that the Empress had been kidnapped and the Imperial forces would be going to war. Although they were all involved in what they considered a domestic war as Braksis had instructed, they knew that the new threat must also be tended to.

As Winton walked into the room, he nodded to the three generals. "Thank you for coming."

The three generals exchanged puzzled glances. Hinbar stepped forward. "If I may, Prince Winton—where is Warlord Braksis? Only he has the authority to redeploy our forces and summon us from the battlefields."

"I regret to inform you that Braksis is dead," Winton coldly replied.

"Dead?" Sevlow repeated. "How?"

"It was an intricate plot staged by the Aezians. Emperor Wei Lau had developed a multi-pronged assault to leave us leaderless and hopeless. Though his operatives were successful, we will not falter as easily as he anticipated."

Sevlow regarded the man for a moment, rubbing his hands through his slicked-back hair. Though it was certainly possible that the Aezians could attack, he felt that it was somehow a faulty conclusion. In his early years working for Emperor Conrad, he had been sent to Aezia as a spy. He found them to be a very noble and honorable civilization, though they did have internal disputes between rival houses and families—nothing that would suggest that they would all unite against another empire though.

"Who else was targeted?" Lowred asked.

"The Empress was kidnapped, as your summons indicated. My own father was murdered in his bedchambers, and Admiral Morex has been reported lost at sea." Focusing his one good eye on the generals, he said very adamantly, "This travesty must not go unpunished."

"Am I to assume that you are now leading the Imperium?" Hinbar asked, not sure he liked the prospect.

"I have been declared the new Emperor until Karleena is safely returned and we are properly wed, as planned."

The generals took in the information, all of them hiding their own feelings on the development. They were military men and professionals. Regardless of their personal opinions and instincts, if the new Emperor ordered them to war, then they would execute those orders flawlessly.

"I have authorized the recruitment of any and all men in the realm that wish to volunteer. The army alone is not enough, but with these volunteers, we have more than quadrupled our forces."

"May I remind the Emperor that we are already facing threats here within the Imperium," Hinbar commented.

"The rebellions have ceased. The people have pulled together in this mutual cause to see the Empress safely returned. There will be no more hostilities."

"What of the orc threat?" Sevlow asked.

"King Garum has sent scouts and informs me that the news of an orc army amassing in Tenalong has been greatly exaggerated. Our paramount concern is the safe return of the Empress, and not running around worrying about small clusters of orc clans."

Sevlow turned and glanced at both of the senior generals for a moment. He did not like this at all. He felt that the threat against the Imperium internally was serious, and that the implications of Wei Lau being involved were lacking evidence and support. This whole discussion appeared to be a gross overreaction, and one he wished there was a voice of reason to somehow respond. He could see in the eyes of Hinbar and Lowred that they agreed.

"General Hinbar," Winton addressed. "With Braksis murdered and Kronos falling while attempting to help the dwarves, I am placing you in command of the Imperial forces. Please finalize all arrangements and make certain that the volunteers are properly equipped. You will be leaving for Aezia within the week."

"As the Emperor wishes," Hinbar bowed.

"Very good," Winton said. "You are dismissed."

The three generals saluted and walked out of the room. None of them felt comfortable with the course of action being dictated to them, but they had no choice other than to obey their new Emperor. They only hoped that when Aezia fell, and they returned, that they did not come to regret their actions.

CHAPTER 53

When Ferceng first came across the orcs, he was in awe. Though he had been told that close to one hundred and fifty thousand orcs were marching, he was unprepared for the columns and columns of armored warriors marching as far as the eye could see. There were more than just orcs: herds of koxlen, flying chimera, and swift moving mantror had mobilized as well.

The orcs were moving swiftly at a jogging pace. Even those traveling with large wagons full of barrels and artillery, such as catapults, were moving swiftly along with the orcs, as they were pulled by large wormlike creatures. They were clearly in a rush to get to Vorstad, and as they all jogged in perfect formation, he thought that their endurance was outstanding.

As he flew over the invading force, Ferceng could not see how the dwarves of Vorstad would possibly be able to withstand such a force. From what he had already known from Braksis, Vorstad has been under siege for months, each attack wearing them down and depleting both their numbers and their defenses. With these orcs bearing down on them, they most likely would be overcome swiftly.

Curious as to exactly what was in the barrels he saw, Ferceng swooped down to do a pass by. He jerked up as an arrow soared towards him. All at once, hundreds of orcs stopped and pulled bows, launching volleys of arrows towards the lone bird.

He could hear them laughing and betting on who would manage to kill him first. Many of the orcs seemed to crave the axe he was holding in his talons as well. As several arrows came close to striking the transmuted Mage Master, Ferceng decided that he had seen enough. He needed to reach Vorstad in time to warn them. If possible, they needed to evacuate. If not, then they may all die at the hands of these orcs.

CHAPTER 54

Travers and Angel paced the hallway, waiting for some word from the generals. Neither one had been informed as to what was happening, only that they needed to return to Trespias immediately. Upon entering the city, they found the streets filled with individuals that seemed almost electric with excitement about the prospect of going to war.

Travers had been assigned to protect Xylona, and knew that the battles with the hobgoblins were not going well. The creatures were relentless, and it took every ounce of their combined strength to oppose them. His cavalry, the dwarves of both Vorstad and Tregador, and the elves themselves, all were powerful forces alone, but together they were impressive. Even then, the hobgoblins attacked them, unfailingly, giving the combined forces neither the time nor the ability to rest.

Angel was not as involved in the war with the forces of evil. Under orders from Braksis, she was establishing a light-foot infantry. Though recruitment efforts had been slow thus far, providing her with only about a hundred volunteers that were being put through rigorous training, she anticipated that their numbers would continue to increase.

Both captains saluted as the three generals approached. Hinbar and Lowred continued on, but Sevlow stopped to relay what was happening. He quickly recapped what he learned from Winton, as well as his own feelings and opinions.

"If we leave, our allies will fall," Travers argued. "What of the unification?"

"Apparently there will be no unification unless the Empress is here to perform it," Sevlow replied. "However, I am concerned about leaving the Imperium undefended." Pausing, he glanced at Angel.

"Captain, he ordered all *men* to go to war. I do not believe he is even aware of your unit."

"You wish me to stay?" Angel asked.

"Not stay, per se," Sevlow answered. "For Trespias is not where you are needed. I think you should take your forces and pull out tonight. Take as many horses as you need from my own regiments. Continue to build your unit, and do whatever you can to help the Imperium. I fear that the Imperium will need your help here far more than it will in Aezia."

"Now you're talking my kind of language," Angel grinned. "Any ideas where we should go first?"

"I would like to learn more about Braksis's demise, as well as the orc city. Perhaps you could go to Falestia, do a little scouting and recruiting, and then head south into Tenalong."

"Falestia, eh?" Angel said. "Home sweet home. I haven't seen the mountains of Falestia in quite some time. You've got a deal, Sev."

"Sev?" Travers asked.

"Got a problem with that, Trav?" Angel replied innocently.

"And she may be the last hope for the Imperium?" Travers asked. "We're doomed."

"As if, big boy," Angel scoffed. "The Imperium has never been in better hands."

"Well, prepare your troops and move out after the sun goes down tonight. Best to leave when Winton will be unawares. I'll make certain that the gates are open for you."

"Thank you, *General*," Angel said more formally, then turned to Travers, "Better?"

"We're doomed," he repeated.

"Captain Travers, you will report back to your unit and inform them that we will be going to Aezia within the week. They have been doing a lot of fighting. Let them have the week off to visit their families, but make sure they are all back before we leave."

"Yes sir," Travers replied.

"Dismissed," Sevlow ordered.

Winton walked into his bedchambers, and paused, smiling as he saw Shiel lying in his bed waiting for him. He licked his lips again as he regarded her. She was lying seductively, with the sheets covering her private parts, but enough being revealed for him to instantly desire her.

"That's more like it," he said.

"I'm glad you approve," Shiel smiled seductively. "I fixed us drinks and candlelight, too," she said indicating the candles and wine goblets beside the bed.

Winton walked over and sat down, not certain what to say. He never imagined that she would come to him willingly.

Shiel sat up, the sheets dropping from her body. Winton took a deep breath as he scanned her form, growing excited with each moment. She slowly rubbed her hands over his neck, and then began to unfasten his shirt. Winton tried to help, but she firmly held his hand and shook her head. "We have all night to celebrate—no need to rush."

"Okay," Winton smiled back, knowing that he was going to enjoy this.

Shiel slipped his shirt off and began caressing his body. "Close your eyes," she said. As Winton did so, she continued to caress him and then began kissing his neck gently.

Slowly she moved her hands down his tanned and muscular body and began to remove his pants. As she did so, he let out a low moan. She removed his boots and pants and then gently helped him to turn over onto his stomach. Once lying flat, she got on top of his back and began to tenderly massage him.

She lightly feathered her fingers over his back and saw small goose bumps appear. She then firmly moved her hands back up until she reached his neckline, and began working her hands in a swirling circular motion. She gradually worked her way down his spine, listening to him gasp and moan in pleasure.

"You are quite gifted," he said.

"I was raised since I was very young to tend to others—massage is something I mastered long ago."

"Well, I for one am glad you did," he said as he began to turn over, his desire to have her no longer willing to be delayed.

Shiel reached out and picked up one of the wine goblets. She slowly took a drink, rubbing her tongue along the top of the goblet. Winton just watched with excitement. She spilt a small amount of the wine on his chest, and then bent over and began to slowly kiss him and gradually remove all of the wine with her mouth. She paused for an extended moment at each of his nipples, gently nibbling each.

As she leaned back up, she smiled at him seductively again, and reached out for the other goblet. "Would you like some too?"

"Oh, yes," he said. Winton took a big drink, and then poured some on her bare chest. He leaned over and began nibbling and sucking upon her breasts. Shiel moaned a few times in pleasure as he did so.

After a few moments, he stopped and just lay with his head between her breasts. "My lord?" Shiel asked. Waiting to make certain that he was not still conscious, she was satisfied and pulled his head back by the hair. "If you ever touch me again, I'll make it so that you will never be able to experience a woman's affections again," she said as she roughly pushed him aside.

She leapt out of bed, grateful that the doctor's sleeping potion had worked, as did her ploy to get him to drink it. She quickly put on a tunic, pants and boots, and then ran to the door where the handmaidens were waiting. "Is everyone ready?"

The handmaidens nodded their agreement and followed Shiel from the Empress's bedchambers. Once in the corridors, they walked confidently, and the only times they were stopped was by guards whistling at them or making insinuations about what they would like to do to them; nobody barred their path though.

The fifteen servants of the Empress stepped into the Chamber and all breathed a collective sigh of relief. They had made it this far.

All that they needed now was to find Angel and hope that she could help them get out of the city. At the other end of the Chamber, Shiel saw two Imperial soldiers speaking. One was a woman, and the other a man.

Rushing over, she stopped in front of them. "Are you Angel?"

The woman turned and looked her up and down. "Depends on who is asking."

"I am Shiel, handmaiden for Empress Karleena," Shiel said. "These are the Emperess's handmaidens."

"Then yes, I am Angel."

Travers stood, his mouth slightly open as he stared at Shiel.

"This lug is Captain Travers," Angel said as she punched him in the shoulder. "He acts like he's never seen a woman before."

Shiel smiled politely, and Travers stumbled on his words. "I'm sorry—I am Captain Travers... a pleasure." As he finished, he winced for his shaky speech, and then bent over and gently kissed her hand.

"What can I do for you?" Angel asked.

"We'd like to join your unit," Shiel replied.

Angel glanced at the other handmaidens and watched them for a moment. Reaching down, she picked up Shiel's hand and examined it. "These are very smooth. You girls have never been big on doing things other than tending to the luxury of the Empress, have you?"

"No," Shiel admitted.

"So then why do you want to become soldiers?" Angel asked.

"Since the Empress's abduction, we have become slaves and Winton has turned us into a harem. We just drugged him and fled. We hope that we can go with you."

"You drugged the Emperor?" Angel grinned with delight at the prospect.

"Yes," Shiel replied.

Travers looked horrified. "Are you ladies all right?"

"We will be fine," Shiel answered sincerely. "Now that we are away from the palace."

Angel glanced over to Travers and smiled. "Drugged the Emperor—my kind of girls. I'm sure I can find some use for all of you—welcome to the light-foot unit."

Shiel released a deep breath that she did not realize she had been holding. "You do not know how much this means to us."

"Don't worry, you'll fill me in on the way to Falestia," Angel winked.

Travers reached his arm out to Shiel. "In the meantime, I have just been put on leave. Perhaps I'll escort you lovely ladies for a day or so."

As Shiel took his arm and walked out with him, Angel snickered and hit him on the shoulder as she followed. "Charmer."

CHAPTER 55

Ferceng was relieved as he saw the opening in the bottom of the mountain that led into Vorstad. He did not have much time to warn and evacuate the dwarves, but at least he did manage to beat the orcs there. He only hoped that they had enough time.

Soaring down for a landing, he began his transformation back into a troll and landed on his feet, shifting his grasp of Carnage firmly to his hands. Quickly moving into the opening, he realized his first mistake, he was a troll and would be perceived as an enemy—he should have remembered that from his encounters with the dwarves of Tregador.

Dwarves started to swarm around him, weapons raised and ready to strike. Vorstad had been under siege so much over the past year; Ferceng silently berated himself for being foolish enough to think he could simply walk right in. His experiences had trained him better than this, but the desperation of the moment had overshadowed all sense of reason.

Hoping to demonstrate his good intentions, Ferceng dropped his axe, raised his arms above his head, and in the dwarven tongue, spoke to the ambushing dwarves. "Greetings dwarves of Vorstad. I am an ally coming with dire news for your king. I assure you, my intentions are true and I will not struggle or confront you."

A gray-bearded dwarf stepped forward. A single patch covered his left eye, with signs of scarring below the black cloth. He wore a stiff, brown, long-sleeve leather shirt and pants, with chainmail draped over his head and chest. These were tucked into studded leather boots and armored gauntlets. A single-bladed axe was held in one hand, with a wooden buckler in the other.

He studied Ferceng with his one good eye. "A troll claiming to be a friend to dwarves? Preposterous. Kill him."

Ferceng lowered his arms quickly and swiped them to the side, mystical energies hammering the dwarves and sending the group hurtling backwards. He watched as the dwarves quickly collected themselves and tried to rise to attack him again. Closing his fist, a mystical barrier covered each of his attackers, preventing them from standing up.

Stepping over to the dwarf that ordered his execution, he glanced down and could see the contempt in the gray-bearded dwarf's eye. "I am a Mage Master and could have done that at any time. My words are true—I come as a friend and have a warning for your king."

The dwarf continued to struggle upon the ground. "You restrain me and expect me to accept you at your word?"

Ferceng unclenched his fist and released the mystical bindings on the dwarves. "I will not use my magic again. If you wish to slay me here and now, then my life is in your hands; though without hearing the news I offer, you may soon follow me into the afterlife."

The dwarf stood up, but his features did not change. If Ferceng was getting through to him, he could not observe that on the expression on the dwarf's rock-hard face. Then, he hoisted his axe up onto his shoulder. "I am Fok, a general of Vorstad and loyal servant to King Chaddrick. Any message you have, I shall hear."

Considering his options for a moment, Ferceng shook his head. "I am sorry, but my warning is for the ears of the leader of Vorstad alone."

"You could be an assassin, attempting to deceive me," Fok theorized.

"If I were an assassin, I would have found a better way in, and this conversation would not be taking place. Instead, the dwarves of Vorstad would be mourning the loss of their king."

"Is that a threat?" Fok asked.

"No, merely a statement trying to prove to you that my intentions are true," Ferceng replied.

Fok shrugged and then turned to walk deeper into the tunnel leading to Vorstad. The other dwarves still had their weapons raised and beckoned Ferceng to follow.

As they approached the Halls of Vorstad, the general turned around. "Wait here."

Ferceng watched him as he walked over to another dwarf that appeared to be directing sentries and soldiers. Glancing around, Ferceng was impressed; although he was here to warn them about the advancing orc threat, the dwarves already appeared to be alerted. He could easily pick out a variety of defenses and traps, and was certain that there were many more that he could not easily see as well.

Fok returned with a red-bearded dwarf, the latter also showing signs of aging, strands of gray scattered through his beard. Unlike Fok, he was more heavily armored in flexible scale, a series of overlapping armored plates sewn into his black leather shirt and pants. Chainmail was draped on top for extra protection. He wore tan leather boots that extended to his knees, with gloves of the same color and material extending over his armor up to his elbows. A helm was upon his brow, with a row of spikes in the center trailing all the way down to his neckline. A tan cloak hung from his shoulders.

"You wish to see the leader of Vorstad?" he asked in a deep and gruff voice. "That would be me: Thron, son of Torrin, protector, and most recently, Steward of Vorstad."

A small smile creased Ferceng's lips. "By any chance, do you have a son by the name of Thamar?"

Thron's eyes tightened in suspicion as he studied the troll. "Thamar is me boy."

"Our sons are allies," Ferceng announced. "There is no reason why we could not follow in their footsteps."

The red-bearded dwarf started laughing in a deep belly roar. Fok and the other dwarves present began laughing boisterously as well. "My son has always been one willing to work with other races," Thron snorted. "I guess it shouldn't surprise me that now he is consorting with a troll."

"My apologies for not clearly explaining myself," Ferceng said.

"My son is Braksis, Warlord of the Imperium."

"Braksis?" Fok asked, his doubts seeming to vanish with the mere mentioning of the name. He and Thron exchanged glances: Lord Braksis was well known to them. After fighting alongside Thamar and the other dwarves sent to find assistance, he had sent soldiers of the Imperium to Vorstad to help face the threat of the orcs and goblins. In the battle where Fok had lost his eye, the general leading the Imperial forces, Kronos, was also lost. Braksis had appeared then, but was not taken aback. He had been adamant that the soldiers remain and defend Vorstad valiantly.

"Braksis is a name that is well known in Vorstad," Thron said appreciatively. "I have heard tales that he was raised by a troll, but never truly believed them."

"They are true," Ferceng replied. "I consider him to be my own."

Accepting his word by seeing the pride in Ferceng's eyes, Thron nodded. "It was a sad day for Vorstad when the messenger arrived recalling the Imperial army to Trespias."

"Their presence here now would be highly valued," Ferceng agreed. "However, I assure you that Braksis did not send for the soldiers. He would not abandon Vorstad like that."

"I believe you," Thron said. "Braksis was a noble soul. He looked to find solutions that many would scoff at, but ones that were vital for success."

"You honor me with your praise," Ferceng said. "As my son had suspected, there is a great conspiracy swirling in motion. Until we can determine exactly what is being planned, nobody is safe."

"Is this conspiracy why the hobgoblins have been attacking Xylona, and the orcs and goblins here?" Thron asked.

"Amongst other things," Ferceng agreed. "Unfortunately, my own boy was lost to this plot."

"Braksis is dead?" Fok asked.

"I do not believe that he is dead," Ferceng confidently replied. "If he were, I would know it. I feel that he still has a role to play in this, but only time will determine exactly what that role will be."

"May it be a role that will lead to glory, as a man like Braksis should have," Thron replied triumphantly. "What brings you here now?"

Ferceng then began to spin a tale that those that heard it truly appreciated. He began his story where Braksis and Solara first returned to his home and informed him of their suspicions as well as what had happened to them along their journey. He then spoke of the apparent death of his son, a moment that quieted the dwarves around him, and saw even a few tears in stone-hard faces. He then discussed his quest to learn the true nature of the Murky Death Clan, an adventure that led him to Grool, and only more dread and concern for the fate of the realm. He then discussed his frantic journey here, pausing briefly to reveal that Xylona had already fallen, and that one hundred and fifty thousand orcs were bearing down on them.

As he finished, he was shocked to see that Thron did not look concerned about his report. The fall of Xylona and the forces approaching them he thought would at least generate some shock and reactions from the battle hardened dwarf, but instead, he just accepted the information as if pieces of a puzzle were finally coming together.

"Thank you for your thorough report," Thron said with a curt nod.

"Forgive me," Ferceng said, "but you do not seem shocked by the news."

"I am not," Thron said. "For in fact, one of my boy's companions had returned with news similar to yours. They took King Chaddrick and his honor guard—kicking and screaming in protest, I assure you, because the king did not have any desire to leave Vorstad before a battle—and marched north two days ago. Those of us left behind have been making every preparation for the oncoming battle."

"There are one hundred and fifty thousand orcs," Ferceng repeated for emphasis. "Don't you think it would be more beneficial to evacuate Vorstad and live to fight again another day?"

Thron and Fok both began laughing at the statement. Thron shook his head. "Only one hundred and fifty thousand? Then they are severely outnumbered, for each true son of Vorstad can easily take on five of those filthy swine without even breaking a sweat!"

CHAPTER 56

"I cannot believe we stopped so close to the Halls of Vorstad," Thamar complained. "Another few hours and we would be there!"

"Ye be sayin' that a few hours ago," Baldock groaned. "We all be pushin' hard to be getting' here this fast. We be needin' some rest. Ye'll be marchin' into yer home soon enough, and ye'll be able to stand strong, proud, and well rested!"

"We could be even better rested in Vorstad though. The food and wine would be glorious, as would be the tales we would weave," Thamar pleaded.

Arifos kneeled down and shook his head. "No, Baldock is right, we will rest now. We do not know exactly what will be waiting for us at Vorstad."

"Even more reason to go now! What if they are in danger? We could help!" Thamar argued.

Arifos snapped his finger, and Thamar's head lowered to the ground, the red-bearded dwarf snoring in an instant and deep slumber. Theiler ran over, his club brandished as he stood defensively between his brother and the Madrew elf.

"No worries, Theiler," Arifos said. "He will awaken shortly, and be well rested."

Theiler did not lower his club, but stared warningly at Arifos until he turned to walk away. Baldock peered over at Thamar and giggled at how easily the sleeping spell worked.

Arifos stepped over to a flat outcropping where Mylvannan was training Ashwin in the handling of her new sword, Martristlit. The two

301

white tigers were watching the elves every move, as if intrigued by their defensive dance.

Mylvannan was moving swiftly, trying to force Ashwin to speed up her attacks. Every night since they fled Trespias, the two had been working hard to improve the young elf's skills. While she was progressing, she still remained little more than a novice. The Frost elf worried that unless she improved quickly, someone may seriously get hurt in combat: either Ashwin, or one of the others trying to go out of their way to protect her. However, she was adamant to learn how to master the blade, and slowly but surely, she was getting better.

Ashwin blocked several attacks by Mylvannan, and then launched into a few moves of her own. She was growing weary with the quick-paced tempo of the duel that he had set, but the Frost elf seemed as if he could continue this pace for hours. Hoping to trick him, Ashwin backflipped, just in time as Mylvannan's sword swiped empty air. She then dropped to the ground and lunged for his legs.

Mylvannan leapt up and spun over her, allowing her to harmlessly pass underneath him. As he began to spin back around, he found her standing closer than he anticipated. Raising his sword, Ashwin quickly attacked with a variety of tactics that Arifos had shown her, switching through a series of combination moves. Mylvannan stumbled back several steps and smiled at her progress. He then threw his sword at her feet, and it dug in between them. Ashwin glanced down, not noticing the Frost elf remove his two serrated daggers, lunge beneath her defenses, and bring the blades us, crossing them at her throat.

"You got me again," she conceded.

"You have improved a great deal," Mylvannan smiled as he sheathed his daggers. "You picked up on the combinations Arifos showed you quite well."

"Thank you," Ashwin said as she returned her sword to its scabbard.

Arifos dropped down to the two of them. "You are not helping her by lying."

"What?" Ashwin asked as she glanced back and forth between the two elves. "What are you talking about?"

"Mylvannan was going easy on you," he said. "Going easy on her will only get her killed. She'll think she's better than she really is."

"She is just learning," Mylvannan objected. "She must learn the techniques before she learns the true pace and ferocity."

"Move aside," Arifos said. "I'll go easy on you too—I promise to only use Skrenlar."

Ashwin watched as Mylvannan backed away. She then pulled Martristlit from its scabbard again and stood waiting for the Madrew elf to attack. Arifos did not keep her waiting long. He moved in swiftly, quickly moving his blade from side-to-side in rapid feints. She tried to defend each one, but was much slower than the pink-skinned warrior.

Arifos continued moving side-to-side, then jabbed his foot out and tripped her. As she fell backwards, he lowered his sword to her throat. "Do you concede?"

"Yes," Ashwin shamefully replied.

"You must be prepared for all things," Arifos cautioned her. "An enemy will rarely fight a fair battle. They will look for every advantage."

"How do you expect her to improve if a battle takes only a matter of seconds?" Mylvannan argued.

"Seconds will increase," Arifos returned as he sheathed his sword and glanced to the sky. A group of birds were flying from the mountain, as if startled. Arifos jogged back to the sleeping Thamar and snapped his fingers.

Thamar sat up and stretched with both hands. "Must have been more tired than I thought," he said with a yawn.

"Those birds..." he pointed, "is their behavior unusual?"

Thamar strained through his sleepy haze to watch the birds fly away. He quickly jumped up and grabbed his mallet, fully alert.

Ashwin stepped up behind Arifos, Mylvannan and the white tigers close behind her. "What does it mean?"

Thamar grimaced. "I may not have the instincts of Grosskurth, but if I am not mistaken, that is a clear sign that the orcs are moving again."

Theiler nodded his agreement with his brother.

"Restin' be done," Baldock observed joyously "Time fer some fun!"

The companions quickly began packing up their few belongings. If the orcs were marching on Vorstad again, they fully intended to be part of the battle.

CHAPTER 57

Thron, Fok, and Ferceng stood together on one of the towering walls defending Vorstad. They scanned the wide caverns where the battle would soon unfold. Thousands of dwarves were moving swiftly, making last minute preparations and positioning themselves. There was not a skeptic or worried face amongst them. The dwarves were partaking in a dwarven battle-hymn as they worked.

Ferceng found himself battling his emotions. From what he had seen, this battle seemed hopeless. There was no possible way that the dwarves could withstand the forces bearing down on them. At the same time, the excitement, the passion, and the methodical way the dwarves were confronting this situation, he found himself growing more optimistic and daring. With the spirit of the dwarves, he wondered if any foe could truly confront them and survive.

That same spirit, he frowned, would be devastating to lose. If Vorstad fell this day, it would be a great injustice to the realm. Tregador may make great weapons and armor, but Vorstad had claimed its fame in battle and glory. This city was full of battle-hardened and tested warriors. They had fought for justice and upheld their ideals for generations. Though the humans were reluctant to admit it, without the assistance of Vorstad, the Race Wars would have ended quite differently.

Now, these proud warriors faced insurmountable odds. Not with fear or trepidation, but with an almost joyous glee as if they were finally about to get what they always wanted. As Ferceng continued to watch, he decided that if he, too, were to die this day, he was proud to do so beside such noble warriors.

From an eastern tunnel, three dwarves darted into the main cavern that served as the home of the Halls of Vorstad. They rushed over to where they saw Thron standing, and quickly ascended to join him.

Thron turned and watched as they ran to his side, then dropped down on one knee and bowed. "What do you have to report?"

"The goblins and orcs of the east are on the move again," said one of the dwarven scouts.

Fok shook his head. "Just like the damned Severed Head Clan to march on us when our attentions are elsewhere."

"Just like the true foe we face, you mean," Thron corrected him.

"This battle is being coordinated by Zoldex," Ferceng concurred. "His efforts are all connected."

"Then let Zoldex feel the sting of the true sons of Vorstad!" Fok roared.

"Yes," Thron agreed. "We will not let Zoldex destroy us without showing him that he has been in a fight. Have the defenses in the eastern tunnels been completed yet?"

Fok nodded, a sly smile on his face. "They have."

"Then take two thousand dwarves with you to properly greet the Severed Head Clan," Thron ordered. "If you are severely outnumbered, though, fall back and we will defend our home from the Halls of Vorstad themselves, if need be."

"You give me two thousand true sons of Vorstad and you think we'll need to fall back?" Fok laughed. "I think not. The orcs and goblins will truly learn what it means to have severed heads this day."

"With honor," Thron said.

"With honor," Fok returned as he grasped Thron by the arm and then walked away. The three scouts fell in line behind him as he began issuing his orders.

"It is not too late to flee before we are completely boxed-in," Ferceng reminded Thron. "By doing so, you would live to fight another day. This war is just beginning. There will be other battles."

"I have fought many battles to defend these Halls," Thron said with pride. "To leave them would be agony, but your advice is sound. With Chaddrick gone, I must consider this situation not only as a warrior, but a leader. As a leader, what would be the best alternative for the most people?"

"To live," Ferceng answered for him.

"Yes," Thron reluctantly agreed. "To live. Very well, I shall order the evacuation of Vorstad. We shall flee today so that tomorrow the banner of Vorstad can be raised over the slain body of Zoldex and his forces."

"A wise decision," Ferceng said, relieved that this dwarf was willing to see reason and not just stubbornly push into battle like so many other dwarves he had known.

Another scout ran up and dropped to a knee before him. Thron glanced down, realizing that his options may have just been taken away from him. "What do you have to report?"

"The orcs, they are within sight," the dwarf relayed. "They will be here momentarily."

"Very well, have the defenders get in place. Tell them I will be there shortly to lead them to glory."

The dwarf jumped up and smiled with anticipation. "Gladly!" he roared.

As he carried out his instructions, Thron took a deep breath and turned to Ferceng. "Too late."

Ferceng nodded his agreement. They were committed. The battle for Vorstad was about to commence.

CHAPTER 58

The dwarves followed Fok into the tunnel heading towards the on-coming orcs and goblins. The further they went, the darker it became, with fewer torches illuminating the area as there were in Vorstad. One section of the tunnel opened up to allow a larger number of troops to walk through at the same time. Before they reached this widened area, he signaled his dwarves where to go, and watched as two thousand warriors practically vanished from sight.

Fok waited until he saw that all of his dwarves were properly concealed before leaving the path himself. He walked over to a slight incline where three dwarves stood over a thick rope, axes ready.

"They're coming," he said.

"How can you be certain?" one of the dwarves whispered back.

"I can smell them," Fok sneered, wrinkling his nose. "On my order."

"Yes sir," the dwarves replied in unison.

He watched from his hiding place as goblins began passing him. As the Severed Head Clan was known to do, their goblin slaves were the first sent into battle, allowing them to fall victim to any traps or defenses before the orcs moved in. Fok did not care about the goblins. They were nothing to his unit. It was the orcs he was waiting for.

As the goblins continued along, he was amazed by how many there were. From all indications, there shouldn't be more than ten thousand goblins left alive in the east, but rows upon rows of the four-foot creatures passed by. Finally, several orcs began passing Fok, and he smiled knowing that the battle was almost upon them.

Glancing back at the three dwarves that were waiting to spring their trap, Fok whispered, "Wait for my signal." He then stepped out of his hiding place full of confidence.

He walked straight into the path of the marching invaders. Several orcs started yelling in their own barbaric tongue, which Fok was glad he never took the time to learn. "You want me you filthy swine, come get me!"

He raised his single-bladed axe and his wooden buckler, waiting for the swarm of orcs to flow over him. He gripped his weapons tightly, swinging at any foe that got close enough to him. The entire time, he continued to watch and wait, not wanting to sound the charge just yet.

His presence had the effect he hoped. The orcs were rushing forward now, charging towards the dwarf rather than slowly and cautiously working their way into Vorstad. When he was satisfied with the orcs' position, he cried out, "Now!"

The three dwarves by the rope began chopping it. The last strand snapped away and the rope was dragged from their sight. As it did so, everyone in those tunnels began to hear a loud rumbling. The orcs closest to it looked up in time to see tons of rock falling down upon them, as if the mountain itself was collapsing.

The rumbling continued for many minutes as the tunnel continued to collapse. Dust and debris rose, permeating the air and making it impossible for anyone to see. This did not stop Fok. He knew that the only thing he could possibly find at this moment were his enemies, and he took the opportunity of their distraction and confusion to continue striking them down as quickly as he could.

As the dust settled, orcs and goblins were in shock, seeing so many of their allies slain, and their forces cut in two. The tunnel they just came through was completely blocked, as if there had never been an opening. One lone dwarf was standing triumphantly amongst them, striking down orc after orc with his ferocity.

Fok extended his blood-drenched axe into the air. "Charge!"

With his command, the disoriented enemies scrambled to try and react in time, but most fell with the first barrage. Two thousand dwarven warriors broke out at them, some from beneath the ground where they were standing, some from the walls around them. To the orcs and goblins, it was as if the tunnel itself had come to life with warriors ready to slay them.

The orc chieftain of the Severed Head Clan, Krug, stepped forward and placed his hand on the rubble that now barred his path. Frustrated, he began pushing at the rocks with all of his might, but soon learned that they were not about to budge. Leaning his head closer, he could hear screams and cries as his forces were being decimated.

Growling in annoyance, he spun around and grabbed an orc standing close to him. "Suffer," he said in a deep voice in his own orcish tongue. "We will make them suffer. Many dwarves will die for this outrage."

The orc nodded enthusiastically, though he reached up and tried to remove his chieftain's hands from around his throat.

"Go—find other tunnels and another way around. Report back immediately for the main force to join the battle," he instructed.

With his order, dozens of orcs began running back the way they had come, all searching desperately for another way to Vorstad.

Krug watched them leave. "Suffer," he repeated as he squeezed the life from the orc he was holding. Dropping the strangled warrior to the ground, he punched the barrier a couple of times, wondering not for the first time exactly how many of his clan mates he would lose before Zoldex was appeased.

"Da, I want to fight!"

Thron paused his preparations and glanced at his daughter in mild frustration. "No."

"But Da, if Thamar and Theiler were here, they would fight by your side," Threll argued. The red-haired daughter of Thron was not willing to concede the point. In the history of Vorstad, many dwarven females had gained fame by fighting for their city. She only wished to do the same.

"No," Thron repeated. "And that's final," he said as he hung four throwing-hammers to his belt by their leather strap.

Threll placed her hands on her hips and glared at him. Like her entire family, she had fiery red hair, flowing in curls to her shoulders. Like Theiler, she had dark green eyes, which now smoldered at her father, offset by the light-blue shirt she wore over navy pants. Like her father, she wore knee-high tan boots, though she did not wear any gloves. Atop of her outfit was a suit of chainmail, and in her hand she clutched a mace—whether he would let her fight or not, she was ready to do so.

"I am prepared to fight," she protested.

"The defenders of Vorstad are known as the true *sons* of Vorstad for a reason," he argued as he placed two daggers into his belt along his back. "I've never heard of the *daughters* of Vorstad before."

"Women have fought, you are just too stubborn to admit it," Threll argued.

"That may be so, but you will mind your father," Thron said with finality in his voice. "This battle will be long, and whether I want you to or not, you will see your fair share of fighting this day. I do not wish for you to rush headlong into it, though."

"Da, I can help."

"No," Thron shouted adamantly. "You will stay within the Halls of Vorstad with the other women and children. If our defenses falter, you will be the last hope for this great city."

Threll bit her lip, and then reluctantly nodded. "I shall not fail you, Da."

Picking up his axe and shield, he walked from his home and moved confidently to the gates. Pausing there, he waited for Ferceng to join him. "I know the dwarven defenses," he said. "How do *you* plan on contributing?"

Ferceng glanced back up at the perch they shared earlier overlooking the cavern. "I will stay by your side for now, but once the battle commences, I shall return to the walls of Vorstad and strike with my magic from there."

"Very well," Thron agreed. "With honor."

"With honor," Ferceng returned.

The two then walked through the dwarven army and stood at the front of the line. There were hundreds of dwarves standing along the sides of the walls, many of these with bows, crossbows, and other defenses. The lines themselves stretched throughout the cavern, with dwarves standing ready with spears, axes, swords, maces, clubs, and shields. Other groups of dwarves with bows and crossbows stood behind this group.

Ferceng knew that this was not the entire army that composed Vorstad. Other units of equivalent size were within the Halls of Vorstad, waiting to charge out when ordered. Hundreds of dwarves also stood along the walls of the city, bows ready to strike from above.

They stood ready, poised for battle. This was the moment when the combatants were fully prepared. They remembered the stories of glory from over the centuries, the times when the dwarves of Vorstad conquered foes far greater in number than their own forces, times similar to what they were about to engage upon now. In these moments before battle, the dwarves knew only victory, glory, and honor. Sorrow, loss, and the aftermath of devastation would only be felt when the battle concluded; but even then, the tales would be told of their victory, of the heroes who fought courageously, and the brave souls that fell would be immortalized for dying valiantly in battle.

The first wave of orcs charged into Vorstad. Thron stood watching them, he and Ferceng the closest to the attacking invaders. He watched them moving in swiftly, noting that their armor and weapons were well-crafted, apparently by dwarves and elves based on the styles and craftsmanship that he saw. The orcs themselves were different as well. Not only did they have better weapons than their cousins in the east, they were also larger, stronger, and if possible, appeared to be more ferocious.

He observed every detail as he unflinchingly watched them approach. Then, raising his axe into the air, hundreds of dwarves revealed themselves directly over the entrance to the cavern. Large urns of boiling oil were tipped over, dropping on the orcs below. A flaming arrow swiftly hit one, igniting the oil and setting hundreds of the creatures aflame. The grayish-brown orcs began screaming and crying in pain. Those that had not been affected by the flames quickly found dwarven archers sending volleys of arrows towards them.

"You *were* prepared," Ferceng said, nodding in approval. "No wonder Vorstad is a city of legend."

Thron watched the orcs scrambling for cover, only to find more dwarves striking out at them. "This is only the first wave," he said. "From here, we truly must be a city of legend."

<h1 style="text-align:center">CHAPTER 59</h1>

Knocking a goblin over with his wooden buckler, Fok swung with his axe and dug it into the creature's chest. Pulling his axe out, he spun around and prepared for the next assault. The remaining orcs and goblins were running in disarray. His strike had been perfectly conceived and executed.

At that moment, he was very proud of his dwarves: they were calm and in control; they moved swiftly to strike down their foes—but did not surrender to berserker rages—maintaining their wits and working together; they moved swiftly as a cohesive unit and showed no mercy as they cut the orcs and goblins down.

Another goblin charged towards him, hoping to take advantage of his apparent lack of attention to the battle around him. The small, yellow-tinged creature was wearing nothing more than rags, and was barefoot at that. He brandished a small rusted dagger. To kill such a pathetic foe seemed demeaning and diminishing, but you ca not always choose your adversary.

Fok dropped down as the goblin leapt at him, watching as it soared over his head, a look of confusion on its face. Fok then spun around and buried his axe in the goblins skull as it tried to turn to face him. Looking at the fallen body, he thought again about how pathetic this foe was.

Scanning the battlefield for remaining adversaries, he found a cluster of orcs. Though they were not much better in terms of honor than the goblins, he was satisfied with the fact that they were bigger, stronger, and a slightly better challenge. He began screaming as he charged towards them, his wooden buckler in front of him, and his axe held back, ready to strike.

The orcs prepared themselves, but Fok charged in swinging mercilessly. He was not alone as dozens of other dwarves saw his charge and fell in step behind him. They crashed through the remaining orc groups and slaughtered them quickly. Only a few remaining foes survived, their numbers dwindling exponentially.

Thron stood motionless watching the remaining orcs as they fled back outside the cavern. His archers along the walls continued their assault, launching arrows after the fleeing creatures. Thus far, not a single dwarf had fallen, whereas several hundred orcs had felt the wrath of the true sons of Vorstad.

A cheer sounded as the dwarves cried out to Mander, the dwarven God of the Mountain. Thron did not partake in the cheer, but admired his dwarves for their spirit and abilities. A dwarf fighting for what he believed in could face insurmountable odds and walk away with a smile on his face and a tale that would be told for generations.

As soon as the last orc left the cavern and the celebratory cheer died down, he ordered his soldiers into formation. A row of dwarves with heavy shields stood in front, brandishing one-handed weapons such as single bladed axes or short-swords. Directly behind them were dwarves with spears. Two more rows of dwarves lined up behind those, wielding bows or crossbows. Closer to the entrance of Vorstad were the warriors with two-handed battleaxes, long-swords, mallets, and maces. This final group would be the ones that would press the attack if the dwarves had to retreat to the protection of the walls of Vorstad.

"Everyone be ready," Thron called out. "That first group was nothing more than a scouting party testing our defenses."

Ferceng flinched at the observation. With an army so large, it was feasible that the orcs could send hundreds to their deaths merely to learn what their foes had prepared to stop them. The true battle would begin shortly. This time, he was afraid that many of the noble dwarves would fall before the rampaging orcs.

Thamar led the companions through the tunnels that he had explored since he was a young child alongside his father. He knew each and every turn as if they were extensions of himself. He could also read disturbances in his surroundings. He could tell just by looking around that large units of orcs and goblins had marched this way—far too many for he and his companions to confront alone.

Pausing, he stopped and sniffed the air. "Something is coming," he said.

Arifos closed his eyes and listened. "There are creatures coming this way."

The companions leaned against the cavern wall, hoping to go unseen until they determined what was approaching. Only about a dozen orcs appeared though, moving swiftly and looking around as if they were desperately searching for something.

Thamar began to laugh and smiled with glee. "These swine will learn what it means to fight a true son of Vorstad!" He then charged around the corner, his mallet held firmly in his hands.

Theiler quickly fell in step behind him, as did Baldock who was laughing joyously himself.

Arifos glanced back at Ashwin, and saw that both white tigers stood protectively by her side. "Do you wish to remain here?"

Ashwin shook her head no, and glanced at Mylvannan for encouragement. The Frost elf nodded his agreement and removed Frostlartil from its scabbard.

"Very well," Arifos replied as he pulled his two scimitars. "Let us show these orcs that to serve Zoldex is to court death."

The three dwarves were the first to reach the orcs. The greenish warriors stopped and appeared stunned to see enemies this deep in the cavern. They quickly pulled their own rusted weapons and prepared for the oncoming dwarves.

Thamar feinted with a high thrust, and then brought his hammer down with a vicious swing at the first creature's foot, breaking it. The orc dropped its sword and started hopping, grasping its foot in its two hands. Thamar whistled to get his attention, then brought his mallet into an uppercut and snapped the creature's neck.

As Baldock was charging towards the foes, he tripped and fell to the ground, his axe and shield spinning away from him. As he began to cuss, three orcs jumped on top of him and started swinging at his illistrium armor, trying to pierce it. Forcing himself up, Baldock spread his arms and knocked the three creatures from his back.

Pulling his sword from its scabbard, he charged forward, knocking one orc down, then swinging at the other and slicing it across the chest. The third one brought a club down on his head. Baldock stopped and repositioned his spangenhelm, then turned around in frustration, glaring at the orc. "Nobody be touchin' me head!" He then rammed his sword into the orc's belly, and lifted it up with both hands, cheering.

The orc he knocked down looked horrified and started to run away. Vella sprung out and brought him back to the ground, clawing and biting at the squirming foe beneath her.

Theiler batted an orc aside with his club, and then spun around and brought it down cracking it on the head, his club splintering in half. The mute dwarf looked stunned that his trusty weapon had broken after using it for so long. In anger, he tossed the club aside and pulled his sword out. He then began swiping at the orc, not caring that the creature had died many strikes before.

Arifos watched the mute dwarf as he continued to strike the dead orc in a berserker rage. He shook his head in disgust: he couldn't understand why the dwarf was so fond of a club anyway. The sword was a much better weapon, especially in combat. Even still, he scanned for enemies and saw that the three dwarves initial assault pretty much cut their foes in half.

Two orcs charged towards him, and he twirled his two blades in anticipation. One swung high and the other swung low, hoping to have at least one hit his mark. Arifos perfectly deflected both attacks, and spun both weapons around in a counterattack. The two orcs also parried and the fighting went back and forth. He considered their form clumsy, but they were at least trying to attack him in unison, hoping to gain an edge.

Against the most famous Madrew warrior, there was little hope of them claiming the advantage. He dropped down and spun, jutting his leg out and swiping the two orcs off of their feet. He then stood back up and brought both swords down, each impaling one of the orcs in the chest. Removing the blades, he glanced around again, pondering which foe, if any, deserved the honor of dying at his hands.

With the familiar chant, "FRAAZAA!" Mylvannan's sword began misting. He swung his honor blade three times, leaving three orcs frozen in his wake, each encased in an icy death cry. Seeing the only other orc close to him turning to run and quickly being hammered down by Thamar, he glanced back at Ashwin to see how she was progressing.

Ashwin was determined to master her sword rather than relying upon her bow. If she felt too overwhelmed, her bow would of course be her weapon of choice, but she wanted to prove to Arifos that she was able to take care of herself. Vella had run off to make a kill herself, but Vaz stayed by her side in case she needed him.

She confronted one orc and began dueling the creature with swords. The orc was much bigger and stronger than her, but she soon saw that it nearly moved in slow motion compared to her bouts with Mylvannan and Arifos. She was able to easily sidestep and dodge his lunges, though the force of the ones she parried had knocked her back. Using her speed in her favor was definitely more preferable.

She concentrated on her foe, trying to anticipate his moves and strikes. Ashwin did not want to be a burden to her companions, and that included becoming overconfident and being struck down by an orc. She could see Vaz in her peripheral vision, watching intently, but also poised to spring at the orc.

Wishing to end this on her own, she braced herself for the creature's next attack. As it lunged at her, she sidestepped, allowing him to pass her, but was unprepared as he swung his fist out and punched her in the face. Ashwin fell backwards but quickly stood up and glanced at Vaz to make certain the tiger would not interfere.

The orc began laughing as it came towards her again. This time, Ashwin moved into motion with one of the combinations she had learned from Arifos. She swung to the left, then the right, then the left, then the right. As the orc struggled to swiftly parry her feints, she spun her sword down and brought it swiping up in an uppercut. The blade pierced the orc's chest, though not mortally, as it tried to dodge backwards.

Pushing the attack, Ashwin stepped in and continued to swiftly move her blade. She was quite pleased to see that several times her sword did hit the orc and drew blood. The creature was slowing even more now that it was wounded, and she had the upper hand.

"End it," a voice said behind her.

Ashwin twirled her blade and brought it down, imbedding it into the orcs chest. She stared at the creature as it gasped and began spitting up blood. A hand grasped her shoulder and pulled her back.

"You did well," Mylvannan said.

Ashwin looked up at the Frost elf and over to Arifos, who was the one who had told her to end it. A single tear was in her eye. "This was the first time I ever killed someone up close like this."

"We know," Mylvannan said sympathetically.

Arifos watched her for a moment, and then returned to the dwarves, biting his tongue rather than pointing out her flaws in the duel. This was her first kill in this manner. As he clutched his swords and felt the warmth they were emanating, he recalled his own sisters and how innocent and full of life they were, very similar to Ashwin. Perhaps he had been pushing her too hard, but in the end, he did not wish to see her come to the same demise as Phistala and Aurlestyl.

Once he reached the trio of dwarves—Thamar and Baldock pulling Theiler from the dead orc—Arifos searched the dark tunnel with his mystical abilities, trying to determine what was down there. Though he could not receive an exact estimate, he knew that more foes were ahead.

"It would be foolish to wander headlong into a force of orcs that far outnumbers us," he claimed.

Thamar glanced up and then over at the bodies that they had killed. "Groups this small are nothing to warriors such as us."

"Not all of these groups will be this small," Arifos reminded him.

"All I know is that my home is being attacked," Thamar sternly replied. "I will fight. Whether it be alone or with you, it makes no difference to me."

"Stubborn," Arifos muttered.

"I will hunt down these orcs and kill as many as I can," Thamar vowed. "The more I kill, the less that will be alive to besiege Vorstad. If I die in this endeavor, I will die happy."

"Yes!" Baldock shouted his agreement.

Mylvannan and Ashwin joined the group, the two white tigers by their sides. Arifos turned and glanced at them.

"Let the durned orcs tremble in our wake!" Baldock cried again. The three dwarves then started down the tunnel once more, each searching for glory and more combat.

Arifos and Mylvannan both shrugged, and then followed their companions into the darkness of the tunnels.

<h1 style="text-align:center">CHAPTER 60</h1>

A most peculiar orc stood watching the entrance to Vorstad as the few remaining orcs he had sent in to test the defenses stumbled out. Their skin was blistered and burning. Arrows jutted from their armored forms as if they were pincushions. Flarg, the orc chieftain in command of the Murky Death Clan, was outraged. Not at the fact that the majority of his orcs had faltered—for that was their role in this battle—but because they had faltered so quickly.

Flarg was one of the tallest and strongest orcs of his clan, a fact that made him the chieftain through the traditional rights of physical combat. In their society, the strongest ruled, and there had yet to be a challenger that could face Flarg in his five-hundred-year rule. His age alone would defy the senses of his foes—most orcs failed to even reach their fortieth year. With the blood of the eternals flowing through his veins, the orc chieftain appeared to be in his prime, augmented with the experiences and teachings of over six centuries of his existence.

His skin color was a charcoal gray, lighter around his left eye. His eyes were a vibrant red that could be clearly seen in the dark. Jutting from his lower lip were two large teeth that he had encased in illistrium, providing Flarg with a vicious bite in close combat. His hair was unique to the orcs around him: like the eternals, he had grown long, wavy lime-green hair. For combat, he wore it tied-back in a braid down his back.

His armor was also much more exorbitant than that of his underlings, though all of the orcs of the Murky Death Clan were garbed in elven and dwarven armor. Flarg had the golden scale armor of an elven noble fastened atop an illistrium-linked hauberk. His shoulders were covered with golden pads with a long elven green cape fastened to them. His arms were protected by golden scale, his hands by studded leather gloves. He wore leather boots laced to his knees, with golden scale fastened to protect his shins. A green belt encircled his waist with a sword sheathed at the side. The blade was a finely-crafted elven blade, and would be recognized by any resident of Xylona as Orfrin, one of the ten famed honor blades.

"Bring the gnome powder," he cried out, deep and authoritatively.

Dozens of orcs rushed into motion, pulling a wagon filled with barrels towards the entrance of Vorstad. Flarg watched as they piled the barrels up along the cavern wall and just inside the entrance. As soon as all of the barrels were removed from one wagon, a second group of orcs pulled another one forward, continuing to add to the growing pile of thick barrels along the base of the mountain.

"Get in formation, and be ready," Thron called out. The dwarves did not need to be told. They were in position and ready to repel the orcish invasion. Though he would never admit it prior to an attack, Thron was proud of the efficiency, devotion, and determination of the dwarves under his command.

"They are planning something," Ferceng cautioned as he studied the opening of the cavern.

"You saw what they were bringing," Thron said. "Any ideas?"

"They could be attempting to use artillery, or unleashing ferocious animals upon us, or a variety of possibilities, too many to name."

"Whatever they bring, we will be ready for them," Thron sternly replied, a comment that received resounding cheers from the dwarves nearest him.

Their conversation was interrupted as a large explosion shook the very foundation of the mountain. The dwarves stumbled to the ground, unable to remain standing. Dust and debris made it hard for Thron to see what was happening as he struggled to stand back up.

He could hear screams and cries, but could not determine where they originated. More rocks started to tumble down, including the stalactites on the roof of the cavern, creating massive spears of death that rained down on the dwarves.

Ferceng held his hands up, forging a protection spell around himself and the dwarves near him, but he had been unprepared for the initial shockwave, and could see many dwarves lying dead near him, jagged edges of stone buried into chests, arms, throats, and heads. Others were injured, but already rearming themselves and preparing for what was to come.

Before the dust could settle, they could hear loud growls, the rumbling of thousands of feet, and the voices of dwarves fighting for their lives. Thron strained to see, but still could not make out anything more than five inches from his head. "They are upon us," he called out. "Archers, fire!"

Wiping the blood of his final adversary from his axe, Fok laughed triumphantly. "That was for all the months those filthy swine have been attacking us!" The dwarves under his command roared and cheered in agreement. Their plan had been perfectly executed, and the orc and goblin threat had been quickly thwarted.

"Should we take the southern passage and go kill the rest?" one dwarf asked as he kicked the severed head of a goblin away from him.

Fok grinned. "Yes—let's wipe them all out and end this threat from the east once and for all!"

More cheers erupted from the dwarves.

"If all of our battles today go as well as this one has, then today will be a swift victory!" Fok raised his axe and called out to inspire his men.

In the midst of their cheering, their voices were silenced as a large explosion and ground-shaking rumbling flowed over them. Several dwarves tipped over and fell to the ground. The warriors exchanged confused looks, none understanding what was happening.

Fok's one good eye widened in terror, "Back to the Halls of Vorstad, quickly!"

The dwarves charged after their general, each hoping that they would reach their homeland in time, each hiding their own fear that the worst thing imaginable may have just happened: Vorstad's fall!

Vaz and Vella had taken the point and were leading the companions deeper into the dark tunnels. Both white tigers were alert and knew that other orcs were nearby. The companions followed closely behind, their weapons raised and ready to strike.

In the distance, a large explosion roared, and even this far from Vorstad, the group could feel the aftershock of the attack. Thamar turned almost as white as Mylvannan and cried out. "No!"

Ahead of them, the two white tigers began to growl a warning.

Arifos stepped forward and peered into the darkness. "I hear many footsteps."

Thamar, still shaken by what he had heard, gripped the handle to his mallet a little tighter and rushed forward without a word, as if reaching the orcs sooner would somehow let him know the cause of the explosion.

The other companions fell in step behind him, pausing when they reached the two white tigers. Arifos swung his hand forward and a burst of flames shot down the tunnel, momentarily illuminating it. In the flickering light, they could see close to fifty orcs charging towards them.

Reaching behind his back, Arifos pulled his two scimitars from their scabbards and glanced at Thamar, seeing the dwarf salivating in anticipation of the fight. "We have found more than a scouting party this time," he called out. "Defend yourselves!"

As the dust began to settle, Thron was rendered speechless. Where before there was the face of the mountain and a narrow passage, now there was a large gaping hole before them. The orcs had somehow managed to tear down a portion of the mountain without collapsing the ledges above it.

Thousands of dwarves were scattered, either dead or unconscious. Those that had been standing along the cavern walls appeared to have taken the brunt of the impact, severely depleting their numbers.

Hundreds of the six-foot reptilian mantror's poured in along the side walls and ceiling, orcs with lances riding upon their backs. The green-skinned mounts had the ability to stick on walls, and the disoriented dwarves soon found themselves being attacked by mantror riders hanging from the very walls and ceiling of the cavern.

"No!" Thron cried out, watching helplessly as dwarves were swiftly struck down. A loud growl diverted his attention as he glanced back at the field before him. A koxlen leapt for him, landing on his shoulders and forcing him down.

Thron dropped, his shield firmly clutched above him keeping the brown-furred beast from fatally piercing him. He struggled to keep his shield where it was, but could see the feet of an orc that was riding the large predator.

Without doing anything, the beast slumped down on top of him. Thron let out a groan as the weight pinned him down. Then, the koxlen was pulled off and he saw Ferceng standing above him with his hand reaching down. His axe had been bloodied. "I owe you one this day."

"This day we shall not keep track," Ferceng replied as he spun to defend himself as another koxlen and rider barreled down towards them. Ferceng reached out with his hand, and the creature lifted into the air before him, clawing desperately as it tried to reach the ground again. The orc rider kept looking around, unable to understand what was happening.

Ferceng then pushed his hand forward and his ensnared attackers launched backwards and into two more koxlen and riders that had been charging towards them.

"Re-form the line," Thron called out to try and get the shielded dwarves to stand before those with spears to attempt a defence against the koxlen attack.

"As you order..." a dwarf started to reply, his words cut off as a koxlen leapt on him and removed his head with one bite.

"No!" Thron cried out as he brought his axe swinging down and digging into the koxlen's furry hide. The rider atop the koxlen swung with a sword and Thron barely raised his shield in time to deflect the blow.

Ferceng slung Carnage over his shoulder and began focusing on magic. He launched small lances of flame towards his targets, engulfing a koxlen and rider with each attempt. As he continued, he realized that he needed to get to higher ground in order to truly help out more.

Glancing at Thron, he watched as the battle-hardened dwarf pulled the orc from the koxlen and buried his axe in the creature's head. The koxlen spun around to attack, but Thron struck with his shield, ramming it in the eyes. Blinded, the koxlen tried to attack any-thing close to it, including another koxlen and rider. The two beasts began clawing viciously at one another.

Thron raised his axe and cried out, "With honor!"

"Wait," Ferceng prompted as he grabbed Thron's shoulder. "Let me try something first."

Thron turned and nodded his agreement, though he quickly lost sight of Ferceng as another koxlen leapt towards him. Thron dropped out of the way and swiped at the creature's back leg, dropping it to the ground. Three other dwarves with spears rushed forward and began stabbing it, leaving an angry orc rider screaming at them. An arrow pierced his neck, and his cries turned into a gurgling moan of death.

The Steward was glad to see the teamwork. They had been disori-ented by the strike, but his soldiers were beginning to pull together again. Wondering where Ferceng was and what he was planning, he glanced around quickly, spotting a large hawk flying to one of the walls of Vorstad. The bird then transmuted back into the Mage Master, and his hand pointed downwards, launching a large fireball.

Thron watched as the ball erupted into flames amongst a large contingent of the koxlen riders. The ferocious mounts began roaring and crying in pain as they burned, their riders squirming and trying to douse the flames themselves.

This attack was followed by lightning bolts lancing towards the mantrors along the walls, striking several and sending them to the ground, sizzling in charred death.

"Good," Thron nodded. Seeing that the orcs were now reeling, he raised his axe in the air and cried out, "With honor!"

Hundreds of dwarves joined in the call and fell in step behind him as Thron led the charge into the orc invaders.

CHAPTER 61

A mantror rider limped from the opening of the tunnels leading to Vorstad; his leg bleeding from a fall after his mount was struck by lightning. He shielded his eyes as he adjusted to the morning light. Seeing Flarg issuing orders to different units, he stumbled towards him, wincing with each step.

Two heavily armored orcs with shields and axes stepped in front of him and barred his path. They were members of the Lathryl, a subset of the orcs that had been mated with captured elves. Each of these protectors adorned their armor, shields, and weapons with sacred elven scripture. They were the most nimble and educated of all of the orcs of the Murky Death Clan. Each member of this group vowed their allegiance only to the Chieftain, pledging their lives in his service. They glared at the injured warrior threateningly. "No minion may have the honor of seeing the Chieftain."

"I have news, dire news," the mantror rider protested.

Flarg glanced up, curious of the report. "He may pass," he said.

The two protectors stepped aside and the mantror rider began moving forward. He paused as he saw dozens of the Lathryl surrounding Flarg, though he had not seen any when he first approached. The warriors had their elven bows drawn, sternly watching him for any sign of treachery.

The mantror rider dropped to his knees in front of Flarg. "My Chieftain, I have news."

"I am waiting," Flarg replied impatiently.

"A Mage," he blurted out. "They've got a Mage."

"I see," Flarg said, considering the implications. "What happened to your mount?"

"The Mage released bolts of lightning. My mantror was slain."

"I see no burns on you?" Flarg observed.

"I fell from the saddle and injured my leg," the orc explained.

"Yes," Flarg said in an uninterested tone. "Thank you for the information."

"It was an honor," the mantror rider said as he began to stand up.

Flarg unsheathed Orfrin and lifted it in the air. The Lathryl released a volley of arrows into the mantror rider.

The orc faltered backwards, stumbling. "Why?" he begged for understanding.

"You abandoned your allies," Flarg said. "Unforgivable." He then swung Orfrin down with a violent swing and severed the mantror rider's head. "He should not have fled. There will be no cowards in my service."

The Lathryl began pounding their fists on their chests over their hearts, a symbol of their agreement with their master.

"Unleash the bargodin," Flarg ordered, addressing the other orc leaders. "Continue pressing the attack—the dwarves will not stand a chance."

"What of the Mage?" one orc asked questioningly.

Flarg roared and slapped the commander across the face. "*I* will deal with the Mage, *you* destroy the dwarves."

"As my Chieftain commands," the orc bowed and returned to his unit.

The orcs were relentless, but the companions were committed and would not back down. Even if they decided to, the two Vorstad dwarves were consumed with berserker rage and would not pause to see reason. Even Baldock appeared stunned at the ferocity of his allies, but admired their skill and determination.

With so many foes confronting them, Ashwin opted to use her

bow, a weapon she was far more familiar and capable with. Her arms were a blur as she unleashed arrow after arrow at the fighting orcs. Her aim was true, and many orcs either fell or were hindered by the sting of her attack.

Vaz and Vella were not as protective when Ashwin was using her bow. It was as if the white tigers knew that she was more confident with the weapon, and understood that they too could engage the enemy without worrying about her safety. The tigers leapt off of walls, barreled into foes, and clawed and bit at orcs until they were dead. Any remaining orcs that were anywhere near the two white tigers quickly turned and fled.

Arifos maintained the calm determination and demeanor he always presented when in battle. His twin scimitars were slashing almost independently of each other as he danced through the orcs, leaving only corpses in his wake. The pink-skinned elf—though one of the highest proponents of not engaging in the battle—was the most effective of the group, swiftly reducing the numbers of their adversaries.

The Frost elf moved slower than his Madrew companion, but with his sword enchanted, he too left bodies behind him, frozen corpses. Mylvannan wondered how much he could use the enchantment of his sword. The Frost Queen had given it to him when he left Akkammanavar. Since then, he has used it many times, but typically only once or twice in a single day. This was already his second time in a matter of mere hours. Thus far, the blade's touch was as chilling as always, but he anticipated that this was one fight that would not end anytime soon.

An orc charged towards him, breaking his concentration. Mylvannan brought his sword up in defense, its chilling effect freezing the blade of his foe. With another slash, the frozen steel shattered under the impact, leaving the orc staring blankly at how quickly his weapon was destroyed. Mylvannan then jabbed his sword into the orc's stomach, and watched as a frost emitted from the wound and quickly encompassed the orc in ice.

The orc then shattered before him, revealing a smiling Baldock standing where the frozen warrior had been. "No time to be observin' yer handiwork—we be havin' more killin' to do!"

The Tregador dwarf then lowered his head, held his shield in front of him, and charged into a group of orcs, knocking several over. Laughing at his pathetic foes, Baldock began swinging his mighty axe, Splitter, and severed the limbs of those closest to him. With the distraction quickly fading, he slowed down his attack and picked his targets more closely, though he still preferred at least five-to-one odds to make his day seem eventful. With orcs, any less would be an insult to the dwarf's fighting spirit.

Thamar and Theiler were working in tandem as they had so many times before. They carved their way through an entire line of orcs, and then spun around to see that almost all of the fifty orcs had already been slain. Nodding to each other, they charged back into the fray, Thamar swinging his mallet, and Theiler his sword.

Several orcs backed away from the unrelenting dwarves and ran further into the darkness of the tunnels. If any of the companions noticed their departure, they displayed no sign of it.

Leading the charge through the orcs, Thron was pleased to see that many of the koxlen and riders had been trampled and slain along the way. These heavily armored Murky Death orcs were bad enough—but paired with koxlen, he liked them even less. With his armies present, the koxlen were manageable, but he knew that he would never want to meet one on the open-plains when he was alone. Their deadliness and ferocity was renowned.

Several bursts of lightning continued to crack as the few remaining koxlen and mantror were killed from afar. Thron tapped his spiked helm with his axe to salute the Mage Master in appreciation, and then prepared for the next assault.

Below him, he could feel the ground shaking again. "What trickery is this?" he called out.

The ground before them opened and a large wormlike creature, with a grooved orange-segmented body, black spots along its top, and two large tusks jutting from the sides of its mouth, rose into the cavern.

It remained there for a moment, and then slammed down, sending hundreds of dwarves scurrying to avoid its monstrous bulk. Though part of it remained within the hole it had come from, it appeared to be well-over fifty feet in length, and almost twenty feet wide.

"Archers!" Thron called out, sending volleys of dwarven arrows piercing the creature.

From the walls of Vorstad, Ferceng bit his lip in frustration. He had seen several of these creatures dragging the wagons on his way to warn the dwarves. Every time they seemed to have a minor respite and victory, the orcs unleashed something even worse upon them.

Taking a deep breath, Ferceng began blowing towards the creature, using his mystical powers to increase the force to a gusting hurricane blast. The wind began pummeling the creature, forcing it to move away from the dwarves, but it did not seem fazed by the attack.

The creature lifted back up again and a greenish liquid sprayed from its mouth, most of which blew wildly in the Mage's attack. Where the green liquid hit, the rock, armor, and any creature that it came in contact with began to smolder as the acidic substance burned through them.

Realizing the danger that this creature could pose, Ferceng began unleashing a volley of mystical attacks towards it. He began with a roaring fireball, and followed up immediately with an ice burst, hoping that the changing temperatures would harm the creature. Seeing that it acted as if untouched, he unleashed a powerful succession of lightning blasts, which resulted in some scalding, but little other effect.

Concentrating on his attack as he had never done before, Ferceng raised every weapon from every fallen warrior, dwarf and orc alike, and sent them hurtling towards the worm. Axes, maces, swords, lances, arrows, spears, and more were all jutting out of the creature. It lifted back up again, this time screeching in agony, but still very much alive.

In desperation, Ferceng concentrated on the ceiling and created a tremor, causing more of the cavern to collapse and cave in. Falling rocks and debris hit the creature, burying it below tons of rubble. As the barrage continued, he focused a blast of light—so pure that it was like the power of the searing sun itself, illuminating the entire cavern as if Vorstad was out in the open—slicing through the rock pile and into the creature, severing it in two.

As the worm stopped moving, Ferceng sighed in relief, hoping that the others he had seen did not begin their attack anytime soon. These things were far too deadly and required too much attention to withstand for long.

Slumping over, he braced himself on the ledge, feeling like he was going to pass out. That last battle had taken a lot out of him. He was alarmed that he was so out of shape with his combat magic. If they survived this, Ferceng was determined to work hard to regain the condition and form he was in when he first left the Mage's Council.

In his peripheral vision, Ferceng saw the worm begin to twitch. He studied it for a moment, and saw that the beast was still alive. Though cut in two, both sides of the worm were moving of their own accord. It was no longer attacking, which he felt was a positive thing, for he wasn't certain what else he could try that might kill it.

By the entrance, thousands of heavily armored orc foot soldiers began charging in, roaring. Ferceng searched for Thron and saw him directing the dwarves back. The enemy forces were too overwhelming. The initial battles may have been won, but the warriors of Vorstad were forced back to defend from the Halls of Vorstad themselves.

The orcs that fled the companions ran straight to their chieftain and told him that a band of dwarves and elves were killing their forces. Krug appeared delighted by the news, as if he was suddenly rejuvenated.

"If they can find a way to us, then we can find a way back to Vorstad," he cheered. "Slaughter them all, but make sure at least one is left alive to tell us how to get around!"

The orcs cheered and charged back down the tunnel to confront the companions. Krug glanced at the debris before him one last time, and then followed his troops, determined to be part of the fall of Vorstad.

CHAPTER 62

After receiving the report that the Mage defeated the bargodin, Flarg ordered his foot soldiers into the underground city. Regardless of how much the dwarves and the Mage accomplished, his army was almost limitless. Still, it was time to request assistance to make the conquest a little easier.

As he walked away, the Lathryl followed in formation behind him. Flarg paused at a grassy knoll and sat down, crossing his legs. Eight members of the Lathryl did the same, creating a near circle around him. The remaining protectors stood around the edge of the circle with their backs to their companions, guarding them from anyone that may attempt to disturb them.

As Flarg closed his eyes and concentrated, the eight Lathryl also closed their eyes and began chanting softly. The orc chieftain focused his attention, and a single name crept into his thoughts: *Zoldex.*

"What is your status?"

Flarg opened his eyes as saw the swirling blue image of Zoldex standing before him. "The invasion is proceeding as anticipated. Vorstad will fall."

"Excellent," Zoldex replied. "I sense that there is more."

"Yes," Flarg said. "A Mage defends Vorstad. Though we will breach their defenses and triumph, his intervention has delayed our victory."

"You wish assistance against this Mage?" Zoldex asked.

"I do," Flarg replied. "The more soldiers that survive, the better our foothold in the south will be."

"Very well," Zoldex said. "Continue the onslaught. I want Vorstad to fall before the sun does this day. The Mage will not be a burden any longer."

"As your eminence commands," Flarg lowered his head in respect. When he looked up again, the image of Zoldex was gone.

With a raging roar, Thamar swung his mallet around and shattered the armor from the last orc. The creature fell back dazed and did not have time to react as the red-bearded dwarf leapt towards him, bringing his hammer thundering down on its head.

Standing up, he roared in triumph. "May ten or ten thousand face me. I am Thamar, thrasher of mine enemies, son of Thron and a true son of Vorstad!"

"He certainly enjoys this," Mylvannan whispered to Ashwin.

"Yes, it is good that he is on *our* side," she smiled back.

"Are there more o' these vermin?" Baldock asked.

"If there is, they will feel the wrath of my hammer," Thamar vowed.

Arifos began to stiffen and studied the dark tunnel. "We have more company."

"Yes! Bring 'em on!" Baldock roared.

"Bring them on, indeed. For Vorstad!" Thamar chimed in, his mallet held ready to strike.

Just then, a swarm of hundreds of orcs began emerging from the darkness. The bluster and confidence of the group quickly dwindled.

"Defensive position," Mylvannan cried as the companions formed a semi-circle. Their foes were overwhelming and seemed never ending. If they were to fall this day, it would be beside noble companions and good friends.

Ferceng monitored the dwarves as they retreated behind the mighty walls that would be the last line of defense for Vorstad. The orcs continued to charge towards them. He knew that Thron needed time to have the massive stone gates sealed.

Digging deep into his soul, he breathed steadily and found the strength to unleash yet another assault at the invaders. A blast of darkness streaked from him and enshrouded the orcs. He maintained the shroud, listening as the armored clanging of the orcs slowed while they defended, in case there were more mystical strikes coming their way.

Ferceng did not wish to disappoint them. If he only encased them in a cloaking shroud, they would quickly be moving again. Instead, he needed to do something to make them feel threatened and fall back slightly.

The Mage Master focused on the darkness and decided that glimmers of light may be precisely what he needs. Small flashes began bursting within the shroud. Each one was quick and sent electrical jolts into those that felt them. Not enough to kill them, but to sting enough to force them back. Even the brightest flash did nothing to illuminate the darkness that Ferceng was casting.

He listened to the cries of shock and pain, and was relieved that he still could help in some fashion. Some of the orcs were not convinced they should pull back and tried to charge through the black shroud. As soon as they reached the end, Ferceng twiddled his fingers, emitting a succession of small electrical globes. As they reached the orcs, they exploded, sending shocking volts of pure electricity through them.

Something pulled on his pants, and Ferceng looked down, being careful not to cease any of his current spells. A small dwarven child that had not yet even grown a single hair on his chin stared up at him. "How is the war going?"

"Your people are fighting most valiantly," Ferceng replied. "Shouldn't you be below, though, with the other children?"

"Me?" the boy asked. "No, I am Prell, son of Reght, a true son of

Vorstad. I will fight!"

"Well Prell, I think you are right," Ferceng replied. "We need warriors like you to defend the Halls of Vorstad."

"Yes," Prell agreed as he lifted a wooden axe, probably little more than a toy or training weapon.

"In that case, the women will need you to protect them," Ferceng said.

"The *women*?" Prell asked skeptically.

"Yes, if the orcs break through the defenses, they will be defense-less."

"I guess," Prell said as he thought about it.

"I can think of no one better to guarantee their safety and help them," Ferceng said.

"Me?"

"Yes Prell," Ferceng said seriously. "Are you up to the task?"

"You bet!" he joyously cried. "Those orcs will never get past me."

"I have every faith," Ferceng said. "Now, hurry to your post."

"Yes sir," Prell said as he jogged towards the stairs.

Ferceng watched Prell as he began to leave. He truly admired these people; their spirit was so strong. The child stopped as if he could no longer force himself to go another step, and soon his whole body began convulsing. "Prell, are you okay?"

The child did not answer. Instead the convulsing continued, and where Prell had been, he transformed and grew into a hideous skeletal Shadow Mage. Ferceng watched in awe, having never before seen one of these creatures. It swung around, a sword held in its decaying hand, and slashed Ferceng across the chest. As the troll fell backwards, he lost his concentration, and the spells inhibiting the orcs dissolved.

"Hurry," Thron called. Most of his dwarves were safely inside the walls of Vorstad, but all of a sudden, the mystical barriers that had been hindering the orcs vanished and the creatures were advancing again.

Arrows were launched from both sides. Thron watched as many of his fleeing dwarves fell before the barrage of the orcs. Glancing up, the red-bearded dwarf strained to see Ferceng. He could not understand why the Mage had suddenly stopped assisting them. As hundreds of dwarves began to fall dead beside him, he vowed that whatever kept the troll from helping them would suffer at his hands.

CHAPTER 63

"By the gods!" one dwarf shouted as they reached the opening of the tunnel and saw thousands of orcs advancing upon Vorstad.

"None of that," Fok ordered as he studied the landscape. He could see Thron surrounded by archers and dwarves with crossbows. They were defending the gates as other dwarves slowly were closing the mighty stone doors.

The cavern was filled with orcs, as if there were a never-ending stream of foes. The vile creatures were trampling over both their slain allies and the noble dwarven defenders without even pausing to notice. As he continued to watch, he was horrified and enraged by the sight. Fok had never been one to pray to either Feldrin or Mander, but looking at the devastation before him, he silently prayed that the gods would not abandon them at this dire time.

"We need to buy them some time," he called out. He looked at his unit, proud to see only eager and determined eyes looking back at him. "For Vorstad!" Raising his axe, he led the charge into the orc forces close to the gates, splitting their attention.

Arifos pulled back on the bowstring of Unamalastra. The string moved as easily as it always did in his hands. Carefully following orcs that were charging towards them, he released an arrow and swiftly pulled another from his quiver. The arrow launched from his enchanted bow with such force that the orc that it struck was lifted from the ground and hurtled back ten yards, knocking over the orcs behind him.

Continuing to aim at those closest, the Madrew elf released arrow after arrow, each hitting their marks. He snorted at the stupidity of his foes as he saw three orcs almost directly in line. Drawing a steel-shafted arrow, he grinned deviously, launching it towards them. The arrow went cleanly through all three orcs, sending the trio flying backwards with the brunt of the impact.

"Impressive, elf!" Thamar cheered.

Ashwin stood on the far end of the companions, who stood in "V"-formation with the two archers at the ends. The armored Baldock stood in the middle with Thamar and Theiler on each side. Next to them were the two white tigers. Mylvannan stood next to Vella on one side, and Ashwin on the other. She, too, was releasing arrow after arrow at the orcs, her arms moving quickly as her volleys launched towards the advancing creatures. Unlike Arifos though, her weapon was not mystically enhanced. At times, it would take two or even three arrows before an orc would fall.

The two archers alone were not enough to repel the attack: the orcs vastly outnumbered them, and no matter how quickly the two elves attacked, the grayish-green-skinned creatures continued to advance. Within moments, they reached the dwarves, who began swinging and striking whatever came within reach of them.

"We must pull back," Arifos called, knowing that they were vastly outnumbered and in a poor defensive position.

Crashing his mallet into the chest of an orc, cracking ribs and drawing blood, Thamar shot Arifos a wicked glare. "I will not leave until every orc that dares to threaten Vorstad feels my wrath!"

Arifos shook his head in defeat and slung his bow over his shoulder. In a swift arc, his arms swung down with Phistala and Aurlestyl in his hands. Knowing that the orcs were too close to continue using his bow, he stepped forward and began swiping his enchanted blades with masterful precision. Each strike was a deathblow, and orcs began piling up around him.

Ashwin was not as confident about surrendering her bow. She took a step backwards to find the safety behind her fighting companions, and continued to launch arrows at the orcs. Each time she reached back, her concern grew—she was quickly running out of arrows. If she ran out, then she would be forced to fight with only the sword, a prospect she was not entirely comfortable with. If only they could survive this confrontation and reach Xylona so that she could replenish the supply of her dwindling stock.

Noticing several orcs pause, she watched as they pulled their arms back, preparing to hurl spears. Ashwin quickly began launching arrows at the group, killing three of them before they had the chance to unleash their volley. The fourth orc released his spear before the arrow hit him. Ashwin saw it coming but her feet did not seem to move quickly enough for her to dodge. The jagged spear dug deeply into her right shoulder, dropping her back with a scream of agony.

Thamar, who slammed his mallet down on the head of an orc, crushing its skull, heard her scream and looked back in terror. The elven princess had fought for his home valiantly, but she was so young and inexperienced. How could he have been so stubborn to force his companions to fight against insurmountable odds, only because he was enraged that his homeland was besieged and there was truly nothing that he could do to stop it?

Seeing her writhing on the ground in agony, Thamar left his position and dropped down by her side. As he saw the blood seeping from her wound, he raised his head howling in despair, "No!"

Taking advantage of Fok's attack, Thron got his remaining dwarves behind the gates of Vorstad. Searching the battlefield for any sign of his long-time friend, he knew that the general would not be walking away from this one.

"Finish closing the gates," he ordered somberly.

"But Fok is still out there!" one dwarf protested.

"Then let his noble sacrifice be an inspiration to us all," Thron sternly replied. "Close the damned gates!"

As the gates began sealing again, he silently mouthed a prayer to Feldrin, the dwarven God of Fury, in Fok's name. If the gods were listening, the general would be imbued with mystical energy to help strike down the orcs with the fury of Feldrin himself.

Fok led his remaining dwarves directly into the throng of orcs. Their battle in the tunnels had been very successful, and almost the full contingent—two thousand true sons of Vorstad—was with him in their final act to help preserve their home. Each and every dwarf would gladly sacrifice his life if it meant the survival of Vorstad. That was the true nature of a Vorstad dwarf: honor, duty, respect, and sacrifice.

Their movements were swift and brutal: the dwarves that Fok had by his side were highly experienced warriors of Vorstad. Like him, most of them were at least three centuries old, and had fought to defend Vorstad from orcs, goblins, and even humans from time to time. They also battled alongside the elves of Xylona against hobgoblins, trolls, and rasplers. These dwarves knew how to fight, and the orcs they attacked would know that they had been in a valliant battle before this day was done.

They sang a dwarven battle hymn as they fought, though Fok could clearly distinguish that fewer and fewer voices were partaking in the song. No matter how experienced or noble his troops were, they were fighting a losing battle, hoping only to achieve a single goal: providing time for the gates to close and the surviving dwarves to prepare more defenses.

Straining to see above the orcs as he continued to strike them down with his axe, Fok watched as the gates slammed together. They had done it. They had succeeded. Even though he could see at least a thousand orcs between him and Vorstad, he knew that his objective was complete. Any orc that he killed now would only help him achieve more glory in the afterlife. If he were to die this day, he knew that he would not be alone.

Stepping forward, he swung his axe, embedding it in the hamstring of an orc. As the creature dropped to the ground, he slammed the axe into its armored chest, splitting the armor and killing the creature.

Another orc charged towards him. He swung his buckler around and defended the attack, following up with a swipe of his axe. The blade caught the orc in its side, and it dropped down, grasping its bloody wound.

A large group of orcs was advancing near him. Fok ran towards them and leapt into the crowd, his axe swinging violently as he landed. Many of the surviving dwarves saw his attack and felt inspired by the general. They charged directly towards the large cluster, and cut them down quickly.

One dwarf gasped and looked down. Fok lay there, his eyes blinking as he strained to fill his lungs with air. A sword had pierced his armor and punctured a lung. "My general!" the dwarf cried.

Fok glanced up, wincing. He reached a bloody hand up and grabbed the dwarf by the head. He lowered him down so that he could hear his final words. The words were barely above a strained whisper, but the dwarf would remember them until his dying breath as well, and hoped that he too could die as honorably.

"For Vorstad, with honor." With his final four words, Fok dropped back, his arm falling from around the dwarf's head and landing in a pool of blood from the slain orcs. His eye remained open, but the light of his life had been extinguished. His mortal deeds of honor and valor had come to an end, his journey leading now to Wolhollm, the great hall of immortality where the souls of heroic and noble warriors would spend the remainder of eternity in a blissful afterlife.

The dwarf who shared the general's final moments picked up Fok's axe and raised it high in the air. "For Vorstad, with honor!" The surviving dwarves rallied around the call, and struck with a fury that was legendary. In time though, they too fell, and orcs continued to advance as if the dwarves had never even been there.

CHAPTER 64

Ferceng leaned forward and clutched his chest, feeling the blood seeping from the wound from the Shadow Mage. The creature was slowly walking towards him, hissing. Remembering what Braksis had told him about these creatures, he reached back and pulled Carnage over his shoulder.

"I have heard about you, demon," he said defiantly. "I am ready."

The Shadow Mage continued towards him, hissing in reply.

Ferceng stood up, pain shooting through him. The wound would definitely need to be tended to quickly, but time was something that he did not have the luxury of with a foe such as this. Holding his axe defensively, he braced himself as the Shadow Mage lunged forward with its sword.

The two blades connected again and again, sparks dancing from their blades with each clash. Tightening his grip on Carnage, Ferceng began to swing harder and harder, hoping to strike and rid the realm of one more demon. In one attack, the Shadow Mage defied its awkward appearance and nimbly moved aside. As Ferceng's back was exposed in the follow-through, the skeletal warrior slashed with his sword, igniting even more pain in the troll as blood began seeping from his back.

With the line crumbling after Ashwin was struck, Arifos somersaulted in front of the group and used his mystical abilities to hurtle the orcs backwards. Seeing the slight gap between them, he quickly erected a defensive barrier. It would not hold long, but it would provide the companions with a minor respite.

The orcs were quickly upon the barrier, striking it with their weapons. Arifos remained before them for a moment, making certain that the shield would hold, then twirled around to see to Ashwin.

Mylvannan had rushed to her side and pulled the spear from her shoulder. The wound was deep and had done damage to her muscles and bone as well. Thamar glanced down at the bloody spear. Like most orc weapons, it was jagged and rusty. With a wound like that, they would have no choice but to sever the elf's arm to prevent the spread of infection.

Ashwin continued to cry and scream. She had never been in such agony before. She felt so cold lying on the stone ground. In her mind, her life was coming to an end. At thirty-five, she was barely an infant in the eyes of the elves, and already her life was at an end. She could hear voices, but had trouble focusing on them.

"We'll have to sever the arm," Thamar said somberly.

Baldock stepped up behind them and held Splitter firmly. "Then ye get out o' the way and be lettin' Splitter here do the job, quick and clean."

"No," Mylvannan replied sternly. Picking up Ashwin's left hand, he squeezed it and tried to reach her. "I know that it hurts, but the ring *should* heal the wound."

"The ring?" Thamar asked.

Baldock looked back and forth between Thamar and Mylvannan, and then placed his axe over his shoulder. If they needed his services, he would be ready.

"Stay with me!" Mylvannan shouted, escalating his voice to get through to Ashwin.

Arifos felt a jolt of dizziness and looked at the barrier. The shields were holding, but the orcs were constantly hammering away at the invisible wall erected before them. "We must leave, *now*!"

"In a moment," Mylvannan said.

Baldock, Theiler, and the two white tigers stepped closer to the barrier, preparing themselves to defend the others if Arifos's defenses faltered. They each knew that Ashwin needed time, and they were determined to provide it.

"It's happening," Mylvannan said with a sigh of relief.

Thamar glanced down at the wound, tears flowing from his eyes, but not caring what anyone else thought about a warrior such as him being emotional. Mylvannan was right—he could see the wound slowly knitting together.

Ashwin continued to cry and scream in agony. Though her wounds were healing, it was an excruciating process. After what seemed like an eternity, she winced and glanced at her shoulder. The pain was gone. As she looked at it, below her torn green tunic, the injury was gone, and not even a scar remained to mark her. "How?" she asked in confusion.

"Your father's ring," Mylvannan answered. "A mighty gift to you, indeed."

Ashwin rotated her shoulder several times, but was amazed that the pain was completely gone. Standing up, she grabbed her bow and glanced down at the teary-eyed dwarf. "I'm ready."

"No," Arifos called back. "We're leaving. To stay here is madness. We will survive this day and strike Zoldex again in another."

Thamar wiped the tears from his face and stood up, his hand tightening on his hammer. He hated to leave his home when it was being attacked, but Arifos was right. "Very well, we're no good if we're dead."

Arifos nodded in respect at the dwarf. He glanced back at the attacking orcs and used his mystical abilities to charge his shield with an electrical shock. As soon as he did so, the orcs all tumbled backwards, yelping in pain. "Now!" he called out. The companions fled the way they had come, leaving their hopes of helping Vorstad behind them.

Thron ascended the stairwell and stood looking down at the orcs. "Archers, keep at them," he called out. "I want vats of boiling oil here too. Drop them down at the swine."

With each command, dwarves leapt into action, efficiently preparing to defend their home. Glancing inside the walls, he saw the Halls of Vorstad, where the women and children stood waiting for the defenses to falter. His own daughter Threll stood in the front, defiantly waiting to strike down the invaders. He did not wish her harm, but was proud of her. She was a good daughter, and an honorable dwarf.

"I want as many dwarves as we can fit up here on the walls," he instructed. "They will try to break through the walls, *and* scale them. We must prepare for both."

Studying the forces coming towards them again, he wondered how they could have been so foolish as to think that they could withstand an army such as this alone. If only reinforcements could somehow arrive in time, either the elves of Xylona or the humans from Trespias. Both were nothing more than dreams though, for he knew neither was coming.

Pondering his allies, he wondered what had happened to Ferceng. The troll had fought valiantly throughout the battle. Without him, they would have suffered many more losses than they had already. However, he had abandoned them when they were pulling back. Too many dwarves died without the cover of the Mage.

Straining to see higher up where Ferceng was standing, his eyes widened in shock, and then quickly set in a hardened rage. The troll was in combat with one of the hideous skeletal creatures, a deadly Shadow Mage. Leaving his own position, Thron rushed towards another stairwell that would bring him to the mystical combatants. He may not be able to do much, but he knew for a fact that Vorstad needed Ferceng's mystical attacks to survive the day. He was not about to let a creature of darkness take him away without a fight.

CHAPTER 65

Ferceng toppled to the ground with the strike of the Shadow Mage. He was at a great disadvantage. It had been many years since he had left the Mage's Council, and the extensive training and skills that he had mastered in his youth were more of a memory than a reality. His defenses and attacks were slow and unorganized. Every movement seemed to be wrong and off-balanced.

The Shadow Mage moved in quickly and slashed down with its swords, slicing into Ferceng's left arm. The troll bit back a scream and forced himself around to defend again. He could not believe that a creature that appeared to be a shadowy skeleton was far more nimble and precise than he.

Deciding to take the offensive, Ferceng reached out and launched bolts of lightning lancing towards the Shadow Mage. The creature kept walking towards him, unaffected by the mystical attack. It appeared to somehow absorb the energy rather than be hindered by it.

Ceasing his attack, Ferceng began a defensive spell to create a barrier around him. Once erected, it would protect him somewhat from the sword slashes. As he began to construct the mystical shield, the Shadow Mage raised its own hand, and Ferceng felt himself battered with torrents of power. The force of the blast knocked him backwards, right off of the ledge.

Falling through the air, Ferceng tried to brace himself, but was unprepared as his body impacted the ledge of a lower level. Lying on his back, he tried to concentrate, but seemed unable to move. The world around him was swirling. He knew that he had to get up, but felt that it would be impossible to actually do so.

Above him, through blurry eyes, he could see the Shadow Mage leap from the ledge where he had fallen from, its sword aimed at his chest to skewer him. As the Mage came closer, Ferceng could do nothing to defend himself. His life had come to an end; his mission was a failure.

The Shadow Mage dropped through the air, a triumphant hiss as it closed in on its victim. Then, a hammer impacted its head and sent the creature plummeting away from the troll.

Thron ran up the last few steps and glanced quickly down at Ferceng, who was struggling to stand up. With deep breaths—in through his nose and out through his mouth—Thron removed another throwing hammer and started twirling it above his head by the leather strap. "I have more where that came from, demon!"

The Shadow Mage stood up, it's glowing red eyes boring into the dwarf. The hammer had impacted its skeletal head, and the Mage's jaw was creaking back and forth as it hung from the right side of its face, part of it shattered by the impact.

Releasing the second hammer, it soared with the accuracy of a skilled warrior and knocked the sword from the creature's hands. Though disarmed, Thron was well aware that the Shadow Mage could still attack him with a variety of mystical assaults; he had to be cautious.

Pulling his axe from behind his back, he firmly clutched it in one hand, holding his shield in the other. In a raging determination, he walked towards the creature, refusing to let the Shadow Mage have a moment's respite. "You distracted the troll. Many dwarves died because of that distraction. Time for you to see what it means to cross a true son of Vorstad!"

Leaping at the Shadow Mage, he brought his axe swinging downward and struck the creature several times, cleaving bones from its body. No matter how hard he pressed the attack though, the demon still stood and appeared uninhibited by the blows.

Raising its hand, a ray of pure black light shot out towards the dwarf. Thron raised his shield just in time, but was still pushed backwards even though he had his feet firmly planted on the ground. Before his eyes, his shield began to glow, and he wondered if this attack could somehow burn right through his shield.

Dropping his axe to try to brace himself, Thron held on tightly. He roared in defiance and took a slow step towards the Shadow Mage, pushing against the force of the constant barrage. Inch by inch, though each step was agony for his muscles, the surly dwarf forced his way back towards his opponent.

The blast suddenly stopped and Thron almost toppled over without the resistance against his efforts. Lowering his shield, Thron risked being attacked by the Shadow Mage if it was faking. He saw it standing up, his axe embedded in its chest.

Glancing backwards, he saw Ferceng kneeling. The troll had managed to regain his senses and used his mystical abilities to send the axe hurtling into the Shadow Mage. Removing another throwing hammer, Thron began twirling it and sent it launching towards the Shadow Mage with deadly force. Part of its head shattered by the impact, but it stood back up, extended its hand, and mystically formed a whip.

The whip was not like a normal weapon. It had five barbed spikes at the end of it, and the entire whip was illuminated by a faint glow. The Shadow Mage cracked the whip in front of it, and the ground shook with the impact as five small explosions erupted on the ground.

"Wonderful," Thron whispered sarcastically.

"Thron," Ferceng called, the effort obviously a strain. "Only magical weapons can destroy it!"

Thron glanced back to see Ferceng struggling to stand up, Carnage being used as a brace. The whip jutted out at him, the five barbed heads hitting his shield and exploding upon impact. Thron was flung backwards, his shield badly scorched with holes in it.

Tossing his shield aside, Thron shook his head to regain his composure, and then glanced at Ferceng again. Ferceng was now standing and threw Carnage to his companion. Thron caught the mystical weapon and could feel the blade's power surging through his fingers. It was as if the axe was calling to him, begging him to use it to slaughter his foes.

Charging forward, he saw the whip lashing out again, and swung the axe with the skill and confidence of a battle-hardened son of Vorstad. The blade severed three of the five barbed heads, the other two exploding on his chainmail. He could feel the blast, but the mystical weapon did not penetrate the scale he wore beneath.

Thron ignored the pain and continued running towards the Shadow Mage. The creature attempted to whip him again, but Thron was already on top of it. He brought Carnage swiping down and severed the skeletal limb holding the whip. With a roar of defiance, he lifted the axe high over his head and brought it swiping down, striking the Shadow Mage on the left shoulder, and exiting from its pelvis on the right side of its body.

Thron continued to roar as the Shadow Mage dropped to the ground in two separate pieces. He raised the axe again, but watched as the body began to crumble into dust. Stepping forward, he kicked the ashen remains, satisfied that the Shadow Mage had been destroyed.

CHAPTER 66

The sounds of the orcs were increasing. The companions knew that the grayish-green creatures were almost directly behind them, gaining upon them. Ahead, light illuminated a portion of the tunnel as they came upon the entrance that they initially ventured through.

"There!" Thamar pointed out.

"The blang durned orcs are still bein' behind us!" Baldock warned.

Arifos paused to study the roof of the cave. "Keep running—I'll stop them!"

Vaz and Vella were the first ones out of the darkness, Ashwin and Mylvannan mere steps behind them. Thamar and Theiler quickly joined them, with Baldock's armor clinking and clanging as he escaped from the tunnel as well. They all prepared their weapons and readied themselves to defend the opening if needed.

Arifos backpedaled towards the opening, waiting for the orcs to come upon him. As he saw the warriors begin to take shape in the sunlight from the entrance, he raised his hands and released a powerful mystical shockwave. The cavern began to shake and the orcs stopped to brace themselves. Rocks from the top of the cave began to collapse, increasing in intensity as it did so.

Arifos back-flipped out of the way of the falling debris and joined his companions. They watched as the cave-in completely filled the tunnel with rocks, dust, and debris. He had succeeded. The orcs were trapped, and they had managed to escape.

Dropping to his knees, Thamar reached out and touched the rocks that sealed the cave. His head bowed, he spoke remorsefully, "I

352

couldn't help them."

Ashwin kneeled down beside him and placed her hand on his shoulder. As the dwarf looked up, she could see even more pain. Though she thought that it was for his inability to help Vorstad, she would have been surprised to learn that Thamar was devastated again by the thought of seeing her hurt and suffering.

"I am sorry, so sorry," he said as he grabbed her tight and hugged her.

"This is your home," Ashwin compassionately responded. "If you did not want to defend it, then you would not be the companion I thought you were."

Thamar leaned back and studied her for a moment. She was right. They all risked their lives when they were on the road, and though he did not wish to see her in pain, he knew that they all were willing to sacrifice themselves in the fight against evil. Cheering up slightly, he nodded his gratitude to the young elf. "I know of another passage. We can see what is happening inside!"

"That would be unwise," Arifos cautioned. "Our supplies are running low. The forces mounted against us are overwhelming."

"You of all people, elf, I would think would love the challenge. I have never seen you turn your back on a threat. And I have never seen a more effective warrior," Thamar said. "Even me."

"You try to humble me," Arifos commented. "It will not work. I would die here if that were what destiny desired of me. However, we are on a more important mission: there is a war upon us, a war against Zoldex. I will die by the Chosen One's side on the day she brings the tyrant down, as it was prophesied."

"Well then," Thamar laughed. "If you are going to die facing Zoldex and it has been prophesied, then whatever you do this day will see you victorious. Come!"

Arifos shook his head. The dwarf did not understand. There was no prophecy determining his death, only that the Chosen One would bring about the end of Zoldex. He just knew deep down that he would play a vital role in the war against Zoldex. He had to. For all of the

Madrew that suffered and did not retaliate, for his sisters and his homeland, he had to play a role in destroying Zoldex.

"Don't worry, my pink friend," Thamar said. "Where I am taking us is nothing more than a window in the sky. We can look down upon Vorstad, but there is no way to intervene in what is happening."

"Lead the way," Arifos replied. Though he was reluctant, he knew enough that to win a war, you must be aware of the forces amassed against you. Any force brave enough to attack the famed Halls of Vorstad must be pretty impressive. The realm would be better-off being aware of the scope of the true threat.

"This way," Thamar said as he and Ashwin led the group up a steep mountain path.

Baldock began to shake his head in disgust. "More blasted climbin'? I need me some new friends!"

Reaching his advance-forces, Krug stopped at the newly caved in entrance. He pounded his fist on it and screamed in frustration. They were now sealed in from two openings. "Find me another way around!" he ordered. "Now!"

The orcs scrambled away, desperately searching for another tunnel. They knew that their leader was temperamental. The orc that returned without finding a way around would be the first to die.

Krug pumped his fist in frustration. His orcs had been the ones besieging Vorstad for so long, and the day that it finally fell, he would be forced to hear about it from others, and not have the honor of being present to help bring an end to the dwarves. The realization infuriated him.

Thron bent down and picked up his own axe, holding both blades in his hand. They felt good in his grip, as if he could take on the entire orc army without working up a sweat. "This blade of yours corrupts the mind."

"Yes," Ferceng answered as he slowly limped over to Thamar. "It is imbued with dark energies. The axe is enchanted to make it unbreakable, but it instills within the wielder dark and sinister thoughts. You probably feel invincible wielding it?"

"I do at that," Thron agreed. "Here. It would be better in your hands. You seem able to control it."

"I am a Mage and understand such things, but it does nag at the back of my mind, too," Ferceng admitted.

"You're hurt," Thron observed. "Badly."

Ferceng knew the truth in the dwarf's words, but did not want to admit how badly his injuries truly were. "I still have some fight left in me."

"No," Thron said shaking his head. Glancing down, he watched as the orcs used a battering ram on the stone gates. Ladders were being carried in to scale the walls. Hooked cables were being tossed atop the wall, orcs trying to scale them. Mantrors were climbing both the wall and the rock face, delivering orcs into the Halls of Vorstad. He even saw mounted three-headed flying creatures, the vicious chimera, attacking the defenders of Vorstad.

"Look about, troll: the battle still rages on, but it is also as good as done."

"I would not expect to hear defeat in the voice of a dwarf," Ferceng commented.

"You do not hear defeat, only realism," Thron differentiated. "Every dwarf—man, woman, and child—will fight until their dying breath to save this city. The end result will be the same."

"I could still help," Ferceng added.

"You can hardly stand," Thron quickly retorted. "Besides, even with a hundred Mages, this battle would still be done. It is time to leave and tell the rest of the realm what to expect. They must be prepared—the unification must succeed."

"It must," Ferceng agreed, "or all of the sacrifices we have made thus far will have been for naught."

"If you see my boys, let them know that I died as a true son of Vorstad, fighting for what I believed in. Let them know that the spirit of Vorstad will never die. It will live on in them."

"I shall," Ferceng promised.

"Now hurry up and get that axe out of here. No use having such a magnificent weapon be lost and claimed by some damned orc."

"Very well," Ferceng reluctantly nodded. "It was an honor to have met and fought by your side."

"Likewise, troll. Now get out of here."

Ferceng transmuted into the form of a hawk again, but the transformation was much slower this time. Feathers were missing and blood could be seen scattered throughout the giant bird. Determination alone lifted Ferceng into the air: and though his flight was much slower due to his injuries, he soared over the orc army and away from Vorstad.

CHAPTER 67

Swinging his axe down, Thron cut another rope, dropping half a dozen orcs back to the ground. "Keep cutting them!" No matter how hard they tried to keep up though, the orcs were upon them.

A chimera flew close to him. The three-headed creature had the forward body of a lion with a lion's head. The fur of the lion extended into the backside of a goat, which was also one of the other heads of the flying monstrosity. The final head was that of a snake, and with the wings, he assumed that the head was truly that of one of the flying snakes of Tenalong.

As the battle continued, he had learned that the chimeras were even deadlier than he had anticipated. Each of its heads appeared to have some kind of natural attack to it. The lion released a deafening roar that was able to crumble stone under the force of its sonic powers. The goat emitted a purple bubbling poison that caused even the strongest dwarf to falter, gasping for air and begging for mercy. The head of the snake emitted some kind of paralyzing venom, which left the dwarves it hit immobilized, trapped in their own bodies, leaving them to helplessly watch what was happening around them.

The head of the snake turned towards him, and Thron swung with his axe, striking it between its reptilian eyes. The entire chimera began shaking and jerked back away from him, exposing its underbelly. Thron picked up his last throwing hammer and released it into the exposed fur. The chimera fell from the sky as Thron roared triumphantly.

A loud shattering caught his attention, and Thron looked down to see that orcs were now charging through the gates. They had somehow managed to breach the defenses. Running to the other side of the wall, he scanned the Halls of Vorstad and saw Threll, her mace ready, lead-ing thousands of dwarves into battle. "With honor," he called out, though none could hear him.

A dwarf fell dead beside him. Thron spun around and saw several orcs standing atop the wall. With another roar from the dwarf, Thron charged, swinging his axe violently as he continued to defend his home.

"Here it is," Thamar whispered as he led the companions into a small tunnel. "This will overlook Vorstad, but there is no way down from here."

Ashwin glanced at Vaz and Vella. "Stay here and guard the en-trance."

The two white tigers turned and lay down by the entrance, appar-ently comprehending her intentions.

Thamar led them to a small ledge, and then kneeled down to look in. What he saw broke his heart and would haunt his dreams forever-more. There were orcs everywhere, both in and outside of Vorstad. Other creatures were flying or crawling on the walls, with orcs riding them like mounts.

"Interesting," Arifos commented.

"This is my home and you call it interesting?" Thamar sneered.

"Look at the orcs," Arifos pointed. "Their armor is finely crafted, as is their weapons. They also appear different than the ones we have been fighting."

"I see elven craftsmanship," Ashwin agreed.

"Armor as if it was bein' forged from Tregador, too," Baldock agreed.

"This is no ordinary band of orcs," Arifos surmised.

Below them, they watched as the orcs suddenly separated, creating an opening for a group of even more heavily armored orcs. They marched straight through the ranks to the walls of Vorstad, and then inside the crumbled gates.

"What was that?" Mylvannan asked.

"If I had to wager a guess, that was the leader and his elite body-guards," Arifos surmised.

"There they are again," Ashwin pointed out. "On the wall."

"What are they doing?" Mylvannan asked.

Thamar turned a very pale white. "They're going to my father."

The battle was not going well. Thron and his fellow defenders were quickly becoming part of the minority. Most of those around him were orcs now. Suddenly, their attacks halted, and they backed away. Thron glared at the orcs, anticipating something sinister. Three other dwarves joined him by his side, the only other survivors upon the wall.

"Be ready, boys," he said.

They all held their weapons steady, prepared for the worst. Each of them had been badly battered and bloodied during the siege thus far, but none of them lowered their gaze or even held the thought of surrender.

A dozen heavily armored orcs approached them and began to encircle them. Thron had been an ally with Xylona long enough to recognize that their armor and weapons were adorned with elven scripture. One final orc stepped forward to approach them. He was taller and looked stronger than the other orcs they had been fighting. He was also much more heavily decorated.

"I am Flarg," he declared in the dwarven tongue. "These are the Lathryl," he added as he swung his arms to indicate his armored warriors. "You are the leader here?"

"How is it that an orc is garbed in elven armor and can speak the dwarven tongue?" Thron demanded.

"We are not what we seem," Flarg replied.

"Funny, you seem like death to Vorstad," Thron sneered.

"That is inevitable," Flarg confirmed. "However, if you surrender, the survivors will be spared."

"If I surrender?" Thron questioned with a sarcastic laugh. "I am Thron, son of Torrin, protector of Vorstad! I will never surrender to the likes of you!"

"As you wish," Flarg dismissed. Raising his hand, the Lathryl all pulled back elven bows with arrows nocked. "Last chance?" Flarg asked.

"With honor!" Thamar cried out, a claim that the three dwarves with him also cheered.

Flarg lowered his hand and the archers released a volley of arrows into the four dwarves, dropping them to the ground. The orc Chieftain then walked to the four bodies and looked down at Thron, who was struggling to stand up, blood streaming from his mouth. "Good-bye, son of Torrin," Flarg said as he thrust Orfrin down into Thron's chest, rotating the blade in a circle until the dwarf's body stopped convulsing and was still.

"No!" Thamar cried out, reaching his hand towards his slain father.

Theiler, though unable to speak looked just as tormented, and acted as if he would leap from their precipice and risk breaking every limb if it meant landing on a single orc and killing it.

Arifos used his mystical abilities to force the two away from the ledge. "Remember his spirit and avenge him later."

"That be my father," Thamar roared. "I demand justice!"

"He be a dwarf," Baldock reminded him. "He died well. He is before the golden gates o' Wolhollm even now. Ye will be seein' him again when yer time is up. That is not this day though."

The Madrew elf did not release his mystical bindings upon the two sons of Thron. "Listen to Baldock—your father died valiantly, the hope of all dwarves. Joining him this day would accomplish nothing. We must get back to Xylona and see the fate of that city as well."

"The fate of Xylona?" Ashwin asked. "What do you mean?"

"I do not think the orcs would have marched here without attacking Xylona first. We must know for certain before we attempt to rally additional allies."

"If Vorstad and Xylona both be fallin', then me father needs to be listenin' and joinin' this here war," Baldock surmised.

"Him and many others, I hope," Arifos agreed.

"Very well," Thamar conceded. "But remember me vow this day. I will meet that orc again, and when I do, it will be *his* blood that will flow as *I* stand triumphantly over his body."

The companions moved out of the opening of the cave and froze as they saw several orcs coming their way. The two white tigers were nowhere to be seen.

"They must have spotted us going in," Mylvannan guessed.

"Let's kill them quickly and quietly. We must get out of here," Arifos instructed.

Thamar grasped his mallet in both hands and charged directly towards the orcs. He had listened and refrained from screaming with his attack. His actions were swift though. He reached the orcs and swung violently, shattering the blade of a sword that was attempting to parry his blow, and then the kneecap of the orc that had wielded it. As the orc fell, Thamar swung the mallet over his head and brought it down, crushing the foe's skull.

Baldock and Theiler were quickly upon the others. Baldock blocked an attack with his shield, and then swung Splitter around catching the orc in its side. As the orc stumbled, he pressed his attack, each time striking the armored orc. As it fell to the ground, he smiled and glanced back deviously at Arifos. "How was that fer quiet?"

Theiler dueled with his opponent, who was very skilled with a sword. They appeared to almost be even in skill. The dwarf decided to try something different and dropped to the ground and rolled, distracting the orc and toppling him over. As he fell, Theiler slashed the sword back and pierced the orc through the back, and into its heart.

"Where are Vaz and Vella?" Ashwin asked.

Arifos listened for a moment and then pointed. "There."

Ashwin followed his gaze and saw that the two white tigers had killed half a dozen orcs themselves. "Good job," she praised them. "Very good."

"Now, let's be off before more decide to explore this path," Arifos commanded. The others agreed and they began to sneak around the orcs as best as they could. Arifos assisted by casting an illusion over their forms. To those that they passed, the companions were orcs just like them, and the white tigers were both koxlen. No other sentry bothered to ask them who they were or where they were going. By night break, they were behind enemy lines and quickly making their way to Xylona.

CHAPTER 68

"That was a laugh," Solara said, mildly shocked.

"It was," Zerilla confirmed as they watched Leora and Trella play-ing. "They are very close in age."

"Leora has been through so much though," Solara said remorse-fully.

"It is the times," Zerilla sighed. "I am fortunate that my children have not really been impacted too harshly by them."

"Things are getting worse then?"

"Much worse," Zerilla replied. "The Empress's kidnapping, King Sarlec's death, Captain Centain's near fatal injuries, the delegates of the races imprisoned, and Winton somehow claiming the throne with the support of Torscen and Garum. Now you tell me that Braksis is dead, too? Things are definitely getting worse."

"I wish there was more that I could do," Solara said. "But Braksis led the military. I only fought by his side. Going back to Trespias now just seems to be a waste."

"You could stay here. I'm sure Captain Vector would be grateful for you to remain as a defender of the city. Most of the Suspintian Guards left when they heard that Winton was looking for volunteers to rescue Empress Karleena. What we have left couldn't even defend us if a thief came to Comonor, much less an attack by hobgoblins or worse."

Solara pondered the words for a moment. If she stayed, it would be much better for both Leora and Sora, but she could not bring her-self to do so. "Are you recruiting?"

"Captain Vector has been accepting any and all help, desperately trying to train children no older than Trong to be soldiers, if they are willing," Zerilla shook her head in disgust. "Thank the gods he is not interested in becoming a fighter."

"He may well have to fight before this is over," Solara cautioned.

"He may indeed," Zerilla whispered. "So how about it? Will you stay?"

"I still have unfinished business," Solara said.

"Rawthorne."

"Yes," Solara admitted. "Are you certain that you have no information as to where I could find him?"

"I only wish that I did, but I do not. If I had to make a guess, I would say he either went home to Falestia and familiar surroundings, or to Tenalong; but where in either location would be but a guess."

"I know someone that might be able to give me the information I seek," Solara said. "I'll look him up. Would you mind if Sora and Leora remain behind?"

"You don't even need to ask," Zerilla smiled.

"Thank you," she said. As she started to stand up, she felt dizzy and almost passed out. "Maybe I shouldn't get up so quickly."

Zerilla smiled at her knowingly.

"What are you smiling about? I have some illness that I can't seem to shake."

"Don't worry, you'll shake it. I'd actually bet that you'll shake it soon, but then you'll notice some other signs."

"Signs?" Solara asked perplexed. "What are you talking about?"

"Solara, I have had five children. I know the signs: you're pregnant."

"I'm what?" Solara asked in shock.

"Pregnant," Zerilla repeated, her smile fading slightly. "I take it that you didn't know?"

"I can't be pregnant, I'm just ill," Solara replied sternly, trying to convince herself.

"Solara, you must not be in denial over this. The baby will come if you want it to or not."

"How could this have happened? I didn't take the ritual of the Essence of the Dragon."

"Essence of the Dragon?" Zerilla asked, confused.

"It is the mystral ceremony administered by the Dragoness when a warrior is ready to provide offspring."

"That sounds so, impersonal," Zerilla said. "If you didn't do the ceremony, have you done anything else recently, something intimate?"

"Intimate?" Solara whispered. Then even softer, "Braksis."

Zerilla leaned back and closed her eyes for a moment.

Solara glanced over. "I am so sorry, if this offends or hurts you, I will understand if you want us—all of us—to leave."

"Don't be silly," Zerilla said, placing her hand on Solara's. "You and Braksis have known each other for years. You two share a very special bond. I would be very happy to see you two together, if he had survived. I am sorry for you. Even more so now."

"But you two were close," Solara said.

"We shared a magical night," Zerilla shrugged. "I would not trade it in for the world. I felt that we had connected in a way I have not done since my dear husband, Noroat, died. However, that was but one night compared to the lifetime you two spent together. I assure you, I am not jealous or hurt in any way."

"I still can't believe it," Solara said. "This has never happened to a mystral before."

"Well, if that is the case, then perhaps you should not go after Rawthorne. Stay here. We will make sure that if there are any complications with the pregnancy that you get the proper treatment."

"There could be complications?" Solara asked worriedly.

"There could be," she admitted, "but don't let that possibility scare you. You may be fine."

"Other than being ill, I still feel like myself. I can still do everything I always could."

"You will find yourself tired more, and soon you'll start to show."

"To show?" Solara asked.

"Yes, you do have a child growing in there," Zerilla smiled.

"I must find Rawthorne quickly then, before my condition impairs me."

"I've never considered my pregnancies as being impairing, but if you are determined to go through with this, then you definitely should either do it soon, or wait until afterwards."

"I shall leave immediately then," Solara said. "Again, I appreciate your hospitality. I also appreciate you looking after Sora and Leora."

"Excuse me?" Sora said from behind her. "You think I'm staying behind?"

"You are hurt and need time to recover," Solara sternly replied.

"Your sister is right," Zerilla added. "You will stay with us."

"I will do nothing of the sort. It has been a week since I was injured. I still may have bumps and bruises, but you yourself said that I was lucky not to have broken anything. I'm fine. I'm not dizzy, I'm not wobbly, and I don't feel like I'm going to pass out." Staring straight at Solara, she lowered her eyes in a glare. "Can we both say the same?"

"Is this like at the farmhouse? Even if I order you to stay you'll follow anyway?"

"You bet," Sora answered.

"Very well," Solara conceded. "You might as well come then." Glancing over at Zerilla. "It looks like only Leora will be staying for now. I promise though, I will be back for her as soon as this is over."

Zerilla smiled compassionately. "You better, because I want to see the baby."

"Baby?" Sora asked with a stunned expression. "What baby?"

Solara and Zerilla smiled deviously and started giggling.

"What baby? What's going on?"

That evening, alone in her chambers, Zerilla held a piece of Braksis's red cloak in her hands. Most of it had been burned while he faced the tragon, but she had kept a piece of it and held it whenever she wished to think of him. As she held it on this moonlit night, a deep sorrow overcame her. Everything she had told Solara was true—she had not known Braksis that long. Solara and Braksis were probably much more compatible. However, that did not change the fact that she loved him deeply. That he had touched her like no man other than Noroat ever had.

Knowing that both men she ever loved were lost to her, she dropped her head into the fabric of Braksis's cloak and cried long into the night.

CHAPTER 69

It had been a long and arduous journey back to Trespias, but Ferceng successfully reached the Mage's Council and had his injuries tended to by the Healers. Their work was quick and efficient, and he felt completely rejuvenated. All signs of his injuries were completely gone, including the scars that normally would be left behind. He had great respect for those with the mystical gift of the healing arts.

But that had been hours ago. Ferceng now paced the corridor, waiting for an audience with the Council of Elders. His news was grave and important. Time was of the essence, but like most individuals in authority, they kept people waiting. What were they possibly doing that was more important than what he had to report to them? Didn't they realize that he would not return to the Council unless it was vital to do so?

Behind him, something collided with the back of his head and he heard a high-pitched scream. Ferceng spun around and saw a fairy falling from the sky, stunned by the impact. Reaching out with reflexes that defied his size, the troll caught the small creature.

"Are you okay?" he asked.

The fairy shook her head and started to blink her light-blue eyes. The six-inch fairy had strawberry-blonde hair tied back in pigtails. Her wings were splendidly colorful with a light purple border, a light-blue hue that matched her eyes blending into the outline, and a yellow interior with small light red spots scattered throughout. By the whiteness of her robes, he knew she was a member of the Mage's Academy.

"Did I win?" she asked, still trying to regain her focus.

"Win?" Ferceng asked.

"Mica," a masculine voice called out.

Ferceng glanced up and saw a sabrenoh. Like his entire race, the boy appeared quite muscular and fit. His skin was golden brown and he had a dark brown mane of wavy hair that flowed from his head down his back. His eyes were yellow and challengingly held Ferceng's gaze.

Two other girls quickly joined them: one, a dwarf with dark brown eyes, charcoal black hair, and a gaze so hard that it would have made Thron proud; the other though, a blonde-haired girl, appeared very familiar to him. Unlike the other three, her robes were almost completely gold. It had a large white star on her chest, with smaller stars scattered throughout. Only a small handful of Mages had ever had that much gold, and none of them ever would have been so honored at this child's age.

"Are you okay?" the sabrenoh asked.

The fairy that was identified as Mica fluttered her wings a couple of times and then lifted from Ferceng's open palm. "Sorry about that," she said with a grimace.

"No harm done," Ferceng replied with a bow. As he raised his head, he held his gaze with the girl wearing the golden robes. "I have seen you before."

"Me?" the girl skeptically asked.

"Yes, as a favor for my son," Ferceng explained. "I summoned images of his friends, and we saw you, along with a pink-skinned elf.

"Kai," the girl whispered.

"Yes, that was it," Ferceng agreed. "I'm afraid I don't know your name though?"

"Don't tell him Kyria!" Mica blurted out and then clasped her hands to her mouth. "Oops."

"Yeah, oops," the sabrenoh said as he shook his head. "Who are you?"

"Once, I was Master Ferceng," Ferceng announced with another bow. "However, I left the Council long ago with no regrets. It is just Ferceng now."

"You said your son was a friend of Kai?" the boy pressed.

"Yes," Ferceng answered.

"I have never heard of Kai befriending a troll," he continued.

"That is because my son is adopted," Ferceng clarified. "My son is Warlord Braksis."

"Braksis?" Kyria repeated, knowing the name well, especially for what he had done to Arkham.

"Do not look horrified. He is a true hero and fought valiantly alongside your elven friend."

"What do you want with Kyria?" the boy asked, grilling Ferceng.

"Nothing—if you recall, your little friend flew into me."

"Sartir, that's enough," Kyria said. Pointing to the dwarf, "And this is Tyrene, the last of our little quartet."

"A pleasure to meet you all," Ferceng said. "I am curious—if you are here, where is Kai?"

"She is gone," Kyria replied.

"Gone?"

"What's wrong, you can't understand her?" Sartir asked. "She's talking clear enough to me."

"My apologies, I was only curious," Ferceng said. "Ah look, the Council of Elders is finally answering my request for an audience. Why don't you run along and play some more."

Kyria glanced up and watched as Master Ilfanti lowered to them on a glowing disc. "Master Ilfanti," she said.

"Kyria," he replied with a wink and a slight grin. "You should probably get going."

"Of course," Kyria nodded politely.

The four kids then walked away, Sartir continuing to look back to try and see what Ferceng and Ilfanti were speaking about.

"She has a lot of gold on those robes," Ferceng said.

"She does at that," Ilfanti replied. "It drove Varitimas mad when she was fitting her for her robes."

"I bet," Ferceng chuckled.

"I also bet that Varitimas would be quite aghast if she saw you *without* your robes on."

"Then we should be off before she sees me," Ferceng suggested.

"Yes," Ilfanti agreed. "I apologize for the delay. Things have been hectic here of late."

"What happened?" Ferceng asked as the two began levitating back up through the Tower.

"During the Founding Celebration, we had some, shall we say, accidents?"

"It sounds more pressing than that," Ferceng probed.

"It was," Ilfanti agreed. "Many students were injured, and then a bunch of things happened at once. Some of those Shadow Mages that Empress Karleena had been speaking about appeared, and the Renegades escaped."

"The Renegades?" Ferceng asked. "I am not familiar with them."

"You shouldn't be. They are a deep, dark secret of the Council. We take great pride in our system, and feel that those that pass the Trial's are ready to advance in their own stature. Every now and then though, something more sinister slips through the cracks. These individuals are deeply rooted in darkness and evil. We do not advertise their existence much, but these individuals do exist."

"And they've escaped?"

"Yes. All nine of them," Ilfanti stated. "Of course, this has taken up a lot of the Council's time trying to ascertain what to do from here. Naturally, we want to recapture the Renegades before they can wreak havoc upon the realm again."

As Ferceng listened, he wondered if this incident too was connected to Zoldex. Was it possible that Zoldex used the orcs for his armies, but was also looking for generals to lead them? Who better than some of the worst Mages; individuals so sinister, that they had been locked away and had their existence denied?

"Here we are," Ilfanti said as he led Ferceng up the golden steps and into the Council of Elder's chamber. "If I may present, Master Ferceng." After making his introduction, Ilfanti stepped over to his seat between Hergzenbarung and Cala and sat down.

Ferceng stepped into the middle of the room and studied Pierce, the eternal that ran the Council.

"You address this Council in *rags*?" Pierce sneered condescendingly. "Have you no respect?"

"My apologies, I meant no disrespect," Ferceng apologized. "However, my news is vital and I wished to report it to this Council as soon as possible. In my haste to deliver it, I did not stop to consider the proper decorum."

"The same Council you turned your back upon," Pierce continued, glaring at Ferceng. "What business could one such as you possibly have with us?"

"Zoldex has returned," Ferceng boldly declared. "He wishes to conquer the Seven Kingdoms. That revelation must be made known."

Pierce leaned back, shocked by the news.

Jeffa launched from his chair and raised his arms, the klatia perched on his shoulder dropped off, unprepared for the Master's quick reaction. "This is preposterous! If Zoldex has returned, we would certainly be aware of it."

"I agree," Ariness said. "I doubt that Zoldex could truly hide either himself or his intentions from us. Do you have some proof to validate your claim?"

Ferceng nodded at the aquatican and then pulled Carnage from his back. Slamming it down on the ground, he yelled out, "Do you need more proof than a weapon that has been mystically enhanced by Zoldex himself?"

Ariness raised his palm and mystically summoned the weapon, guiding it until it was close enough for him to reach out and grasp it. As he glanced at the axe, he nodded his agreement. "The blade is most certainly enchanted. A dark spell as well, though what Mage did the deed is not clear."

After making his observation, Ariness released the axe and sent it hovering back to Ferceng in the middle of the room.

The newest member of the Council, the photon Cinzia, leaned forward. "Forgive me for my ignorance, but there is clearly a Dark

Mage at work here. Whether it is Zoldex or another, should we not vest resources to discover the culprit?"

"I second the motion," Cala called out. "We must know precisely what is going on before we can properly respond to the threat. I for one do not wish to be caught unawares simply because we think we are right."

"Here, here," Ilfanti cheered, his gaze settled on Pierce.

"Oh please," Promethisus, the albino centaur, sneered. "Haven't we heard this before? Isn't this why we are helping the damned humans in the first place? We're already allocating resources."

"Not enough!" Herg roared as the lupan jumped up from his seat.

Ilfanti stood up and beckoned everyone to settle down. "Why don't we let Ferceng fill us in on what he knows before we argue amongst ourselves?"

"I agree," Ariness said. "Please continue, Master Ferceng."

"This was first brought to my attention months ago when my son, Warlord Braksis, returned home with dire news. He had been piecing together a puzzle where the forces of evil were aligning against the noble races. Gradually, the conquest was progressing."

"This is not new to us," Promethisus uttered in mild annoyance.

"An uprising led the Imperial forces to the harbor town of Arkham. There, a man that had once been a common fisherman wielded an axe—this axe," he clarified as he held Carnage up, "—and claimed that Zoldex had promised him glory and victory.

"In this same battle, my son had his own sword—one I forged for him with illistrium—destroyed. He then separated from his troops and returned to me, stopping at Vorstad and Xylona—both under siege as he had been told."

"So the orcs and hobgoblins have decided to go to war—how does that connect with Zoldex?" Jeffa asked.

"The invaders cheered in the name of Zoldex. Shadow Mages were also at each site," Ferceng explained. "My own son faced one during this journey."

"How do we know Shadow Mages are truly linked with Zoldex?"

Senix, the avarian, asked. "Could they be the ones behind the enchantment on the axe? Unlike Zoldex, we see them appearing throughout the realm. That would make sense to me."

"Then why do the Dartian hunters, the Arkham fishermen, the Severed Head Clan and Murky Death Clan orcs, assorted goblins, and hobgoblins all claim to follow Zoldex?"

"You said Murky Death Clan?" Ilfanti asked. "We have heard the rumors of such a city before. Do you have evidence of its existence?"

"I do," Ferceng said. "I have been to Grool myself, though the quantity of orcs is far more staggering than we had ever imagined."

"Impossible," Pierce said shaking his head. "Orcs could never multiply so quickly and without anyone else's knowledge."

"It is not impossible," Ferceng said, "as I said, I have been there myself. The city is being controlled by an eternal that has sworn allegiance to Zoldex."

"An eternal?" Pierce scoffed, disbelief clearly etched on his face. "You were amusing until this latest lie."

"It is no lie. The eternal has been feeding the orcs the blood of other eternals. They are bigger, stronger, smarter, and live longer."

"Who is this alleged eternal?" Pierce asked.

"A man named Benatar."

"Benatar?" Pierce pondered. "I do recognize the name. If memory serves, he was a Eurillien Knight—one of the soldiers of my people—but still more of an outcast, a rebel that followed his own ideals rather than that of the kings."

"He is there, and as I said, he claims to be preparing his army for Zoldex."

"That is still no proof that Zoldex has returned!" Jeffa objected. "Only that one man feels that Zoldex is here. Perhaps the warriors all feel that Zoldex will return, and this eternal has somehow forged an alliance in Zoldex's name."

"Even if that were so, we should still become involved," Ilfanti said. "A unified front against the realm is a frightening prospect."

"What else do you know, Master Ferceng?" Ariness prompted.

"After leaving Grool, I saw that Xylona had fallen, and helped defend Vorstad, but it was no use. The dwarves, too, have fallen before the armies of Zoldex."

"Are you certain?" Senix asked, his mouth suddenly dry as he struggled with the thought.

"Yes," Ferceng declared. "I was fortunate to get away to be able to spread the news of Zoldex's siege. We must prepare. The unification must go through as planned."

"The races fighting side by side with humans?" Promethisus asked. "Then the realm is already lost."

Pierce raised his hand for everyone to quiet down. "The news of the orc army is of course dire. However, I see no substantial evidence that Zoldex has returned. If he were here, I would know. As such, we will no longer involve ourselves with the affairs of the realm. Once Askari and Cicero return from their mission, I will order them to remain here."

"How can you do that?" Ilfanti demanded. "The realm needs us now more than ever!"

"If the presence of Zoldex is positively affirmed, then we will bring him before this Council to face the penalty for his crimes—the same as any of the Renegades, who are our *first* priority."

Ferceng glared at Pierce, disgusted with the final decision. "Benatar claimed that Zoldex has legions coming here to reinforce his conquest. I only pray that by the time the Council decides to become involved, it will not be too late."

"What do you think?" Cala asked.

"Pierce is being stubborn and foolish," Ilfanti answered.

"What can we do though?" Herg asked.

"Something," Ilfanti said. "We must do something."

"It is too bad that the Empress has been kidnapped," Cala said.

"At least she was trying to unite the races—something that Winton seems opposed to doing."

"Yes," Herg agreed. "Let us hope that this war that is being declared on the Aezians will quickly retrieve the Empress."

"Wars have a way of lingering," Ilfanti replied with the wisdom of one who had seen and experienced more than one war. "And they rarely turn out the way we hope."

"Convenient timing," Cala mumbled.

"What was that?" Ilfanti asked.

"I just think that the Empress was kidnapped at a convenient time. As if it, too, was part of this master-plan that Master Ferceng was alluding to."

Ilfanti started to walk away, determination and purpose in his step.

"Where are you going?" Cala asked.

"The library," Ilfanti shouted back.

"The library?" Cala asked as she glanced up at Herg, who merely shrugged in reply.

"There's something I just remembered that may be able to help us out. I need to research it though," Ilfanti explained as he hurried down the hall, his two taller companions struggling to keep up.

"Hold up," Herg shouted. "We'll help!"

CHAPTER 70

Winton stood on the terrace of the palace overlooking the bay. He watched as thousands of soldiers boarded hundreds of Imperial Gallies and set sail. It was a glorious spectacle of the might of the Imperium, and he was certain that the war with Aezia would end quickly and prosperously. Nothing could hope to face a force so strong.

Things were progressing relatively well for the new Emperor. Captain Centain was still breathing, but he was drifting further and further away each day. Captain Adonis had left Trespias, and the investigation into the murders of his father and Sharnesta appeared to be forgotten as well. Even if not, almost every member of ISIA had joined the army being sent oversees, leaving Adonis too understaffed to really consider building a case against him.

The threats implied by Lady Salaman had also ceased, though he was not naïve enough to think that the Hidden Empire would forget about his debt to them. Even Zoldex had stopped contacting him, allowing Winton to run the Imperium as he felt was best. The only thing that truly bothered him was the disappearance of Shiel and the rest of his harem. The thought infuriated him, but as Emperor, there would be other servants that would satisfy his urges.

The doors behind him burst open and Winton turned to see two Mages walking in. One was Askari, the aquatican he had seen the image of in the Corryby. Just as he had assumed, the man was striking, bold, and full of confidence.

The Mage along with him was his younger apprentice, Cicero—a wraith with shadowy skin so dark that Winton strained to see him until he emerged from the shadows of the room and entered the sunlight.

His shining yellow eyes appeared to glow even in the darkness, and glared directly towards him.

"Master Askari, Apprentice Cicero, an honor to finally meet you in person," he said.

"You must stop what you are doing at once," Askari demanded. "We have spoken with Emperor Wei Lau. He was not involved in the abduction."

"Perhaps you are mistaken," Winton said.

"There was no deception. The Aezians did not abduct the Empress," Askari boldly declared.

"I am sorry, you have obviously been duped. Perhaps an Aezian Mage has somehow distorted your perceptions," Winton said. "I will listen to this no longer. We are on the dawn of a great time for the Imperium. We will strike the Aezians swiftly and demand retribution. This act will prove to the world that the Imperium is not a nation to be taken lightly."

"Of course," Askari said. "It will be a nation of fools, led by a fool, that does not know who its own enemies really are!"

"Your services are no longer required, Master Askari," Winton said. He turned dismissingly and continued to watch the fleet sailing in the harbor. "Good day."

Askari and Cicero exchanged a glance, and then walked out of the room. As they left, the aquatican mystically slammed the two doors shut behind him.

"What is going on, Master?" Cicero asked.

"I wish I knew," Askari answered. "I fear that the true deceiver is not Wei Lau, but Winton himself."

"I admit, I am having similar thoughts, Master," Cicero concurred. "What will we do now? Just let the Imperium go to war?"

"There is little we can do to avert the war now," Askari concluded. "We must return to the Tower and report our findings to the Council of Elders. They will decide how to proceed."

"Yes, Master," Cicero nodded in agreement.

"Excuse me," a whisper summoned them.

Askari turned and saw the doctor. "May we help you, doctor?"

"I would be tortured if they knew I was here, but there is something I am hoping you could do for me," he said nervously.

"Name it, doctor," Askari said. "If it is within our power, we shall do so."

"The Captain of the Guards, Centain, was badly injured when the Empress was abducted. He is dying and there is nothing I can do. Perhaps you could save him?"

Askari rubbed his chin for a moment in contemplation. "Take us to him and we will see what we can do. No promises."

"Oh, thank you, this is more than I had hoped already."

The doctor quickly hurried down the hall, the two Mages calmly walking behind him. Centain was known to them. He was an honorable man, unlike the new Emperor. If they could save his life, they would make every effort to do so.

CHAPTER 71

"So who is this Palmer-guy again?"

Walking with the reins of Myst in her hands, Solara glanced back at her sister. "Do you have selective memory?"

"Hey, don't blame me—I was hit in the head a few times, if you recall," Sora argued.

"And whose fault is that?" Solara asked sternly.

"Mine," Sora sarcastically replied.

"Exactly," Solara grinned. "Palmer was a former Captain in the Imperial Army. He's one of the knights that joined Braksis to reclaim the throne of Falestia from Rawthorne, and then fought by his side against various warlords. He's very loyal to Braksis. Around the time that Emperor Conrad gave command of the Imperial Army to Braksis, Palmer decided to leave the military when he met and fell in love with a farmer."

"A farmer? Is that what he is now?" Sora asked.

"Yes," Solara answered. "And the last time I saw him, he was quite happy with his decision."

"So how did he meet this farmer anyway?" Sora asked.

"Ellie had been previously married, but her husband grew frustrated with his life as a farmer. He aligned himself with the Hidden Empire seeking better rewards and riches for his life. He abandoned his wife and two infant daughters.

"His wife was not happy with his decision. She dropped the children off with her mother, and then went after her husband. She got lost in the Tenalong swamps, and found herself in some trouble."

"What kind of trouble?" Sora asked.

"Rasplers," Solara answered. "She said that she wandered into a den of the reptilian creatures, and they attacked her. Captain Palmer had been escorting Emperor Conrad to Fenland, and overheard the screams. He could not risk splitting his forces, because the Emperor's life was his first priority, but he personally went to investigate."

"What were the rasplers doing to her?"

"Nothing from what he saw, Ellie was tied up. He rode in on his horse, kicked a few rasplers over without drawing his sword, and rescued the woman. It was love at first sight after that. Both were very taken with each other."

"What about the husband? Not that I care about the intricacies of human relations, but aren't you only supposed to take on one mate?"

"Yes," Solara agreed. "That was never a problem though. Ellie's first husband was found dead in the streets of Fenland. The local constabulary theorized that he had been trying to pick the pocket of the wrong individual, and was killed for it. Too many in Tenalong are corrupt—you need to choose your enemies wisely."

"Then Palmer just married Ellie?"

"It wasn't that quick. Each time he had his leave, he journeyed to her and spent it with her. Ultimately, he did give up his commission and remained by her side."

"And I haven't regretted it a day since," a male voice called out.

"Palmer!" Solara called as she saw the man and hugged him. He was very large and muscular, standing a foot taller than Solara. His face was stern and hard—even though he appeared pleased to see her—as if he had the features of a dwarf. His hazel eyes held the gaze of Sora even as he was holding Solara. His chestnut hair was closely cut to his head, and standing almost straight up as if his hairs were small needles or spikes. The sleeves to his beige shirt were torn, allowing his bulging biceps to reveal themselves. He also wore blue pants that were torn into shorts and boots that were laced up slightly higher than his ankles.

Palmer lifted her up in a big bear hug. "It's good to see you Solara. It's been too long."

"It has," she agreed. "I wish it was under more pleasant circumstances though."

"Does that mean that we won't be preparing two more place settings for dinner tonight?"

Tiot barked, and Palmer glanced down at the timber wolf. "I stand corrected, three more settings."

"We are in a rush," Solara replied.

Sora stepped forward and pushed in front of her sister. "We would love to stay for dinner, thank you for the gracious invitation."

Palmer gave her a lopsided grin. "She reminds me of you when you were that age."

"No way!" both mystral answered at the same time.

Palmer laughed and shook his head. "Sisters?"

"Sisters," Solara answered with a nod.

"Will you stop and rest?"

"You really should," Sora prompted, her eyes focusing on Solara's abdomen.

"Very well, if it is not an inconvenience."

"It is not," Palmer said. "Come—let's go tell Ellie, and then we can catch up."

The former Captain led them back to his farmhouse. It was a cozy little home, though Solara wasn't sure she would like the location for herself: they lived practically on the border between Suspinti and Tenalong. They also were the only farmhouse for miles around, and being so close to Tenalong, she wondered if they experienced raids or had problems.

Seeing Palmer though, she doubted that the man would present the easiest target in the realm. He looked even stronger than he had before he left the military. She saw him pause at a small barn and, peeking in herself, could see more weapons and armaments than an Imperial supply bunker would have. This man may be a farmer now, but the blood of a warrior still surged through his veins.

Ellie had reacted just as graciously as Palmer, welcoming the mystral into her home. She indicated that she would prepare something special for them that night. As Solara watched the two together, she could see how very much in love they were. They were tender, with small touches and smiles here and there. The two were an inspiration and symbol of what the potential of a relationship could be, even if a mystral never supposed to understand such things.

Palmer also was overjoyed to introduce his first-born child, his son Conrad, to them. He said that he had named the boy after the Emperor in honor of what the man had achieved in his lifetime. Though Conrad was his only child, one could never tell by looking at Ellie's two daughters that they were not Palmer's own. They were truly a happy little family.

As the evening wore on and the children were sent to bed, Palmer led Solara and Sora into a separate parlor where they could speak. Ellie soon joined them, telling them that Tiot and their dog Corrie were out back playing together.

"So, might as well tell me what brought you here?" Palmer began.

"I was wondering if you still kept your ear to the ground?" Solara asked. "You do seem pretty isolated out here."

Ellie chuckled at the thought. "Don't worry Solara, he may not be in the military anymore, but Palmer makes sure he knows everything that he can."

"What do you want to know?" Palmer asked.

"Did you hear that Braksis was killed?"

"Rawthorne and Durgin were teamed together to go after him. Allegedly, they succeeded, though no body has been found."

Solara lowered her eyes somberly.

Palmer studied her for a moment. "Did you two finally hook up?"

"Excuse me?" Solara asked.

"Hun, you can't ask a woman that," Ellie scolded.

"Sure I can," Palmer laughed. "We all thought that the two of you would wind up together years ago. Did you?"

"Yes," Solara answered. "I'm carrying his child even now."

"That's great," Palmer said. "Congratulations."

"He's dead," Sora sternly said, defensively. "How is that a good thing?"

Palmer held her gaze with one equally hard and unyielding. "No body has been found. This is Braksis we're talking about. He'll pop up again when he's needed the most. Trust me."

"I pray that you are right," Solara said.

"Durgin is dead?" Palmer asked for confirmation.

"Yes," Solara answered.

"And you want to know where Rawthorne is?"

"Yes," she said again.

"Knowing where he is is the easy part. Getting to him will be hard," Palmer declared. "Not only do you have to worry about the increased presence of hobgoblins in these parts and the trolls in the swamps, but your destination will be full of foes that will be perfectly happy to kill you both without batting an eye."

"Where is he?" Solara boldly asked.

"He's with Lady Salaman and the Hidden Empire," Palmer answered. "Apparently, they are going to try and help him to reclaim the throne to Falestia. You may be better off delaying your plans until he is in a less defended location. Bide your time."

Solara reached down and rubbed her abdomen. "No, I must do this soon."

"Then we will leave at first light," Palmer said.

Solara glanced at Ellie and saw the fear in her eyes at the statement. "That won't be necessary."

"I think it is," Palmer replied. "If there's no time to get Reister, Valgaror, Centain, Atherok, Shalin, and Niyilka together for this, at least you'll have me."

"You're leaving out the Falestian Knights," Solara said with a slight laugh, remembering her former companions.

"Purposefully," Palmer held her gaze. "I will join you."

"I cannot ask you to do this," Solara said. "You have a new life now, a life here with Ellie and your children. This is where you belong. If there is fighting to be done by you, it will be here, defending your home and loved ones."

He sat in his chair for a long moment without saying anything. He felt the need to go. It was an overwhelming urge that fueled him in a way he hadn't felt in many years. However, Solara's words rang true, and he also could see the expression on Ellie's face. She would support him, wish him well, and tell him to come home safely to her, but he could sense that she was afraid that his former life would finally call him back into service and away from her.

"Very well," Palmer finally said as he stood up. "I have a map in the other room. I'll give it to you."

Solara watched as he walked out.

Relieved, Ellie leaned forward and patted Solara's hand. "You must have faith," she said. "Vengeance is not the answer."

"It's my answer," Solara said coldly.

"Here you go," Palmer said, handing the map to Solara. "This is pretty accurate. I did a few reconnaissance missions when I moved here to learn the layout of the land. This will lead you directly to the lair of Lady Salaman."

"Thank you," Solara said more pleasantly. "May you and your family fair well in these tumultuous times."

"We will do well," he said. "Be careful yourself. The trolls in the swamps have banded together in greater numbers than ever before and have been attacking anything they come across. Avoid them if you can."

"We shall attempt to do so," Solara agreed. "Come Sora, we must be off."

Sora stood up and pleasantly thanked the two for their hospitality. They then prepared their horses and summoned Tiot, and headed into the darkness of the night, their quest for vengeance almost at an end.

CHAPTER 72

The flight from Vorstad to Xylona heightened the growing dread and depression of the companions. They had discovered large patrols of hobgoblins that they either had to avoid or fight along the journey. Their supplies were running low, and all of them were fatigued by the constant alertness and potential for battle.

Thamar and Theiler were both far more somber than usual. Their father had been slain before their eyes, their home conquered, and they could only assume that their younger sister had also perished in the skirmish.

Thamar no longer told stories or acted invincible as he often did. If nothing else, he was humbled by the scars of the memory. He provided his feedback and thoughts, but he rarely made suggestions any longer, leaving the leadership of the group to Arifos.

Ashwin noticed the change and had been the most sympathetic to it. She wondered if the others ignored it because they had all suffered losses at one point in their vast lives and knew that a few words and actions would truly be small solace in light of such a tragedy. They were there if the sons of Thron needed them, but they did not overly venture to try and console them.

She hoped that she would never become as hardened or impassioned to disaster and tragedy. She could still vividly recall the death of her cousin, and the lasting mourning in her heart. She knew that the others did not readily accept what happened at Vorstad, but they at least appeared unbothered by it.

When they finally reached Xylona, Ashwin herself became visibly distraught. There were no signs of elves at all, only the vicious hobgoblins that were scattered throughout the trees of the once-proud city. Even more of the vile creatures were along the ground and patrolling the area. Her darkest nightmare suddenly sprang to life as the fate of her own family was thrust into the vast depths of the unknown.

"What now?" Mylvannan whispered.

"Tregador," Baldock said. "We must be goin' to me home. There we can be resupplyin' and gettin' more assistance."

"I agree," Thamar stated. "Tregador did send soldiers with Baldock to help fight the hobgoblins. With what we know now, they will certainly need to be informed."

"How do we get through though?" Ashwin asked. "Look at all of them."

"We will need to go further into Tenalong and try to get behind their lines. Then we can head north," Arifos suggested.

"Agreed," Thamar nodded. "Let us be off then."

"No," Arifos said. "Look at the hobgoblins here. There are fewer patrols. These hobgoblins are more intoxicated than prepared for any kind of problems. I would bet that we could rest right under their noses and they would never know."

"Ye want to be stayin' here?" Baldock snorted.

"Yes. We are drained, we need our rest," Arifos firmly declared.

"He speaks the truth," Mylvannan concurred. "Look at them, they are not looking for spies now."

"Very well," Thamar said. He then leaned back and closed his eyes. "Wake me when it's time to go."

Arifos removed his quiver and bow, and also lay Skrenlar down on the ground. He then began scanning the hobgoblins.

Mylvannan grabbed his shoulder from behind. "What are you planning?"

"We need supplies," Arifos replied. "I will get them for us."

"Be careful," Mylvannan said. "Do not let them know of your presence."

"If I am caught, Unamalastra is yours, my friend."

"Then your bow will be waiting for you, for you shall not be caught," Mylvannan declared.

The two exchanged a nod and then Arifos darted silently across the open grassland to one of the trees. Without a single hobgoblin seeing him, he summoned his mystical abilities to help him leap further up into the tree. Clinging to the trunk of the tree, he remained there, studying the creatures both above and below.

In silence, he inched his way up the tree and stopped below one of the vine-woven bridges that connected the buildings of Xylona. He could hear hobgoblins crossing the bridge above him. Creeping out slowly, he grasped both sides of the walkway with his hands and released his legs' grip on the tree. Hanging from the bridge, he began to quickly move below it, listening closely to make certain that no alarm was sounded because of him.

At the end of the bridge, he waited and listened, hearing nothing from above. Rocking back and forth gently, he flung himself out and somersaulted up onto the bridge. As he landed, he scanned both sides and then moved swiftly from where he landed.

He walked into one of the buildings and darted for cover as he heard two hobgoblins laughing. They entered the building and remained there, talking for several minutes. Arifos stayed still, not moving a muscle as he watched them. They were each carrying a bottle of elven spirits, and were quite intoxicated. One of them collapsed on top of the other, and Arifos darted from the room without notice.

He avoided several other hobgoblins, managing to reach a supply building. Inside, he was dismayed to see that very little remained. Most of the food had already been eaten or destroyed. He did manage to find a small handful of muffins though, and placed them in a satchel to bring with him.

Strapping that to his belt, he made his way swiftly towards the armory. Though he himself was skilled with the blades and would not need to rely heavily upon arrows, Ashwin did not share his confidence. If he could find full quivers, he would take them with him.

As he stepped into the armory, he saw that most of the weapons had been removed. Whether they were taken by the elves or were stolen by the hobgoblins he did not know. However, there were still a few bows, daggers, swords, and—most importantly—quivers with arrows.

He placed three over his shoulder and hoped that they would be enough to get them to Tregador without needing to supply again; though, unless they stopped at Turning Leaf, he knew that Ashwin would not be as happy with the less-detailed and skilled dwarven arrows.

"Halt!"

The voice made him jerk to a halt. He had been so cautious, and was disappointed with himself that he had been caught by a hobgoblin that he did not detect first. Arifos pivoted around, not reaching for a weapon because he was confident that he could use his mystical abilities as an advantage. As he finished his turn and glared at the hobgoblin, he saw a streak of white and black plow into it, knocking the hobgoblin from the ledge. Turning to regard him, he saw the emerald eyes of Vaz watching him.

"Good boy," Arifos said as he rushed past the white tiger. "Time to leave."

Below, he could hear several shouts as hobgoblins began to surround their fallen ally. He also heard distinctive laughs from below. Perhaps they thought that he had been intoxicated and fell from above. Regardless, Arifos did not wish to remain where he was. He and Vaz moved swiftly, but still came across several other hobgoblins.

Using the example that Vaz set, Arifos decided that uninjured hobgoblins that were unconscious would not rouse suspicion. He therefore used his mystical abilities to hammer the hobgoblins with invisible force, sending them crashing into trees and walls. If that failed, he would force the trees themselves to strike the hobgoblin from behind. Each time, the creatures fell unconscious, with no external markings to show that they had been attacked.

Arifos descended the tree quickly, and was amazed to see that Vaz had found a way down quicker than him. The two then returned to the rest of their companions, and ducked into the cover of the trees.

"You made it," Mylvannan said.

"I did not find much—only some muffins and arrows," Arifos explained.

"They will do," Mylvannan said, considering the supplies.

"Wake the others," Arifos prompted. "It's time for us to leave."

The two elves then began gently nudging their companions to rouse them. Baldock was the only one that gave them any trouble, swinging his fists without ever opening his eyes. Mylvannan finally poured some water on his head, which got him hopping and screaming, though Thamar and Theiler jumped on top of him and held his mouth so the hobgoblins would not hear. With Baldock awake, they began moving south, further into Tenalong.

CHAPTER 73

Maps may call it Border Town, but it would be more accurate to refer to it as Swindler's Domain. The small town was located on the edge of the swamps of Tenalong. The advertised allure was that Border Town could provide you with safe transportation to anywhere within the realm—especially the swamps, their main attraction. Instead, the decrepit town was in shambles, consisting of several wooden buildings that were infested with a wide variety of insects and looked like they would crumble under a mere touch.

The citizens of Border Town were little better. They wore rags for clothing and appeared as if they had not bathed in years. Most of them were missing teeth, and those that still had them looked as if their teeth were moldy and rotting. The stench of the residents alone was enough to make a grown-man nauseous, and they resembled the unkempt goblins more than humans.

The streets were filled with beggars and the homeless. Street urchins could be seen around every bend, always watching the newcomers, undoubtedly hoping to pick a pocket or scavenge the remains of any weary traveler that was somehow unfortunate enough to be rendered unconscious.

The three legitimate businesses in town—though even those maintained exorbitant prices that were grossly inflated—were the tavern, the barn, and the docks. The tavern provided the most service to the town and visitors, boasting a good warm drink and bed to sleep in. Of course, they did not advertise the fact that their drinks were close to ninety-percent watered-down, the sheets on their beds were never changed, and the only person that could receive a good night's sleep was one that was willing to share their bed with various insects and other wildlife of the swamp.

The barn was in the best shape of the three establishments. Old Man McCurty took great pride in his mules, and made certain that all of his provisions came from neighboring Danchul and Suspinti, not relying on anything from Tenalong. McCurty was probably the last honest man in Border Town, remembering the golden days of the area before the Hidden Empire demanded a cut of everything, and the more criminal elements began to migrate west. He ran his establishment along with his five sons and three daughters. For each mule that was rented out, one of his children would be sent along as an escort and tour guide, making certain that his precious pack mules were returned. His wife was famous for her home-cooked meals, and she made certain that all of the clients of her husband's business were treated like family.

The docks, on the other hand, were in no better shape than the rest of the town. Small rowboats and dinghies were tied up for travelers to rent as they journeyed into the swamps. Each boat looked as if it were over a hundred years old, and that even a single passenger may break the rotting hull. Even still, the signs by the docks guaranteed a safe and sturdy ride, with protection against the trolls and rasplers of the swamps.

When Adonis and the ISIA agents he brought with him arrived at Border Town, he saw several residents scurrying away, attempting to avoid being seen by the law. Others sat there with blank expressions on their faces, just watching the newcomers. A few came right up to them trying to sell a variety of items: daggers, stones that they claimed were valuable, assorted trinkets, and other items that Adonis presumed were stolen. Adonis kept waving them away and continued on to the tavern.

Darkler was a little less amused, and actually pushed a few peddlers aside, scolding and threatening them. He had been raised in Tenalong and was not willing to put up with the riffraff that remained there. To him, these individuals deserved their miserable lives for not standing up to try and change things; as such, he refused to allow them to hinder him in any way.

Doctor Podeis appeared the most affected by the spectacle. He was sworn to help and save people, and seeing so many in pain, so many suffering, it broke the man's heart. How people could live like this, he could not fathom.

As the quartet entered the tavern, they easily found their five companions, the best-dressed individuals in the place. Nextra stood up and walked over to them quickly, gaining the attention of every man in the bar as they salivated over her.

"Is he?" she asked.

Adonis nodded. "He is."

Nextra shut her eyes and leaned into the Captain, tears beginning to flow. "How?" she whimpered.

"Poison," Adonis said. "I'd like your take on it if you can."

Nextra wiped the tears from her eyes and leaned back. "I'll do whatever I can to help nail the bastard that killed Sarlec."

Adonis knew her sincerity. When he had first met Nextra, she was in the arms of King Sarlec, being given a tour of the palace. The Danchul King was so taken by her, that he was considering remarrying after being a widower for so long. Adonis had been more cautious though, and conducted a detailed background on the woman. What he had found was disturbing.

Nextra had been born to aristocracy in Dartais, part of a very prominent family. Her every whim and desire was hers for the asking. However, that was not enough. She knew that she was a very beautiful woman, and began to use that to manipulate and seduce others—first her own family, and later expanding her sights, exploiting other members of nobility on her island home.

Though everyone she knew regarded her as an angel, they were all blinded and could not see her darker, more secretive side. Nextra kept her true desires and intentions very close to herself, allowing people to see only what she wanted them to see. That was, of course, until the wife of her father's close-colleague returned home to find her husband in bed with the nubile girl.

Disgraced by the scandal, Nextra's parents turned their backs on their daughter and disowned her. She remained on the streets for a short time, earning a roof over her head and a meal with various erotic acts, but soon grew tired of how she had fallen so far from grace. Deciding that it was time to make a change and attempt to reclaim the stature she had lost, she relocated to Danchul where she would have a fresh beginning.

Her decision had been quite advantageous. She selected several marks from the wealthiest individuals in the realm, and had amassed a fortune by doing so. When she arrived at Larcridge, she was adorned in such elegant gowns and jewelry that the only suitable place to offer a roof over her head was the castle, and as a special guest of King Sarlec.

Sarlec was a powerful King, leading the most prosperous kingdom in the Imperium; Nextra could not have chosen a better mate. Sarlec was quite taken by her early on, and when Imperial business called, he asked her to join him.

When Adonis learned this—though the trail had been well hidden with alter egos—he confronted and arrested her. King Sarlec was dismayed to learn that Nextra did not really love him, but wished to see no harm come to her. He ordered Adonis to release her, an act of kindness that shocked Nextra, and apparently had been a life-altering incident.

After leaving Trespias and Sarlec behind, Nextra honestly tried to make a new living for herself. She met and fell in love with an inventor who had a fascination with chemical compounds. Intrigued—and hoping to merely spend more time with him—she watched him while he worked, and he explained everything to her. One day though, one of his mixtures proved fatal, and Nextra was left alone grieving.

This was after ISIA had already been formed, and when Adonis went to investigate, he was shocked to see Nextra at the scene. He instantly thought that she was behind the murder, but soon realized that she had made an attempt to change her life, and was innocent. He then decided to take a chance, and offered her a position in ISIA, which she reluctantly accepted, but later decided that she had made the right choice.

"We detected traces of a potent poison," Adonis explained. "It was located in the wine."

"Do you know the composition?" Nextra asked.

"Doctor Podeis can fill you in on some more of the details."

"Why don't we get some fresh air?" Podeis suggested as he escorted Nextra outside to talk.

Adonis watched them leave and wondered if he had made a mistake those many years ago. Was it possible that Nextra had truly loved Sarlec? Had her deceptions come to an end? Or could the King have been her latest target? The way she had reacted to the news of his death, he wondered.

Dozzer and Tink were both at the bar talking. Darkler quickly joined them. He ordered a real drink, and explained that if it were watered down, he would make the barkeep sorry. As the man poured the drink, his hands were shaking, for the reputation of the short man preceded him.

Quince and Ortrill were sitting at a table waiting for them. Adonis and Cylnta walked over and sat down. As he stared at Ortrill, he wondered what would be next. His spiked hair was now two-toned, with an aqua-blue blending into a bright and vibrant pink.

"Nice hair," Adonis said sarcastically.

"Thanks," Ortrill beamed. "I kind of like this one."

"I'm sure," Adonis replied. "What have you heard since arriving here?"

"A lot of talk about going to war with the Aezians, and that all men of fighting-age were expected to volunteer to go fight," Quince reported.

"It doesn't look like that message reached here," Adonis observed.

"Who would want these people?" Ortrill asked with his nose scrunched.

"What else?" Adonis asked.

"Lady Salaman is apparently busy. I have heard a few stories since I've arrived," Quince reported.

"Such as?" Adonis pushed.

"Well, there's the assassination attempt on Warlord Braksis by the newly appointed Emperor, the recent attack on the Hidden Empire by Mages, a plotted coup to take over the Falestian throne, and her normal clutches on King Garum."

"Busy lady," Adonis said. "Tell me more about the assassination attempt."

"According to my source, Winton—when he was still a Prince—approached the Hidden Empire to hire assassins to kill Lord Braksis: an attempt that failed."

"He must have loved that," Adonis said.

"I'm sure. Since he didn't have any more money to safely fund a second attempt, Lady Salaman arranged protection for him."

"At what price?"

"My source indicated that Lady Salaman knew that Winton would quickly rise in stature, and by doing so, he could repay them then."

"Just like Garum—a pawn," Ortrill added.

"Is there a link to the murder of Sarlec?" Adonis asked. "Was there some plot to have Sarlec murdered and the Empress kidnapped?"

"It would make sense," Quince agreed. "But I find no evidence of a plot against Karleena. The Hidden Empire certainly could have provided the poison to Winton, though."

"So what do we do, boss? Go arrest Winton?" Ortrill asked.

"That could be tough with what we have. He has just been crowned the new Emperor," Adonis explained. "We need something more solid to dethrone him."

"Time to make a visit to the Hidden Empire then?" Ortrill asked with a large grin on his face.

"Only you would be happy about going into a den of criminals," Quince said in disbelief.

"Not so," Ortrill laughed. "Darkler will be all over this one, too!"

"The sad part is that he's right," Quince conceded. "What do you want to do, sir?"

"We'll have to go in, but I want to hear what else you've learned.

What about this 'coup?'"

"My source indicates that Rawthorne, the former King of Falestia, has gone to the Hidden Empire with the request of aid in regaining his throne. Apparently, he has killed Lord Braksis and demands to be a lieutenant in her organization for his accomplishments. As such, he'd have the right to request aid in his conquest."

Adonis and Cylnta exchanged a glance. "I hope that for the sake of the realm, Braksis is not truly dead, especially now. What about the attack by the Mages?"

"This one is priceless," Ortrill laughed. "The Hidden Empire was besieged by children!"

"Children?" Adonis asked skeptically.

"This one was not as easy to get details on. But then again, if it's true, I'm sure Lady Salaman doesn't want the news to spread," Quince explained. "Apparently, a few young Mages infiltrated the Hidden Empire and rescued a slave-boy."

"Like I said, priceless," Ortrill laughed again.

"May our mission there be as equally successful," Adonis said.

A loud scream from the bar caught their attention. Adonis glanced over to see Darkler holding the barkeep's head to the bar. "You call this *the good stuff?*" He then pulled the man's head up and forced him to drink some of it. "How do you like it?"

"Sergeant, at ease," Adonis called out.

"Sorry sir—this pathetic excuse of a barkeep was trying to cheat me," he explained. Seeing Adonis's expression, he lifted his chin. "You're ready to go?"

"Yes, gather everyone up and get started. I want to get out of the swamps as soon as possible."

"Where are we headed?" Darkler asked as he released the barkeep's head.

"It's time to learn about the Hidden Empire's involvement from the source itself: we're going to the lair of Lady Salaman."

Darkler smiled sinisterly and then cracked his knuckles. He liked being home. It was time to remind the Hidden Empire what exactly that meant.

CHAPTER 74

Sitting alone on the throne, Winton stared at Ochroid, the famed blade of Conrad, and wondered if he too would one day be hailed as a great man. With Sarlec as a father and Karleena allegedly his mate-to-be, he was also guaranteed prosperity, but that was only if the realm failed to learn about his connections to Zoldex and the Hidden Empire—something that was an ever-growing concern.

Two knocks on the door caught Winton's attention, and he called out, "Enter."

Prime Minister Torscen walked in and bowed before him. "My Emperor."

"Rise, Torscen," Winton declared. "What news do you have?"

"Apparently, my lord, the Mages took Captain Centain with them."

The news was not good. His anger was growing. Centain was one of the few that knew for a fact that he and Karleena were not betrothed. In the hands of the Mages, he would be exposed quickly, for Centain would certainly make a full recovery. Zoldex would be most displeased.

"Is this news unwelcome?' Torscen asked.

"Not at all," Winton lied. "I hope the Captain makes a full recovery."

"Very good," Torscen said.

"Is there anything else?" Winton asked impatiently.

"I have received reports that the Falestians and Dartians have failed to assist us in our war efforts," Torscen reported. "Apparently, King Lorrents and King Palenial have ordered that all volunteers join their own kingdoms' military forces."

"It will have no impact on the war," Winton brushed away the concern.

"Should we not seek an audience with them?" Torscen asked. "They are no longer supporting the Imperium. It would not surprise me if they attempted a revolution to separate themselves from the rest of the government."

Winton glanced at the Prime Minister, seeing the man's concern, but not really caring for the news.

"If they do, Suspinti may be quick to follow," Torscen continued. "I would advise you to summon the royal families again, now that things have settled down."

"I will consider it," Winton said.

The doors slammed open and nine individuals, all of various races, stepped into the room. As they entered, a cold chill flowed throughout the room as if the grip of death was looming in the air.

"What is the meaning of this?" Torscen demanded. "Who dares disrupt my counsel with the Emperor?"

"I dare," a cold and chilling voice declared. A figure cloaked in dark robes entered the room and stood in the middle, approaching the two. Winton instantly recognized his blood red eyes and distinctive voice.

"The unification talks have been disbanded," Torscen continued. "You are not welcome here!"

"I am welcome wherever I wish to go."

"And who are you to make such a claim?" Torscen demanded, wondering where the guards were.

"You may call me Master."

Torscen scoffed at the idea, an action that would be his last. The cloaked figure clenched his fist, and the Prime Minister before him began to writhe and scream in agony as every bone in his body was ground to dust. As the man's fist opened, the lifeless form of Torscen slumped to the ground.

"Welcome, Zoldex," Winton declared with a bow. "Who are

these individuals with you?"

"Let us say..." Zoldex paused to contemplate, "they are your new ministers."

"Ministers," a black-bearded dwarf repeated, laughing at the concept.

"Is that all you will tell me?" Winton asked.

"They are the leaders of my cause. Outcasts of the Mage's Council, like myself. Their vengeance will bring about the destruction of the Mages, and then we shall form a new Council in our own image."

He realized that Zoldex was not going to provide him with any further information as he hoped. Regarding each of them individually, he studied their features and tried to absorb every detail.

The first was a dwarf, his stern brown eyes embedded in his hardened face, with a thick and bushy black beard and hair. He was wearing black garments decorated with skeletal forms crafted in illistrium on the top of his head, his shoulders, the middle of his belt, and on his knees. Beneath his tunic, Winton could see fine-mesh illistrium chainmail covering his body. His knee-high black boots grew wider and puffed out at the top; his elbow-length gloves did the same. He held a large double-bladed battleaxe in both hands, decorated with similar skeletal designs along the head as on his outfit.

Next to him was a most unusual sabrenoh, her appearance frightening, instilling terror within him. She had pale white skin with blood-red hair and vibrant red eyes. She still wore the robes of the Mage's Council, but they were as red as her hair. A black belt bound her robes, and fastened to it were a sword and a whip, both with intricately-designed handles.

The third Mage was a female wraith that resembled the Apprentice of Askari. She had the same dark, shadowy skin, pointed ears, fangs, and glimmering yellow eyes. Her hair though had white highlights and streaks amongst the sea of black. She too wore the robes of a Mage: the white and gold standard that all Council Mage's wore. She was adorned with exquisite jewelry and other fashionable baubles. Winton spotted several small stilettoes and daggers on the insides of her sleeves as well.

Next to her was a creature he could only assume used to be a sar-nal. He shared the brown-pigmentation and the large intimidating frame of the Falestian cave-dwellers, but his head was badly burned and appeared almost skeletal. Two eerily glowing red eyes glared through the holes of his skull as the creature took long and loud breaths. His clothing was skin tight and binding, straps laced around his body, fastening the fabric to him. Across his back was a mace, though Winton felt that this one would be dangerous enough with his bare hands alone.

Though he had never met Lady Salaman personally, the first Mage on the other side of the room had to be a gorn like her. He had light-beige fur all along his body where it was exposed by his white and gold Mage's robes. The fur was longer on the back of his head and flowed down his back. His eyebrows and chin also had longer fur than the short cropped beige that was on the rest of his face. He also had pointed ears and fanged teeth, which he seemed particularly pleased to display to Winton.

The sixth Mage did not look to be in the proper place at all. He was a satyr with dark brown fur along his goat-like legs and similarly tinged hair dangling down his back. His skin was reddish, and made the horned creature appear like a demon. This one did not wear any garments at all except for a single belt, eight pouches and a slingshot fastened to it.

Standing next to him was a troll that was more than double his size. The troll was a dark grayish-green, covered with stringy gray hair. His outfit was taken from an ensemble of human garments, and Win-ton thought that they were the most mismatched and ridiculous combi-nation he had ever seen. He wore a red plaid shirt that was far too small and had the buttons straining to remain fastened around him. His pants were brown and torn at the seams. His feet were partially breaking through the black boots he had on. The only thing that looked like it fit well was a lupan-fur cloak that was draped over his shoulders. He also looked as if he was a walking armory, with a mis-matched pair of swords strung across his back, two more fastened to his waist. He also had several daggers and knives of different sizes, a mace, and a halberd in his hands.

The next Mage looked very similar to the Bounty Hunter that had kidnapped the Empress. He was a celestial with black hair, yellow eyes, and a nearly transparent form with the unsettling effect of a galaxy swirling within his head. He, too, wore the normal robes of a Mage.

Turning around, Winton saw that the final newcomer was an elf. He was sitting comfortably on the throne, his feet dangling over the armrest. He had long, flowing blonde hair, sky-blue eyes, and the face of innocence. If not for his solid black leather outfit and matching black cloak, Winton would have thought that this elf was like any other he had ever heard about: true, just, and noble. An honor blade of Xylona was lying across his lap, and two rapiers were holstered on his belt.

After examining each of the new Mages, Winton returned his gaze to Zoldex. "I am uneasy."

"Why are you uneasy?" Zoldex asked.

"We are doing too much too soon," he explained. "Our deception will be exposed."

"Whether we are exposed or not is no longer relevant," Zoldex said as he walked towards a window in the room. "The tide has changed."

"What are you talking about?" Winton demanded.

Zoldex pointed out the window to the water below.

Winton walked over and gazed outside to see what he was indicating. As he saw the harbor, his eyes widened in shock—ships of unfamiliar design stretched as far as the eye could see. As he glanced over the scope of these vessels, he had to admit that they far surpassed the forces he had just sent to war. "I don't understand," he said in a whisper.

"How little you truly understand," Zoldex scolded him. "Did you believe that my interests only extended to those within the borders of the Seven Kingdoms? Foolish whelp. My will has spread throughout the world."

"The world?" Winton asked, not happy with what he was hearing.

"Behold—the legions of Zoldex."

CHAPTER 75

"Does this ever end?" Baldock asked as he scanned the marching orcs.

Thamar's expression did not change. Since leaving Vorstad, he had been stern, hard, and cold, but even he had to agree with Baldock's blunt question. They had seen the invasion of Vorstad, and the forces amassed. They wove their way through the hobgoblins in the South and North Horwood Forests, and Xylona. Now, more orcs—all garbed in the fine dwarven and elven armor as those that had besieged Vorstad—were marching in a near endless succession.

As he watched the orcs pass, he realized that even if the unification had succeeded, the realm still would not have been prepared to face an army so vast. The sacrifice that his father and all of those that fought at Vorstad to try and help dwindle their foes and defend their homes had been in vain. A waste. There was no way that the fifty thousand dwarves—even though they were proud, Vorstad dwarves—could ever have succeeded against forces so grand.

"What are those?" Ashwin asked, pointing through the foliage where she was hidden at several large creatures. There were three of them in all, standing close to twenty feet in height and twice that in length. Their bodies were separated into three parts: a large rounded head with a long neck; the main body with pincers at the end of two short arms, and six thick and hairy legs attached to the thorax; and an abdomen that resembled a long round tail. Each of them were tinged lime-green on the topside, with an orange underbelly. Their eyes were large black orbs that reflected images around them.

"I have never seen anything like it," Arifos said as he regarded the

403

giant insects.

"Nor have I," Mylvannan agreed.

"I do not like it," Arifos added with concern. "These creatures work for Zoldex. Their usefulness must therefore be nefarious."

"Nothing we can do about it," Thamar commented, an underlying tone of defeat and resignation in his voice.

Ashwin looked at him sympathetically, but could see by his reaction as he quickly looked away that the dwarf did not want her compassion.

"Baldock is right," Mylvannan said. "There does appear to be no end in sight. We cannot remain here much longer, for we will surely be found."

"The tigers and I have scouted further down, and these orcs are wide-spread. We may not be able to get around them as easily as we had hoped," Arifos explained.

"What do we do then, wait here?" Ashwin asked. "Mylvannan just said we'd be found."

"We must risk the swamps," Arifos concluded.

Thamar snorted and lay down next to his brother, who was sound asleep as if he had not a care in the world.

"What is it?" Ashwin asked.

"You wish to exchange one enemy for hundreds," he said. "If we go into the swamps, we will face near-death at every turn. If we aren't lost to the bog, then we could fall to the trolls, rasplers, snakes, and thousands of other wildlife that call the Tenalong swamps home. And if we survive all of that, don't be counting your blessings too soon, for the swamps belong to the Hidden Empire. We may wander aimlessly from one threat to another, but Lady Salaman will know exactly where we are, and she could order her people to strike at any time."

The Madrew elf began to grin deviously.

"What are ye smilin' at, elf?" Baldock asked.

"If the Hidden Empire controls the swamps, then we should thank them for the gracious hospitality we received in Trespias," he said.

"Ye want to be facin' the Hidden Empire?" Baldock asked.

"Yes," Arifos said. "Unless you dwarves have had your fill of battle and wish to lie down and die. If so, we can stay here; but if its glory—and retribution—you seek, come into the swamps with me."

"No one be callin' *me* a quitter, elf!" Baldock shouted a little louder than any of his companions would have liked with the orcs so close. "Let the durned Hidden Empire learn what it is to be facin' me and me Splitter!"

"How about it, Thamar?" Ashwin asked, kneeling down next to him.

Thamar kicked his brother in the leg to wake him up. He then lifted his mallet and rested it on his shoulder. With a lingering glare at his companions, he turned and led the group into the swamps, leaving the advancing orcs behind him. Let the swamps try to defeat them—Thamar would prove that there was still a true son of Vorstad left alive to lay claim to the name.

CHAPTER 76

"He calls this a map?" Sora scoffed at the thought. "We have been walking in this crud for hours!"

Solara lifted her leg, the dense mud they were walking in bubbling around her. Every step they had taken was a chore, for with each one, the two mystral and Tiot found their legs sinking to their knees. It was a long and slow process, but they were advancing and following the map that Palmer had provided them.

"Better this than that," Solara gestured towards the murky water with algae draped across it. All around them, trees rose from the swamp. The bases of the trunks were wide at the bottom and they rose straight up with lush leaves only at the top of the trees.

The three never felt alone: they could hear animals all around them; the constant melody that made up the life of the swamp soon became an accustomed aspect of their journey.

The insects were maddening. Time and again, the two women swatted at the backs of their necks, their arms, their heads, and numerous other places as they found small winged creatures digging into their skin and draining blood. How anyone could live in these swamps was beyond them.

More than once, Sora had complained about the fact that they left the horses with Palmer and his family, but the former Captain insisted that the swamps were no place for their mounts; now that they were knee-deep, she finally had to agree with him. Although, she thought that it would be far better for the horse to be knee deep than her.

"How deep is that water?" Sora asked. "Maybe it's better than this."

"No," Solara said sternly. "Palmer has scouted the swamp. If this is the path he recommends, then this is the path we will take."

"This is horrible though," Sora protested.

"We have a larger clearing up ahead," Solara pointed out, trying to sound optimistic. "At least we haven't come across any of the trolls he warned us about yet."

"*Yet*," she repeated sarcastically.

Solara did her best to ignore her sister's tone. Though she had insisted on coming with her, she found Sora to be quite sarcastic, demeaning, and in many instances, aloof. Not for the first time, she wondered how many lives Durgin had ruined that day he came into their lives. She was ashamed to admit it, but she was so focused on her duty to Braksis, that she never considered the anguish that Sora must have been feeling as well.

"This can't be healthy for the baby, you know," Sora added, ending the silence.

Solara paused and felt her abdomen. Though she was trying to deny it, she had begun to show signs of her condition. Even though she was as physically fit as she was, a slight rounding had begun to appear. If she could not kill Rawthorne now, then she knew that she would be forced to wait until after the baby had been born—something she hoped that she would not have to deal with; no, the murderer would meet his demise by her hand within a matter of days.

"Did you hear me?" Sora prodded.

"I heard you just fine," Solara said. "Keep moving. We're almost there."

"Don't say I didn't warn you if the baby is born with scales and a tail," Sora snickered.

"Don't be ridiculous," Solara shot back. "The baby won't change its appearance because of this."

"How do you know?" Sora shot back instantly. "No mystral has ever had a child from a man before. How do you know what it will look or behave like?"

Solara had to admit that she did not know. She had assumed that the child would be like any other, but Sora could have a valid point.

After this was done—regardless of the outcome—they would reclaim their horses from Palmer, return to Comonor for Leora, and then she would go back to Ferceng's cave and remain there until the baby was born. She trusted that the Mage Master would know precisely what to do—whatever complications may arise.

"One thing is certain," Sora added. "Soon, you're going to be a porker."

"A porker?" Solara asked, insulted by the insinuation.

"Oh yeah," Sora grinned mischievously. "Once you are, that's what I'll call you."

"How mature," Solara said.

"Just saying it as I see it," Sora replied, flattening her nose with her finger and making pig sounds.

"See, we made it," Solara said, ignoring her sister.

Sora forgot all about her little insult as she took her last step out of the thick mud, relieved as she set foot on the more solid ground. "Can we rest here?"

"Yes," Solara said as she reached over and helped Tiot out of the mud. "We should rest."

"You'sss will not be resssting here," a rasping voice warned them.

Solara stood fully erect and pulled her elongated mystral sword from its sheath. Standing ready, she scanned the figures leaping from the water and landing all around them.

They had thick, scaly hides that were tinged either greenish-brown or greenish-yellow. Their eyes were slit like a snake's and rested above a slightly-elongated snout. Every few seconds, a long, split tongue would flicker in and out of their mouths. Their necks were large and thick, the scales along the sides and nape far more pronounced than along the front—as if the scales were an armored collar protecting the neck. Their bodies were large and imposing, the shortest of the group was slightly over seven feet tall. Their fingers and toes were both clawed, and the backs of their hands also had a much larger claw so that if they balled their hands into fists, the claw would be a piercing weapon. Long, powerful tails wove behind the reptilian creatures.

"What are they?" Sora asked as she held a glaive, ready to throw.

"Rasplers," Solara informed her disdainfully. "A hunting party."

One of the rasplers stepped forward. His scales were the palest of the group, almost beige. In his hands he held a large menacing spear that had a single blade jutting from the top, and two rounded blades arching down.

"What are you'sss doing here?" the raspler asked.

"We are seeking the right of vengeance on a cowardly man that murdered my mate while he was unarmed, and now hides behind Lady Salaman."

The raspler turned and signaled his pack with a series of quick moving hand gestures. When he completed, the others dropped back and returned to the water, swimming away as their tails propelled them quickly through the swamp. "Lady Sssalaman," he repeated. "The Hidden Empire is our enemiesss too."

"Then perhaps we are allies against a common foe?" Solara speculated.

"Perhapsss," the raspler replied.

"I am Solara, this is my sister, Sora, and the wolf is Tiot."

"Ssshressstellisssshar," the raspler hissed back.

"Shrestellishar," Solara repeated as she nodded towards the raspler. "A pleasure."

"Come, I'sss ssshall lead you'sss persssonally," Shrestellishar prompted them. Without waiting for an answer, he started to walk deeper into the swamps, leading the way.

"What do we do now?" Sora asked.

"I guess we follow him," Solara shrugged. "Like he said—he'll lead us personally."

"After you, sister-dear," Sora replied sarcastically, trying to hide her dissatisfaction with following the raspler.

"But of course," Solara sang back, jogging to catch up to their guide, realizing that allies often were found in the most unlikely of places.

CHAPTER 77

Shrestellishar was true to his word, safely leading the mystral and timber wolf to the lair of the Hidden Empire. He had taken a much more direct course than the map had indicated, but he paused frequently to point out the dangers and things to avoid.

The lair was little more than a single stone structure in the midst of the swamp. Though large, the round building had no windows built into it. The top of the building had several outcroppings with guard towers.

As she studied the base of operations of the feared Hidden Empire, Solara was not impressed. She had thought that the lair would have been much more awe-inspiring, even regal. After all, Lady Salaman had her grasp on almost every criminal element in the realm. You would think that that would be a profitable enterprise.

"From thisss way, the guardsss do not watch," Shrestellishar informed them.

"Why not?" Sora asked.

"Path leadsss to Fenland," he explained. "Guardsss watch the road."

"And coming in through the swamp is not expected?" Solara speculated.

"Ssswamp isss dangerousss," Shrestellishar agreed. "Lady Sssalaman thinksss we'sss won't bother her."

"Then we thank you for guiding us this way," Solara said appreciatively.

"How do we get in?" Sora asked.

"There," Shrestellishar said as he pointed. There was a small gate,

410

hardly noticeable if they did not know where to look. It was well-concealed to the casual eye. "They thinksss it'sss a sssecret."

"Well, we're glad that you know about it," Solara said as she started to step from the swamp and head to the gate.

Shrestellishar reached out with lightning-quick reflexes and stopped her. "Thisss isss where we ssshall part," he said. "We'sss wisssh you luck with your vengeance."

"We thank you for getting us this far," Solara nodded.

Shrestellishar then released her and watched as she led Sora and Tiot over to the gate. Within a matter of moments, the trio disappeared into the lair of the Hidden Empire.

Arifos paused and studied the two women as they ran. He did not recognize the blonde-haired one, but the other was unmistakable: Solara. Though they had met only once at Xylona, he was certain that it was her.

The companions had been wandering the swamps for days. What they had hoped would be the easier path, proved not to be so. Since entering, they had several near encounters with trolls, but had managed to avoid them all. Each time they were forced to divert their course, and now, none of them truly knew where they were.

Seeing Solara, Arifos felt that it might very well be the first positive sign they had since their journey had begun. A known-ally of Thamar, and of the Imperium, made her a welcome sight indeed. The fact that she also was in the swamps that they were lost in, certainly added hope that they would manage to find their way out.

Where was she going though? The structure had several guard towers atop of it. Was this the lair of the Hidden Empire that Thamar had warned them about, or was it something else? If it was the Hidden Empire, was Solara attacking them, or in league with them?

Reaching the conclusion that it was not his place to speculate, he reached out and tapped Thamar to gain his attention.

"What?" Thamar barked challengingly. His demeanor since leaving Vorstad continued to be worrying; but the elves all agreed that, in time, Thamar would come to terms with the death of his father and the destruction of his home. It may be a long time, but they opted to be patient and supportive, giving him that time.

"Do you know what that complex is?"

Thamar strained to see, but his eyesight was not as keen as the Madrew elf's. "If I had to wager a guess, I'd say that it was the Hidden Empire."

"As I feared," Arifos said.

"We must avoid it," Thamar decided. "We'll sneak around and none will be the wiser that we were here."

"It may not be that easy," Arifos replied.

"Speak, elf," Thamar ordered. "What are you hinting at?"

Baldock and Ashwin both turned to regard the conversation. They were closest to the two and were concerned by the harshness in Thamar's tone.

"I believe Solara is an ally of yours?" Arifos asked.

"And a friend," he confirmed. "What is it to you?"

"She just went inside that structure, along with another woman and a wolf," Arifos informed him.

Thamar's eyes widened. "Solara and Tiot, here?"

Theiler stepped up and pulled his sword from its sheath. He nodded at his brother and stared sternly at the lair before them.

"Secrecy be damned," Thamar cried out. "We shall not let an ally face a den of vipers alone!"

As they stepped into the darkness of the tunnel, Solara unsheathed her drantanas. She glanced back at Sora, and watched as her sister removed the bow that Atindra had given them and nocked it with an arrow. Tiot stepped in front of them and led the way through the darkness.

The trio stayed close together, their eyes trying to adjust to the darkness, but having not even the slightest illumination to do so. They could be walking directly into a series of booby traps, and be none the wiser until it was sprung. Knowing where they were, Solara would not be surprised if the floor opened beneath them and they fell into a pit of spears.

They walked in silence for what seemed an eternity, cautiously making their way through the tunnel. They reached a wall and could see that the passage would allow them to go either left or right. To the right, they heard moans and cries, but they could also see the flickering of torchlight.

Deciding to risk the path that led to the torchlight, Solara beckoned Tiot to lead them forward. Solara resheathed one of her drantanas and removed a throwing knife in case there were any guards posted nearby. She hoped that a swift and silent attack would prevent any alarms from being sounded.

Once they reached the torch, they found no guards—only small cages with people locked inside. There were several rasplers and humans, a pair of dwarves, and an elf. One of the humans reached his hand out of the bar and tried to grab them.

"Help us," he pleaded. "Please!"

Sora stepped towards the cage, but Solara held her arm out to stop her. "What?" Sora shot her an angry glare.

"What if the cages are somehow rigged?" Solara cautioned. "If we release them, it could bring the Hidden Empire down upon us."

"No," the human cried. "Just let us out."

Solara's heart broke as she watched them. They were all badly battered and bruised. They were also much thinner than she thought they should be, practically skin and bones. She assumed that their captors did not treat them well at all.

The elf did not move, but held her gaze knowingly. Though her garments were in tatters, Solara could see that at one time they had been highly fashionable and regal. They were a mixture of blue and purple, with some signs of silver as well. This was one of the High elves of Turning Leaf.

"I'm sorry," Solara said. "We will free you if we can, but not now."

The elf slowly bobbed her head in acknowledgement and acceptance. "Until we meet again."

Solara started walking back down the corridor again, Sora remaining behind, in shock that they were not rescuing the prisoners. The human that had reached out did so again. "No, don't leave us!"

His words echoed after them as they continued into the lair. Solara wondered if she had made the right decision. She did not wish for the freed prisoners to alert their captors, but the cries of the human may be even worse. Pushing her doubts aside, she continued on. Her priority was Rawthorne. She vowed that, after he was dead, she would return this way and free the prisoners.

"You certainly put on an entertaining show," Rawthorne said in admiration.

Lady Salaman smiled as she watched the spectacle before her. Several of her men had returned from Trespias with news that they could not reach Winton. She did not take too kindly to their failure and decided to feed them to her pet, Kargle.

Kargle was a torsneg, a vicious—and deadly—three-headed snake from the swamps. Its bite was venomous, and those that were pierced only had moments before it reached their nervous systems. The torsneg was fifteen feet long, and found a variety of ways to play with its prey, including wrapping itself around its meal and crushing them in its constricting vice. It also moved swiftly, eliminating any hope one may have of escaping.

Not that anything that faced Kargle could ever escape. Lady Salaman had a dome built as an arena. The bottom was filled with the murky swamp water, with a round cage providing room to try and evade the pet. No matter how many go in, none have ever walked back out.

The spectacle was one that was well enjoyed by her minions, but also held a sense of foreboding, for none knew what would cause Lady Salaman to grow enraged and offer you to her pet. Not that Kargle was her only form of intimidation: Lady Salaman herself was a gorn, and she could make a grown man shrink with a glance. Covered in varying shades of brown fur, most of her body was a light brown, though it was much darker on her head and trailing down the midsection of her back. Her eyebrows and the fur on her chin were also longer. She had canine ears that jutted from her head and twitched slightly as she listened to things around her. Her nose was short and embedded in her face. Her teeth were sharpened and fanged; she often licked her lips when looking at those that stood before her, as if she wished to leap upon them and begin devouring them.

Like all gorn, Lady Salaman had a symbiotic relationship with her outfit. At most times, it only covered her private parts, revealing almost all of her muscularly furred body. In the times when she experienced danger, the symbiote would become defensive and create a thick exoskeleton that could rival even the strongest of armors. Not only was this form of armor strong, but also highly resistant to mystical assaults, making a gorn almost impervious to combative magic. The symbiote could also develop spikes and jagged edges on command, creating razor sharp weapons for the gorn to face their foes with.

Gorn are never found together unless it is their time for mating rituals, typically between their second and third century of life. During these times, the parents of the gorn would arrange a mating with another family. After the mating is complete, the two offspring would form a new family hierarchy, and their parents would be disposed of—unless there were other siblings that required pairing as well. The mates would remain together until their offspring reached the age of majority—which for gorn was twenty-five—and then all three would go their separate ways until it was time to arrange a marriage for their own child.

As such, the entire race is full of lone individuals existing independently. Even so, others regard them as hostile, warlike, intimidating, and ruthless. A gorn is never to be trusted, but is definitely a creature to watch out for and be cautious of.

Standing by her side, as he almost always did, was Larude. He was the first to join her cause, and was her most loyal lieutenant. As such, he had become her right-hand man and, quite often, her enforcer. Larude was never seen without his battle armor on, his true heritage never revealed. He wore black-gold armor, glistening with golden emblems of serpents along his chest and knees. His faceplate revealed none of his true features, and had golden scales surrounding the edges of the helmet and encircling the dark orbs that covered his eyes. A dark-green scaled-tunic was fitted loosely over his armored chest and fastened by a black belt at his waist. A matching hooded cloak was clasped on his neck by a golden snake brooch.

Rawthorne stood on her other side, and all three were surrounded by photons. The photons were garbed in navy blue and white robes. Each held a bladed staff and had a gladius short-sword fastened to their belts. Photons were generally regarded as honorable and noble, but they had forged an alliance with the Hidden Empire and provided the bodyguards for Lady Salaman.

The arena was full of thieves, assassins, bounty hunters, mercenaries, enforcers, guards, information brokers, and numerous other individuals that were allured by lives of crime. Unlike the rest of the realm, there was no prejudice in the Hidden Empire. The arena was littered with humans, photons, orcs, goblins, hobgoblins, giants, rasplers, trolls, and several other individuals from a variety of races. They all adhered to only one rule: Lady Salaman's word was law.

In the dome, only three of the messengers were still alive. Two were attempting to climb the chain mesh gate, with the third struggling to run through the murky swamp to reach the edges himself. He never made it as Kargle grabbed him from below and dragged him under the water. Those in the arena cheered as they saw his crimson blood bubble up where the man had been dragged under.

"Let me out!" one man was crying. He had climbed close to where

Lady Salaman sat and was reaching towards her through the steel-barred dome.

Larude stepped forward as if he would push the man back in, but Lady Salaman stopped him. "Let him cry for help, it is of no consequence."

"Please, I will go back and force an audience with Winton!" he cried again.

Lady Salaman smiled expectantly at the man. He was a fool to try and gain her sympathies. Especially when that meant that he would remain stationary.

From the water below, the three-headed Kargle leapt straight from under the surface. All three heads bit into the man at the waist, and then dropped back down again, bringing his severed lower body with them.

The man stared at Lady Salaman, blinking in shock. His hands were trembling, trying desperately to hold onto the bars. His last sight was of the crime-lord purring over his demise.

Kargle leapt up again, this time, digging its teeth into the man's back and dragging him completely under the water with it. Only one of the nine that had entered the arena was left alive. He, too, would feel the torsneg's chilling embrace.

A tail shot from the water and knocked the last survivor down. Kargle then wrapped around his body and began to crush every bone. His dying scream of agony was like a symphony to the criminals cheering for his death. As Kargle began to devour the man's lifeless body, Lady Salaman stood up and returned to her audience chamber.

Larude, Rawthorne, and the photons followed her closely, with others gradually returning to whatever they had been doing before the nine messengers were dropped into the dome. "This lack of respect from Winton is most discouraging," she said.

"A boy who knows not what it means to be King, much less Emperor," Rawthorne concluded. "After we remove King Lorrents and I am King again, perhaps then I will challenge Winton for the Imperium."

"You are very presumptuous," Lady Salaman declared. "I have not yet decided that you will even be a king again."

"I killed Warlord Braksis!" he screamed. "By my own hands he died. I have nothing left to prove."

"Winton had requested aid of me. He hired assassins to kill Braksis. Low-paid assassins that would never succeed," Lady Salaman explained. "He then requested protection from us, an arrangement that my faithful lieutenant, Xyphin, oversaw. Whether you killed Braksis or not, Winton still owes a debt of allegiance to me."

"But he is a fool," Rawthorne objected.

"Fool or no, he belongs to me," Lady Salaman said sinisterly. "His new reign as Emperor should therefore be most prosperous."

"He is not listening to you," Rawthorne objected.

"Kabilian," Lady Salaman called out.

The assassin stepped forward and bowed. "Yes, your excellence?"

"You gave him the message I sent?"

"Of course, your excellence," he stated. "I would not send another message though if I were you."

"You dare?" Larude barked in his deep and muffled voice.

"Let him speak," Lady Salaman said as she held up a finger.

"Rawthorne is right: Winton is a fool. Let me go back," Kabilian offered. "This time, instead of giving him a message, I'll turn him into a message."

"Your offer amuses me," Lady Salaman grinned at the thought. "But I do not wish to lose an Emperor just yet. Rawthorne, I want you to go to Trespias. Make sure Winton knows that we demand payment for supporting him."

"I should be King of Falestia, not an errand-boy!"

Lady Salaman stood up and struck Rawthorne in the face, knocking him to the ground. "Your insolence will not be tolerated. Perhaps Kargle will have a tenth snack today?"

Rubbing his chin, Rawthorne looked up from the ground. "That will not be necessary."

"Patience, Rawthorne," Lady Salaman declared. "When you came to us with news of Braksis's murder, you requested assistance in reclaiming the throne of Falestia. I allowed you to stay and promised that when the time was right, you would rise in power again. Do not question or doubt me again."

"My apologies," Rawthorne said, struggling to sound sincere. "When do you wish for me to leave?"

"Immediately," Lady Salaman said.

"Did you hear that?" Sora asked. "He admitted that he killed Braksis."

"Yes," Solara agreed. "It's deeper than that though. Winton is now Emperor? And he is the one that hired the assassins? It was as we thought: the 'son of Sar'—as the assassin started to say—was really the 'son of Sarlec.'"

"Does that mean we try to kill the Emperor too?" Sora asked, sounding skeptical.

"No, we cannot face the entire Imperium right now," Solara replied. "Rawthorne must die first."

Pulling back on the bowstring, Sora aimed for Rawthorne's heart. "One shot is all it would take."

"No," Solara decided. "We will wait until he is on the road to Trespias. Then we can challenge him without having so many foes to face."

As they stealthily returned the way they had come, neither noticed the shadowy form of the chiroptera, Xyphin, hanging from the ceiling, his ears twitching as he listened to their conversation. Their presence was no longer hidden.

"Come on," Thamar called out. "They may need us!"

"Thamar, no!" Mylvannan warned as he scanned the watchtowers above. "The guards will spot us!"

"Too late," Arifos warned as the bells began clanging. "We have been seen."

Two large doors opened and warriors started charging towards them—orcs, humans, goblins, and hobgoblins. As the companions drew their weapons and prepared to defend themselves, each had the thought deep down that at least these orcs did not resemble those fighting at Vorstad. These were normal, ordinary orcs: orcs that were about to learn what it meant to fight a group with pent-up frustration and anger.

Solara heard the bells clanging and tensed immediately. She glanced at Sora and Tiot to see if either of them knew what had caused the commotion, but neither appeared to know what was going on.

A ray of black light shot down and separated the two mystral. Only their training and reflexes kept them from being impacted by the blast. Solara held her drantanas ready and looked for the source. She saw a chiroptera drop for the ceiling and call out, "Intruders!"

From all around the room, she saw faces looking up at her. She caught the glare of one: Rawthorne. As she stared back at the man, she could see that he was visibly shaken. He did not expect to see her again, certainly not here. A smile quickly creased his face as dozens of Hidden Empire thugs began climbing the stairwells, approaching the three intruders.

"Well, so much for subtlety," Solara called out as she leapt from the second-story, spun in the air, and landed on the ground facing Rawthorne. Even outnumbered, when she was certain that she herself would perish, she knew that it would not be before Braksis was avenged.

CHAPTER 78

As the Hidden Empire lackeys charged towards them, Mylvannan dropped back, issuing commands to the rest of the group. Thamar took the point and had both Theiler and Baldock on his sides, slightly behind him. Vaz and Vella were on the opposite sides of the two dwarves, creating the now-familiar defensive "V"-formation. Mylvannan stood in the middle, behind Thamar, Frostlartil aimed at the advancing creatures. Slightly behind him were both Ashwin and Arifos, their bows nocked and drawn.

"Fire!" he called out.

The two elves began launching their arrows towards the advancing masses. Ashwin moved quickly, releasing arrow after arrow at anything that came near the group. Arifos was being more selective, using the stronger draw weight of Unamalastra to eliminate as many of the larger orcs as possible. Each orc hit was launched backwards with the power of the blow, often rendering several of those behind them unconscious.

"On my order," Mylvannan called out to the dwarves and white tigers. "Steady."

The two archers continued their attack, striking as many foes as they could. This battle would soon be a physical one in close-proximity—and the fewer the opponents, the better.

Arifos watched as an orc picked up a goblin and hurtled it towards them. Undoubtedly, they hoped that the goblin would distract the archers and give the others time to reach the dwarves and attack. The Madrew elf would not be baited though. He aimed carefully at the screaming goblin as it flew towards them, and released an arrow. The tip entered the goblin through its open mouth, and jerked it backwards as it burst through its upper spine and continued on until it hit the orc that had thrown it. With a grin of satisfaction, Arifos pulled another arrow and sent it towards his next target.

"Steady," Mylvannan called out again, making certain that his companions held the line as long as possible.

Though they were the smallest creatures advancing, the goblins were the first to reach the dwarves and white tigers. Ashwin began to focus her arrows on the smaller creatures, and was also much more efficient with eliminating them, for a goblin took only a single arrow or two, whereas an orc, hobgoblin, or human sometimes took three or four arrows before they stopped advancing. Even still, there were too many of them for her to pick-off before the goblins were upon them.

"Now!" Mylvannan cried out.

The second the order was given, the dwarves and tigers stepped forward and began to attack the goblins approaching them. Thamar began the battle as he brought his mallet slamming down on the skull of the green-skinned creature closest to him, hammering it into instant oblivion.

The companions were swift and highly-skilled. They moved as a team, covering each other whenever one of their backs was turned, as if they had always done so. Even so, the attacking Hidden Empire guards were not deterred. They would soon learn the error of their ways.

Sora watched dumbfounded as her sister spun through the air, and landed on the ground in a roll. She shot upwards again, her arms moving independently, and striking down the first two foes that were closest to her. She could not believe that Solara would attempt such a reckless maneuver, but they were committed now.

She saw a man running towards Solara from behind with two daggers in his hands. As Sora fumbled to pull her bow and nock it, she was simply amazed as her sister twirled one of her drantanas and jabbed it backwards without even looking. The blade could be seen jutting from the back of the man right before Solara drew it out again to defend against the next attacker.

Without delaying further, Sora began launching arrow after arrow at the criminals below. Whenever one of them closed in on Solara, she aimed for them. Otherwise, she was not selective, striking anything in the lair that dared to even look her way.

Absorbed by her attack, she failed to spot a mercenary sneaking up to her until she heard Tiot growl and leap at the man, his jaw clamped shut on the mercenary's neck. Sora said a silent prayer of thanks to the timber wolf, and then launched several arrows at others that had been following the mercenary.

Though she would chastise herself later for not being able to absorb her surroundings as well as Solara, or having a sort of sixth-sense to know when danger was coming, she was quickly struck by a furry fist. She dropped to the ground, her bow spinning away from her. Looking for her attacker, she saw the same bat-like creature that had sounded the alarm flying away from her. As it turned to swoop down again, she braced herself for the attack.

Crick watched as Xyphin struck the mystral and knocked her backwards. As the bow spun away from her, he glanced at his own wretched hobgoblin bow and decided that it was time to procure the more finely-crafted mystral version.

He no longer feared being injured, especially in this battle. The dwarves had done their work well. He was covered from head to toe in a solid suit of illistrium armor. The sparkling exterior was engraved to resemble the scales of a dragon, with a full dragon emblem upon his breastplate. His helmet encased his head, with the jaws of a dragon's fanged mouth open wide enough for him to see through, two dragon wings extending from the sides.

The Tregador dwarves had performed exceptional work, even his weapons had become part of the suit of armor he now wore: around the calves of each leg, small loops were forged into the armor to hold his mystral throwing daggers. Similar holders were mounted across his back, one for each of his drantanas. His two ornamented mystral quivers were fastened to his waist, one on each side of his body. Strung over his shoulder were his hobgoblin bow and an illistrium kite shield, engraved with the same image of the dragon that was carved into his breastplate.

With the armor and weapons he wielded, Crick no longer felt like a hobgoblin. He felt nearly invulnerable. As he began to advance towards the stairs to go after Sora's bow, Kabilian stopped him.

"We will collect the mystral weapon's when the day's events are through," he said.

"I want the bow," Crick growled with determination.

"I know you do, my friend," Kabilian said. "For now though, unless we are specifically ordered otherwise, we are to play the role of the silent observers."

"Why?" Crick demanded. "Why are we not fighting?"

"I only fight if it's in my best interests to do so," Kabilian explained.

"How would us being ordered be in your best interests?" Crick asked, still confused and trying hard to grasp what Kabilian was getting at.

"Why, that is simple, my friend," Kabilian smiled. "If we are asked, then Lady Salaman will owe us. That is not a bad proposition."

"We could fight now, and she would still owe us," Crick surmised.

"Look at her," Kabilian pointed. "She is sitting on her throne, feeling comfortable and confident. Untouchable. She is being attacked, but does not think that her life is in jeopardy. If we fought now, it would be for nothing. Let the less skilled members of the Hidden Empire falter. Then we will go in and mop up the mess, gaining more prestige and rewards for ourselves."

Crick glanced up and watched as Xyphin spun around to dive at Sora again. He bit his lip in anticipation—the bow would be his, he just needed to be patient.

A sarnal stepped before Solara, clearly expecting to bar her path. What the seven-foot creature did not realize though, was that he blocked her from Rawthorne, and anything that dared to do that, would share his fate. The brown-skinned creature swung a mace at her. Solara dropped to the ground and rolled, knocking his feet out from under him. Spinning back up, she jumped on top of the sarnal, straddled him, and then dug both drantanas into his chest.

Flipping off of the sarnal, she withdrew the blades and landed several feet in front of Rawthorne. The man was watching her with admiration and anticipation. As she stepped towards him, the photon guards of Lady Salaman moved to intercept.

Solara stepped back to give herself more room, and scanned the pale warriors with burning heads. These would not be like the others she had carved her way through to get to Rawthorne. They were far more experienced and skilled; she could see that in their eyes. Even still, they were but a distraction from her true goal, and she refused to be distracted for long.

Lady Salaman watched the exchange between Rawthorne and Solara. As her guards moved in to intercept the anticipated mystral assassin, she kept her gaze intently on her new ally, and watched him, as he appeared to grow increasingly more excited.

"You know this mystral?" Lady Salaman demanded.

"Oh yes," Rawthorne replied. "This is the servant and protector of my late cousin."

"Why is she here?" Lady Salaman pressed.

"She must be here to avenge Braksis," Rawthorne surmised. "Magnificent, isn't she?"

"Magnificent?" Lady Salaman asked.

"Yes," Rawthorne answered in appreciation. "It's a shame that she was sworn to Braksis and not me. I could use such a woman, in many ways."

"I'm sure you could," Lady Salaman answered with no hint of annoyance or disapproval. "I am not pleased that you have brought enemies to my very doorstep."

"My apologies," Rawthorne declared, taken aback for a moment, pulling his eyes away from the raging battle between Solara and the photons. "I had no way to anticipate her actions here this day."

"Nonetheless, if this is not resolved quickly, you will find yourself as an outcast to the Hidden Empire."

Rawthorne glared defiantly at the crime-lord and watched as she rubbed a small talisman carved to resemble Kargle. She held his gaze unflinchingly, and he knew that if Solara succeeded in wreaking havoc on the Hidden Empire, he would be the next bout of entertainment in the dome with Lady Salaman's pet serpent.

Turning away from the crime-lord, Rawthorne raised his mallet and advanced towards the combatants. He was determined to kill Solara as quickly as he did Braksis, and maintain his favor with Lady Salaman. After all, her support would be instrumental in reclaiming the Falestian throne.

CHAPTER 79

The companions continued to fight. Their sheer determination and skill kept them ever-moving forward, whereas the forces against them at many times dropped back rather than risking their lives. Dozens of the Hidden Empire lackeys fled into the swamps rather than continuing the battle against the dwarves, elves, and tigers; they were the smarter ones. Those that remained found themselves hammered by Thamar, struck by Baldock, slashed by Theiler and Mylvannan, clawed by Vaz and Vella, or pierced by Arifos and Ashwin.

Even without those that darted into the depths of the swamps, the companions were still vastly outnumbered. That fact did not bother any of them—since they had banded together to travel to Trespias for the unification talks, they seemed to always face insurmountable odds; and even though they had setbacks—such as the death of Heirn and the fall of both Vorstad and Xylona—they managed to persevere.

Ashwin paused and lowered her bow. The foes furthest from them were turning around and returning to the lair of the Hidden Empire. "Arifos, what do you make of that?"

Arifos launched three more arrows, killing those closest to them, and then watched as a few more of their opponents returned to the compound. "They must be distracted by Solara," he theorized.

Thamar turned, overhearing the comment. His eyes grew with shock, and then narrowed, his growing rage building inside. He let out a wailing battle cry and charged straight ahead, striking anything in his path, pushing some creatures aside.

The companions all paused, shocked by the berserker rage of their ally, and watched as he made his way safely through the enemy forces and into the Hidden Empire lair.

"Are we goin' to be lettin' him have all o' the fun?" Baldock cried out as he lifted Splitter high and then charged the enemies just as Thamar had done.

Arifos slid his bow over his shoulder and pulled Phistala and Aurlestyl from their sheaths. He beckoned Ashwin to do the same, and waited as she lifted Martristlit and held it firmly in both hands. He then nodded to Mylvannan, who called out for them to charge.

Baldock was the furthest ahead, but Vaz and Vella quickly caught up to him. Theiler, Mylvannan, Arifos, and Ashwin took a little longer, still striking down as many foes as they could. Each time they felt overwhelmed, Arifos used his mystical abilities to batter the foes away and clear a path. Even so, the companions quickly realized that until they defeated their adversaries outside, they would be of no help to their allies inside the enemy compound.

Sora watched as Xyphin closed in on her. At the last possible instant, she pulled her two glaives from her belt and sent the first one spiraling towards the chiroptera. Sora stared in disbelief as the bladed weapon halted in the air mere inches from Xyhin's chest. He was a Mage!

"Impressive," Xyphin said. "Your aim is true."

Sora, reared back and released the other glaive as hard as she could. In a rebellious roar, she cried out, "Catch this!" As the blade was still hurtling in the air, Sora drew her drantanas and jumped from the stairs towards the Mage.

Xyphin managed to stop the second glaive as easily as the first, but he could barely believe his enhanced senses when the image of the leaping mystral came to the blind Mage. He quickly tried to fly higher to avoid her, but was not quick enough to evade her completely, barely quick enough to save his life.

The drantanas barely missed the chiroptera's stomach, and dug into the creature's left calf. Sora's momentum kept her in motion, gravity pulling at her towards the ground, the two blades slicing down his leg as she fell.

Sora tried her best to somersault and roll as she had seen Solara do, but she hit the stone floor hard. She lay there for a moment, and then heard her glaives clanging to the ground. Forcing herself to stand up, she felt renewed vigor as she watched the bleeding chiroptera fly up through an opening in the ceiling and flee to safety.

Taking a deep breath and revolving her back several times to try and reduce the pain from the impact, she bent over and reclaimed her glaives. Deciding that she would join Solara and help her against the photons, she paused as she saw Tiot severely outnumbered back on the ledge she had leapt from.

Her actions were instinctual as she launched the glaives at the foes on the ledge. The blades struck the two foes closest to Tiot, and then spiraled back down to her grasp. She loved her glaives, especially when they worked the way she wanted them to. Seeing that Tiot still required more assistance, she replaced her glaives on her belt and charged back up the stairs, her drantanas drawn and hungrily craving to sink their teeth into another foe.

The photons were skilled—too skilled, she feared. They had been battling for several minutes already, and she had been unable to ascertain a weakness in even one of them. They were well organized, fighting as a team, and were highly adept swordsmen. How the Hidden Empire could employ individuals like that, she knew not.

The battle quickly turned into a defensive one, with Solara doing everything in her power to stand her ground. She did not like the turn of events. She knew that with the numbers amassed against her, she needed to keep pressing and moving forward. To falter backwards was certain defeat.

Making matters worse, she could spot Rawthorne in her peripheral vision. The murderer was circling around the battle, sizing her up as he waited for the opportune moment to strike. She only wished that she had a chance to do the same to him. As long as he was killed, then however this day turned out would be acceptable.

From the doorway, she heard a familiar call from her past—one that invigorated her and gave her hope and confidence. Perhaps she would survive this day yet.

"You face Thamar, son of Thron, thrasher of mine enemies! Tremble before my wrath!"

Solara grinned triumphantly at her friend's announcement. All she could visualize was the ten battle-starved dwarves of Vorstad she had met that stormy night long ago coming to her aid once again. The tide had turned: the Hidden Empire had no chance at all. The thought almost made her laugh heartily, but she suppressed it. She would wait until after Rawthorne was dead before rejoicing.

CHAPTER 80

Thamar's call was quickly answered as several orcs charged towards him, their rusted blades ready to strike. The Vorstad dwarf tightened his grip on his hammer, a slight smile of anticipation creasing his lips.

Feeling almost joyous, Thamar charged forward and met the orcs with his mallet swinging violently. The first orc was battered to the ground, convulsing as it gripped its ribs. The second dropped as Thamar struck with a low blow, crippling the creature. The final one was slightly more skilled, but Thamar's ferocity was not about to be abated. He shattered the rusted weapon with one strike, and then ripped his mallet straight up, cracking the orc's neck with a mighty uppercut.

The battle was a quick one, and Thamar stood in the midst of it for a moment, relishing his victory. To him, every orc that fell was a slight atonement for what had happened to his father and to Vorstad. He had failed to help his beloved people on the day his homeland fell, but he would not do so again. The rationalization pierced his bloodlust and brought him back to the calmer demeanor he typically represented himself as. He spotted Solara and could see that she was vastly outnumbered. As long as he breathed, he refused to allow another person that he cared for to perish as he stood by and watched.

Two humans, with mud-crusted clothing and blades as rusted as the orc's, confronted him. With his faculties returned, he would not let them distract him. The dwarf charged forward, emitting a bloodcurdling roar, and knocked both men from their feet as he hurried to join Solara.

Once he reached the flaming-headed warriors, the group opened up and split their ranks to focus on both threats. Thamar liked the new odds—he had seen Solara holding her own against six, and now that she only faced three, she would undoubtedly be victorious. As for him, three opponents was almost laughable after everything he had been through lately.

"It's good of you to join me, my friend," Solara thanked him.

"What are friends for?" Thamar asked as he parried a thrust from a photon's gladius.

"Where are the other dwarves?"

"Other dwarves?" Thamar repeated, not certain he understood.

"You know: your brother, Detroz, Graf?" she clarified. "The others."

"Alas, I know not their fates. Only my brother is with me, along with a dwarf from Tregador, a trio of elves, and two magnificent cats."

Solara managed to exploit a weakness in one photon's defenses and dug a drantana into his chest. The photon dropped back, his wound smoldering and smoking with a dense red blood that set anything it touched ablaze.

The other two still facing Solara grew enraged. The flames on their heads changed from a clear blue burst to a crackling yellow. Their eyes also began to glow, a small trail of smoke seeping from them. As they stepped forward to confront her again, their blades burst into flame

"This is fun," Solara sarcastically commented.

Thamar started to emit a deep and heartfelt belly laugh. He then swung his mallet around and knocked a photon back. "It does my heart good to fight by your side again."

"Well, things were looking pretty hopeless for a while there—hopefully together that will change."

Thamar considered the words. She was right: he had been so depressed and absorbed with the loss of his father and homeland, he had been making reckless decisions and foolish mistakes—he was acting as if he wanted to join his father. It was not his time to make the eternal journey to Wolhollm yet. Even if he and Theiler were the last two true sons of Vorstad, he would make sure that the name of his proud city would be remembered. He would fight valiantly, and let his deeds speak for him. He too, was glad that he had been reunited with his old ally.

"Good doggie," the man said as he held the spear at full length, backing Tiot into a corner. "We're not going to hurt you."

"You're at least right about that."

The man spun around in time to see Sora's drantana slashing down towards his face. He managed to dodge slightly, but the blade cut deep and left a gash from his forehead down to his left cheek. As he dropped back screaming, Tiot leapt forward and bit into the hamstring of a second man, who screamed just as loudly as his partner.

Sora punched the man in the face, and with his arms waving to desperately try to maintain his balance, he fell from the ledge, landing on the floor below with a hard impact. She waited for a moment to confirm that he was unconscious, and then bent down and patted Tiot on the head. "Good boy."

Glancing over to Solara, she watched as her sister struck a photon and he fell back, smoke and flames lancing from the wound. She did not recognize the dwarf by Solara's side, but it was evident that they were fighting together. Satisfied for the moment that her sister was safe, she scanned the balcony for where her bow had fallen. Several men were still standing near there. "Shall we reclaim my bow?" she asked.

Tiot stiffened slightly and then ran off towards the foes. Sora stood up, the pain from her fall only slightly nagging her, and ran after the wolf, her swords twirling.

A second photon broke away from the attack, leaving a pair of guards to face each of the foes. He grabbed his injured companion and dragged him back to where Lady Salaman was sitting, still calmly watching the fight before her.

"Lady Salaman, you should be evacuated for your own safety," the photon recommended.

"There is no need for concern, Neuss," Lady Salaman replied. "These few are nothing but entertainment."

"There are more outside of the lair," Neuss objected. "We must get you to safety."

"I will not leave my own base for the likes of a handful of heroes," she yelled, her nostrils flaring with her temper.

Larude pulled his sword and nodded to Lady Salaman. His weapon was one that most in the Hidden Empire tried to avoid. Though the man was deadly enough, there were rumors that his blade had a bloodlust that could not be satiated, and would hunger for all of their lives. The sword was named Zloreskalaza, the skull cleaver. The entire hilt was an array of finely-crafted skulls, with a fanged skull in the middle. Each end of the crossguard had a sharp blade, allowing the wielder to strike in several ways.

As soon as Larude unsheathed Zloreskalaza, the two eyes on the fanged skull began to glow with an eerie yellow, the illumination spreading and flowing over the entire blade. Lady Salaman nodded her approval, and Larude stepped forward to join the fray.

CHAPTER 81

Ashwin swung Martristlit, and had her blow parried easily by the man she fought. She brought the sword slicing down, but again he deflected it without much effort. She stared into his face and saw the man smiling at her, knowing that he was the better swordsman. His teeth were discolored and he had black gums. She could not help but wince whenever he grinned.

The man grew tired of the fight and began initiating several offensive strikes of his own. Ashwin did her best to remember what Mylvannan and Arifos had taught her. Compared to them, this man moved practically in slow motion, but she still did not have the confidence that a true swordsman needed to survive.

The tip of his sword breached her defenses and slashed her cheek. Ashwin dropped back, her hand reaching for the bleeding wound. Breathing deeply to steady herself, she took her hand away, wincing at the sight of her own blood, and firmly clutched her honor blade with both hands.

The man before her was still grinning, but his smile quickly began to fade. "What devilry is this?"

Ashwin smirked knowingly—the sting to her cheek was already fading, her father's ring was working again. She knew that the wound was healing directly before the man's eyes, and it was something that unnerved him. "Not devilry, witchery!"

"A witch?" he gasped. "You're a witch!"

Ashwin could see the terror in his eyes, and used it to fuel her own action. She stepped forward and kept moving her blade from side-to-side in quick motions, watching as the frightened man kept faltering backwards, barely dodging each blow.

As the battle continued, she could see how much confidence—or, rather, a lack thereof—could impair your abilities. This man had clearly been the more skilled of the two, but now he was acting as if he had never held a sword before in his life.

The man tripped over the body of one of his slain allies and fell flat on his back. His sword was knocked from his grasp, and he stared up at the elf, pale as the clouds. "Please don't hurt me."

Ashwin lowered her sword to his neck, and let it rest slightly nicking his chin. "Why should I spare you?"

"I do not wish to be damned for eternity," the man cried.

"The only way to spare your soul is to improve your life," Ashwin declared. "Leave this place, now."

"I will, I will," the man stammered.

"If I ever see you again, do not make me regret my generosity."

"You won't," he promised. "I have an aging mother: I will go to her, and be a good son."

"You better," Ashwin said. "For with my witchcraft, I will know. And if I see you acting like a ruffian, I will return and claim your soul for all eternity."

"I will, I will," the man promised, frantically.

Removing the sword, Ashwin stepped back and allowed the man to regain his footing. He stood up, never taking his eyes from her, and then turned and fled into the swamps.

As she turned around, she bumped into Arifos who was standing behind her with Vaz by his side. "A witch?"

"It worked," she chuckled. "He did have more skills than me with a sword."

"Innovative," Arifos replied. "I like it."

"Are ye goin' to be talkin' or fightin'?" Baldock cried out.

"Come," Arifos prompted. "We have defeated their welcoming party. It is time now to join Thamar inside. Are you ready?"

"Yes," Ashwin said with a deep breath to steady herself. "I am ready."

"Good," he replied. "Come."

Arifos and Ashwin rushed to catch up with the others. Vaz was far faster and reached the doorway and entered the lair along with Vella, the dwarves, and Mylvannan. As they stepped inside, they could see the ensuing chaos: Thamar and Solara were fighting a quartet of pale-skinned warriors with flaming heads; dozens of spectators were circling them like vultures; on the upper level, another mystral and Tiot were fighting as well.

"Choose your targets," Mylvannan advised.

Theiler rushed forward towards the crowd where his brother and Solara were fighting. He clearly intended to fight by his brother's side. Vaz and Vella, both of whom recognized Tiot from the palace, rushed up the stairs to join the battle there. Mylvannan and Baldock moved forward to intercept several individuals that were coming towards them.

Arifos remained behind with Ashwin. "You did well in the yard," he said.

"I am not as skilled as you," she replied.

"Very few ever could hope to be as skilled as me," he returned, his words were serious and factual, not conceited in any way. He spoke as a warrior that had earned his reputation and honed his abilities through centuries of proving himself. "Remain here and use your bow. If you are in danger, call for help." He waited to make certain that she understood and would comply, and then joined Mylvannan and Baldock, his two swords dancing an intricate waltz of death.

The two photons facing Solara were more vicious than they had previously been. Though it was taxing her to defend against them and their flaming blades, she also could see that their attacks were not as coordinated and precise as they had been before. The longer the battle continued, the more the heat emanating from her foes was making her perspire and tire.

Stepping back into a defensive posture, she felt the mace of the fallen sarnal scrape against her boot. Without even looking at it, she positioned her foot and flung the mace forward towards the photons. As the two guards brought their blades up to defend themselves, Solara dove in low and slashed her drantanas towards their hamstrings.

One managed to evade her strike, but the other dropped to the ground, the same steaming red ooze coming from his wound. A fire began to rage where he was kneeling as the blood continued to splatter and drip on the ground.

The other photon stood several feet away from her and slashed his sword down. As soon as the blade was pointed towards her, a beam of yellow flame burst from the sword and directly at her.

Solara back-flipped out of the way, though she could still feel the singeing burst on her stomach. As she hurtled backwards, she dropped her drantanas and pulled several throwing knives from around her leg, launching them towards the photon. As soon as she hit the ground, she reached forward and reclaimed her swords, then leapt towards the photon again.

The photon was stumbling backwards; two of the three blades had struck him on the chest. Dropping to his knees, he raised his sword again to try and launch another volley of fire at Solara. He was unable to remain upright, and faltered backwards, sending the stream of flame directly into the ceiling.

Solara quickly searched for Rawthorne, and saw him standing behind the pair of photons still fighting Thamar. Unlike the two she had fought, these still had a crisp blue flame issuing from their heads, and they were fighting as skilled as they had when the battle first began. Thamar was doing everything in his power just to hold his ground.

As she took a step forward, she heard several grunts to her side, and turned quickly to defend herself. She need not have bothered, as she saw Theiler punching one of the thieves closest to Solara and then rushing over to his brother's side.

Moving quickly to join them, she slowed down as she saw the darkly-clad armored figure step forward and push the two photons aside. "Defend Lady Salaman. These belong to me."

Sora took a step closer to one of the thugs she was facing, and suddenly ducked as a large white and black tiger leapt over her head and slammed into the man she was about to attack. Sora turned and looked as a second white tiger leapt over her and began to attack her foes as well.

The two white tigers moved in swiftly, ignoring Sora as they began to strike the Hidden Empire men on the ledge. The two batted, clawed, bit, and rammed into them. Tiot fought directly alongside of them, giving those that were closest to the steps a reason to turn and flee from the trio of animals.

Sora watched them fighting in awe: they were amazing. Spotting her bow, she took advantage of the minor respite and reclaimed it, along with half a dozen arrows that had fallen from her quiver. Glancing at Tiot and the two white tigers, she could see that the battle on the ledge had already come to an end, and they had won.

Searching below for her next target, she saw Solara had now been joined by yet another red-bearded dwarf, and the three were preparing to confront a duo of warriors, one of which she knew was the man they had come to kill. There were others fighting now as well: two elves and a dwarf were moving through foes as easily as a baker might cut through bread; another elf stood by the doorway launching arrow after arrow at Hidden Empire minions.

Realizing that Solara was fine for the moment, Sora decided that there were other matters to attend to. Glancing down the tunnel she and Solara had come from, she remembered the prisoners and aimed to set them free. Jogging quickly so that she could return as soon as possible, she ventured into the darkness.

Tiot spotted her running down the tunnel and then followed her.

Vaz and Vella both exchanged a glance with each other. They then kept looking back and forth between the battle raging below and Tiot running down the tunnel after Sora. After several moments of pondering what to do, both white tigers entered the darkness and followed the mystral and the wolf.

CHAPTER 82

Kabilian was almost salivating when he saw the companions he had encountered in Trespias enter the lair. He had hoped that he would meet up with them and all of their mystical items again one day; this was as ideal a location as any. Surely, at least some of them would fall victim to the Hidden Empire.

As he watched the forces of Lady Salaman running in disarray, he questioned whether they would be able to handle this at all. The companions were good. He knew that. They had forced their way out of Trespias, and the Hidden Empire had supplied the forces there as well.

"Crick, it appears that we may have to intervene after all," Kabilian said.

Anticipation was clearly readable in the hobgoblin's expression. Crick glanced over at Solara, standing alongside the two dwarves, and then up to where Sora had just vanished. "I will go after the younger one first."

"No, no," Kabilian tried to calm him. "We will get the mystral items soon enough. But first, I have need of you."

"What?" Crick asked impatiently.

"All in good time," Kabilian sung. "Be ready."

Crick watched as the assassin reached into his pouch and removed a small pearl. Kabilian raised the gem to his forehead, and four small legs dug into his head. Before Crick's eyes, Kabilian's features began to change. His hazel eyes darkened into a deep blue indigo. His long, auburn hair shortened and lightened into a honey-blonde. His ears began to extend and became pointed like that of an elf. His face began to narrow and soften into the features of an elven male. Even the scar upon his face vanished with the transformation.

The transformation was not only skin-deep: Kabilian's wardrobe began to blend into a myriad of green patterns, his black boots turned completely white. Kabilian scanned himself and nodded his approval. "The deception is nearly complete."

If Crick had not seen the transformation himself, he would not believe that the man before him was his ally. Even his voice had been altered. The tone was almost musical in nature as if he truly were an elf.

Kabilian rubbed his forehead a bit, and then lowered his arms behind his back—several bindings appeared around his arms and legs, a scrap of cloth also formed around his mouth, gagging the assassin. His clothes grew dirtier, as if he had been dragged forcibly through the swamps, and even tore in certain spots. Small wounds and bruises also began to appear, making the elven figure appear to be close to death.

"How is this possible?" asked Crick, dumbfounded by what was happening before him.

With the gag over his mouth, Kabilian answered only with his eyes, an expression of triumph and guile in his look. He then strained to glance towards the door, and saw that his efforts had proved successful.

Ashwin carefully selected her targets. They were vastly outnumbered, but it appeared that many of the individuals within the lair of the Hidden Empire were striving to stay out of the way of the combatants. She did not wish to reward them by launching an arrow in their direction; instead, she watched for any potential foe to draw a weapon or advance upon her friends, and this was whom she struck at.

With her bow drawn, she continued to scan the room and search for her next target. She was not prepared for what she saw. Bound and gagged on the ground alongside the side wall was her father, King Echalas of Xylona.

Lowering her bow, Ashwin began running towards him. To her

amazement, she was left alone. None of the criminals near her even delayed her advance. She dropped to her knees, tears in her eyes as she looked down at her father. His gaze was as peaceful and calm as ever.

"Father," she said as she unfastened the gag around his mouth. "What happened?"

"Attacked," he moaned, the word filled with such pain and anguish that she could feel his turmoil. "Xylona, destroyed."

"I know father, I was there," she said. "Thank the gods that you have survived."

"I will not live long," Echalas said. Each word was heavily accented and separated by painful pauses as he struggled to continue. "You must be Queen now."

"No father," she cried as she gently rubbed her fingers through his hair. "We'll get you out of here."

"It's too late for me," Echalas wheezed. "Now go."

"The ring can save you," she said with hope.

"My ring?" Echalas asked. "Yes, that may save me after all. Please child, give it to me."

Ashwin sighed with relief. She reached down and removed the ring. "This will heal you," she said as she reached out to place the ring on his finger. "It will make you stronger."

Echalas struggled to raise his finger for her to put it on, his hands shaking. His eyes were fixated on the black-golden band as she began to place Imperius on his finger.

"Ah ha!" Baldock cheered as he sunk Splitter into the chest of another orc. "Give me one or one hunnerd and I'll be kickin' all o' yer backsides!"

The dwarf spun around and slammed his shield into the face of a goblin, and then brought Splitter down, ending the creature's life. As he started to cheer again, he could see that those near him had started to back away. Glancing around, he saw Arifos and Mylvannan both still fighting valiantly. They had meshed into a good fighting group. He was proud to be amongst such fine heroes.

Feeling that something was missing, Baldock looked back towards the doorway and saw that Ashwin was no longer there. As he ran towards the door, a human leapt out at him. Baldock did not even look as he swiped at the man with his shield and battered him out of the way. "A friend o' mine may be in need, I have no time fer ye!"

Once he reached the spot where Ashwin had previously been, he was relieved to see that there were no signs of blood or a struggle near the elf. Searching for her, his eyes widened in disbelief as he watched her rubbing her hands through the hair of the man he had fought in Trespias.

Though he did not understand what was happening, he started to run towards them, calling her name. Ashwin did not respond at all, though he watched as she removed her ring and started to put it on his finger. She must be under mind-control, he deduced.

As he closed in on them, he jumped forward and pushed Ashwin away. The ring clanged to the ground and rolled away.

"What are you doing?" Ashwin cried out. "My father needs that!"

"That is not yer father!" Baldock roared.

Ashwin stared at the dwarf, and then looked back at her father. He looked paler and closer to death than ever. "How can you say that? Look at him!"

"I'm lookin'," Baldock said as he stood up and held his shield in front of him. As he stood, the visage of Echalas faded and was replaced by that of Kabilian.

Ashwin stared at the man in shock. She could not understand what had just happened. How had this man tricked her?

Kabilian reached up and felt for the pearl on his forehead. He then glanced down at his wardrobe and shrugged. "I'll have that shield, too," he said as he removed the pearl and dropped it in his satchel. He then pulled out a highly ornamented silver scepter with images of ice surrounding a large blue diamond at the tip.

"Over me dead body," Baldock replied.

"That is my intention," Kabilian returned as he pointed the scepter towards Baldock, and a torrent of small, jagged ice shards launched towards him.

Solara joined Thamar and Theiler and stood with their weapons drawn and ready for the new threat. Larude and Rawthorne were walking straight towards them, their weapons also in position to strike.

"Rawthorne is mine," Solara practically growled.

Thamar nodded. "Then armored-boy here is ours."

Without delaying any further, the two sons of Thron charged the armored lieutenant of Lady Salaman, their weapons swinging when they reached him. Rawthorne broke off away from them and advanced towards Solara. He knew who his foe was this day.

Thamar lunged his hammer and Larude jumped back and out of harm's way. "Think you're quick, eh?" Thamar asked mockingly.

Theiler swept right past his brother and swung his sword with a vertical slash. Larude parried the attack and returned with one of his own. The two continued striking each other, their swords sparking.

Thamar barreled in again himself, his mallet swinging before him. Larude attempted to block the attack, but the red-bearded dwarf hammered his sword away.

Rather than giving ground, Larude pivoted and brought his fist right up into Theiler's ribcage, two claws extending from his gauntlet dug into the dwarf's side. The dwarf blinked several times and dropped his sword. Larude then pulled his fist and the claws from Theiler, and the dwarf slumped down in front of him.

Solara and Rawthorne sidestepped, circling around each other, watching and measuring their opponent up. Neither advanced, waiting for the first move to be made.

"I was wondering if you would come after me," Rawthorne said. "What took you so long?"

"I had to kill your companion, first," she replied harshly.

"Durgin?" Rawthorne laughed. "He was a coward that trembled at his own shadow."

"You can tell him that you think so when you join him in the fire-pits of Tanorus," Solara threatened.

"Oh, ho," Rawthorne laughed again. "Braksis's pet mystral thinks that she can beat me?"

"I know I can beat you," Solara replied confidently.

"He could never beat me: not when I killed his family and took the throne, not even when he came to reclaim it. He needed an entire army to bring me down," he explained. "And he certainly couldn't beat me the day I killed him."

"Murderer!" Solara screamed as she stepped forward, slashing with her drantanas. She was far quicker and more skilled with the blades. Her reflexes, even though she was hampered by her condition, were far superior to his as well. However, Rawthorne was bigger, stronger, and far more physical. As the two began the battle, both soon realized that neither combatant would gain a significant advantage over the other, nor would this battle end quickly.

The ceiling above the combatants was crackling with flames. The ground where the photons had fallen had also been ignited. Even the far wall where the first flame burst had hit was now burning. Lady Salaman was not pleased with her domain being violated, and now destroyed by the consuming flames.

"We should get you to safety," Neuss repeated, trying once again to get the gorn crime-lord away from the combatants.

"No," Lady Salaman sternly replied. "We are not leaving until I see exactly what I need to."

Neuss glanced at the other two remaining photons. None of them were pleased with the decision. Accepting the decision though, the trio each firmly clutched their gladii and observed the battle to see if they would be needed again. They had sworn an oath of allegiance to Lady Salaman. Though half of their numbers were dead, they would all fall before allowing any harm to come to her.

CHAPTER 83

"FRAAZAA!" Mylvannan cried out, enabling the mystical enchantment of his sword. He had presumed that this fight would be a long one and had hoped to refrain from using the chilling effects of Frostlartil, but they were severely outnumbered and he could use every advantage that he had.

With his blade crystallizing and releasing a chilling, frostbitten mist, Mylvannan braced himself as a giant stepped towards him. Of all of his companions, he had been the only one to face a giant before, the vicious Frost giants of the Mourning Mountains. Those behemoths were much larger, more cunning and deadlier than the one facing him now, but as Mylvannan glared up at the eighteen-foot-tall creature, he could not see that much of a difference.

He and Arifos had been fighting orcs, humans, and a few trolls. Then, the crowd had opened up as the giant stepped forward. This particular giant was loosely garbed in the pelts of rasplers, including reptilian-hide boots. He had long gray hair that hung in knots from his head. His lime-green eyes bore into the Frost elf. He held no weapon, but with his size and strength, his body alone was a weapon.

Mylvannan had not seen a giant since leaving Akkammanavar. The presence of one was quite shocking to him. He had heard some of the Tregador dwarves speaking of giants up north in Falestia, but that did not explain the creature's presence here.

Glancing to find Arifos, he saw the Madrew elf still engaged in combat with several orcs and humans. This battle was to be his alone. He remembered the lessons of his father, Rillvennen: when facing a giant, if there was no way to avoid the conflict, then the best thing to do was to use the creature's own strength against it.

A giant was larger and stronger. One hit from the creature would mean certain death for an elf, even one with a finely designed mithril breastplate and boots. However, the giant would either try to squish him, swat him away, or hurl objects at him. Instead, Rillvennen had taught that if you could get close enough to a giant to strike it from below, using the speed and skill of a Frost elf, then even the largest foe would fall.

He trusted in the wisdom of his father's teaching. Rillvennen was a highly-skilled hunter and warrior of Akkammanavar. Even when Mylvannan was just a small child, his father would take him with him to teach him the dangers of the icy terrain, and how to survive. The two had slain many Frost giants over the years, and never before had they an enchanted weapon such as Frostlartil.

"This is your only warning, giant," Mylvannan called out. "I have slain many of your kin in my youth. You will be no threat. Leave here and live, or stay and perish. I leave the choice to you."

"Funny elf," the giant snickered as he bent over and tried to pound Mylvannan into the ground with his fist.

Mylvannan did not expect the giant to heed his warning. As the giant began his attack—which he had to admit was much quicker than he anticipated—Mylvannan spun to the side, and as the fist hit the ground, he jumped on top of the hand and thrust Frostlartil down.

As the sword dug into the giant's thumb, its enchantment began to encase the thumb in a block of ice. The giant pulled his hand back quickly, causing Mylvannan to fall backwards and crash to the ground.

He spun around and stood up quickly, bracing for the next attack. He watched as the giant kept shaking his hand in an attempt to free his thumb.

"Stings," he said. "You'll pay for that!"

Mylvannan was not pleased with the initial result. Frostlartil may have stung the giant, but he had hoped to encase its entire hand—and perhaps even its arm—in ice. Perhaps relying on a mystical weapon was not the way to deal with a giant after all.

The giant reached up and hit the stone ceiling several times, dislodging part of the roof. As the pieces crumbled, he tried to grab as many of the falling rocks and debris as possible, and dropped them into a pouch on his belt. Holding one of the stones in his hand, he glanced down at Mylvannan and pitched the stone as hard as he could.

Mylvannan sprung away, closer to the giant. Glancing back, he saw that the stone had actually embedded more than halfway into the ground. He certainly could not survive an attack of that magnitude.

Continuing forward, he slashed the giant's ankle with his sword, splitting through the raspler-skinned boots and showing signs of freezing underneath. The giant raised its foot and began hopping on its other one as he clutched his ankle.

Taking advantage of the opening, Mylvannan cautiously moved to where the giant's foot was moving up and down. He knew that without even trying, the giant could step on him here, but this was also an opening that he could not pass up.

Holding his sword firmly, he jabbed Frostlartil forward and dug into the giant's heel. As with the previous attacks, ice began spreading from the wound. This time though, the giant fell forward and Mylvannan was unable to remove his enchanted blade from the wound.

As the giant fell, the impact sent a shockwave throughout the lair, causing all combatants to momentarily pause and glance towards the behemoth. The giant lay sprawled out on the ground, face down, as he screamed in agony.

Mylvannan reached down to his belt and unsheathed his serrated swords. Having Frostlartil, he did not often resort to using the weapons more common amongst his people, but these two swords were the weapons he had first learned how to fight with. As he held them in his hands, it was as if they were old friends calling to him.

Mylvannan leapt up onto the heel of the giant and ran up his body until he reached the giant's head. Bending down by the giant's ear, he spoke slowly and clearly. "I will let you leave even now if you chose to do so."

The giant started to roll over, hoping to crush Mylvannan beneath its back. Mylvannan though had exceptional balance and managed to walk his way around the giant's body and stay upright on his chest.

"I gave you two chances," Mylvannan reminded the giant.

The giant brought its hands thundering in from his sides towards his chest. Mylvannan back-flipped out of the way and winced as he could hear ribs cracking from the violent pounding the giant just administered to himself.

As the giant began screaming again, Mylvannan twirled his two swords and dug them into the giant's chest. He had hoped to reach the giant's heart, but apparently his swords were not long enough. The giant was wheezing and struggling to breathe. Mylvannan watched the creature's hands, preparing himself to leap if he needed to. The giant was visibly weakening—his own attack trying to kill Mylvannan one last time must have done more damage than either thought, one of the broken ribs puncturing a vital organ: the giant was dying right before his eyes.

Wanting to reclaim his sword before going back into battle, Mylvannan darted back down the giant's leg. He was relieved to see that its foot was lying flat, and not resting on the heel. Resheathing his serrated swords, he grabbed the hilt of Frostlartil with both hands and started to pull. The blade was frozen inside the giant's foot.

Placing his own foot onto the giant's heel for leverage, he continued to pull, but his sword would not budge. A wailing cry from Thamar refocused the Frost elf. As he searched for his allies, he watched as a dark armor-clad warrior stood above the body of a motionless Theiler.

"No!" Thamar cried out as he watched Theiler crumple to the ground. "My brother!" He rushed forward and pushed Larude aside with all of his might, forcing the armored warrior to fall to the ground and slide several feet away.

Thamar turned pale as he watched Theiler look up at him, dazed.

He reached down and could feel the warmth of his brother's blood on his hands. Clutching his brother tightly so that he would not be alone in the end, tears began flowing from the dwarf's eyes.

Theiler slowly reached up and brushed a finger against Thamar's cheek, and as he looked down at his dying brother, he could see that Theiler was smiling. His arm then fell limply to the ground and his eyes closed. Thamar began breathing very heavily through his nose, his rage beginning to consume him. He knew that in that last moment, Theiler was trying to convey that he had died as a dwarf, in battle and with honor—the only way that a true son of Vorstad ever hoped to die, earning passage to Wolhollm and spending the afterlife with all of the slain heroes that had fallen before.

As Thamar released his brother's body, he firmly clutched his hammer and stood to face Larude, who was feet away watching the spectacle. There was another credo of the dwarves: the right of vengeance. Larude would learn what that meant this day. With a roar of defiance, Thamar charged the Hidden Empire lieutenant, his rage and anger over this entire quest building and ready to be unleashed upon this one foe.

Ashwin dropped to her hands and knees and started to crawl after her father's ring. She was not about to lose such a precious gift because some assassin with a fancy towards mystical items had tricked her.

Kabilian kept launching his ice darts at Baldock. The dwarf was using his shield to block most of the attacks, but several shards were shattering off of his armor. Realizing that the ice would not be enough to defeat the armored dwarf, Kabilian reached into his satchel and removed a second scepter. This one was gold rather than the sleek silver of Blizzard. The highly ornamented golden images swirled into flames that encased a red ruby at the tip.

"Let me introduce you to Inferno," Kabilian laughed as he lowered the second scepter in his other hand and it began to emit a succession of flaming bursts towards Baldock.

Baldock held his shield firmly, but could feel the force of the two scepters. The mixture of heat and cold seemed to be having a much deeper effect than either alone could ever hope to. As he took a step towards Kabilian, both scepters stopped launching their endless stream of fire and ice.

Glancing over his shield, he saw that Kabilian's attention was focused on Ashwin. He took a step towards her, almost forgetting about Baldock completely. That was a mistake that Baldock was not going to allow the assassin to forget. Charging forward, he tackled Kabilian, knocking him to the ground.

Kabilian dropped both scepters and hit the ground hard. This position with the dwarf was becoming uncomfortably familiar. However, he had more important concerns at the moment. Spotting Crick staring at the battle between Solara and Rawthorne, he called to his partner, "Get the ring!"

Crick was oblivious to the plight of Kabilian. He was fixated on the battle between Solara and Rawthorne. After Sora had fled down the tunnel, he grew enraged that her mystral armaments would not be added to his own, particularly her glaives.

Solara was not going anywhere though. The two were fighting and appeared to be at a draw, neither gaining any ground on the other. Both were highly skilled fighters. He only hoped that Rawthorne would win so he could claim the mystral's weapons for his own.

"Crick, get the damned ring!"

Reluctantly, Crick turned away from the battle he was watching. The anger in Kabilian's voice could not be ignored. He looked over to see Kabilian beneath a heavily-armored dwarf, squirming to try and get away.

Stepping to help, Kabilian shot him a glare of pure disdain. "Not me, the ring!"

Following the gaze of the assassin, he saw Ashwin crawling along the ground after the small black-golden band. If the ring were all that Kabilian wanted, then he would get the ring so he could get back to trying to procure the mystral's weapons.

Bringing Phistala and Aurlestyl slashing down in two arcs, he dug a cross into the chest of the orc before him, and then kicked the fighter away. Arifos was amazed by what was happening: their foes clearly outnumbered them, but they were dwindling quickly. That fact was a good thing, but he could not understand how a thriving criminal organization could have been so successful with such unskilled riffraff in its ranks.

He had even observed Mylvannan single-handedly slay a giant—no easy feat, but like all of the other foes aligned against them, it had fallen far quicker and easier than he thought it ever would.

Taking a moment to observe the battle, he spotted Thamar fighting a black armored warrior, with Theiler lying limply on the ground. Mylvannan was rushing towards them. Perhaps he did not give their foes enough credit. If Theiler had been slain, this would be a tragic day indeed—he had found the silent dwarf to be quite resourceful and skilled.

Solara was fighting a larger man herself, though the battle seemed to almost be a draw as neither of them seemed to be able to gain an advantage over the other. Baldock was lying on top of a man and struggling to hold him down. An odd tactic, he thought. Ashwin was crawling along the ground, a heavily armored hobgoblin in pursuit.

He saw no sign of Vaz and Vella, but knew that the two white tigers could certainly take care of themselves. Deciding that Ashwin and Baldock needed the most help, he used his mystical abilities to knock several individuals out of his way with a swipe of his hand, and then ran towards them. A few foes still returned to bar his path, but he quickly used his swordsmanship to show them the error of their ways.

"Looks like we may have to settle for a stalemate," Rawthorne sneered.

"We will have an ending," Solara promised. "Blood *will* be spilled this day: *your* blood."

"Ooh," Rawthorne mocked with a fake shiver. "Scare me some more."

Solara dove into a series of battle maneuvers, striking at Rawthorne with the skill of a highly-trained mystral warrior. Even though the man wielded a cumbersome mallet, his bulk-strength allowed him to twist and turn it with such skill that he easily parried each blow.

The two continued, losing sight of anything else in the lair. Small cracks of flames rained down upon them, but neither seemed to notice as they danced their waltz of death, each searching for an opening within the other's defenses. The battle had become almost surreal, as time seemed to slow and focus only upon them.

Deciding to take a risk, Solara opened her defenses to try and draw Rawthorne in. The large man took the bait and struck out, knocking one of her drantanas from her hand. At the same time, she swiped with her other one and dug into his wrist, forcing him to drop his mallet as well.

Rawthorne did not appear deterred at all. He swung out with his other arm and backhanded her across the face. Solara tumbled to the ground, dropping her second drantana.

Standing up to face him again, she drew her elongated mystral sword and set herself into a defensive posture. Rawthorne backed off several steps and reached down to pick up Zloreskalaza, the sword dropped by Larude. As soon as he did, his arm began to convulse and pure shock flashed over his face.

Solara studied him for a moment, puzzled by what she was witnessing. Still holding her sword steady, she bent over and reclaimed one of her drantanas, sheathing it in its scabbard. Rawthorne was glancing down at the sword in his hand, consumed by the blade. Sidestepping without taking her eyes off of the man, she reached down and re-claimed her second drantana as well.

She was not certain what was happening with Rawthorne, but she had come to kill him, and she was not about to abandon that quest. Stepping forward, she slashed with her sword, and was disappointed as Rawthorne, still acting shocked and disoriented, perfectly parried her blow.

Yes.

Rawthorne could not understand what was happening. Ever since he had picked up the sword of Larude, the blade had been speaking to him. Not to him, but through him, implanting its thoughts and impulses directly into his mind. The effect was chilling, his sword arm growing numb as he held the mighty weapon in his grip.

Strike her down. Kill her. Slaughter her. Let me taste her mystral blood.

Rawthorne continued to parry, still trying to come to terms with what he was hearing. The sword was ravenous, desiring the blood of his foe even more so than he. He did not realize that such a weapon existed.

Let her learn why I am Zloreskalaza, the skull cleaver. Let her learn what it means to experience death.

As Rawthorne listened to the dark impulses, he had to agree. Whatever this sword was, it was as if they had a like mind. They both craved the death of the mystral slut of his cousin; and they were both going to get exactly what they wanted.

CHAPTER 84

The fire was starting to pick up in intensity. As a Frost elf, Mylvannan felt weaker when in close-proximity to high temperature climates. The flames were certainly increasing the temperature and taxing his limits. If he had not been a half-breed by an elf of Xylona, he was certain that he would have already succumbed to the heat.

Sweat was pouring down his face and gave him the appearance of one that was practically melting. His breathing was heavy and intense as he moved closer to the flames where his companion lay motionless. Regardless of the personal consequences, he would not succumb to his limitations. He would reach the dwarves in time.

Thamar was battling the armored warrior that had struck his brother down. As Mylvannan strained to see through the smoke, he could tell that Thamar was in a deep rage and would not rest until his vengeance was wrought. He was certain that the dwarf would succeed in his endeavor: Thamar was a true warrior that has seen centuries of conflict, and in many instances, fought his way through it.

Reaching Theiler, Mylvannan bent down, removed his glove and gently touched two fingers below the red-bearded dwarf's chin. Though it was very faint, he could feel the pulse of the carotid artery. Theiler yet lived, but was hanging on only by a thin thread.

The flames were closing in on them, as if with a mind of its own, looking to devour the two companions. Mylvannan would not allow that to happen. He grabbed Theiler by the shoulders and started to slowly drag him away from the flames. He could see Theiler's face begin to contort and wince in pain, but that could not be helped. If the dwarf remained where he was, there would be no chance of saving his life.

A trail of blood marked the passage of the two. Mylvannan watched it with growing concern. Too much blood. He wasn't certain that the Frost Queen herself could save Theiler with his injuries this extensive. Even still, he was determined to get the dwarf to safety.

"That's as far as you go."

Mylvannan tensed as he heard the voice behind him. Gently lowering Theiler's shoulder to the ground, he turned and faced his new threat: the creature before him looked as if he had been a freak accident of birth, for what species he was no longer appeared certain. He had the face and body of a man, though darker in skin-tone with two horns jutting from the sides of his head and hair that appeared to be more of a brownish-orange fur. His muscles were much bigger than any human Mylvannan had ever seen, and his ears were also pointed like those of an elf or a cornal.

The man smiled, revealing sharp, carnivorous teeth, certainly much pointier than that of a human. His eyes were vibrant silver, and were glimmering in the firelight. He raised his hand and started to flex his fingers, showing long, razor-sharp fingernails.

"I intend to pass," Mylvannan said, trying to sound authoritative and strong even though the heat sapped him.

"I'm sure you do," the horned man replied. "I can't let you leave this party until Lady Salaman gives you permission."

"She already has," Mylvannan acted confused. "Didn't you hear?"

"Don't play coy with me," the man roared. "After I bring the two of your corpses to Lady Salaman, today is the day that the name Ravinder will grow in fame."

"So you're looking to make a name for yourself?" Mylvannan asked.

"I am," Ravinder said, his fangs clearly visible with his expression.

"The folly of youth," Mylvannan replied, shaking his head.

"Youth?" Ravinder cried out. "I am eighteen years old!"

Mylvannan shuddered at the thought. This boy stood close to nine feet with such well-developed muscle-tone that he could probably lift a wagon on his own. To think that he was only eighteen and still had much growing to do was unimaginable.

"Yes Ravinder, the folly of youth," Mylvannan repeated. "Eighteen is nothing. I myself have seen one hundred and eighty-nine winters. Trust me when I tell you: you make a name only by your deeds and actions, not by trying to gain favor with a tyrant."

"I will gain my name by deeds: by the deed of slaying you!"

"You would fight an elf that killed a giant mere minutes ago?" Mylvannan asked, one eyebrow raised in astonishment. "What makes you think you would fare any better?"

"Blarg was stupid," Ravinder surmised. "I am not."

"Oh really?" Mylvannan asked. "Then why are you here?"

"What?" Ravinder asked. "What do you mean?"

"Why are you here," Mylvannan repeated, "in a den of vipers that exist only to stab one another in the back, all in the name of impressing one woman?"

Ravinder glanced around for a moment, considering the words. Most of his companions were fleeing as quickly as they could. Several were still fighting the intruders, but as he looked around, he also saw one man stab another in the back. That was not the worst of it: a few hobgoblins had circled around a pair of humans and were jabbing them with spears. All around, it was as if the Hidden Empire was fighting amongst themselves.

"You see now?" Mylvannan asked.

Ravinder seemed shaken by what he was witnessing, as if his entire set of core beliefs and principles were being challenged.

"There is a better way," Mylvannan added.

"How?" Ravinder asked, clutching his fists in fury at what he was witnessing.

"The Seven Kingdoms are at war," Mylvannan explained. "What happens here is truly trivial. What is yet to happen will determine the fate of us all."

"What do you suggest?" Ravinder asked, the slightest hint of amusement and interest spreading over his face.

"Leave this place," Mylvannan professed. "You are young. There is time. You may not be tainted by the greed and hate that permeates this place."

"And do what? Join you?" Ravinder laughed.

"Why is that thought so humorous?" Mylvannan asked.

Ravinder stopped laughing and looked at Mylvannan for a moment. "You would have an enforcer fight by your side?"

"Not an enforcer," Mylvannan clarified. "You."

"No!" Ravinder cried as he leapt towards Mylvannan.

Mylvannan crouched down, unable to pull his weapons in time. The large creature was exceptionally fast and agile. He heard a ripping sound followed by the clanging of a fallen sword, but did not feel the impact from the creature. Glancing up, he saw Ravinder standing above him, his arm bloodied to the elbow.

"What?" Mylvannan asked as he looked to try and understand what happened. Lying next to Theiler was a hobgoblin with a gaping hole in its chest. "You did that?"

"He was attacking you from behind," Ravinder explained. "He was without honor." He then sniffed his hand several times and began licking the blood. "Even his blood tastes tainted by his deed."

"Thank you," Mylvannan exclaimed. "That was a deed that will help you grow your name."

Ravinder glanced down and scowled at the elf. He was not convinced by what the elf said. He only knew that there were rules to combat, and sneaking up to strike someone from behind was prohibited. That was why he called out to the elf in warning, giving him a chance to prepare for battle.

"You are much bigger and stronger than I," Mylvannan said. "Could you help me with my friend?"

Ravinder did not move, considering what it would mean if he did assist the intruder. If he did, his life in the Hidden Empire would be over; he would return to the realm as not only an outcast because of his appearance, but also because he turned his back on the one organization that was willing to accept him for whom he was. Was he ready to do that?

"Please," Mylvannan added. "My strength is failing with the fire."

"You admit a deficiency?" Ravinder asked. "What is to keep me then from killing you as easily as I did your attacker?"

"Honor," Mylvannan said. "Would you really strike a foe that was not at his peak ability? Would you not rather fight me as I was when I defeated Blarg?"

"So you wish a delay to our encounter," Ravinder surmised. Reaching down, he picked up Theiler and cradled him in his arms. "Very well—a delay you shall have."

Mylvannan pondered the words for a moment. He was not certain whether he got through to him or not. Was he now their ally, or was he just biding his time for a chance to test himself against the companions when they were not fatigued and weakened? As Ravinder started towards the entrance with Theiler in his arms, Mylvannan decided that time would sort out the enforcer's intentions.

Baldock rammed his fist into Kabilian's face and then pulled back to repeat his blow. "Yer not even payin' attention to me attack!"

Kabilian pulled his eyes away from Ashwin and Crick and gave a look to Baldock as if the dwarf was nothing more than a nuisance. "I could end this any time I wish," he boasted.

"Ye won't be vanishin' from beneath me this time!" Baldock roared.

"Oh, foolish dwarf," Kabilian said as he shook his head. "I have already hurt you in ways that you cannot possibly fathom."

"What are ye gettin' at?" Baldock demanded.

"Tregador is nice this time of year," Kabilian said. "I truly did like it. Your father gave me such a warm welcome when I arrived. He thought we were companions. Poor deluded fool."

"Yer lyin'," Baldock replied.

"Am I?" Kabilian asked with a snicker. "If so, then how come my companion is wearing armor crafted by the same dwarves that crafted yours?"

Baldock took his eyes off of Kabilian for a moment and regarded the armored hobgoblin. The suit was clearly well-designed, and also of high-grade illistrium. There could be some truth to what the assassin was saying.

"I'm sorry to inform you that your father's gullibility did him in in the end," Kabilian beamed, proud of what he was saying.

"What are ye sayin'?"

"I came as a friend, was welcomed into your father's home and to his table, and then showed both your father and your idiot brother why I am an assassin-extraordinaire!"

Kabilian began laughing as he saw Baldock turning to regard the armor worn by Crick again. It was as if the dwarf was clinging to some hope that the armor was not actually from Tregador, but the skill of the artisans was staring him directly in the face. The suit of armor was not only dwarven, but forged by the dwarves of Tregador.

"Don't worry, I left the Queen alive. She seems to have enough reason of her own to despise you. I figured that by leaving her alive, it would be an added torment for you."

Baldock raised both fists, an unbridled fury coming over him. Kabilian just shook his head as he forced his knee forward and kicked the armored dwarf off of him. Unbalanced, Baldock stumbled off and crashed into a wall, the torch resting on it falling to the ground. The liquor and spirits that had been shattered when dropped by members of the Hidden Empire celebrating the show in the arena quickly burst to flame, adding to the chaos of the lair.

Kabilian was pleased with his work. He quickly pulled the cork from a healing potion and drank it. The pain in his right eye where Baldock hit him quickly began to fade. As he regarded Baldock one last time, he snickered to himself: when last they met, he was unaware of who the dwarf was. To him, information was power. Now that he had power over the Tregador dwarf, he could afford to toy with him and kill him at his own leisure. For now though, the ring was more important.

Ashwin sighed in relief as the ring stopped rolling and tipped to the ground. She reached out for it, but pulled her arm back quickly as an arrow perfectly entered the opening of the ring, pinning it to the ground.

Glancing back at her attacker, she saw Crick as he began to pull another arrow from his quiver. As he aimed it at her, she knew that without the ring, this time if she were hit, her life would be forfeit. The realization had a calming effect upon her, as if the ring had been a crutch allowing her to keep from truly developing her own abilities.

Unsheathing Martristlit, she held her sword ready, waiting for Crick's next move. Crick released a mystral arrow, and Ashwin raised her sword slightly, deflecting the shaft. As she did so, almost instinctually, she realized that Mylvannan and Arifos's training sessions really had helped. She just never felt like she needed to rely upon those lessons before now.

Crick placed his bow over his shoulder and then pulled his pair of mystral drantanas from their sheaths along his back. He twirled his blades for several seconds and then stepped towards Ashwin.

For the first time in her life, with an honor blade in her hand, she felt as if she was ready. She would not fail. The hobgoblin would try, but he would fail in defeating her. The confidence was surging, inspiring. She stepped forward swinging her sword, and the battle began.

Running down the dark tunnel, it seemed like an eternity until Sora reached the prisoners again. She knew that she was doing the right thing, but she hoped that no harm would come to Solara without her and Tiot there to fight by her side.

"Thank the gods, you have come back!" one of the men called out.

"Stand back," Sora instructed as she removed her dagger and started to hit the lock with the pommel.

Tiot and the two white tigers paced back and forth behind her impatiently. As Sora continued trying to break the lock, she could tell that the three animals wished to be back in the lair fighting alongside their allies.

"It's not working," she said in defeat.

"There are keys," the man said.

"Why didn't you say that to begin with?" Sora asked in frustration. "Where?"

"The back wall," the man said as he pointed behind her.

Sora jumped up and ran to a hook on the wall. There was a ring with dozens of keys on them. As she rushed back to the lock, she fumbled with the keys trying to figure out which one would work.

The man kept fidgeting, impatiently watching as she tried one key after the other. "Can't you hurry this up?"

"I'm going as fast as I can," Sora screamed. "There are a lot of keys here. Wait a minute, I think I got it."

The man's eyes illuminated with joy as the lock opened and Sora started to pull it from the bars. He would never make it from the cage and to freedom though—a bolt launched out from the tunnel and pierced him in the chest. He faltered backwards and collapsed to the ground, struggling to try and pull the shaft from his body, to no avail.

Sora turned around and spotted several men and a pair of hobgoblins approaching. One of them raised his crossbow and aimed it directly at her.

"Time to die, girlie."

The flames were dancing all around them. Small debris fell and singed their bodies as the two warriors moved back and forth, neither willing to give an inch. Their movements were becoming faster, almost as if the two were able to read each other's mind and anticipate their tactics.

"I told you that I was nothing like that pathetic excuse of a cousin of mine," Rawthorne taunted.

"You are not even a fraction of the man that he was," Solara replied as she slashed her sword in several easily blocked arcs.

"To face me is to face your death," Rawthorne boasted.

To face us is to face death, the sword corrected. *She cannot hope to persevere.*

"Quiet, this is my moment," Rawthorne screamed at his sword.

"You are losing your mind," Solara commented. "Just as Durgin did before I dug my two swords into his chest and cut the life out of him."

Do it now! Zloreskalaza demanded.

"Say hello to my cousin," Rawthorne roared. "You are about to join him!" As he said it, he stepped forward and went into a series of motions with Zloreskalaza, forcing her backwards several steps.

Solara braced herself and tried to stand her ground, keeping the larger man's advances at bay. His physical presence was overwhelming when he went into a marching fury like that. She did manage to barely recover and reclaim the initiative. "You are mistaken, Rawthorne—don't you see the flames? They are the harbingers of death coming to claim you for their maiden-master!"

Both heard a loud cracking and stepped back and away from each other as they glanced upwards. It was fortunate that they did so: the ceiling above them, raging in flames, finally gave way and fell to the ground, separating the two with a wall of debris and fire.

The two shielded their faces and backed away before turning to confront each other again. There was no way to get through the barrier.

"Looks like we'll have to finish this another time," Rawthorne laughed boisterously. "Kill you later!"

No, kill her now! Zloreskalaza protested.

Solara watched in horror as the man turned and walked away, vanishing in the smoke that permeated the room. "Rawthorne!" she called after him, but the man was gone. Her vengeance was insatiable. She had failed in her mission. She had failed Braksis.

CHAPTER 85

He was closely monitoring what was happening between Crick and Ashwin. Kabilian was rather shocked to see the young elf fighting so well. She clearly had been trained in the art of swordplay since last they met. Even so, she was no match for his hobgoblin companion, and soon that fact would dawn on them both.

Keeping his eyes intently on the duel between the two, he reached down and reclaimed his two scepters, returning them to the satchel upon his belt. He could see confidence exuding from Ashwin. It was as if she had suddenly gained faith in her own prowess and abilities. It would not matter in the end. She was without her ring, and without that, she did not have the experience and skill to survive the day.

Taking his eyes from the fight, he licked his lips as he spotted Imperius pinned to the ground by a mystral arrow. Crick was quite a shot, Kabilian thought. He did well in choosing the hobgoblin as his companion. Though he, too, was young for his race, he displayed many qualities that set him apart from other hobgoblins. It was this that Kabilian would foster and see grow. Crick would become a great warrior in time.

Quickly moving through the spreading flames, Kabilian reached the arrow and bent down to pull it from the ground. The fire was closing in on the ring, although it wouldn't matter now that he was about to claim it for his own. With this ring, he would be invincible. Not only was he an assassin-extraordinaire, but now he could not be physically harmed, making his deed an even easier one.

As he pulled the arrow from the ground, the ring clattered back down by his feet. "Come to your new master," Kabilian said as he

464

reached for the newest of his mystical artifacts.

Two bodies slumped down in front of him, inches from his fingertips. Kabilian glanced up and saw the pink-skinned elf standing above him, his two scimitars soaked in blood. Arifos's gaze was firmly set on him, a silent challenge declared.

Kabilian refused to give up on the ring, but as he stretched a little further to reach for it, the assassin found that he could not get close enough to it. "What sorcery is this?"

"The ring does not belong to you," Arifos replied.

"What did you do?" Kabilian demanded.

"I have placed a protection spell around it," Arifos answered. "It will not dissipate unless I will it, and I will never will it for you."

"Then perhaps it will dissipate with your death!" Kabilian bellowed in anger.

Kabilian back-flipped and landed on his feet, standing directly before the Madrew elf with only the two bodies of Arifos's most recent kill and the ring before them. He reached down into his belt and removed his two jewel-hilted daggers.

Arifos regarded the man for a moment. His eyes lowered to the two daggers. He was shocked that the man would bring two knives into a sword fight when he had an honor blade of Xylona clearly visible in its scabbard.

He knew that this man was the one that had fought Heirn and almost bested the elf if not for Baldock's interruption. Since the Madrew elders had first sent him to this realm as part of the Triad, he had fought alongside the elves of Xylona. He found Heirn to be an elf of honor, courage, and considerable abilities. To lose him to the Shadow Mage was a noble sacrifice, but to have almost been beaten by a mere man? Arifos knew that he must not underestimate his opponent.

Kabilian whispered a short incantation as he moved into an offensive stance, his two daggers extending in length to actual swords. The enchantment managed to surprise Arifos for a moment, but he recovered and defended against the strike.

The two then began fighting in what onlookers would call an inspirational battle. Four swords were moving as if of their own accord. Sparks danced from their blades. The two combatants never remained in the same place for more than a second. Neither of them would be surprised again, nor would they underestimate their foe.

Baldock stood up and started to shake his head to try and regain his focus. The world was spinning all around him. He could see the flames encompassing him where the torch had fallen and struck the ale. The lair of the Hidden Empire was burning to the ground. Soon, all that would remain is ash.

Finding a small opening in the fire, Baldock rushed through it. He could feel that even his illistrium armor had begun to heat up with the exposure of the flames. He had to be careful not to touch any of his allies until the armor cooled down again, or else he may scald them.

Of course, that was not a concern where Kabilian was concerned. The assassin would pay for murdering his father and brother. He would see to that personally. Slinging his shield over his back by its guige, he clutched Splitter with both hands and searched for the assassin.

He found him fighting against Arifos. The two were moving at a swift pace, striking hard and viciously. He had fought by Arifos's side for some months now, but he was awestruck by the spectacle before him. Baldock wondered just how skilled the Madrew elf truly was? Even so, he would not let Arifos have all of the fun. Kabilian had a lot to answer for, and he aimed to ensure just that.

"This way, elf," Ravinder called back over his shoulder. He reached the double doors of the Hidden Empire compound and glared back, waiting for Mylvannan. As he watched, he was amazed at how slow and cumbersome the elf looked. His strength had been almost completely sapped. That was a weakness that would one day prove the Frost elf's undoing.

Mylvannan reached the door and nodded for Ravinder to continue out into the swamp. The large man followed, showing no exertion at carrying the unconscious dwarf. He heard a growl from before him, and strained to focus his eyes, only to see some of the soldiers he had fought in Trespias barring their path.

"They are the ones from Trespias," Darkler called out, pointing towards Theiler and Mylvannan. "Get them!"

"Belay that order," Adonis shouted loud enough for all of them to hear.

Ravinder was still holding Theiler, but his eyes were moving quickly, like a predator sizing-up its prey. As he took in the details of the newcomers, he began determining the order in which he would kill them.

Adonis regarded the horned man for a moment with skepticism, but then walked past him and over to Mylvannan. He could see that the Frost elf was struggling to even stand at the moment. Extending his hand, he offered assistance to the elf, who stared at him for several seconds before collapsing into the ebony-skinned Authority agent's arms.

Helping Mylvannan walk further away from the Hidden Empire lair, Adonis lay him down next to Doctor Podeis.

"Captain," Darkler protested. "What are you doing? We should be arresting them!"

"Open your eyes, Sergeant," Adonis said. "The Imperium is being taken over by Winton. We are at war with a neighboring nation that we had never had a problem with. The one thing that keeps popping up in our investigation is that the Hidden Empire is involved. We come here to investigate further, and find the same group that was fighting the Hidden Empire's men in Trespias doing the same here."

"Perhaps you are being naïve," Darkler added. "What if they are part of the Hidden Empire and we are helping them?"

Ravinder started to laugh. "That was a funny one, little man," he said. "The elf part of the Hidden Empire." He began laughing again, even louder than before.

Darkler glared at the large man, a threatening look in his eyes. He was certain that this creature was part of Lady Salaman's followers. If only he could be unleashed, he would show this creature why Lady Salaman ordered his obedience, or his death. He may be small, but even in his youth, the crime-lord had seen how dangerous he had been.

"I stand by my own instincts and observations," Adonis concluded. "The Empress's white tigers would not fight by their sides if they were evil. We are all but pawns in a greater game. Until we figure out who all of the players are, we certainly must not fight amongst ourselves."

"Zoldex," Mylvannan whispered.

"What?" Adonis asked.

"Zoldex," he repeated with more conviction.

"Are you certain?" Cylnta asked. "He has returned?"

"Yes," Mylvannan winced.

Adonis glanced at Cylnta for an explanation.

"A long story short," Cylnta began, "Zoldex was one of the eternals that discovered the mystical spring that introduced magic to the realm. He wanted to use the magic to conquer the land, whereas Pierce wanted to forge what is the current day Mage's Council. Pierce won, and Zoldex was banished."

Adonis ruffled his fingers through his goatee for a moment pondering the words. "That was a long time ago," he said. "Surely Zoldex would be dead."

"No," Cylnta disagreed. "Pierce and the others from the expedition are mostly still alive. Eternals have vast life spans."

"Then if he is back, he could be trying to do what he could not at the time," he surmised.

"The news does not bode well for the realm," Cylnta warned.

"When did he return?" Adonis asked.

"I know not how long he has been back, but he has been coordinating most of the attacks that have befallen the Seven Kingdoms," Mylvannan explained.

"What attacks?" Adonis demanded. "Arkham? The Dartian Plains? The kidnapping of the Empress?"

"Yes," Mylvannan answered. "And more."

"What else?" Adonis pressed.

"Vorstad and Xylona have both fallen," Mylvannan answered. "We are certain that there is more, but to speak of it would be without firsthand knowledge."

"Very well," Adonis said, not happy with what he was hearing.

Quince and Adonis both stepped aside a moment to confer. The two discussed the possible implications of such news. Their investigation had led them here, but if a Mage was manipulating them, then even the Hidden Empire may be innocent of the crime they were being blamed for.

The news about Zoldex coordinating the events that have befallen the realm of late certainly did put things into a new light. Neither of them could accept the fact that a man like Winton could turn from a disinterested prince that had favor of many ladies, into the Emperor of the Imperium practically overnight. He, too, could be a pawn of the Mage.

As the two discussed these possibilities, they decided that the best course of action was to forge an alliance with the allies that appeared to be combating Zoldex, and then refocus their efforts. This was no longer about the murder of King Sarlec or the abduction of Empress Karleena: this was about the future of the entire realm.

Walking back to the rest of his agents, Adonis glanced up at Ravinder, who was still holding Theiler defensively. "Doctor Podeis, if you could see to the injuries of the dwarf and the elf?"

"Of course," Podeis replied. "If you would?" he said as he gestured for Ravinder to put Theiler down.

Ravinder shot a glance to Mylvannan who nodded his approval. He then kneeled down and lowered the injured dwarf with a gentleness and grace that seemed to defy his appearance and size.

"Could you tell us what is going on in there?" Adonis asked Mylvannan.

Being away from the heat of the flames, Mylvannan's voice was already sounding clearer as he gradually began to regain his strength and vitality. "My companions and I were trying to move north, to spread word of the fall of the south."

"This is Vorstad and Xylona?" Adonis asked to clarify.

"It is," Mylvannan confirmed. "The orc army was practically never-ending, and we lost hope of circling around them. As such, we opted to risk the dangers of the swamps to reach our destination.

"We came across this structure and saw a companion of the dwarves. A mystral warrior known as Solara."

"Solara is here?" Adonis asked, visibly shaken by the news.

"She is," Mylvannan informed him. "We saw her, another mystral, and a wolf entering the lair. We then moved in so that they would not face the Hidden Empire alone."

"Do you know why they are here?" Adonis asked.

"I do not know," Mylvannan replied earnestly. "I only know that as an ally of Thamar and Theiler, we refused to let her face danger alone."

Ravinder was watching Mylvannan as he spoke. It was as if he was hanging on every word, absorbing the details. Mylvannan glanced at him and could not read his expression. Was he listening to the words and somehow finding a new calling in life? Or was he absorbing every detail to determine how best to take advantage and defeat the companions? He wished that he knew for certain.

"How many of you are in there?" Adonis wanted to know.

"Two elves, two dwarves, two mystral, two tigers and a wolf," Mylvannan relayed.

"Very well," Adonis said as he turned to face his team. "Quince, Darkler, Ortrill, Dozer, Cylnta and Nextra are with me. We will go in and assist our nine allies and try to pull them out. This structure is burning down quickly, so we will have to get in and out. Any questions?"

Mylvannan stood up and walked to join them. "I will show you the way."

"No," Adonis said. "My people are trained for this. Besides, you appeared very weak when we first saw you. Continue to regain your strength, stay here and help Tink guard Doctor Podeis. We will bring your friends out to you."

"They are my companions," Mylvannan protested. "I will not abandon them."

Ravinder stepped directly behind Mylvannan, his arms crossed and his eyes boring into Adonis. He was acting very defensively, but Adonis could sense that the horned-man was ready to try and slay them all if he felt that Mylvannan was being harmed.

"This is a rescue operation," Adonis explained. "The fight is as good as done."

"I have some cold water," Doctor Podeis offered. "Perhaps it will help you recover more quickly, and then you may be able to assist in the rescue efforts."

Mylvannan considered the doctor for a moment and then nodded his agreement. "Very well; but when I am recovered, I will be joining you."

"If anything happens to Doctor Podeis and Tink, I am holding you responsible," Adonis replied with a threat implied. "You will wait before going in until this position can be better defended."

"If anything happened to your men, it would be because of your own orders," Mylvannan said.

"Orders that include you remaining here and defending them," he repeated to emphasize his point. "I'm certain that in your hands—both of your hands—no harm will come to them."

Mylvannan nodded. "Very well, we will remain for the time being."

"Good," Adonis said with a grin. "I'd hate to have to risk losing Crimbaya to your ice weapon as I did the other sword the last time we faced each other."

Mylvannan grimaced as he thought of his own enchanted sword, Frostlartil, most likely lost to him forever. He watched as Adonis led his people into the lair, and then turned to see how Theiler was doing. The doctor had removed the dwarf's tunic, chainmail, and undershirt and was examining two deep wounds.

Praying to the Frost Queen for help, he hoped that his companion would be spared this day. Too many dwarves had already been slain at Vorstad. Theiler, if fortunate, would not be joining them so quickly.

Rawthorne was admiring the sword in his hands as a viselike grip grabbed his wrist. He glanced over and saw Lady Salaman staring at him. The voice of the swords started ringing inside his head again. *She dares to touch you? One swipe of me and* you *will run the Hidden Empire.*

"She is not dead yet," she calmly stated.

"She will be when next we meet," Rawthorne said, his eyes holding hers.

Do it, strike her down! The sword prompted.

"Very well," Lady Salaman said as she released his wrist. "After this is over, I want you on your way to Trespias immediately, as planned."

Are you going to let her talk to us like that? The sword asked.

Rawthorne would never have the opportunity to answer either of them. He heard the cracking above him and glanced up just in time to see the ceiling cave in upon them. Several things grabbed his attention at that moment: three photons were lunging towards Lady Salaman as they tried to push her away from the debris; his new sword was screaming for him to slay the photons and Lady Salaman, for they were all easy prey right now. The most damning thing though, the last thing he saw, was Solara glaring at him through the flames as he was buried alive beneath burning debris.

Thamar charged and battered the armored warrior with his mallet again and again. The armor was well-forged, but under the dwarf's rampage, it was beginning to dent and even shatter in places. Beneath it—if Thamar paused long enough to notice—he would have seen that Larude had purple skin.

Larude did not want to admit it, but without Zloreskalaza, he was faltering and would not be able to sustain many more of the dwarf's attacks. Only one other time had a dwarf ever bested him in combat, and that was the infernal Mage Ilfanti. He refused to let Thamar have a similar claim.

He distended the claws from his second gauntlet and charged forward, swinging both arms at the dwarf. Thamar swung with his hammer, shattering two of the claws, leaving Larude with only the blades on his right gauntlet remaining.

"You killed my brother," Thamar growled again as he stepped forward, his mallet swinging yet again, knocking Larude to the ground with the blow.

As Larude lay on the ground, he heard the photons shout and glanced over to see the ceiling collapse over Lady Salaman. With her in danger, he could not sustain this battle. He must put an end to it and rescue his mistress.

Thamar stepped forward, his mallet held high to bring the final deathblow to the battle. Larude extended his arm and a clear mist sprayed out at the dwarf, hitting his face with poisonous venom.

The dwarf dropped his mallet and clutched his face, screaming. Larude smiled beneath his helmet in satisfaction as he saw Thamar's face begin to blister below his hands. He would be blinded as well, and in time, would perish from the venom.

Bending over, he whispered in the screaming dwarf's ear. "Now you can join your brother." Leaving him with his taunt, Larude darted away in hopes to find his mistress alive.

Sora tensed and silently berated herself for not having one of her weapons in her hand. Her swords remained sheathed along her back, her glaives upon her side, and her dagger was lying next to the cell she just opened. While she was trying to free the hostages, she had not considered that an enemy would come upon her, and she was not prepared.

One of the hobgoblins aimed the crossbow directly at her, and as she watched, she could see his finger beginning to tighten. The scene was almost surreal. She could see her death clearly as the bolt would be launched and would strike her, but there was also nothing she could do. Funny, she thought, that her life would end here, and like this.

Vaz and Vella leapt into action. The two white tigers struck swiftly as they typically did. The bolt launched and flew wildly as Vaz swiped the hobgoblin across the chest with his forepaw.

The bolt did not miss them though; it launched out and pierced Vella in her right shoulder, barely missing her head by inches, and toppling her backwards. Vella did not wish to give up, and stood back up, emitting a roar.

Vaz turned momentarily, and then jumped on top of the hobgoblin that had attacked Vella. He dug his teeth into the burly humanoid's neck and kept biting until he could no longer feel the hobgoblin squirming beneath him.

Tiot and Sora also moved quickly when the two white tigers had advanced. Sora had her drantanas out and was dueling with the other hobgoblin. Tiot had jumped and sank his teeth into one of the humans.

The hobgoblin that Sora was fighting appeared distracted, worried. His allies had all faltered quickly, or were crying in pain even now. His movements were not as accurate as they should be, and he soon joined his companions as Sora slashed both blades across his chest and he dropped back, bleeding.

The wounds were not enough to kill the orange-haired creature, but Vaz jumped on top of him and bat his head back and forth several times with his front paws until this hobgoblin joined the other in death.

Sora dropped down and looked at the bolt jutting from Vella. Blood had soaked through and soiled her beautiful white and black fur. Vella kept trying to move, but faltered backwards and could not gain her footing.

"What do I do?" Sora cried out. "Somebody help me!"

CHAPTER 86

Confidence was vital in any contest, but it could only take you so far. Ashwin could see that she was beginning to falter before the hobgoblin, and no matter how hard she tried, the armored creature was beginning to overpower her.

Not only was he heavily armored, larger, and stronger than she was, but he also was striking her with two swords compared to her one. He clearly was not as skilled as Arifos with the twin blades, but she was no Arifos herself.

The hobgoblin swung both blades again, and she deflected them—barely. She diverted her attention and tried to see if there was any chance of gaining assistance. She could not locate the tigers, Mylvannan, or the dwarves from Vorstad. Arifos was currently fighting the same man that had deceived her into thinking he was her father. Baldock was rushing towards them.

The hobgoblin thrust with both swords, which Ashwin blocked—again, too close for comfort. Then, the creature did something she did not expect—he kicked forward with his armored leg and struck her in the stomach.

Ashwin fell backwards, struggling to breathe as the wind was knocked out of her. Crick stepped forward as he twirled his drantanas. Trying to regain her footing, Ashwin found her leg stuck, pinned between some debris that had fallen earlier in the battle.

As she watched the hobgoblin, she knew that the creature did not care if she was helpless or not. He would strike and take her life without batting an eye. "Help!" she cried out as loudly as she could. "Please, help me!"

Solara watched as the ceiling collapsed on Rawthorne. She kept straining to see through the flames and smoke for any sign to confirm that the man was either alive or dead. The pile he was buried under was aflame itself, and she could see no movement. That fact did not convince her though that the man was actually dead. Like Durgin, she wanted to watch the life drain out of him.

"Help!" a cry called out. Solara glanced and tried to see through the smoke for the source. "Please, help me!"

Glancing back at the unmoving debris, Solara bit her lip and started towards the sound of the voice. Though she could not see exactly where the plea for help was coming from through the smoke, she sensed that it was one of Thamar's companions. She could not let an ally suffer because of her own vendetta against Rawthorne.

As she moved, the smoke grew denser and she began coughing as she tried to find the one in need. Dropping to her knees, she found that the air was not as polluted, and she spotted an elf sprawled out on the ground, an armored hobgoblin bearing down on her.

With her goal in sight, Solara moved swiftly and hoped that she would make it to the elf's side in time.

Arifos also heard the call from Ashwin, but was unable to find even a moment's break in the battle between him and Kabilian. For a human, the man was very skilled and nearly his equal, something he found unnerving since he had spent so long trying to improve his own abilities so that he could be the best warrior ever known in order to face Zoldex. Now, a mere human was proving to be his equal.

"Soon your associate will be overcome and the ring will be mine," Kabilian gloated.

"Do not count your victory before you have earned it," Arifos replied as he initiated a complex tactic that he was certain would overcome Kabilian's defenses. The assassin's hands moved swiftly though and countered every strike to perfection.

"My victory is assured," Kabilian laughed triumphantly.

"Not so fast!" Baldock cried as he rammed into Kabilian from behind. The assassin crumpled over and landed on his chest. His two swords spinning away from him and reverting back to daggers.

Arifos glanced at Baldock. "My thanks," he said.

"He be mine," Baldock growled.

"No," Arifos sternly objected. "You must help Ashwin. I can handle this."

Baldock glanced back and forth between Kabilian and Crick. He wanted to continue to strike Kabilian, but his sense of honor and responsibility would not allow Ashwin to suffer for his desires. "Ye better be kickin' his durned arse fer me then!"

With a torrent of cussing, Baldock lifted Splitter over his head and leapt towards Crick and Ashwin.

Arifos turned towards Kabilian again and mystically forced the two daggers back towards the man.

"I don't understand?" Kabilian asked.

"This duel will end honorably," Arifos replied.

Kabilian grinned. If that was what the elf thought, then he was doomed.

"Will he live?" Mylvannan asked.

"I have bandaged him and sealed the wounds," Doctor Podeis replied. "I have given him some medicine, but he would benefit from a trip to Shimendyn or from a mystical potion."

"You have none?" Mylvannan asked.

"I'm afraid I don't," Podeis replied, "though I'm beginning to think that I'd be wise to make a trip to Shimendyn myself and stock up."

"Perhaps we shall when this is over," Mylvannan surmised. "Together."

"Perhaps," Doctor Podeis smiled. "Here is the water I promised."

"Thank you," Mylvannan said sincerely as he uncorked the bottle and began drinking. "This is invigorating."

"Before seeing you, I have never met a Frost elf before," Podeis explained.

"That does not shock me," Mylvannan replied. "My people prefer to remain secluded in their own homeland. If not for my mother being from Xylona, I myself never would have wandered from home."

"Curious?"

"Yes," Mylvannan confirmed. "I grew up as a Frost elf, but wished to learn about the elves of Xylona as well. Because my mother is from there, I am not as susceptible to the heat and can withstand even the most humid days. Fire, though, is still very sapping."

"I can imagine," Doctor Podeis smiled pleasantly. "So what is the story with your friend over there?"

"I'm not entirely certain I can refer to him as a friend," Mylvannan said as he glanced at Ravinder in concern.

"What do you mean?" Doctor Podeis asked.

"Back inside the compound, he meant to kill me and Theiler as a gift for Lady Salaman. I was already weakened and tried to talk him out of it. It worked, but I do not know his true intentions."

Doctor Podeis considered this for a moment. "We shall watch him then. Let his actions prove where his heart is."

"Yes," Mylvannan agreed. "I hope he proves to be noble."

"Well, if he can put up with Tink, he certainly has patience," Podeis joked.

The two watched as Tink paced around the horned man, talking non-stop.

"I designed these myself," Tink said as he pulled two small silver items from holsters on his belt. They appeared to be similar to crossbows, but forged out of steel instead of wood, and they also lacked the string that would launch bolts. Like a crossbow, they had handles with triggers on them.

"I call them projectile launchers," Tink continued. "I saw some designs that Vingalli was working on and decided to complete them myself. They are really quite innovative."

He placed one of the projectile launchers back in its holster and then held the other one up. "See this little crank? After I shoot a steel dart, I rotate this in a complete circle, and another dart automatically rises up into the shaft. The cable to launch it is also pulled back and reset inside the shaft so that it will launch."

Tink looked up at Ravinder for a moment and then continued, oblivious to the look that the man was giving him. "You're probably wondering what the cable is made of, aren't you? Well, the cable is a hardened, elastic-type of a rope. It will actually give these babies twice the impact of a crossbow, both in speed and distance of the darts.

"Impressive, aren't they?" he asked as he glanced up again. "I'm planning on making at least one of these for every member of ISIA. It takes a long time to make, and forging the darts just right is a pain, but I think its well worth it, don't you agree?"

Ravinder crossed his arms and looked away, hoping that the inventor would grow weary of his own voice and find something else to do.

"So, enough about this, what about you?" Tink asked.

Ravinder started to look skyward, not answering the question.

"Your horns, your teeth, your ears, your skin, your size, your claws, your hair," Tink started listing off. "What are you?"

Ravinder emitted a low, feral growl at the annoyance, but refrained from looking down again.

"How come you don't wear a shirt?" Tink asked. "Can't find one big enough? Maybe you can't get it over your horns?" After waiting for a moment with no answer, he continued. "The pants are interesting though. Very tight fitting. No boots I see. Are the claws on your toenails too hard to be cut? Is that why you are barefoot?"

Ravinder glanced down again, breathing more deeply.

"So what do you like to do for fun? Me, I like to tinker with things, but that's why I was named Tink, by the gnomes that raised me. How about you?"

"I like to rip the hearts out of the chests of people who annoy me, and then eat them while it still beats in front of their dying eyes."

"Wow," Tink said. "Does a heart still beat after it's been pulled from someone's chest?"

"Ask me any more questions and you may find out," Ravinder threatened with a scowl.

"All I was trying to do was get to know you better," Tink frowned. "Kill a guy for trying to be nice."

"If you insist," Ravinder said as he stood up and glared down at the man.

"Ravinder," Mylvannan called out. "Be good."

Ravinder glanced back at Mylvannan. "We were only," he paused searching for the right word, "playing."

Mylvannan and Doctor Podeis shared a concerned glance. They would indeed have to watch Ravinder closely—very closely.

Crick stood above Ashwin, a maniacal gleam in his eyes. He stopped twirling his two swords and prepared to drop them down into the elf's chest. She was not a mystral, but she was one of the mystral's allies, and would die just as they would.

A battle-cry from behind startled him. Turning to see what it was, his eyes widened as the armored Baldock soared towards him. Crick started to leap aside, but Splitter rammed down and dug into his leg.

Crick fell and looked at the armor. It had protected him for the most part, but the axe had still managed to cut through. The dented armor was also cutting off the circulation in his leg; he stood up and toppled back over as soon as he put weight on it. He let out a cry of agony in the shock at the attempt.

Ignoring Baldock, who was kneeling by Ashwin and helping to free her ensnared leg, he tried to crawl away. He soon found that crawling was not as painful as standing, and decided that he would be able to escape like this and hide until his leg had healed. Either that, or until Kabilian could give him one of his vast healing potions.

Two red boots stood directly in his path. Crick slowly followed them up the legs and kept going until he saw Solara staring down at him, her elongated mystral sword resting snugly by his throat.

"I believe those swords belong to me."

Adonis winced as he stepped closer to the flames. The entire compound was now ablaze, and their time was running out. "Cylnta, can you do something about this smoke? We need to at least be able to see."

Cylnta stepped forward and started blowing a gentle breeze from her mouth, her breath mystically magnified thousands of times, gradually blowing the smoke from the room and dousing some of the fire.

"This won't last long," she explained. "Smoke is a natural side effect of the fire."

"Understood," Adonis acknowledged. He scanned the area and saw that four of the companions were close together and still engaged in combat. One of the dwarves was writhing on the ground in agony. There was no sign of the animals and the second mystral.

"Quince—take Dozzer and Nextra over there and get the dwarf out of here. Darkler and Ortrill—you guys have mop-up duty—anyone that is still willing to fight, show them the error of their ways. Cylnta and I will try to get the rest of the companions out of here."

"Yes sir," Darkler said with a lopsided grin.

Ortrill nodded enthusiastically as he pulled his two swords and prepared to swing into action.

Cylnta stared at the stairs at the back of the chamber. "I am needed elsewhere," she said cryptically.

Adonis followed her gaze and nodded his agreement. "Quince, change in plans. You go with Cylnta. Dozzer and Nextra, you're on your own."

With everyone in agreement with their assignments, the members of ISIA split up into their designated teams and moved in to help as best they could. None of them realized at this moment that all of them would find more than they bargained for in this rescue mission.

CHAPTER 87

The elf may be an idealistic fool, Kabilian thought, but he certainly was skillful with a blade. He had to admit he was enjoying this fight. It had been centuries since he had fought a foe that was worthy of his attention. The brunt-blow of Baldock did not count. The dwarf was a battering ram that had taken him unawares. Arifos was a finely forged blade being wielded by a master.

Under more ideal circumstances, this would be a battle that he would cherish. As it was, things were not going well. Not only did the two have each other to contend to, but they were also forced to struggle to find room to maneuver without setting their clothing or bodies aflame.

He remembered when he looked through his magic-detecting ruby that Arifos himself was a Mage, and he also wielded three enchanted weapons—his two scimitars and his bow. As a collector of mystical artifacts, Kabilian wondered if he had been too focused on Ashwin's ring, and should instead have begun with Arifos.

Imperius would have been an immense tactical advantage in this encounter. The ability to not be physically harmed when fighting a foe so proficient would have been crucial. As it was, he was wearing the Ring of Dexterity, providing him with enhanced speed and skill of his hands and body. Ironically, even with that powerful ring, one that has served him well through many battles, he was still only managing to break even in this duel.

As they continued to fight—their hands a blur as their swords moved through a series of formations—Kabilian pondered what powers the swords that Arifos wielded contained. Could they be the reason that he was fighting so well?

The thought left him as soon as he conceived it. Whereas he was sweating from the heat and the strain of the battle, Arifos was not even winded. Clearly the elf was the one with the true talent. His swords must somehow play to those strengths, but not enough to provide him with an added edge.

Realizing just how hot he really was, Kabilian knew that he needed a moment's respite to utilize another mystical potion. He raised one hand up with his sword still in it, flicking his wrist—a small drug-tipped dart launched from his mystical bracers at the Madrew elf.

Arifos did not even slow down or pause. He countered the move easily by crossing his two scimitars and deflecting the small dart with his blades. He then slashed them both out again and was back into battle with Kabilian without missing a beat.

The assassin still needed time. He went into a series of strikes trying to force Arifos back, and then backpedaled several steps himself, though the Madrew elf did not take the bait and stayed with him.

Sighing in frustration, Kabilian raised his wrist again and continued the motion several times, launching dart after dart at Arifos. The sword in his opposite hand shrank back down to its original form and he tucked it in his belt. He had to move quickly—no matter how many times he used his mystical bracers, Arifos deflected the strike and managed to gain ground.

Fumbling around in his satchel, his concentration diverted, Kabilian had trouble summoning the image of the item he sought to recover from the mystical pouch. Growling with impatience, Kabilian finally found what he was looking for: a small vial of a sparkling pearlescent-blue liquid. He flicked the cork and drank the contents. It took only seconds, but he could feel the effect that it was having on him. The sweat on his brow diminished, and though he was still standing close to a raging fire, he could no longer feel its warmth.

The potion of Chill would not save him from being burned, but it would make him immune to the ever-increasing temperature of the Hidden Empire compound. Without the cork, he placed the vial in the mouth of a dead goblin, careful not to spill any more of the contents. If he were able to, he would return for it when this battle was through.

Picking his jewel-hilted dagger up again, Kabilian spoke the incantation and watched it grow to a full-length sword. He was ready to continue the engagement with Arifos. Dropping both arms into a defensive posture, he stopped launching mystical darts at the elf and waited the two seconds before Arifos was upon him again.

"You rely too heavily on magic," Arifos cautioned. "It will be your undoing."

"And you do not rely on it enough," Kabilian countered. "You are a Mage and do not seem inclined to use your powers."

"My powers are there if I need them," Arifos said as he deflected several strikes from Kabilian. "I prefer to use finesse and master my own abilities. You never know when your magic will fail, but your own innate abilities shall never abandon you."

"Are you trying to teach me or fight me?" Kabilian sneered as he brought both swords down, trying to swipe the legs out from under Arifos. Arifos twirled his two swords and slammed them down, easily parrying the attack.

"You are a good fighter," Arifos declared. "But you rely on magic to enhance your skills. I do not."

"You wound me," Kabilian said with a mocking expression of sorrow. "Was that supposed to hurt me?"

"No," Arifos said. "It just means that the outcome is predetermined. Sooner or later, you will run out of mystical weapons and potions. The spells will wear off. I will still be as I am, and as such, will be your better."

"We shall see, won't we?"

"Yes," Arifos agreed. "We shall."

"Kabilian!"

The shout caught him by surprise, though his foe did not notice it. He continued his battle as if unaffected by the call, but recognized the voice of Lady Salaman. If she had actually requested his aid, then her plight must be severe.

He split his focus momentarily, trying to gain some insight beyond his current encounter. He saw Crick on the ground with Solara standing above him, a sword to his throat. Baldock and Ashwin were walking towards the ring and both appeared unharmed. Others were also joining the fray now. Two men in the red garb of ISIA were cutting through the remaining combatants from the Hidden Empire as if they were practice dummies.

He still was not certain where Lady Salaman was. The area where her throne had been was buried and ablaze. If she was there, she certainly would need assistance for she must have been buried alive. However, he had made a large investment in his time and efforts to recruit Crick as his partner. He was not about to let the hobgoblin perish in his first real skirmish.

Dropping back, he resumed launching darts at Arifos. As before, the Madrew elf deflected the darts easily.

"Are you running out of ideas?" Arifos asked.

Kabilian reduced the size of one of his daggers and returned it to his belt. He then reached up to his face and started to pick at the scar he had below his right eye. He winced, but the scar began to pull away from his skin, leaving a red mark where it had been.

Arifos watched the assassin as the scar was being torn from his face and couldn't understand what Kabilian was doing. Several more darts launched at him in succession and he continued to knock them from the air with his swords.

"Shall we continue this another time?" Kabilian asked as he ripped the last piece of the scar from his face and then threw it at Arifos.

Swiping with Phistala, Arifos hoped to cleave the scar in two and keep it from him. Instead, it stuck to his sword and continued to soar towards him, expanding like an elastic. Part of it touched his right shoulder, and stuck to him. Arifos tried to sever the substance in two with Aurlestyl, but the sword did not cut the substance, and that too became bound.

As he struggled to get free, the sticky substance continued to touch him in other spots and bind him further. He even tried to use his own mystical abilities, but as flames launched from his fingertips, the goop increased in size exponentially and ensnared him even more.

Kabilian frowned as he stood over Arifos. "You shouldn't have done that," he said. "I was going to take your swords and bow. Now they are as stuck as you are."

"Sorry to disappoint you," Arifos sneered as he continued to struggle.

"No matter, I shall claim your weapons when we meet again," Kabilian said confidently. "Until then, keep them safe."

Arifos watched as Kabilian leapt over a small wall of flame. No matter what he did, he could find no way out of this trap. He was officially out of the fight; and unless one of his companions came to his aid, odds were that the fire would end his life as well.

Lady Salaman pushed one of the dead photons away from her. They had been her loyal servants until the last. It was most unfortunate that only those six had pledged their allegiance to her. It would be many years before she found bodyguards that trustworthy again.

She had called to Kabilian, but the assassin did not come to her aid. She would be forced to try and free herself. She grabbed onto the doorway that led to the arena, and pulled herself up. The effort was agony. Sharp, shooting pain flashed through her trapped leg and almost overwhelmed her. She was a gorn though, and refused to give in.

She continued to pull herself free—she had almost fainted from the last attempt, but made it. As she examined her leg, she could see that it was lopsided by the knee: it was badly broken. She would need to get out of here and either find a mystical Healer to reset the bone or take time to rest and heal properly.

Glancing at her domain crumbling around her, she wondered if she would be able to do either. This morning she had been a crime-lord, one of the most feared women in the entire realm; now, she was little more than a cripple trying to claw her way to safety. Oh, how easily the mighty have fallen!

The rubble before her began to shift, and she watched as Rawthorne came bursting up, his arms outstretched and forcing the debris from him. He let out a roar of defiance, informing the gods that they failed in their attempt to kill him. His entire body was covered with soot. His hair had been slightly scorched, but the man was a survivor, and this was not his day to die.

"Rawthorne," she beckoned him. "I believe it is time to leave."

Rawthorne stared down at her with spite and scorn. He despised the woman, even more so now that her empire was falling. He may not need her help after all. Turning away from her, he searched the debris until he found the intricately crafted skull-hilted sword. As he reached down for it, he could hear Zloreskalaza calling out to him, summoning him.

She is weak. Unworthy of us.

"She is," he agreed.

"Rawthorne?" Lady Salaman asked, not certain of who he was speaking to.

Strike her down, now! Zloreskalaza prompted. *The Hidden Empire is gone. We shall rebuild it ourselves.*

"Yes," Rawthorne agreed. He stepped closer to Lady Salaman, the sword firmly clutched in his hands.

"To whom are you speaking?" Lady Salaman demanded.

"It no longer matters," Rawthorne said.

Lady Salaman could see Rawthorne's intentions in his eyes. As soon as the realization came to her, her symbiotic suit became protective, expanding into a hardened, thorn-encased armor. "You cannot harm me!"

She does not know what she speaks of, the sword whispered. *But she will learn.*

"Your symbiote can't save you," Rawthorne said. "You are injured. Weak. You can't even defend yourself."

From the flames leapt Larude, crashing into Rawthorne from behind. Rawthorne stumbled to the ground and glared at the lieutenant. "You will pay for that!"

Look at him - his armor has been compromised! He, too, has become weak. I can't believe he wielded me for so long!

"I will not let you harm Lady Salaman," Larude said. "My sword has corrupted you."

"I am not corrupted by anyone," Rawthorne growled as he lashed the sword at Larude.

Larude caught the blade and held on tightly. Rawthorne could see blood dripping from the gauntlet where the sword had cut through, but no matter how hard he tried, he could not move the sword further. Larude shot out with his second hand and punched Rawthorne in the nose, dropping him down, blood seeping down to his lip.

As Rawthorne fell backwards, Larude reclaimed his sword and stared at it for several moments. The master and weapon were waging an internal war inside his mind. The blade must be controlled, and he had to teach it who its master was.

Rawthorne watched Larude as he was trembling. As soon as he had released the skeletal hilt, he lost the link with the sword. He could no longer hear its words inside his mind. That was something he hoped to remedy.

Larude lowered the sword so that the tip of the blade rested under Rawthorne's chin. "The sword has influenced you. Do not let it dictate your fate. Lady Salaman still has need of you, and if you accept that, you will be spared this day."

Rawthorne considered the words, and then glanced at Lady Salaman. She was eying him coolly. "Very well, I will not fall victim to the sword's influence."

"Excellent," Larude said as he removed the sword from Rawthorne's neck. "What are your orders?"

"It is time to leave," Lady Salaman instructed. "I will need help walking."

"I'll help her," Rawthorne said as he reached over to lift her up.

As he did so, the thorns shrank back into the symbiote and vanished.

"Larude, make sure you don't forget Kargle on your way out," Lady Salaman instructed.

"As you wish it, so it shall be," Larude bowed.

"How are ye now?" Baldock asked.

"Better, now that I'm not stuck," Ashwin said. "Thank you, Baldock."

Baldock turned away as he tried to hide his blushing cheeks. "We should be gettin' back into this. Are ye up fer it?"

"Just as soon as I get my ring," Ashwin agreed.

Baldock walked over to where it was and picked it up for her. The protective shield that Arifos placed around it dissipated beneath his gauntlet. "Ye be keepin' this safe. Don't ye be lettin' no illusions or deceptions be foolin' ye."

"I won't," Ashwin said. "I promise."

"Good, then let's be gettin' back into this here fight," Baldock beamed with excitement.

"Oh no," Ashwin cried as she watched Arifos struggling with the sticky substance. "We must help Arifos."

"I'll lead the way," Baldock said. "And if any o' these durned fools dare to be gettin' in me way, then they will be feelin' Splitter this day!"

Solara examined Crick's suit of armor and the weapons he had amassed. The armor was definitely dwarven; but with the exception of the bow, all weapons were mystral.

"I overheard a bunch of hobgoblins cheering about killing a mystral," she said. "With all of those weapons strapped to you, were you involved?"

Crick looked up and frowned. He had been involved, though it was a Shadow Mage that killed the dark-haired mystral months ago.

He found it ironic that the death of that one mystral would possibly cause his death when it was Solara herself that he had claimed most of his weapons from.

"Speak up," she demanded.

"My clan did face a mystral," he said.

"What happened?" Solara asked.

"We were raiding a village in Suspinti. She was a Mage that had been passing through. She was in the wrong place at the wrong time."

"Oh," Solara said. "So you think that I would be perfectly willing to accept that you struck at a village of humans?"

"That is not what I meant," Crick said. "I did not like what my people were doing, so I left."

"I supposed to believe that?" she asked.

"It is true," Crick said. "The mystral had been defending a small hut with children. After the Shadow Mage had killed her, I walked into the hut and saw the kids. They were terrified and screamed when they saw me. I could not do it though. I used my mace and created an opening in the back of their hut. I then turned and walked away."

"Did they make it?" Solara asked.

"I know not. The entire village was burned down. I only hope that they did flee through the opening and manage to evade the rest of my tribe," Crick said. "I do know that there were no stories of children being found by any other hobgoblins after the raid."

"This doesn't explain where you got the mystral weapons," Solara said as she dug the tip of her sword a bit deeper into his throat.

"I was sent to find a scouting party in the Suspintian Woods. I found them all dead, but some mystral throwing knives were left behind. I remembered the dark-haired one from the village and took them as my own."

Solara was quiet for a moment. She did not know if she believed the hobgoblin about the children and the village, but she remembered killing the scouting party. That much of his story at least was true.

"So that accounts for some throwing knives. What about the rest?" she continued.

"My tribe attacked the home of the mystral. I did not wish to face the warriors I was becoming drawn to, and waited until the battle was done. Then I gathered all of the fallen weapons I could."

She remembered that battle well: a hobgoblin bola had given her a concussion, or else she may have reached Durgin in time to spare the farmers. It would also explain why he had her swords.

"What about the armor?" she pressed.

"Kabilian brought me to Tregador and they forged it for me," he said.

Solara did not recognize the name, but the armor did resemble the fine craftsmanship of Tregador. It was certainly plausible. "Yet still I find you in the den of vipers," she said. "Tell me why I shouldn't slit your throat right now?"

"I'll give you a reason," Kabilian said as he stepped before her, slightly behind the kneeling Crick. "The man you are after is getting away."

Solara followed his pointed finger and could see Rawthorne assisting Lady Salaman as they fled through a back door. The sight of the man still alive provoked a myriad of reactions. She was enraged that he yet lived, but also felt relieved that she still had the opportunity to mete out her own version of justice.

Kabilian was watching as well, and was not pleased by what he saw. As Rawthorne helped Lady Salaman from the compound, he could see her gaze firmly set on him. The look was of sheer contempt. His actions this day may have just made him one of the most wanted men in the realm—Lady Salaman would not rest until his head was served to her on a platter. He grinned to himself: it would be an interesting challenge.

Solara glanced back at Kabilian and then down at Crick. "If you are not who you claim to be, I will be back for you." She then removed her sword from his throat and ran after Rawthorne.

Sora finished opening all of the cages. She hoped that the prisoners could somehow help her with Vella, though she was uncertain how anyone could do so without the proper medical equipment.

The prisoners were growing more anxious as she had been fumbling with the keys. They could all smell the burning wood and bodies from the inner complex, and they all wanted to escape before the fire consumed them as well.

The humans fled in panic as soon as their cages were opened, much to Sora's dismay; the three rasplers, two dwarves, and elf remained behind. The dwarves scoured through the fallen weapons of their slain captors and each claimed one for their own.

The elf stood tall and regal, as if she were a member of aristocracy and expected respect from those around her. When the dwarves were done with making their selections, they both dropped to a knee in front of her and lowered their heads. The elf immediately took command of the situation.

"You three rasplers pick up the tiger and come with us. Prohammer and Dawar, you two will scout ahead and make sure the way is clear," she ordered.

"Yes, eminence," Prohammer bowed.

Sora glanced up at the elf with tears in her eyes. She was grateful that somebody seemed to know what to do. She hoped that the elf was making the right decisions.

"I am Shanavie," the elf said. "A High elf of Turning Leaf. Prohammer and Dawar are my entourage."

"Dwarves serving an elf?" Sora asked. "A Turning Leaf elf?"

"A long story that we do not have time for," Shanavie replied. "Come, we must get your tiger out of here."

Sora glanced back down the hallway towards where she had left Solara. She hoped that she was making the right decision and that her sister would be all right. Two figures emerged from the darkness, one was human, the other reptilian. She drew her drantanas and stood ready to face them.

"No need to fear," Quince said. "We are allies."

"How do I know that?" Sora asked.

"We are companions of Solara, the mystral that you came here with," Quince explained.

Cylnta watched her closely, and then smiled knowingly. "We are friends of your sister."

Sora watched them and then glanced at Shanavie, who only shrugged.

"We have a doctor outside," Quince said as his eyes quickly scanned the group and noted their injuries. "He can tend to all of your wounds, including the tiger's."

"Very well," Sora said. She could see that neither Vaz nor Tiot appeared agitated or threatened. These two must be whom they claim. "We'll trust you."

Shanavie pointed down the hallway and the three rasplers started walking after the dwarves, Vella propped atop of their shoulders. Sora followed with both Tiot and Vaz walking close to her.

Cylnta and Quince remained behind the group. Cylnta was particularly interested in the High elf. She had not heard Shanavie provide introductions to Sora, but she knew who the elf was; her exploits over the past six hundred years were required reading at the Mage's Council. She hoped that, when this was over, she would have time to actually meet the legend she once had to study.

CHAPTER 88

Life was cruel. First his brother lost his ability to speak. Now, he lost his ability to see. The pain was overwhelming. Thamar felt as if his entire face was melting. He could feel it blistering beneath his fingers. His eyes were swollen shut, but even in the rare moments he could open them, the world around him was dark.

He had heard the elves telling Theiler that when you lose one of your senses or abilities, other attributes are honed even more sharply to help you adapt. Though he was blinded only for a matter of minutes, he had to admit, that the sound of the crackling flames closing in on him was maddening.

Standing up, he tried to walk blindly, one hand stretched forward, feeling for either the fire or something that could help him find his way out of the lair. He could not believe that he—a true son of Vorstad—would find death, not at the blade of an enemy as his father had, but by flames and his own inability to find a way out.

In truth, he was wandering aimlessly. For all he knew, he was walking around in circles, no closer to finding his way back outside than if he stayed where he was and just accepted his fate. But that was something he could not do. He was Thamar, son of Thron, and like his father before him, he would die before giving up, regardless of the odds.

He could hear a pair of footsteps approaching him, one sounding much larger and heavier than the other. Crouching down, he started patting the floor looking for his fallen mallet. He may not be able to see, but if he could, he would still fight.

"There he is," a deep voice called out.

Too late, Thamar realized. He stood back up and grabbed his two daggers from his belt. He would have preferred to die with his hammer in his hands, but he would fight to his dying breath with his daggers.

"Whoa," a feminine voice gasped. "We're here to help you."

Thamar listened. The two had stopped moving. He could not tell where they were unless they moved. Tensing, he waited to spring as soon as he sensed that they were closing in on him.

"Put the knives down," the deep voice encouraged.

"I'll put them down," Thamar said. "I'll put them down your throats when you come near me!"

"I said we were here to help," the female voice replied.

"I know my allies, and you are not one of them," Thamar said.

"How does Adonis expect us to get him out of here?" the woman asked.

"I'd hate to have to try and knock him out," the man replied.

"Did you say Adonis?" Thamar asked.

"What of it?" the woman shot back.

"The same Adonis that fought by Braksis's side and was the protector of Emperor Conrad?"

"He's one and the same," the woman replied. "He's also my boss, and he ordered me to get you to safety."

Thamar lowered his two daggers. "An ally of Braksis is an ally of mine."

"I'm Dozzer," the man said. "Pleased to meet you."

"Would you stop being polite and just pick him up so we can get out of here," the woman shouted.

"Don't mind her," Dozzer whispered as he picked Thamar up. "Nextra just prefers missions where she can get a little more close and personal, if you know what I mean."

Thamar snickered at the thought. "Can you see my mallet?"

"I see it," Dozzer said.

"Can you reach it?"

"I have it," he said. "Come on, we're out of here."

Dozzer lifted Thamar up in one arm and held the mallet in the other. Nextra waited a moment to make sure he was ready and then she led the way back through the flames to the entrance, Dozzer close behind her.

"That's fifteen, my hairy little friend," Ortrill laughed as he dug his left sword into the chest of an orc. His blades were uncommon compared to the other members of ISIA: they typically wielded long, narrow blades, whereas Ortrill preferred thicker, shorter swords. They were heftier than a normal blade, but he fought with such precision that none would ever notice the difference.

"Fifteen, my behind!" Darkler sneered as he dropped below the lunge of a hobgoblin and dug his dagger into the creature's side. "More like five."

"Count the bodies, if you dare take a moment to look," Ortrill laughed as he leapt and spun over two goblins, landed behind them, and rammed his two swords into their backs. "Sixteen and seventeen!"

Darkler glanced over and smirked. "If you're killing goblins, I'll give you the higher count."

"Oh, touché," Ortrill said. "Only two goblins, we'll strike them from the record." He then spotted a pair of humans and charged towards them. The two men screamed and ran away. "Drat!"

"What's the matter, are they afraid of you?" Darkler asked.

"I thought it was you they were supposed to be afraid of?" Ortrill replied with a sullen frown on his face.

Darkler jabbed his blades several times into the chest of an orc until the creature slumped forward in death. "They do fear me," Darkler said. "And with good reason."

"Yeah, well now they fear me, too. How sad!"

"Behind you," Darkler pointed out.

A sarnal ran towards Ortrill with a mace raised over its head.

"Oh goodie," Ortrill called as anticipation returned to his eyes. "Hey, ugly—this isn't personal."

The sarnal brought the mace down and Ortrill deflected it with one sword, while bringing the other slashing towards the brown-skinned creature's side. The blade dug deep and Ortrill could feel his sword strike the bone.

"Ooh, that had to hurt," he said. "Let me end the pain."

The sarnal dropped its mace and reached for Ortrill, grabbing the man by the neck.

Ortrill looked at him blankly. "Is this supposed to scare me?"

As the sarnal began to squeeze, Ortrill shrugged as if he wasn't bothered at all and brought his two swords swiping together, slicing through the muscular creatures arms. The sarnal dropped back screaming as Ortrill shook his head.

"Pathetic."

A dagger flew past Ortrill's shoulder and hit the sarnal in the chest, dropping it to the ground in death. Darkler stepped forward and pulled it out. He rubbed the blade on the sarnal's pants and then glared at Ortrill. "Stop playing with your targets and just kill them."

"That still counts as eighteen," Ortrill said as he stuck his tongue out at Darkler.

"Whatever," the sergeant replied. "Let's go check on Mylvannan's companions. They look like they might need a hand."

"Oh sure," Ortrill mockingly sneered. "Change the subject. Admit it: I had more kills than you."

"Come on," Darkler said again.

The two walked over and paused before Baldock. The dwarf glared at Darkler, remembering him from Trespias. "What do ye be wantin'? A rematch?"

"We're here as allies this time," Darkler said.

Baldock eyed him suspiciously, but then shrugged in agreement. "That durned assassin used some kind o' mystical bindin' on Arifos here. We can't be gettin' him free."

Ortrill and Darkler exchanged a quick glance. They were the brawn of the group; mystical traps were Cylnta's department.

"I have an ally that might be able to help," Darkler said. He pulled out his modified corryby and held it close to his head. "Cylnta."

Ashwin and Baldock exchanged a glance and they both shrugged. To them, this human must be a little insane. What would talking to an orb do to help their friend?

"Yes, Sergeant?" the voice of Cylnta spoke clearly through the orb.

"Impressive," Baldock nodded his approval.

"One of the allies of Mylvannan is stuck in some kind of sticky goop; it's mystical. Any chance you can get back in here?"

"I'm heading towards Doctor Podeis now," she said. "I'll make my way towards you soon."

"Thanks, Cylnta," Darkler said. He then returned the corryby to a pouch dangling from his belt and nodded reassuringly to Ashwin and Baldock. "We'll be able to help him soon."

"Here," Kabilian said as he handed a small vial to Crick. "Drink this."

Crick looked at the glowing blue liquid in the vial and then quickly drank the entire thing. He started to feel a burning sensation in his injured leg almost immediately. "You poisoned me?" he moaned.

"Give it a second," Kabilian instructed.

The pain began to fade and Crick could no longer feel the pain from his wound. The armor was still cutting his circulation off a bit, but the injury itself was gone.

"See," Kabilian said. "All better."

"The mystral could have killed me," Crick said. "But she didn't. Why?"

"She either liked the story you told her, or her lust for vengeance was too great to worry about you."

"I didn't tell a story," Crick said. "What I said was true."

"It matters not," Kabilian said. "You'll have many mystral to kill in the days to come."

"No," Crick said adamantly. "I want their weapons, yes, but I do not wish to see them harmed."

Kabilian stared at his companion in disbelief: this was something he would have to work around. He guessed that they could just stay away from the mystral, but if not, the mystral certainly would be opposed to an assassin. Odds were they would come against the maiden warriors again one day. Having a partner that refused to harm them would be rather difficult. It could be a weakness that Kabilian would have to decide not to live with, though that would mean that Crick would be the one that ceased to live.

"We shall debate this another time," Kabilian said as he reached into his satchel and removed a large tooth.

"What are you doing?" Crick asked.

"Something to remember me by," he said as he tossed the tooth to the ground several feet ahead of him. He then spoke a quick incantation and watched as the tooth grew into a fully developed forty-foot silver dragon.

Smiling triumphantly, Kabilian wrapped one arm around Crick and grasped his amulet with his other. The two then teleported away, leaving the dragon to mask their escape.

Solara reached the same spot where she had stood before. The door where Rawthorne fled was so close, but she could find no way around the flames without badly burning herself. She could not believe that the man had eluded her grasp twice in the same day.

An arm wrapped around her waist and started to pull her backwards. Solara began to struggle until she recognized the voice of Adonis. "Solara, we must go, now!"

"No, he's the one that killed Braksis," she protested. "I must avenge his death!"

"We'll get him later," Adonis promised. "This place is coming down all around us. We must get out of here while we still can."

Solara gave in and agreed to go with Adonis. They would indeed see Rawthorne again, and when they did, things would end much differently. Her silent vow was interrupted as a roar—so loud that it made her clutch her ears to block the sound—erupted from the mouth of the dragon.

Her first thought was that they were about to face another tragon, for it sounded like the beast that she and Braksis faced at Comonor. What she saw though was amazing, and also slightly disturbing. A silver dragon was issuing a warning. It was magnificent and beautiful, just as she always imagined one of the famed dragons would be, but it also appeared ready to strike. Her loyalties were torn, even as Adonis rushed towards the mighty lizard, his sword brandished in his hand.

CHAPTER 89

"Um, that's a dragon," Ortrill pointed out.

"Oh really?" Darkler sarcastically replied. "What gave you that idea? Idiot."

"This one's all yours, Sergeant," Ortrill grinned as he beckoned Darkler to go first.

"Hey, look at the bright side," Darkler stated. "At least with it being inside, it can't move around as much."

"I hate to break it to you," Ortrill commented, "but there is very little 'inside' left. If we don't get out of here soon, dragon or no, we'll be burned alive."

"Something is better than nothing," Darkler growled.

"Well, since you put it that way," Ortrill shrugged. "The only problem is that we're stuck inside with it."

"Would ye two quit yer durned squabblin' and get out o' me way?" Baldock shouted as he pushed past the two ISIA agents.

"Of course," Ortrill said with a bow as he stepped aside.

"That's better," Baldock sneered. Holding Splitter in one hand and his shield in the other, he emitted a dwarven battle cry and charged the silver dragon. Once he reached it, he swung Splitter at the creature's chest, hoping to end the encounter with one swipe. The blade hit its mark, but the creature's armor-like scales prevented the axe from causing any damage.

Pulling Splitter back, he swung several more times, each attempt to no avail. "Would ye bleed, ye durned dragon?"

Ortrill and Darkler exchanged a glance and wry smiles. "The runt's got spirit," Ortrill admired. Twirling his two blades several times each, he followed Baldock's lead and charged the dragon, swiping his swords in hopes of piercing its strong external layer.

Darkler glanced down at his two daggers and shrugged. He might not be able to do much, but he was not one to ever back down from a good brawl, even if it was with a dragon.

Glancing back to see Ashwin, he motioned towards Arifos. "Try to get your companions out of here. We'll try to hold the dragon off."

Ashwin grimaced at the thought. "I wish you good fortune," she said.

"Thanks," Darkler snickered. "I'll need it." Taking a few deep breaths and shifting his grip on his daggers so that he could swipe his blades in a backhanded thrust, he charged in and joined his allies.

As the human joined the other two in combat, Ashwin could not help but think that the trio were mad. To fight a dragon? They must be insane.

Scanning Arifos, she saw that he had finally stopped moving. By doing so, the sticky substance the bonded him had stopped spreading. Reaching down, she firmly grasped him by the shoulders and started to drag him away. Though the Madrew elf weighed only one hundred and twenty-five pounds, the substance on him, his armor and weapons made him far too heavy to even budge for the smaller elven female.

Frowning in frustration, Ashwin tried to pull her hands away as she looked to try something else, only to learn that she too was now ensnared. "Oh no," she gasped. "I can't move my hands!"

As Sora reached the doorway, Quince held his hand out to help her up. She nodded her appreciation and then turned to make certain that the rasplers were able to get Vella out without harming her further as they climbed up the steps.

Shanavie remained behind the rasplers, directing them as they were stepping outside. The two dwarves pushed Quince aside and reached out to help steady the rasplers and help if they could. Within moments, they were all outside of the lair and in the open night.

"The doctor is around this way," Quince said as he waved the ras-plers around a bend.

Shanavie reached a hand out and grasped Sora by the shoulder. She stopped and turned to face the High elf. Tiot also paused and watched the exchange, his hair standing on end as if he expected trou-ble.

"This fight here is yours," Shanavie explained. "There is no place here for my entourage and myself."

"But they imprisoned you," Sora protested. "Surely you wish to see your captors brought to justice."

"Justice," Shanavie repeated. "It is merely a concept that has only meaning for the party wronged. I seek no retribution."

"Then you are more lenient than I," Sora stated.

"Perhaps," Shanavie said. "You are young. If you were to reach my age, things may appear quite differently."

"Eminence," Prohammer spoke out in a typically gruff dwarven voice. "We be needin' to be gettin' ye out o' here."

"Yes, Prohammer," Shanavie said. "I shall be ready in a moment."

"Where will you go?" Sora asked.

"I will go where fate has dictated," Shanavie replied.

"That is pretty cryptic," Sora said in disgust. "There is a war com-ing. We can use all of the allies we can get."

"You would call me an ally without even knowing me?" Shanavie asked.

"I felt that you were honorable," Sora answered with a shrug. "That is why I saved you."

"And for that I am in your debt," Shanavie bowed.

"You also might help us gain the aid of the elves," Sora suggested with a glimmer of hope.

"Unfortunately, child, you are mistaken," Shanavie said. "I was ex-iled from Turning Leaf almost four centuries ago."

"Exiled?" Sora asked. "I don't understand."

"There's no time for you to understand," Dawar growled impatiently. "We need to leave."

"You're a dwarf, why would you flee from a fight?" Sora challenged.

"I am Dawar, son of Drewellin, a true son of Vorstad. I have seen more fights than you could possibly dream of," he sneered.

"Dawar," said Shanavie sternly. As the dwarf shuffled away to join Prohammer, Shanavie continued. "I found Dawar long ago. He had been sent to help Xylona in a scouting mission into Tenalong. His entire party was captured by trolls. He still does not talk about it, but he was forced to watch as, one by one, the trolls grabbed the captured dwarves and elves, and ate them.

"When a former companion of mine—a noble ranger that has been dead for decades—Prohammer, and I found them, Dawar was the last dwarf alive. After we rescued him, he pledged his allegiance and his blade to our cause. For a while, the four of us made quite a team."

"Prohammer speaks much differently," Sora observed. "Is he from Tregador?"

"No," Shanavie said. "Carnelian, though they do have similar dialects."

"Eminence," Prohammer called to her.

"My entourage is right," Shanavie admitted. "It is time to leave. Until we meet again."

"Will we meet again?" Sora asked.

"You yourself said that there was a war brewing," Shanavie explained. "We undoubtedly will meet again."

Sora watched as the elf joined her dwarven companions and the trio soon vanished in the night. After they were gone, Sora wondered if she had made a mistake. Vella was wounded, and she had abandoned Solara against insurmountable odds, all to save the prisoners. Yet those same prisoners just fled, not even pausing to help their rescuers against their captors. If anything happened to Solara, she knew that her decision would plague her for the rest of her days.

"This is ridiculous," Mylvannan protested. "You and Dozzer are back. You bring my injured friends to me, and still you have the audacity to tell me that I am not to return to the compound and help my friends?"

"Those were your orders," Nextra said.

"To Tanorus with the orders," Mylvannan sneered. "Adonis has no sway over me. My friends need me."

Doctor Podeis glanced up from his work on Thamar's face and frowned. "Do not forget that the flames will weaken you again. It will sap your strength and odds are, your friends will need to help you more than you will be able to help them."

"As long as my friends are in danger, I cannot stand idly by," Mylvannan protested with conviction. "We all heard the roar of a dragon—they are most likely fighting for their very lives this moment."

"Most likely," Nextra agreed. "But think about what the doctor said: do you wish to be a burden to your friends instead of an ally?"

"Woman, if I perish to save even one of my friends, then so be it," Mylvannan sneered. "The sacrifice would be well worth it."

Thamar coughed a couple of times and tried to sit up. He was still blinded and could not see, but his hearing was fine. "It was an honor to fight by your side," he said. "If you will act as my eyes, I will be your strength."

Doctor Podeis shot a concerned glance at Mylvannan and shook his head. Mylvannan picked up the meaning and kneeled down, grasping Thamar's hand. "No, my friend, you must get your rest. We will fight by each other's side again one day."

"I may be blind but I'm not dead yet!" Thamar roared in protest. "I am Thamar, son of Thron, thrasher of mine enemies!"

"Yes you are," Mylvannan agreed.

"How hard would it be to fight a dragon?" Thamar asked. "I don't need me eyesight for that! It's so damned big that wherever I swing my mallet, I'm bound to hit it!"

"Doctor," Quince called out. "Vella needs your assistance."

"The Empress's white tiger?" he asked. "Of course, of course—bring her over here."

The rasplers did as beckoned and lowered Vella gently to the ground. Podeis immediately began to examine the wound. "I'll need my scalpel to get the bolt out—the tip looks barbed."

"Where is it?" Mylvannan asked, concerned for the cat that had fought so valiantly by his side.

"In my bag. Over there," Podeis pointed.

Mylvannan fumbled through the bag until he found the instrument. He then brought it over to Doctor Podeis and handed it to him.

The doctor took the scalpel in his right hand. With his left hand, he began to stroke Vella behind the ear and spoke softly in a very soothing tone. Vaz paced behind the doctor, his eyes never leaving Vella.

Podeis then lowered the scalpel and cut incisions in four directions around the arrow, creating a small cross on the white tiger. With each slice, Vella shuddered and moved slightly, but she managed to remain where she was without interfering with Podeis's work.

Sora and Tiot reached the group and spotted the doctor working on Vella. She hoped that he would be successful in his efforts—she did not wish to see harm come to any creature. Two red-bearded dwarves were also lying near the doctor. One had his top off and was heavily bandaged; the other's face was all blistered and an irritated red. She recognized the latter was the dwarf that came to help Solara—she wondered if he knew her fate.

She slowly walked over and sat next to the dwarf, careful not to make any sounds or cause a distraction for the doctor. Although Thamar was blind, his face turned towards her and his eyes glared directly at her. "Who's there?"

"I am Sora," she said. "Sister of Solara."

"Solara," Thamar smiled. "You are fortunate to have one such as her for your sibling."

Sora listened to the words and remembered how harshly she had treated Solara when she had first returned to Dragon's Myst. She had been cold and harsh, trying to punish Solara for leaving her alone after their mother died at the hands of Durgin. Now, she only prayed that she would see her sister alive once again.

"Do you know anything about my sister?" she asked.

"We were fighting together," he said. "It was almost like old times. But we were separated and faced our own foes."

"What happened?" she pressed.

"When my own brother fell, I'm sorry to say that I lost track of everything in there except for the villain that I thought killed him. I do not know how Solara fared."

"You should let him rest," Dozzer said as he reached his hand out to help her up.

"Thank you," Sora said to Thamar. "Thank you for coming to her aid. Thank you for fighting by her side. Thank you for everything."

"She is my companion," Thamar shrugged. "I did not join her for gratitude."

"Well, know that you have earned mine."

"Please," Dozzer said again.

"Do *you* know anything of my sister?" Sora asked as she glanced up at Dozzer.

"She must still be in there," he guessed.

"Then that is where I belong," Sora said.

Mylvannan pulled his gaze from the doctor's work and listened in on the conversation. Tink could hand the doctor the proper tools; he, too, belonged inside.

"I can't let you go back in there," Dozzer said.

"Just try to stop me," she spat back and pushed by him.

The former Lumnia player looked at Quince for orders. The commander gestured to look at Mylvannan, who also stood up and started to join Sora. Vaz stopped watching Vella and joined the trio, Tiot already standing at Sora's side.

As they walked past the rock where Ravinder was perched, Mylvannan expectantly glanced at the man. "Are you coming?"

"Are you paying?" Ravinder asked in reply.

"No money," Mylvannan answered. "This is for honor."

"You forget where you found me elf," Ravinder said. "I find no honor in fighting the Hidden Empire."

"The Hidden Empire boasts the possession of a dragon?" he asked. "I didn't realize that they did."

Ravinder considered that for a moment; he had never heard of them owning a dragon before. Of course, Lady Salaman did enjoy unique pets; perhaps that was what this was. "No money, no me."

"Here I thought you wanted to earn a name," Mylvannan commented. "Perhaps I was mistaken."

"Perhaps you were," Ravinder growled back.

"A shame, as this would definitely be noteworthy—a grand name, indeed, for the one who fells the dragon."

Sora glanced at Mylvannan with a puzzled expression. She didn't understand why he was trying to convince the creature to join them—if the thing wanted to fight, it would, for its own ideals and reasons, nobody else's.

Ravinder dropped his feet from the rock and walked over to join them. "I'm not doing this for you."

"I know," Mylvannan replied.

"Maybe I'll find some of Lady Salaman's treasury before this place completely burns to the ground."

"You may indeed be that fortunate," Mylvannan said.

Quince watched the exchange, sensing a sinister vibe from Ravinder; he did not trust the man. Regardless, his own people were still inside. The mystral may be young and stubborn, but she was right about one thing: if they were in need, he would do everything in his power to provide it.

"Nextra, Tink—you two stay here and help the doctor. Dozzer, Cylnta—you're with me," he ordered.

"Don't forget the elf that Darkler contacted me about," Cylnta reminded the commander.

"Understood," Quince replied. "We'll get him out."

Solara stopped short, watching the dragon fighting the dwarf and two men. The dragon was beautiful, even more so than she imagined one of the famed beasts would be. Its silvery scales seemed to sparkle with the illumination of the fire. If the beast wasn't fighting and creating such havoc, she would think that it was majestic.

The dragon's head was rounded, its mouth and snout slightly extended from its face. Its eyes were yellow with black slits that were set deeper in its head. Two small horns jutted from its forehead, with four lower to the sides and two much longer ones extending from the back of its head. Its neck was heavily protected with larger and thicker scales, the back of which was spindlier with spikes that jutted from it. Its shoulder blades led to two wings that were closely tucked along its body at the moment. Two arms also came from the shoulder and bent down. Each hand had three long fingers with pointed claws and an opposable thumb. Its underside was smoother, like that of a snake, with horizontal scales that stretched from one side to the other and encompassed its chest, belly, and the bottom of its entire tail. The dragon's back had a single row of large spikes that trailed down its backbone, jutting from larger and thicker scales. Its hind legs had three clawed toes and one additional toe at the back of its foot. Its tail was longer than the entire body of the dragon. The back of which, like its neck, had smaller thick scales and spikes that jutted from it all the way down to an arched tip that appeared to be as sharp as a well-honed double-bladed axe.

Its tail flapped around and swiped at Baldock, who barely dodged in time, wincing when he saw that the statue he was crouching in front of was severed in two just above his head where the dragon struck it. His eyes widened as the tail flung straight at him again, and he dodged aside hearing the remains of the stone statue shattering behind him.

Darkler had been running to help Baldock—he had seen the dragon's second swipe with its tail. He had hoped to push the stunned dwarf aside, but instead became a victim as one of the dragon's back legs kicked out like a horse and knocked him backwards.

Ortrill fared little better. He moved to the side of the dragon and figured that he was safe for a moment while he devised his strategy; the silver dragon did not give him the respite. It extended its wing horizontally and hammered into the master-swordsman, battering him backwards.

"Stop!" Solara cried out. She did not know why a dragon was here, but they were the protectors of the realm, noble beasts that forged a bond with the mystral. From the tales she learned when she was young, a mystral could communicate with a dragon.

Ortrill and Darkler, both of who were forcing themselves back up from their recent attacks, glanced at Adonis and saw him beckon them to stand down. Whether the mystral could get through to it or not was irrelevant. At that moment, they were both grateful for a moment to recollect their wits.

Solara walked forward, her two palms outstretched to show the dragon that she meant no harm. The reptile stopped attacking and looked as if it had calmed down. It lowered its head so that it could look directly at Solara at her own height.

Baldock rubbed his eyes to see if he was really seeing this or whether he was imagining it: the dragon had completely ceased its hostilities! Glancing back at the shattered statue, he decided that was a good thing. Even with all of his bluster, he had to admit that having a dragon as a friend rather than a foe was a much more desired relationship.

"That's it," Solara smiled as she reached out and gently rubbed the dragon's nose. "We're not going to hurt you."

The dragon pulled back slightly, and then swung its neck like a club and slammed into Solara, sending her hurtling through the air. She did not fly that far, but she landed awkwardly on the back of her neck, her consciousness fading away.

"So much for that idea," Adonis called out. None of the others needed any further prompting. The four of them moved forward, engaging the silver-scaled dragon for the second time.

CHAPTER 90

Mylvannan stepped through the doorway and could feel that his strength was already beginning to flee him once again. The flames were higher and fewer spots in the compound were unaffected. Even so, he knew that he could not fail his friends.

"You do not look well, elf," Ravinder observed.

"I will be fine," Mylvannan replied. "I wish to get to Blarg again. Can you see him?"

"I can smell him," Ravinder said with his nose curled in disgust.

"I guess that makes you the guide, then," Mylvannan grinned.

"You are not going to help the others?" Sora asked incredulously.

"We will," Mylvannan assured her. "My sword is mystical: it has the ability to turn things to ice. With this raging inferno, my sword will be an invaluable asset."

"Let me guess," sarcastically said Sora, "—the sword is with Blarg?"

"It is," Mylvannan confirmed. "We shall not be long."

Ravinder narrowed his eyes and displayed a lopsided grin. "Unless I decide that it is time for our rematch."

Mylvannan studied the larger creature for a moment and then shook his head. "There would be no profit and no name in it. You will not harm me now."

"Perhaps," Ravinder replied, his grin broadening.

"We will join the battle soon," Mylvannan told Sora reassuringly.

"The smoke is so thick," Sora said as she coughed several times. "How am I to find the others?"

"Trust in the tiger," Mylvannan advised. "I found Vaz to be quite intuitive when it came to knowing where he needed to be to help the most."

"Good luck then," Sora offered.

"To us all," Mylvannan replied as he clutched Sora by the arm in a parting shake. He then followed Ravinder into the smoke and flames, leaving Sora and the two animal companions behind.

"Can you lead the way?" she asked Vaz.

The white tiger turned and headed in the opposite direction that the elf and horned-creature went. Sora and Tiot followed, though they moved slowly with the fire bursting around them and debris from above caving in every few seconds.

They reached a small clearing and Sora strained to see through the smoke. She thought that she could make out a red-armored form. "Solara?" she called out. Tiot darted forward and stopped by the figure on the floor, and began licking her face.

"It is Solara!" Sora shouted, horrified. Her sister was slumped to the ground, unmoving. Vaz was moving further into the compound, but Sora no longer cared. Her sister was either hurt or dead.

Dropping to her knees, she glanced at Tiot who was still licking Solara's face. "Is she still alive, boy?"

Tiot barked once in confirmation and then continued to lick Solara.

Sora examined her sister and found a lump on the back of her neck, a recent wound by the looks of things. She was relieved to find no blood, at least not externally. Taking a deep breath, she began coughing again from inhaling the smoke.

"We need to get her out of here," Sora explained frantically to Tiot.

Tiot stopped licking Solara's face and bit into one of the straps for her scabbards. He then started to move backwards slowly, gradually dragging Solara with him.

"Good idea," Sora said. She moved to Solara's feet and lifted them up so that they could move her sister more easily. Somewhere behind her, she heard the dragon roar again. With a grimace, she realized that it would be her that failed to join Mylvannan in battle. She wished him well and hoped that they would meet again one day.

Quince led Dozzer and Cylnta back into the compound. The smoke was worse than it had been when they first arrived. "Cylnta, can you blow the smoke away again?"

"Of course," she said as she called upon her magic to create a gust of wind and sweep the room clear of smoke again.

"How about these flames? Any water spells?" he asked.

"That would be more difficult," Cylnta replied. "I need moisture in the air to create a water spell. I'm afraid the flames have removed the moisture."

"Very well," Quince conceded. He examined the landscape and spotted the dragon with ease. It was standing in the midst of fire, apparently not feeling its effect. Adonis, Darkler, Ortrill, and one of the dwarves were engaged with it, though they did not appear to be doing all that well.

"There are the elves that need assistance," Cylnta motioned towards Ashwin and Arifos. "Looks like they're both bound now."

"No," Quince replied. "Our first priority is the dragon. We'll need your help with that. You can use your abilities to try and free the elves afterwards."

"The elves may be able to help," Cylnta objected.

"Perhaps, but by then Adonis and the others may already be dead," Quince decided. "No, we will help with the dragon and then try to free the others."

"They may perish in the fire," Cylnta protested.

"Very well, Dozzer, get them to safety. Cylnta and I are going to help against the dragon."

"Yes sir," Dozzer replied. He then moved swiftly, defying his vast size: his years as a Lumnia middleback had been most advantageous. He zigzagged around the walls of flame as if they were opposing players trying to claim him. He did not pause, and within moments, he was with the elves.

"I'm here to help!" he called out.

Ashwin glanced up appreciatively at him. He was also shocked to see that Vaz was sitting by her side, watching his every move. The cat was acting quite protective of the elves.

Bending down, Dozzer studied the sticky substance that was binding the two.

"Don't touch it," Ashwin cautioned. "It will ensnare you as well."

"Is your companion still alive?" he asked, for the substance completely covered Arifos's face. As if in response, Arifos's foot moved, and the goop slowly moved down his leg to bind it further.

Standing back up, he began to look around at the walls, hoping that he could find something that had not yet burst into flames. A relieved smile creased his lips when he spotted a banner from the royal family of Tenalong hanging on a wall.

"I will be right back," he said. He rushed over to where the banner hung and pulled at the bottom. With his second yank, the clasps broke and the banner fell to the ground in ripples. Dozzer gathered it all together and, folding it as much as he could, placed it under his arms, and then ran back for the elves.

Vaz stepped in front of him and he looked at the tiger with curiosity. He was here to help, why was the tiger stopping him? Vaz then reached up with a claw that had a small cork on the end of one claw. With the danger that the rest of the companions were in, he was shocked that the tiger would distract him for an inconvenience.

Trying to get past the white tiger, Vaz emitted a roar of defiance and barred his path again. "What is it?" he demanded.

"Take the cork," Ashwin advised.

"What for?" Dozzer asked impatiently. "I need to get you out of here."

"Over there, in that goblin's mouth, you'll find an uncorked vial. That is the cork for it."

"I don't see the relevance?" Dozzer asked, but then gave in and pulled the cork from Vaz. He then leaned over and removed the vial from the goblin's mouth and saw that half of the contents were still there. Placing the cork in the neck, he pocketed it.

"Now can I save them?" he asked the tiger.

Vaz seemed appeased. He turned and ran deeper into the lair in the direction of the dragon.

Dozzer still did not understand, but accepted that perhaps he never would. He then dropped the banner over the two elves and used it to protect himself as he picked them up.

"You two are lucky I work out," he said. "With the banner and whatever is stuck to you, you're much heavier than I would have imagined."

Though he felt the strain, he managed to get the wrapped elves up and onto his shoulder. He then headed back towards the entrance, much slower than before.

"Are you certain?" Mylvannan asked, his movements slowing by the heat.

"Would you stop asking me that?" Ravinder shot back in frustration.

The two stopped where they were as the spell of Cylnta flowed over them and blew the smoke away. Mylvannan peered down and saw that he was mere feet away from Blarg's nose.

"Told you I was certain," Ravinder replied impatiently, his arms crossed in mild annoyance.

"I must get to his feet," Mylvannan explained.

"You know the way," Ravinder replied.

The two followed the scorched giant until they reached his feet. The smell of burnt flesh was almost overwhelming, but the two managed to somehow block it out and continue on. They reached the foot where the sword was, and Mylvannan was relieved to see that the ice had melted in the heat and his sword was easily reclaimed.

"I hope that is worth it," Ravinder said.

"It will be," Mylvannan nodded. "It will be indeed."

He used the giant's foot to pull himself up and get a better view. He spotted the dragon. Every second that he remained here, he felt weaker and weaker. It did not matter though—he now had his sword, and soon he would be in battle again. He would find the strength to move on.

Ravinder watched him closely. No matter how confident Mylvannan acted, he could see right through the elf. The doctor had been right: the heat was too much for him. He would not truly help his friends; he would be a burden to them. If he did so, Ravinder knew that he would just as soon kill Mylvannan and take his chances on his own rather than be hampered by a weakened ally.

Returning to the entrance was a slow and painful one. Sora and Tiot had both been burned numerous times as they tried to drag Solara to safety. That fact barely even registered though as they remained focused on the task at hand.

As they reached the entrance, Sora spotted Dozzer moving towards them with a large roll of fabric and four feet sticking out from the end. "What is that?"

"Elves," he replied. "Your sister?"

"Yes," Sora confirmed. "She's hurt."

"Come then, we'll get them all to Doctor Podeis. He is quite skilled."

"He better be," Sora threatened.

"It looks like you could use some treatment yourself," he said as he spotted some blistering and scorch marks on her body.

"I'm fine," she replied.

"Spoken like a true athlete," he laughed.

"An athlete?" she asked.

"I used to play Lumnia. The best players would play through injuries no matter what. They just wanted to make sure that they won, and felt that, even hurt, they were still invincible."

"I see," Sora said.

"Sort of like the Frost elf. He knows that returning here will weaken him, but he will not rest while his friends are in need."

From Dozzer's pocket, the vial of the potion Chill dropped out as if it had a mind of its own. Dozzer frowned and put it back into his pocket. The vial slid back out again. "What is up with this thing?"

"It looks like a potion," Sora shrugged.

Inside the banner, Dozzer could hear the muffled voice of the male elf. He could hardly make out the words, but one of them did sound like "Mylvannan."

"Is it possible for a Mage to lift objects that they can't even see?" asked Dozzer.

"I don't see why not," Sora shrugged, though she really had no clue.

"I wonder if the elf is trying to tell me to give this to Mylvannan?" he speculated. He then scanned the room until he spotted Mylvannan looking out over the fire on the foot of a giant. "There he is."

"What are you going to do?" Sora asked.

Dozzer put the two elves down and then held the potion in his hands. "I was great at this with a ball. I hope that my aim with a vial is as true." Placing both hands to his mouth to try and create a micro-phone effect, he yelled as loudly as he could, "Mylvannan!"

Mylvannan heard him on his fifth attempt, and turned to look at him. Dozzer then threw the vial with all of his might. He was afraid that it wouldn't make it, but as it began to dip, it suddenly evened out and soared right into Mylvannan's waiting hands. He glanced down at the banner with the elves inside and knew that somehow, this was the doing of Arifos.

Mylvannan studied the vial for a moment, and then a thought entered his mind as clear as day. *Drink it.* Without hesitating, he pulled the cork from the vial and drank the sparkling pearlescent-blue liquid. As he did so, he felt his strength begin to return. The flames that were tormenting him no longer had any affect at all. Now, he could help his friends without worrying about being a hindrance.

CHAPTER 91

Baldock jumped from side-to-side, trying to avoid the dragon's tail. He hoped that with one swing of Splitter, he could sever the tail in two. Thus far, the dragon hadn't slowed down enough to give him the chance to even try.

Adonis, Darkler, and Ortrill moved back to join him. They hoped that at least one of them would manage to strike while the others were acting as bait. The dragon seemed to know this and kept trying to force the quartet apart.

When Baldock spotted Mylvannan, he felt that they might actually stand a chance. Perhaps the elf could freeze the dragon in its tracks and end this skirmish right here and now. He certainly hoped so—he was beginning to feel his own skin blistering beneath his scalding armor.

"Elf, will that blasted enchanted sword o' yers stop this durned thing?"

Mylvannan could see the hope in his companion's eyes. He did not want to disappoint Baldock, but when he fought Blarg, his sword hardly had an impact at all. The dragon was much larger than Blarg.

Even so, he had to try. "Only one way to find out," he yelled back. "FRAAZAA!"

"Stupid," Ravinder said behind him.

"What is stupid?" Mylvannan asked as he prepared to charge.

"Let me count the ways," Ravinder mockingly replied. "First, the dragon will stop you before you even reach him. Second, your sword will not have the effect that your dwarven friend hopes. Third, you'll make it even angrier."

"First," Mylvannan said to argue the point, "you are going to make sure I get to the dragon unhindered. Second, I know that my sword will not have the impact that Baldock hopes for. And third, if the dragon is angry, then at least it won't be thinking."

"Still stupid," Ravinder replied. "And what is this about me making sure you get to the dragon unhindered?"

"You're the distraction," Mylvannan smiled.

"You will definitely be paying when this is done," Ravinder sneered.

"I have no gold to offer," Mylvannan shrugged innocently.

"There are other ways to pay—and let me assure you, you shall do so!"

"After you," Mylvannan beckoned him forward.

Ravinder darted out and sprinted towards the dragon. Mylvannan moved almost as swiftly behind him, watching the dragon closely for any movement. Ravinder then leapt up and grabbed on to one of the dragon's wings. He let out a cry as if he were a lion and then dug his claws into the wing.

The dragon stood straight up and started to flap its wings, trying to shake Ravinder off. The horned creature would not release his grip. He dug the nails from his fingers and toes into the wing and solidified his grasp.

As the dragon was flapping wildly, Mylvannan managed to get underneath it and swipe his sword at its less protected belly. The dragon roared in pain, and Mylvannan was pleased to see that the scales began to ice over and become frostbitten.

"It's working!" he cried out.

The dragon flapped its wings harder, lifting it slightly from the ground and impacting the stone ceiling. More debris showered down, causing everyone in the room to shield themselves as a torrent of stones rushed down upon them.

Ravinder struggled to maintain his grasp, but a piece of the ceiling struck him on the back and he slumped to the ground. He struggled to get up again, but he felt numb below his neck. For a warrior such as him, the thought that he could be paralyzed was terrorizing.

The dragon turned in the air and started to drop to the ground again. Mylvannan looked up and realized that he was directly beneath the dragon and would be squashed when it landed. Vaz leapt out and knocked him aside, saving his life at the last instant.

"That be havin' an impact," Baldock beamed. "Good one, elf!"

The silver-scaled dragon then reared back its head, and leaned forward as two streams of flames burst from its nostrils. Baldock raised his shield and winced as the flames poured all around the edges and hit part of his armor. The stream seemed as if it lasted forever.

Once the flame burst stopped, Adonis, Darkler, and Ortrill looked over their bodies, pure shock on their faces as they wondered how they had just survived the blast. They had seen the flames coming straight for them—it was as if they, too, had shields before them.

"You can thank me later," Cylnta said behind them.

"Cylnta," Ortrill laughed. "Am I glad to see you!"

Adonis rushed back to Cylnta. "It's mystical," he said, pointing at the dragon. "Can you somehow dissipate it?"

"Dissipate it?" she asked. "I have never tried something like that before."

"There's a first time for everything," Adonis explained. "We're not even breaching its defenses. This is a losing battle."

"I will try," Cylnta promised.

"Good, that is all we can ask," he said. "Ok men, we need to give her the time she needs. Let's do it!"

All at once, they all rushed forward to press the attack. Adonis, Darkler, and Ortrill remained by its tail, trying to sever it as Baldock originally planned. One by one, each of the ISIA agents were battered away by the dragon.

Mylvannan moved over to its hind leg and tried to freeze it. As he was swinging his sword, the leg kicked out, knocking him backwards and away from it.

Vaz leapt up and onto the back of the dragon, raking his claws over the heavily scaled dragon. The dragon kept twitching, but it was unable to force the tiger from its back.

Baldock rushed to the front and tried to attack the dragon's throat again, hoping to have better success. As he brought Splitter slamming into the dragon, it emitted another ferocious roar and then lowered down and scooped Baldock up into its mouth.

The dwarf was repulsed as he saw the large teeth continuing to come down towards him, trying to crunch him to death. He held his shield up to protect himself, but he could feel that the teeth that dug into him were piercing even his durable illistrium armor.

Mylvannan's eyes widened when the dragon reached down and took Baldock in its mouth. His companion was certainly doomed. Then he heard the familiar gruff and taunting voice of Baldock.

"Is that the best ye got? Bring it on!"

Darkler limped over and helped Ortrill up. "Are you all right?"

"My arm," Ortrill said. "It's broken."

"My ankle is sprained," Darkler said in reply. "We can't give up though: the dragon just ate the dwarf."

"It ate him?"

"Yes," Darkler said. "Come."

The dragon suddenly roared in agony and started to swing its head back and forth quickly. All of the heroes that were still conscious looked up and could see Baldock holding onto the hilt of his axe, which was embedded into the roof of the dragon's mouth. His legs were dangling freely, the inertia from the speed of the dragon thrashing its head about keeping him in the air. If he let go of his axe, he would be flung as if launched from a catapult.

"Quit squirmin', ye blasted reptile!"

Darkler and Ortrill exchange a glance and both snickered. "I definitely like this one," Ortrill said.

Right before their eyes, the dragon faded away as if it had never been. Only the single enchanted tooth remained, falling from the dragon's mouth and clanging to the ground, its powers no longer imbued with mystical energies. Without the substance of the creature to hold Baldock aloft, he hurtled through the air towards one of the remaining walls.

"Oh crud!" he shouted as he flew. A loud, clanging bang rang out as Baldock impacted the wall and vanished behind a river of flames.

Cylnta reached her hand out to Adonis. The Captain allowed her to help him up. Blood was stemming from a gash in his forehead.

"One dragon dissipated," she said and then collapsed into his arms, the strain from the effort overwhelming her.

Adonis glanced around and found Quince rushing towards them. "Get her out of here," he ordered.

"Yes sir," Quince replied. He then cradled Cylnta in his arms and made his way towards an opening in the compound that was formed when the dragon had taken to flight.

Ortrill helped Darkler over to the wall of flame separating them from Baldock. The two peered through it but could not see the dwarf. Was he even alive? If the impact didn't kill him, the flames could have just as easily.

"How do we get to him?" Ortrill asked.

"Like this," Mylvannan cried out as he swung his still-enchanted sword at the flames. Before their eyes, the fire he hit solidified into ice and spread throughout the area, stopping the fire closest to them.

"Impressive," Darkler said. "I'm glad you don't hold grudges from our battle at Trespias."

"It has already been forgotten," Mylvannan assured him. He glanced over at the edges of his ice and saw that the fire on the sides was already beginning to melt it. "We must hurry."

Ortrill lifted his sword with his good arm and broke his way through the ice. Baldock was sitting against the wall on the other side, his entire suit of armor covered in saliva and soot. "There he is!"

Baldock raised his head after a few bobs and opened his eyes to look at his saviors. "Did I get it?"

Ortrill laughed at the absurdity of the question. "You got it."

Baldock smiled triumphantly and then passed out.

Adonis joined them and looked at the dwarf. Noting that his own men were injured, he reached down and tried to pick the armored dwarf up himself. With his heavily plated armor, he was unable to do it alone. "I need help."

"Mylvannan sheathed Frostlartil and grabbed Baldock's legs. "Someone make sure that you get his shield and axe. If you don't, we'll never hear the end of it."

"I got it," Darkler said as he flung the shield over his back and grasped the axe in his hand. As he did so, his ankle suddenly did not feel as hurt, and he swore that his entire body somehow felt reinvigorated.

Mylvannan heard a sizzling and got the distinctive smell of burning flesh. He glanced down and was horrified to see that the heat of Baldock's armor was burning through the white gloves he wore beneath his gauntlets. The potion he drank may keep him from feeling the heat, but he could see that his hands were still burning.

As they started to leave, Vaz darted in front of them and began to lead them away. He paused only once in his path, directly before Ravinder.

Ravinder strained to look up. "A little help would be nice."

"Ravinder!" Mylvannan called out. "Are you hurt?"

"It appears that I may be paralyzed," he said, doing his best to keep the fear from his voice.

"Darkler, Ortrill," Adonis called out and his two men helped Ravinder as well. Neither was strong enough to carry him, but Vaz lay down next to the larger man and they managed to lift him onto the tiger's back.

Vaz then retook the point and led them from the burning lair of the Hidden Empire. They had survived the criminal element, mercenaries, and even a dragon. Still, the flames threatened to consume them. Three times Vaz had to pause as he was leading them and find another way to go. Ultimately, the injured group reached the doorway and hobbled out into the clear night air.

As they did, they all stopped and stared blankly ahead. Would this night never end? Dozens of rasplers surrounded them. They were encircling the entire compound of the Hidden Empire.

"Stand ready, men," Adonis instructed as he and Mylvannan lowered the unconscious Baldock to the ground.

"Captain," Darkler spoke up. "I lived with rasplers for a bit. Perhaps I can speak to them."

Adonis knew that his sergeant had spent several years with the rasplers. It was a time when Lady Salaman had placed a death mark on his head. Instead of fleeing into the Seven Kingdoms as the bounty hunters had presumed, he had ventured into the swamps and met these lizard men. He had even learned their language.

Reaching down, he held the hilt of Crimbaya just in case they could not get out of this by talking. "Try," he instructed.

"Wait!" a female voice called out. Adonis searched and saw Sora calling to them, Nextra by her side. "They are friends."

"Friends?" Adonis asked as he scanned the reptilian creatures, all holding large axes and spears.

"Yes," Sora said. She stepped next to one of the rasplers and took his arm. "This is Shrestellishar, and he is our friend. We helped to save some of his people and his pack came to make sure we did not need further assistance."

"The myssstral ssspeaksss the truth," Shrestellishar declared. "We alssso caught sssome of thossse that tried to essscape."

Adonis followed the gaze of Shrestellishar and saw close to fifty orcs, goblins, hobgoblins, and humans surrounded by rasplers. Nodding in approval, he took his hand off of his hilt and extended it towards the raspler. "I am Adonis, Captain of ISIA. A pleasure to make your acquaintance."

CHAPTER 92

As he stood atop a hill watching the events as they unfolded below, Kabilian had to admit that he was shocked by the outcome. Though he was unable to witness what had happened inside the Hidden Empire lair with his mystical dragon and his foes, he had seen it crumble large sections of the complex and attack viciously. Somehow, though, they had apparently defeated it.

He watched as the so-called heroes of the realm limped from the burning lair. Very few had emerged completely unscathed, but none of the wielders of the fabled mystical items had been mortally wounded or slain. Though disappointed by not being able to claim the items as his own, he was also relieved in a way.

These magic-wielding warriors had gained his admiration—even the loud and annoying Baldock. They deserved better fates than to fall victim to a dragon that he summoned as a distraction. They deserved to die in combat, face-to-face, with him introducing them to their makers.

The thought was a pleasant one. The companions may escape this day, but tomorrow would weave a different tale. With the Ring of Eternity on his finger, Kabilian had ceased aging long ago. When it came to tomorrow, he had endless opportunities to seek the right moment to face these particular foes again.

He was certain that Crick would remain by his side in these conquests. The hobgoblin was like a sponge, trying to learn new ways and leave those of his people behind—though he did still have trouble with certain concepts. Kabilian also knew that he would ultimately face the mystral again, for Crick would undoubtedly wish to increase his armaments from the warrior women. The hobgoblin's newfound respect and pledge not to harm any of them may make things a little trickier, but they would pursue them in the future.

The apparent newfound allies of the heroes intrigued him as well. It was something that he had not expected, and in truth, never would have fathomed. Rasplers were known enemies of man, elf, and dwarf alike, yet they were assisting the injured and helping to heal wounds. It was an alliance that was worth noting—and Kabilian always made certain that he had accurate information with most matters he looked into.

"You lost your dragon," Crick said slowly, as if he was afraid that the revelation would enrage his companion.

"That I did," Kabilian agreed. "It's okay. I still have another."

"Another dragon?" Crick asked in awe. "You control the mighty beasts that the mystral ride?"

"Yes, like the mystral *used to* ride," Kabilian said to appease his companion. "I acquired two of the mystical teeth at the same time. Losing one is a blow, but certainly not something that is too hard to accept. Replacing the scar will be much more difficult though, if not impossible."

Crick watched the man for a moment, giving him several minutes to think in silence. He knew that Kabilian was in deep contemplation as he studied the survivors below. Ultimately, he broke the silence with a question that was nagging at him. "What do we do now?"

"Now, we're free agents," Kabilian shrugged.

"Free agents?" Crick asked, struggling with the concept. "What does that mean?"

"It means that we are no longer aligned with the Hidden Empire," Kabilian explained. "By not going to Lady Salaman's assistance when she called, we will no longer be welcome here."

Crick was confused by the implications: why would Kabilian wish to remain aligned with the Hidden Empire? It was nothing more than a smoldering ruin. With his people, if a tribe was destroyed, then a rival tribe would absorb the survivors, increasing their strength and numbers. If any leaders from the original tribe survived, they would be slain to prevent any future revolts in the new hierarchy.

"We are loners now," Kabilian continued. "Reporting to no one. Now, we'll do what we want, when we want."

"Perhaps you can do that, and not have to look over your shoulders for the rest of your lives," a voice commented from behind.

Kabilian drew Pandring and spun around, ready for battle. In the dead of the moonless night, it was hard for him to make out the features of the newcomer. He was wearing shadow-black clothing with purple outlines. The only feature that Kabilian could clearly make out was his vibrant yellow eyes as they peered through the veil of darkness.

"How is that?" Kabilian asked, his sword still poised ready to strike.

"My employer could be considered a, shall we say, rival of Lady Salaman. She is willing to make certain accommodations to ensure that Lady Salaman never bothers you again, and at the same time, allow you to be as independent as you desire."

"I'm sure," Kabilian said dubiously. "At what price?"

"No price," the man replied. "One day my employer will have reason to call upon your services, and you shall return her favors in kind."

"Right," Kabilian said sarcastically. "And who exactly is your employer?"

"I'm afraid that my employer would like to keep her true identity anonymous. I'm sure you understand."

"Then at least tell me who you are," Kabilian prompted.

"Who I am is unimportant," he returned. "What is important is this generous offer."

"No," Kabilian said. "Not interested."

"Do not be so hasty in your judgment," the man cautioned.

"You wish me to accept an offer of a new allegiance with a rival criminal organization, yet you do not reveal the name of the head of that organization, nor even the name of her herald? I think not."

"I see that this is a sticking point," the man replied. "I would not wish to have you make your decision solely on the lack of a name. I am Archer."

"And your employer?"

"Shall remain anonymous," Archer sternly returned. "Some things will not be revealed."

"I could make you tell me," Kabilian said, a gleam of anticipation in his eyes.

"You could try," Archer replied. "However, I take my vows very seriously. You would not be successful."

"I have not yet met an individual that I could not, shall we say, persuade," Kabilian grinned. "I do not expect you to be the one to change that trend."

"Try if you must," Archer said. "You will find me most unaffected by your attempts. When I make a vow of secrecy, I keep it."

"Fair enough," Kabilian said, though he did not truly believe that this man would be able to refrain from answering his questions for long if he was being tortured. "What's the catch? Why does she want us?"

"My employer has foreseen that you will play a pivotal role in the events that will unfold. When that time comes, she merely wishes to make certain that you are able to fulfill your role."

"She has precognition?" Kabilian asked, intrigued by the possibility that Archer's employer was a Mage.

"Amongst other gifts," Archer admitted. "Do we have a deal?"

Kabilian pondered the implications of Archer's words for a minute. He was to play a pivotal role in the events that would unfold. What was that? Which side would he be on? Did it have to do with the takeover of Trespias, or was it something more diabolical? Either way, he was not pleased with the fact that his fate was apparently written. He was a master of his own fate. If that proved to not be so, Kabilian knew that he must discover what his destiny truly was, and quickly.

"I won't be dictated to," Kabilian commented, probing for more information. "If she wants me to do things that I am not willing to do, I won't do it."

"Then we have no problem," Archer replied, brushing off the concern.

"Is this a once-in-a-lifetime offer?" Kabilian asked.

"No, you need not make a decision this day," Archer admitted as he glanced back and forth between Kabilian and Crick. "Though there is a definite time-constraint. Your foreseen role will be upon you sooner than you may think. My employer would, of course, like you to be under her guidance when that time comes."

"Very well," Kabilian said. "I hate to disappoint your employer, but for now, the answer is no. We'll take our chances on our own."

Crick glanced over and was shocked. This new employer was like a new tribe absorbing the old. Why were they not going willingly?

"That is most regrettable," Archer said. "That too, I'm afraid, is as my employer foresaw. In time your position shall change."

"Perhaps," Kabilian said, wondering again who exactly this mysterious employer was. "Come when you have need of me. With more specifics, I may give you a decision that is more agreeable to your employer's wishes."

"As you wish," Archer said, his voice starting to fade as he backed into the darkness and vanished from sight.

"What was that all about?" Crick asked. He still could not understand why Kabilian did not agree. Just as his people absorbed their defeated foes into their ranks, were they not better off in larger numbers?

"I'm not certain," Kabilian said. "But I intend to find out."

"Why did you not agree?" Crick pressed, seeking to understand the decision.

"I did not just get out from under the thumb of one crime-lord to get under another's. We will stay independent for now, and let the future unfurl, as it will.

Crick watched Kabilian as he sheathed his sword and went back to watching the survivors below. He still did not completely understand, but he also knew that he had abandoned his own people, and as such, abandoned their beliefs. Perhaps being absorbed into another criminal organization was not the way to go. Perhaps Kabilian was right, and they were better off alone. Accepting this to be true, he realized that he still had a lot to learn in life, and hopefully Kabilian would be a good mentor in his endeavors to do so.

Kabilian continued to watch the figures below. Some were grouped together and talking, others were off by themselves—all of them watched as the Hidden Empire lair continued to burn in the night. The future was not yet written, regardless of what Archer said. Smiling to himself, he thought that perhaps the future was written, for it was obvious that one day he would confront the companions again—and on that day, their mystical weapons would exchange hands.

CHAPTER 93

The lair of the Hidden Empire burned long into the night. Those that had partaken in the battle all sat watching as the flames continued to rage. None of them had come out unscathed—physically or mentally—but they had survived. The question on everyone's minds: what happens now?

Doctor Podeis had his work cut out for him, but in time, even he managed to find some time to rest, his patients all stable. The rasplers had helped quite a bit as well, a fact that was clearly apparent with Thamar.

The red-bearded dwarf sat with his companions watching the fire burn. His eyesight had not yet completely returned, but he could see shimmering lights in front of a darkened background. A slimy greenish-yellow substance that looked like bile and smelled worse than a goblin's den covered his face. The rasplers assured him that it had great healing properties and that the red blistering of his face would not leave scars.

His brother was also awake now, a new set of bandages wrapped around him. The blood had finally stemmed and he was slowly on his way to recovery. Podeis made certain that he checked on Theiler every thirty minutes or so.

The sticky goop that had bound Arifos and Ashwin was removed shortly after Cylnta had gained enough strength to try to counter the spell. The two elves were very grateful. Arifos had not stopped moving since, including several sprints by himself to clear his mind and find harmony with his body.

Baldock finally awoke, famished. Doctor Podeis made him strip out of his armor and they placed it into the swamp water to help it cool down. Beneath the armor, his companions all laughed at his pale white skin that looked completely awkward with his heavily tanned face. He brushed off the laughs with a shrug and feasted on food provided by the rasplers. He ate as if it was the first time he had ever done so.

Vaz remained protectively by Vella's side. Doctor Podeis assured Ashwin and Sora that the tiger would be all right and just needed rest. She acted as weak as a kitten, but both women felt that the tiger was exaggerating the severity of her condition to gain more sympathy from her mate.

Solara sat silently next to Thamar. The two held hands and did not speak. Tiot was also with them, his head resting comfortable on Solara's thigh. For those that knew Thamar, it was an awkward silence, as he rarely refrained from telling stories. In their own way though, they were both finally mourning their lost loved ones, taking comfort in the presence of each other.

Mylvannan had his hands tended to and bandaged. He sat with Ravinder, poking and prodding the man with a small stick. Though Doctor Podeis said that there was nothing he could do, they found Ravinder twitching and moving several hours later, which was why Mylvannan was having fun with him. Ravinder assured Mylvannan that he would pay for this. The elf laughed and taunted the horned man in reply. Each time, Ravinder seemed to regain more and more motion. Doctor Podeis was amazed at the rate of recovery and commented more than once that Ravinder had phenomenal recuperative abilities.

Darkler's ankle started to bother him again as soon as he gave the axe back to Baldock. The dwarf didn't seem to know what he was talking about when he mentioned that it was enchanted, but affirmed it definitely was an amazing axe. Doctor Podeis wrapped his ankle and told him to stay off of it for a while. He did his best to listen and sat down with three of the rasplers that he had known when he lived among them.

Ortrill had his arm in a sling and then went straight to sleep. Tink sat close by him and kept tossing small stones at the swordsman. Every time he woke up, he looked around and then went back to sleep. Minutes later, the inventor would do it again. Dozzer watched on and was amazed that not even once did Ortrill scream or protest. It was as if the two were playing a game and trying to see which one would last the longest.

Adonis had some bandages around his head and sat with Quince, Cylnta, and Nextra. They had discussed the feasibility of trying to incarcerate the prisoners that the rasplers had rounded up, but—in the end—decided that they did not have the ability to do so. Garum was corrupt, so bringing them to Fenland would be a waste of time. With most of ISIA off to war, they also did not have the resources to bind them at Trespias. Ultimately, they decided to let the rasplers determine the fates of the prisoners.

Even with the Hidden Empire burnt to the ground and its operatives rounded up, they all knew that Lady Salaman would be back. She had eluded the rasplers and was still at-large, along with some of her most loyal lieutenants. Whether she came back here or found a new lair, the Hidden Empire would be built again. The only unknown with that was whether or not the crime-lord would still have enough influence when she rebuilt, or whether some other despot would come to power.

Tales were eventually told throughout the night. The adventures, tragedies, and experiences that each had been through over the past several months were relived in the somber voices of the speakers. Even Thamar, when he spoke, talked slowly and without the excitement that Solara remembered from the first time she had heard him tell his tales.

They all felt closer that night. They had begun from very different places and with different goals, but all ultimately wound up fighting for the same cause. Their goals were just, and as they spoke, more of the mystery of what was happening had unfurled. Still, the one question that remained unanswered: what happens now?

CHAPTER 94

The room they were in was truly majestic. It was as if the walls themselves were made from solid crystal. The floor was white with golden designs crafted into them, and the ceiling looked as if it was an open blue sky filled with white clouds. Ilfanti paced the room anxiously. He had made a decision, and all that he needed to do now was implement it.

His fellow Council of Elders members, Cala and Herg, walked into the room with Master Askari, Cicero, and Captain Centain, who had undergone a complete recovery thanks to the Mage Healers. The six of them were about to conspire a plot that would not be favored in the Mage's Council, but one that all of them felt was vital to the survival of the realm.

With all of them in the room, Ilfanti waved his hand and the hallway closed, leaving only the crystal walls completely encircling them. He then closed his eyes and raised his arms outwards. Ten rays of yellow light shot from his fingertips and struck the crystal walls—an almost prism-like effect reflected the light and turned the entire room into a warm, glowing radiance.

"It is safe now," Ilfanti said.

"What was that?" Cicero asked.

"This will protect us from any prying eyes or ears," Ilfanti said. "While within the light, we are safe from being overheard."

"Then you intend to go through with the plan?" Herg asked.

"I do," Ilfanti said. "I see no other alternative."

"If only Pierce had not declared that the Mage's Council was now sealed. Without his directive, we cannot do this without violating the laws of the order," Cala explained.

"It does not matter," Ilfanti said. "We have all seen how badly things have become. The news from Master Ferceng and Master Askari has confirmed a lot of what we thought was happening, but would not admit."

"Zoldex is indeed back, and he is looking to claim the Seven Kingdoms as his own," Askari said.

"Yes," Ilfanti concurred, "though I fear that it will go deeper than that. Perhaps even the Mage's Council itself will be threatened."

"Do you think he would really challenge us?" Cala asked.

"He was banished by Pierce," Ilfanti pointed out. "If I were him, I would want vengeance on the man that banished me."

"As would I," Centain said. "I want to return to the palace and bring Winton to justice. I know everything that he has been up to thanks to my bond with the Harlocten plants. He must not get away with this."

"He will not," Ilfanti promised. "But everything must be done perfectly; timed perfectly."

Centain clenched his fist in frustration. He could not stand to think of Winton sitting on the Empress's throne.

"We must be prepared for two things," Ilfanti explained. "First, we must find the Empress and bring her back. When she was kidnapped, the unification fell apart. To survive this ordeal, we cannot allow that to happen. Karleena must return and see her dreams reach fruition."

"She is not in Aezia," Askari pointed out. "No matter what the palace has declared."

"Winton is up to something," Centain agreed. "He must be in league with Zoldex."

"Whether he is or not," Ilfanti said as he lifted his finger, "the return of the Empress will force him to relinquish the throne."

"What is the second thing, Master Ilfanti?" Askari asked.

"Until we recover the Empress, we must find a way to confront Zoldex and help the rest of the realm."

"This will be most difficult with Pierce's current decree," Cala reminded them.

"But not impossible," Ilfanti grinned. "Askari—you and Cicero were instructed to assist the Empress in the unification, correct?"

"Yes," Askari nodded. "But that mission had been completed when Winton dismissed us."

"I say it's not," Ilfanti sternly replied. "Follow your initial directive. Help the Empress the best you can. At least, until she tells you herself that your services are no longer required."

"A deception?" Askari asked, glancing at his apprentice and hoping that their mission here was not corrupting Cicero.

"Call it 'following through with something you started,'" Herg grinned.

"Very well," Askari agreed.

"I would recommend that you start helping by returning to Aquatica," Ilfanti said. "From what we know, your sister may have sustained severe injuries. Go to her, help her, and make sure that Aquatica is safe from the influence of Zoldex."

"That is not helping the Empress," Askari pointed out.

"Sure it is," Ilfanti shrugged. "Sovereign Arianna is involved in the unification talks. As such, the directive expands to ensuring the presence of the aquaticans in all such negotiations."

"Thank you," Askari said, relieved that he would be able to try and help his sister and make certain she was all right.

"How are we going to find the Empress?" Centain asked.

"That will be my task," Ilfanti said.

"I am her protector. The job falls to me," Centain objected.

"Not this time, I'm afraid," Ilfanti said. "We are not after the Empress yet. Instead, my research has revealed a mystical item known as the Orb of Prophecy that will allow us to determine her true whereabouts. I will be going after it."

"I could come with you," Centain offered.

"When we go after Karleena, you will be by my side. For this though," Ilfanti began grinning, "it's my specialty."

"I don't understand," Centain said.

"Ilfanti was something of an adventurer during his Paladin years," Cala explained.

"More than that," Herg said. "He was a regular treasure hunter, seeking priceless relic after priceless relic."

"Exactly," Ilfanti said. "This will be like returning home for me."

"Be careful, and don't be too cocky," Cala cautioned. "It's been three centuries since you've stopped your wild days."

"Perish the thought," Ilfanti said. "I've never stopped being wild. Perhaps I haven't been out in the world, but I also have not lost a step. I will be fine."

"How long will this quest take you?" Centain asked.

"It will not be short, I'm afraid," Ilfanti said. "If I can acquire a fast ship, I can reach Egziard in about four months. From there, I will need to make my way to Ramahatra, which will take probably another month if the desert is accommodating."

"So the earliest you could be back is ten months?" Centain asked, not happy with the fact that the Empress would remain lost for so long.

"Actually, it will probably be longer than that," Ilfanti said. "I have learned that when it comes to Egziard, time has a way of flowing as quickly as the sand in the wind."

"Wonderful," Centain sulked.

"Do not worry," Herg tried to cheer him up. "Ilfanti has allies there. That may help to speed things up."

Centain glanced up, an eyebrow raised.

"It's true," Ilfanti said. "An old friend of mine, Osorkon, and I spent many years locating lost tombs, bringing some wondrous artifacts out for the dwarves of Memtorren. They remain as some of their most prized possessions, a lure for those to see from miles around."

"This Osorkon is still alive?" Centain asked.

"I certainly hope so," Ilfanti laughed. "We have a lot of catching up to do!"

"What am I to do then?" Centain asked. "How will I meet you upon your return?"

"I have been in contact with the Elandeeril of Faylinn. They have agreed to allow us to converge there for our meeting. Upon my return, the Elandeeril will help me to communicate with all of the individuals that must attend. They will then be guided to Faylinn."

Ilfanti walked over and stood before Centain, a knowing look in his eyes. "I trust that you will know how to get there without my message?"

"Yes," Centain admitted.

"Then perhaps it is time for you to return there and visit your ancestors. The Healers have returned your health, but you must reclaim your vitality on your own. The elves can assist you."

"Very well," Centain nodded.

"Excellent," Ilfanti said. "Then let the three of you be off before anyone notices that I placed a similar protection spell along the western stream to allow you to leave the Mage's Council undetected."

Askari, Cicero, and Centain all bowed and began to walk out. The wall reverted back to a hallway to let them leave. As soon as they exited, Ilfanti sealed it again.

"Are you sure about this?" Cala asked.

"I am," Ilfanti said.

"You'll be removed from the Council," Cala warned him.

"I never wanted to serve on it anyway," he said. "I agreed to it as a condition to train you."

"And I appreciate that," Cala said. "But still, you are well respected and a great Council member: to lose you would be tragic."

"It is still a Council, not a dictatorship," Ilfanti reminded his elven friend. "There must be a vote to remove me."

"I know where my vote stands," Herg said.

"Mine too," Cala agreed.

"See, two already in my favor," Ilfanti's face broadened into a wide smile. "For now, just tell Pierce that since the three of us always agree, I gave you two permission to vote for me: the two of your votes will just have to count as three."

"I'm sure that will go over real well," Herg snickered.

"Pierce isn't going to like this," Cala warned one last time in protest.

"By the time he finds out, it will be too late to do anything," Ilfanti said. "Besides, Zoldex is his ancient foe. If he is too set in his ways to realize that he will be challenged, then we should not be following his lead anymore anyway."

"Are you really as confident about finding the Orb of Prophecy as you sounded?" Herg asked.

"Oh, I will find it," Ilfanti said. "What else I find with it will be the question."

"You are worried about Ramahatra?" Herg asked.

"Not worried," Ilfanti said brushing off the concern. "It's just that first I need to find it. Then, when I do, the people there are fanatics. They won't want to give up the Orb just because I tell them its vital to the future of the Seven Kingdoms."

"I'm sure you'll think of something," Cala said. "You always do."

"Yes, it will be just like that time in Cortrel when I saw a jewel the size of a goblin's head in the hands of an evil tyrant. I knew immediately that it was mystical by the way it radiated and that I needed to get it away from him and make sure that the people—who were quite poverty stricken—managed to gain a fair-footing with their self-proclaimed master."

Cala and Herg both listened to Ilfanti for hours as he retold a story that he had told many times in the past. This was the dwarf that they knew, the storyteller who relived his glory days in elaborate tales that had diabolical fiends, noble goals, vast treasures, the mysteries of the unknown, and always a damsel-in-distress. They both hoped that his return to his former occupation would not be a bad one, and that he would find the success that they all knew he needed to claim—the lives of all of those who lived in the Imperium depended upon it.

EPILOGUE

"The horses are growing weary," Shiel observed.

"We will be in Brigdin soon," Angel explained.

"Are you sure it exists? I've never heard of it."

"It exists," Angel confirmed. "You'll not find it on any map, and that's exactly the way the people want it. It's a haven for pirates and outcasts—ruffians. We'll have to be cautious going in."

"You're sure that this is a good idea?" Shiel asked pensively.

"If the rumors are true," Angel grinned.

"A woman that can best any man," Shiel said, repeating the story they had heard. "One that is the child of a giant and a barbarian."

"So the story says," Angel nodded.

"How can a barbarian and giant mate?" Shiel asked. "I don't even find the tale believable."

"It does sound a bit farfetched," Angel agreed. "But I am from Falestia. I know that the barbarians and giants have struggled over the open-range between the Kreblahn and Ordell Mountains for centuries. It's possible that during one such raid, a giant did indeed capture and rape a female barbarian."

"Perhaps," Shiel said, though she was not convinced.

"Well, we'll see soon enough," Angel said.

"As long as we survive the experience," Shiel argued.

"Hey, you're with me," Angel grinned. "No worries."

"That's easy for you to say," Shiel sighed.

Seeing that the former handmaiden was concerned, Angel decided to change topics to something that would be less intimidating. "By the way, I love what you and your handmaidens did with my uniform."

"You can't call the little that you have left a uniform," Shiel snickered.

Angel glanced down and could not see what Shiel was talking about. She had asked the handmaidens to modify her wardrobe into something fitting for her personality, and she thought that they had done an exceptional job.

The black leather bodysuit that all Imperial soldiers wore beneath their armor had been completely cut down. Now, the skintight garment was sleeveless and also ended directly below her chest. The collar still extended half way up her neck, with two gold bars on the right side of her neck indicating her rank as a Captain in the Imperial Army. Elbow-length black gloves covered her arms with white armor plating over her wrists. Though her shoulders and upper arms were bare—allowing her thorn-slash tattoo to be clearly displayed on her left arm—she did have white-armored shoulder protectors. A black cloak with a green satin underside—resembling the colors of the Imperium—was fastened around her neck by a round emerald and black clasp.

Her skintight black leather pants fit firmly at her hips and covered her legs down into her black boots. White-armored plating was fastened over her shins and knees. The armor covering her knees and shoulders both had finely crafted and detailed emblems of the white tiger carved into them. This was an idea of Shiel's that Angel had liked. They were sworn to serve the Empress and preserve the Imperium, so as such, they took on the symbol of the Empress. This emblem was found on all of the units' armor and shields.

Two white straps with emerald designs were clasped to her belt, which was emerald and had a black outlining. Each strap held the sheath of a modified drantana to the left side of her leg, one slightly higher than the other. The two blades had black and white woven hilts with an emerald pommel. She had a matching hilted dagger fastened to a clasp around the back of her calf.

"It's better than what you're wearing," Angel shot back.

Shiel had to admit that Angel was right. She had never professed to be a fighter, and her garments clearly displayed that. She was wearing a long white gown with her hair pulled back and tied into a ponytail. A matching shawl was resting on her shoulders. Her neck had an elegant necklace hanging from it, a gift she had received by her mother when she was very young.

Like Angel though, Shiel, too, had a modified drantana. A wide belt was laced across her waist, making her gown look as if it were two separate pieces. A drantana was strung to one side, and a dagger to the other. She did not feel comfortable using the weapons, but she had been improving steadily since they had left Trespias.

"I prefer to at least try and remain *somewhat* elegant," Shiel shrugged.

"Hey, that's your choice," Angel said. "When every man in that place starts ogling you and tries to steal your necklace, don't say I didn't warn you."

"Sounds just like the kind of place *you* would fit it," Shiel observed with a wry smile.

"It does, doesn't it?" Angel snickered. "Look, there it is."

The two rode into Brigdin and left their horses tied to poles. The town, if it could be called that, was little more than a dozen taverns, assorted merchant shops, and one shipyard. Those that lived in Brigdin had their own facilities within their workplaces. Visitors either rented a room from one of the taverns, slept in their own boats, or on the muddy streets.

Brigdin was loud. Bar fights could be heard throughout the streets—windows, bottles, and wooden chairs breaking. Drunks could be seen at almost every turn, either passed out, mugging those weaker than them, or vomiting.

Shiel felt very exposed walking through the streets with Angel. From the dark alleys, eyes peered out and followed the two women. She saw men that looked as if they had not bathed in years suddenly emerging from small holes and rotted buildings. They all looked hungrily at the two.

They spotted one building that looked far-better preserved than the others, a fence surrounding it and guards posted at a gate. The house itself was three-stories-high and had smoke pouring from a chimney.

"What is that?" Shiel asked. "It seems out of place."

"That would be the overseer," Angel said. "All of these little un-marked towns have one. Whoever lives there runs this town. They get a percentage of every coin spent, and they also uphold the law—so to speak."

"What do you mean?" Shiel asked.

"They'll only interfere and have their own private enforcers be-come involved if an incident breaks-out that disturbs business—wouldn't want to have their pockets a little less-lined in gold."

"I'm surprised that this is actually in the Imperium," Shiel said. "I thought that things were better than this."

"They are, for the most part," Angel said. "These towns are all over, though. They attract the less desirable elements. Since they are only harming themselves, most people feel that these towns should be left alone."

"Where do we find Otkatla?" Shiel asked, hoping to leave this place as soon as they could.

"Find the loudest bar fight, I would wager," Angel shrugged.

At the end of the muddy road, a window shattered and a man rolled out into the street.

"Might as well try there first," Angel suggested.

The two walked over to the tavern and stepped inside. If the woman inside was not Otkatla, then they would settle with the woman they found. She was seven-and-a-half feet tall and had cropped brown hair, as if she was trying to pass for a man. Her skin held a dark, tanned complexion. Her face was set in a leering scowl that appeared stern and focused.

One man was trapped at her hip in a headlock. The woman they presumed to be Otkatla was punching him in the head with her fist as another charged towards her. She whipped the man around and flung him into his companion, both crumbling to the ground. Two large and muscular men closed in on her from behind.

"Should we help her?" Shiel asked.

Angel grabbed a seat, sat down and put her feet up. "Hell no," she said. "This is too good to pass up."

"She could get hurt," Shiel protested.

"She started it," Angel said. "Besides, we'll consider this an audition."

The two men grabbed Otkatla by each arm and held her so she could not move. Another rushed towards her, a barstool in his hand. He brought the stool crashing down over her head and Otkatla stumbled a bit, blood beginning to stream from her nose.

"Again," one of the men said.

The two men forced Otkatla back up again as the third man grabbed another barstool. He went to crash that one down as well, but Otkatla strained and forced both men before her with a cry to the barbarian god of Earth, Wind, and Fire, "Xeorn!"

The two muscular men bumped heads as she whipped them into each other, and wound up with the barstool breaking over them as well. As they slumped to the ground, Otkatla reached out, grabbed the third attacker, lifted him over her head, and threw him through a decrepit wooden wall.

"Not me place!" the bartender cried out. "Not again!"

A pair of men, who looked almost as large as the two she rendered unconscious, slowly approached her, their fists up to defend themselves. Otkatla watched them for a moment, and then leapt forward. She landed on her hands in front of him and sprung back up, her feet connecting with each man in the chin.

Several others fled the bar and she watched them go. One man was not as wise, though. He grabbed a bottle and tried to sneak up on her. He crashed the bottle over her head, and an infuriated Otkatla swung and backhanded him across the face, twirling him in the air with the power of her blow.

Angel began clapping her hands.

Otkatla glared at her. "Who are you?" she demanded.

"My name is Angel," she said. "And I have a proposition for you."

"I'm not interested," Otkatla sneered.

"Don't be so hasty," Angel replied. "What can this life possibly be like? Bar fight after bar fight? Where is the challenge? Where is the fun?"

Otkatla glared at her for a moment. "What do you suggest?"

"I've started a military unit that is full of women. The Seven Kingdoms are at war. We are all that remain to stand in the way. Join us."

"We're not at war," Otkatla shook her head thinking that she was being duped.

"You may not think so this far north, but we are indeed at war," Angel said. "I could use you."

Otkatla turned her gaze on Shiel. "Are all of your warriors as pretty as that?"

"Some," Angel agreed.

"Then your army is doomed," Otkatla replied as she backhanded her nose to wipe some blood away. "She doesn't look like she could even hold her own against a rabbit."

"Even more reason for you to join us and help train the unit," Angel said. "What do you have here that is so important?"

Otkatla glanced around the tavern. The barkeeper was hiding behind the bar. She could hear his whimpering over the repair costs he'd undoubtedly be paying yet again. Other than the three women, the rest of the tavern was empty of life, her unconscious foes lying where they fell. Life here was one big battle: a daily battle for survival.

She had been an outcast from her own people. Though the barbarians said that they accepted her, she could see it in their eyes and the way they treated her: the genes of the giant that had bedded her mother tainted her. No matter what they said, she was an outcast, and Brigdin was just one destination where an outcast wound up. A place where people did not ask many questions, and the strength in one's arms often indicated the hierarchy. Even so, very few wanted to succumb their highly developed senses of value to a woman, which resulted in more fights in whichever tavern she visited.

She wondered if starting over with Angel and her companion would be so bad. Joining the military did not sound very appealing. It fact, it sounded very restricting—but when she studied the garb of the two before her, she thought that perhaps this unit was not as structured and formal. It would indeed feel good to actually be wanted some-place.

"Fine," Otkatla said.

"You'll come with us?" Angel asked.

"Yes," Otkatla replied.

"Not so fast, Otkatla," a man said from the doorway. "You'll be spending the night in the tank for this."

"I don't think so," Angel said. "This woman is coming with me."

"And who are you then?" the man asked.

"I am Captain Angel, a representative of the Imperial Army."

"That's fine and well, Captain," the man said. "But you have no jurisdiction here. You can pick up your prisoner in the morning."

"Otkatla is not my prisoner," Angel said with a harsh edge. "She is to become an officer in the Empress's army."

The man glanced at his partner and both started laughing. "I'd like to see that."

"Do not worry," Otkatla said. "I am used to this. It has become my nighttime home."

"That's because you do so much property damage," the guard shook his head.

"I'll see you in the morning," Otkatla said.

"We'll be waiting," Angel replied, not happy with the way this was turning out.

The two followed the guards out of the tavern and watched as they brought Otkatla over to a hole dug in the ground. They forcibly pushed her inside and then slammed an iron-barred lid over the top.

"Are we going to stand for this?" Shiel asked.

"No, we'll wait an hour or so and then get her out," Angel replied. As she glanced at Shiel, she paused. "You look like you've just seen a ghost."

"I think I have," Shiel said. "Is that who I think it is?"

Angel followed Shiel's finger, and her mouth dropped open. "It is!"

The man had not noticed them yet. He was garbed predominantly in black with baggy pants flowing into knee-high light-gray boots. He had a black surcoat with golden shoulder pads, and silver plated armor was woven into the front and back of his jacket. His hands were covered in the matching gray gloves as his boots, as was his belt, which was fastened over his surcoat. A sword was clasped to the belt and hung along his left side. His hair was a light-brown shade and it flowed wildly in disarray. A goatee of the same color encircled his mouth.

Angel started running towards him, but the man spotted her and ran further away himself.

"Don't let him get away," she cried out. Shiel was directly behind her running just as fast.

The man rushed towards the docks, and Angel thought that they had him for sure. He was out of places to run and the crowd was thick around the boats. The man wove in and out of them without slowing a step.

Angel and Shiel were not as fortunate. They had to push and shove their way through the crowd at times. For a moment, they lost sight of the man. Then they saw him, one hand holding on to a mast of a ship, and the other waving to them.

"Better luck next time, Imps!"

The two watched as the ship continued into the harbor and out to sea. It was a pirate ship. Neither could explain how this had happened or why, but they were both certain: the man was Braksis.

The war for the Imperium has begun!

A year has passed since the forces of Zoldex first began arriving in Trespias. The time for his conquest has come! The dark Mage has waited long enough. His forces are vast and strong, and he is confident that nothing will stand in his path.

Follow the adventures of the heroes of the realm as they try to preserve the Imperium and confront Zoldex's forces. Their hearts are true and their intentions noble, but will that be enough to overcome such overwhelming odds?

Find out as this epic saga continues in

Fall of the Imperium Trilogy
Book III

THE SIEGE OF ZOLDEX

By
Clifford B. Bowyer

The Empress has been kidnapped while in the midst of trying to unite the races. Her true whereabouts are unknown, but her return is vital to the survival of the Seven Kingdoms.

One elf, the Mage Ilfanti, is determined to find Karleena and return her to the realm to face the threat of Zoldex and fulfill her dream of unification. His mission will be not be an easy one. He must journey far from the Imperium in search of a mystical artifact that will allow the wielder to have any one question answered. That question: "Where is Karleena?"

Follow Ilfanti as he returns to a life of an adventurer and battles against time to save the Imperium. Will he be able to find the mystical artifact and locate the Empress in time?

Find out in

ILFANTI AND THE ORB OF PROPHECY

By
Clifford B. Bowyer

Check your local bookstore, order here, online at
www.SilverLeafBooks.com, or call our Toll Free
number at: 1-888-823-6450

The Imperium Saga: Fall of the Imperium Trilogy

___0-9744354-4-9 # 1:   The Impending Storm $27.95

___0-9744354-5-7 # 2:   The Changing Tides $27.95

Please include $3.95 shipping and handling for the first book and $1.95 each additional book. Massachusetts residents please add $1.40 sales tax per book.

The Imperium Saga: The Adventures of Kyria

___0-9744354-0-6 # 1:   The Child of Prophecy $5.99

___0-9744354-1-4 # 2:   The Awakening $5.99

___0-9744354-2-2 # 3:   The Mage's Council $5.99

___0-9744354-3-0 # 4:   The Shard of Time $5.99

Please include $2.25 shipping and handling for the first book and $.50 each additional book. Massachusetts residents please add $.30 sales tax per book.

Payment must accompany orders. Please allow 4 to 6 weeks for delivery.

My check or money order for $__________ is enclosed.
Please charge my ❏ Visa ❏ MasterCard

Name ____

Address ____

City ____________________ State/Zip ______________

Credit Card # ___________________ Exp. Date ________

CCV # ________ Signature ___________________________

Make your check payable and return to:
Silver Leaf Book, LLC
P.O. Box 6460 • Holliston, MA 01746